# A TREACHERY OF FRIENDS

## CJ CARVER

BLOODHOUND
— BOOKS —

First published in 2023 by Bloodhound Books.

www.bloodhoundbooks.com

Print ISBN: 978-1-916978-11-9

# PRAISE FOR CJ CARVER

'A terrific, heart-stopping page-turner... and a heroine with guile as well as guts'
**Harlan Coben**

'Do I recommend CJ Carver? Hell yeah! One of my top crime thriller writers'
**Crime Book Junkie**

'My goodness, I couldn't put this book down... amazing. Didn't see that coming...'
**Josée McClure**

'I've been a fan of Harlan Coben for years and never found an author to compare until now... Deserves ten stars not five'
**Amazon Customer**

'Just when you think you have it figured out, you're blindsided again'
**Deborah L. Mull**

'Mesmerised by all the twists and turns and what a surprising ending. One of the best reads in a long time'
**Doris Johns**

'I hated to see it end!'
**Carol**

'Wow! Just wow! Great read in one day! Do not usually leave a review but just had to... really fantastic'
**Kindle Customer**

'Thrilling... atmospheric, beautifully paced... a fantastic book'
**The Mystery and Thriller Club**

*Janet. This one's for you, with love.*

# 1

OXFORD 2003

W hen Sidney Scott was eight, her father showed her his favourite magic trick.

It was a mid-winter weekend, a sopping wet afternoon with rain dribbling down the windows and the steady drip-drip of an overflowing gutter beside the back door. Sid sat at the kitchen table, colouring in a horse in her pony fun activity book. Chestnut coat, black mane and tail, and she was wondering if she should give it a tan saddle and bridle, or be more adventurous and make them red or purple, when her father came and scooted the cat off the chair beside her, and sat down.

'Shuffle the cards.' He passed Sid a deck.

She put her felt pen down and reached for the cards. She wasn't great at shuffling but with her tongue pressing against her lower lip, she did her best before passing it back.

'Cora,' he called.

'What is it?' Her mother's voice drifted down from the study. She was ordering stuff online for her shop in town. Joss-sticks, scented candles, dream catchers, anything woo-woo, as her dad would say, but with a twinkle in his eye.

'I need you to shuffle.'

'Oh. I thought you might have lost something. Hang on...'

With his small, bright brown eyes and slightly dishevelled air, Sid's dad resembled an amiable bear, a bear that could, however, drive Mum and her mad with his absent-mindedness. He'd mislay keys, spectacles, his wallet, with monotonous regularity. The refrain, 'Have you seen my...?' would have them rolling their eyes, but they'd always chip in on the hunt for whatever it was he'd mislaid.

Her mother arrived in a flurry of tinkling bangles and patchouli. She was almost as bad as Sid at shuffling but Dad looked happy when he took the cards back, fanning them out, face-up. 'All different, and all well mixed up now.'

He put the deck face-down and squared it neatly on the table.

'Now,' he told Sid. 'Cut the deck into two while I look away.'

Dutifully, she did as he said.

'Without showing it to me, remove the card you cut to and have a look at it.'

The eight of clubs.

'Now replace the card and reshuffle the pack so we don't know where the card is.'

Both Sid and her mum shuffled. By this time, Sid was riveted but her mother stood behind her father with an amused expression. When her father took the deck back, he began to deal the cards face-up onto the table. 'Try not to react when you see your card, okay?'

Sid was holding her breath as she watched, determined

not to respond but she was sure something must have showed in her face when he dealt the eight of clubs, but to her amazement he didn't stop, he just kept going, creating a messy pile on the table between them. Finally, he dealt the last card, leaned back and crossed his arms.

'I bet you tonight's washing up that the next card I pick up will be your card.'

'Deal,' Sid said. She didn't hesitate. She *hated* washing up.

She was preparing to crow, because her father hated washing up almost as much as she did, when, to her astonishment, he reached forward and plucked her card from the pile. 'Eight of clubs, right?'

She shot to her feet so hard she almost toppled her chair over. 'How did you *do that*?!' She picked up the deck and checked, but they were all different, seemingly genuine. She checked her card but couldn't see any marks. She flipped through the deck again before looking at him, her mouth hanging open.

He laughed. 'It's easy. I'll show you.'

'Michael,' her mother said gently. 'Leave some magic for her.'

He twisted in his seat and looked up at her. 'But she needs to learn that even magic can be explained.'

'She's just a child. Magic's fun.'

'Magic is nothing but a trick of the mind. I don't want her misperceiving the world or being controlled by others.'

'So says the scientist,' her mother said.

'So says Mystic Meg.'

Her mother gave a snort and rolled her eyes as Dad put his arm around her waist and drew her close. He was chuckling.

'Please show me,' Sid said. She was wriggling with anticipation.

Her father looked up at her mother, waiting for her consent.

'Please, *please*,' Sid begged. 'Then I can trick Aero.'

Aero was her best friend at school, nicknamed after the Aero peppermint chocolate he never seemed to be without.

Her mother sighed. 'I just think it's a shame to take the mystery out of life. Not everything can be explained.'

Her father arched his eyebrows but, surprisingly, he didn't say anything.

'Oh, go on then,' her mother capitulated, 'but just the one trick, okay? Or she won't have a spiritual bone in her body.'

With her mother upstairs, Sid's father proceeded to show her not just that one, simple trick, but another where he asked her to choose a card from the pack, write her name on it, and fold it into four. He made the card disappear, and then revealed that it had been magically transported into her mother's jewellery box upstairs. Which was locked.

Something happened that day. Sid could never explain it, but she became hooked on the science behind magic and the paranormal, and when her father disappeared six years later, she honestly thought it was another trick and kept waiting for him to reappear, *ta-da!* When he didn't, life became monochrome without him.

Her mother visited clairvoyants, psychics and tarot card readers to try and find her husband while Sid railed at her that they were just fleecing her with lies. They didn't argue all the time, but Sid never let her mum trot off to yet another psychic without protesting she was wasting her money.

When her mother fell ill, diagnosed with cancer, nobody seemed surprised. They talked about the horror of being abandoned, the stress of being on her own with no support for bringing up her daughter, the trauma, the strain and grief.

Four years after her father disappeared, Sid's mother did the final disappearing act, and died.

Her mother had told Sid to listen out for her when she'd gone, that she'd send her daughter a message, and even though Sid didn't believe in ghosts, she still kept an ear open, just in case, but her mother never contacted her.

Which, as far as Sid was concerned, simply confirmed that ghosts didn't exist.

# 2

## WILTSHIRE, PRESENT DAY

Sid was fast asleep when the phone rang. Pitch dark, country dark, not a pinprick of light. Her consciousness struggled to heave itself from a vat of dreamless treacle. She groaned. Fumbled her fingers over the bedside table and managed to knock over the glass of water.

'Fuck.'

She found the lamp switch. Flicked it on. Picked up her phone. Two minutes past seven in the morning. For a moment she couldn't believe it. It felt like the middle of the night and Tank seemed to think so too. He'd scrambled up the stairs and was now standing in her bedroom doorway yawning widely, his long pink tongue curled between rows of shiny white teeth. Sometimes, like now, she couldn't believe she shared her cottage with a dog. A *huge* dog at that; an attack dog. A bullmastiff. She'd never had a dog before and when her landlord – a down-to-earth, no-nonsense farmer – had insisted she take Tank in for a fortnight, she'd only done it to prove she *didn't need* a guard dog. Ha ha. Because here Tank was eight years later, greying around the muzzle, a little fatter, a lot more spoilt, and completely part of the furniture.

She squinted at the phone's display. *Number unknown.* She couldn't think who it might be. Nobody rang her outside work hours. She switched it to mute before shoving it aside. Another nuisance call, no doubt. She'd been getting loads recently. *Been in an accident? Been mis-sold an insurance policy?* She really must do something about it.

Tank flopped on the floor, gave a sigh. He obviously wasn't ready to go out yet and although she didn't have to get up for another hour or so – the joy of being self-employed – she was now too awake to go back to sleep. Her mind was already flitting over her presentation to a group of psychology students at Bath uni that morning. Would they be open to her explaining that as far as she was concerned, the paranormal didn't exist? That it was the human psyche that created things that went bump in the night?

At her last talk, a woman had called her the Devil's Mouthpiece before storming out, unable to believe her pet psychic – who'd also been in the audience – had been using nothing but a box of common psychological tricks to convince her that she was talking to her dead mother.

Why did people believe they were talking to the dead? Why did they believe in ghosts? Questions like these were Sid's bread and butter. She was fascinated by uncovering the psychology that made people believe they were experiencing the paranormal which, nine times out of ten, turned out to have a sound scientific answer. Some people called her a ghostbuster, but on BBC Radio Wiltshire last year, they'd called her a supernatural scientist.

Ha! Don't make her laugh. Scientist she was not. She did one term at uni before dropping out. But at least now she could see why her mother had put her faith in the paranormal rather than face the truth that her husband had abandoned her. It was all about comfort.

Kicking the bedclothes back, she pulled her father's oversized dressing gown over her pyjamas. Pushed her feet into a pair of sheepskin-lined Ugg boots. The heating hadn't come on yet and the floorboards were freezing. In the bathroom she switched on the boiler before heading downstairs. Tank mooched along behind her.

While he sniffed and peed in the back garden, she brewed some tea and lit a cigarette, moving to the window to watch the blue tits and goldfinches come and go from the feeder. When she caught her reflection, she shifted so she couldn't see it anymore. Her face was thin and unsmiling. She looked angular, unapproachable. The woman she used to be – warm, lively, fun; she'd vanished when she'd overheard the gang talking about her in the pub. Not that she blamed them as much as herself. After her mother died, she'd gone off the rails in a spectacular fashion. It may have been a coping mechanism but when she looked back, she cringed. She'd been so reckless, so *stupid*. Little wonder she couldn't bear to look at herself.

She drank her tea and finished her cigarette. Beyond the drystone wall, the rolling fields were empty of Jersey cows, who were being wintered indoors. She missed seeing them but it wouldn't be long before spring was here and they'd be browsing past her garden, huffing and swishing their tails and filling the air with the sweet smell of grass and warm cow hide.

Her cottage, a tiny two-up two-down, apparently used to house a farm worker, his wife and five kids, which made Sid feel strangely selfish moving in on her own. Her favourite room was the kitchen with its wood-burning stove and original 400-year-old timber beams. She'd sit at the table and plan out her next gig, be it spending a sleepless night in Hampton Court Palace, supposedly one of the most haunted buildings in Britain, or travelling to the Isle of Wight to investigate a psychic dog. The one thing you could say about her job was that it was never dull.

In the garden, a sparrow darted from the hedge to the feeder. There was something comforting about the rhythm and movement of the countryside, just yards away. She used to live in Jericho, in Oxford. She'd been a townie, nipping to the pub once or twice a week, partying, clubbing, but now? She'd be in her jim-jams by nine in the evening watching whatever Netflix had to offer. She frowned. Perhaps she should move. But where to? Why? She was content here. At ease.

A scratching at the back door reminded her to let Tank in, give him his breakfast. While he ate – extremely noisily as usual, pushing the tin bowl across the stone flagstones to jam it against the skirting board – she picked up her phone to check her emails. Four missed calls, all from the same *number unknown*. Perhaps it wasn't a nuisance caller after all, but she still couldn't think who it might be. She was gazing nonplussed at the phone when it rang again. This time, she answered, but she didn't say anything.

'Hello?' a man said. 'Hello?'

'Hello,' she responded.

She thought she heard him say, 'Thank fuck for that.'

'I'm sorry?'

'Miss Scott?' the voice asked. 'Miss Sidney Scott?'

'Who is it?'

'My name is Detective Kelly. I'm from the Gloucestershire Police.'

It was like being doused in ice water. Her father was still listed as missing. Had they found him?

'What's it about?'

'Are you Miss Sidney Scott?' His voice held weary impatience.

'How do I know you're a policeman and not some scammer?'

She thought she heard another 'fuck,' then, 'Trust me, I'm a policeman. I need to come and see you. This morning, if possible. You're at Nook Cottage, Neston, am I right?'

'I won't be in.' Her voice was crisp, covering her lie. She had no intention of having a stranger in her home, Tank or no Tank. She wondered if she could hear the detective grinding his teeth.

'Perhaps you could come to the station?'

She dithered briefly before saying, 'I'll be at Bath university, if that helps.' She could purloin an office if necessary. 'Newton Park campus.' She gave him directions.

'I'll be there in an hour.'

'I'll be there at midday.' She was firm. There was no way she was going to compromise her course until she knew what was going on.

'Can't you make it any earlier?'

'No.' The word came out more abruptly than she'd planned, but she seemed to have lost the art of feminine, polite niceties after living alone for so long.

When he didn't say anything, Sid hung up.

She felt odd, her hands disembodied from her arms as she put the phone down. He hadn't mentioned her father. Why not? Was he alive? Was he dead? Out of nowhere she felt the urge to cry. Shit, *shit*.

Real fear opened inside her, dark and cold, like an underground river that never sees the sun.

She'd always held out the hope her father was alive. That maybe he'd knocked his head, lost his memory, forgot who he was. She'd pictured him working in another country, sharing a beer with another physicist at the end of the day, maybe in Melbourne or Singapore. She'd imagined him married to someone else. Maybe with another kid or two. Then she'd imagine the police or Missing People finding him and putting them in touch. Dad ringing her. Asking her how she was. What grades she'd achieved at uni.

*I dropped out,* she'd tell him.

She'd imagine his response. Horror, dismay, disbelief.

*But you were going to be a lawyer. Fight for the underdog. It was what you always wanted to do.*

*I couldn't concentrate.*

*What a waste.* He'd shake his great shaggy head. *All your education, thrown into the bin.*

In her imaginary conversations she never told him about Mum's illness. Instead, she'd dream about him introducing her to his new family. Pictured them all getting along brilliantly, cooking together, laughing and holidaying in the sun. She'd fantasise that she had a family again. But if he was dead, then she couldn't do that anymore.

3

Sid struggled to concentrate on her talk that morning. She kept seeing her father's face out of the corner of her eye, bearded and affable. He would have enjoyed her talks but her mother would have been saddened.

*Leave some magic for her.*

Sid was giving a demonstration on fortune-telling, and how easy it was to convince strangers that you knew everything about them. 'Double-headed statements,' she explained, 'are the stock-in-trade, because people invariably only focus on the part of your description they can relate to.'

She turned to Clare, her guinea pig.

'You love routine,' she told her. 'But at other times you love being impulsive and free.'

Clare's face lit up. 'That is so *true*! Everyone knows how spontaneous I am!'

'You can be incredibly creative, but you also have a down-to-earth streak.'

'Creative, that's me all right.'

Sid went on. 'I'm getting the impression of some kind of change coming into your life...' When this didn't produce any kind of reaction, Sid added, 'Perhaps a journey of some sort?' Clare remained unmoved. Sid said, 'Hmmm. I'm thinking it might be an upheaval in a relationship?'

As soon as Sid mentioned the relationship upheaval, Clare's expression darkened, becoming introspective.

Sid made a mental note, moving on swiftly. Later, when she confidently announced that Clare was having relationship difficulties with her partner, Clare was dumbfounded.

'It's all about watching the body language,' Sid said, winding up her demo. 'Noting when your client smiles or tenses up. Then you can tailor your suggestions. This is why palmists, for example, want to hold your hand. They can feel your responses much more easily.'

The students erupted into excited chatter. Everyone had an experience they wanted to share. As she put her crystal ball away – props were always fun – Clare came over.

'My mum has someone who talks to the dead. Is that a hoax too?'

'I'm afraid it probably is.'

'She really believes it.' Clare pulled a face. 'What should I do?'

'If it doesn't do any harm, I wouldn't worry too much. But I'd definitely intervene if it turns disturbing or upsets your mum.'

Sid picked up her handbag and jacket, and headed to the Commons. In the centre, several students were adorning a huge Christmas tree with handmade decorations. Lots of merriment and youthful spirits made

Sid feel every one of her twenty-eight years. She said goodbye to Clare when she saw the detective walk through the door and look around. She knew it had to be him by his greying hair, his self-containment. He was also the only person wearing a jacket. She started walking towards him, watching as his gaze settled on a middle-aged female lecturer with whom she had a passing acquaintance. He gave the lecturer a wave and she waved back, and at the same time a man said, 'Sidney Scott?'

Startled, she switched her head around to see a beanpole of a man with coat-hanger shoulders and a shock of blond, almost white hair. He wore little round specs and jeans, sneakers and a sweatshirt. A tatty black backpack was slung over one shoulder. He looked like a Swedish student.

'Detective?' She tried not to seem surprised but something must have sounded in her voice because he looked at the man in the jacket and then back at her. He smiled.

'You thought that was me?'

For the first time since she could remember, she felt flustered. 'No. Yes. I didn't expect...' She waved a hand at him. 'Such casual attire.'

'And I didn't expect...' He made a gesture at her hair.

Once, her hair had hung to her waist but now it was cropped close to her scalp.

'Your website has an old picture of you,' he added.

His eyes slid to the side of her neck, where the tip of her tattoo ended, or began, depending how you looked upon it. She'd started it after her mum died and finished it just after her twentieth birthday. Eighteen months of inking and healing, during which time she and her tattoo artist got to know each other pretty well.

Detective Kelly looked away, clearing his throat. 'You have an office here?'

'I've borrowed one.' She pointed at the lifts. 'It's on the second floor.'

She led the way. Even though she wore baggy cargo pants and a shapeless top, she could feel him watching her. Her waist, her hips, her legs. She winced. She used to enjoy a man's attention but not anymore.

The office belonged to a psychology lecturer who was currently at lunch. As usual, it was a mess of notebooks, box files, cardboard files, pens, books, and stacks of paper littering every surface. Sid removed a handful of notebooks from a swivel chair and slipped them onto the windowsill. She took the other swivel chair on the other side of the desk and placed her hands in her lap, where he couldn't see the way her fingers had clenched together. Christ, she could murder a cigarette.

'Do you have some ID?' she asked.

He reached into his back pocket and withdrew a warrant card, pushed it across. She looked it over carefully, memorising his warrant number before returning it.

He surveyed her steadily. His calm demeanour sat at odds with the frustrated man who'd said *fuck* on the phone. 'You don't live in Oxford anymore.'

'No.'

'When did you move from Juxon Street?'

She saw no reason not to answer. 'Eight years ago.'

'And you moved directly from there to where you are now?'

'Yes.'

'Have you lived anywhere else?'

'No.'

'Just two addresses,' he confirmed.

'Yes. Juxon Street was my childhood home.'

'Do your parents still live there?'

She stared at him. This wasn't about Dad?

'Why do you ask?'

He tilted his head on one side. 'Did they move from Oxford too?'

'Not exactly.'

He raised his eyebrows, waiting.

A rush of something close to euphoria swept through her. Her mind became a single long jamboree. *This isn't about Dad, this isn't about Dad.* Which meant they hadn't found him. Did this mean he was alive? The jamboree abruptly cut into a single, long and all-too familiar shriek. If so, then WHERE THE HELL WAS HE?

The detective leaned forward a fraction. 'Are you okay?'

Yes. No. Never.

She took a deep breath. Let it out. Tried to lasso her emotions. 'Sorry.' Her tone was brittle. 'You see, my father disappeared fourteen years ago. My mother died of cancer four years later.'

He blinked. 'I'm sorry. That must have been tough.'

*If only you knew.*

People said, surely, she'd have got over it, come to terms with it after so long, but she never had. Her world had fallen out of orbit, lost its rhythm, and she'd never regained it. Perhaps if she knew what had happened to Dad it might have helped, but as it was, some days she felt as though she was sleepwalking through life, pretending to be alive.

'Tell me about your father,' he said.

'Is it relevant?'

'It might be useful.'

*To what?* she wanted to ask, but decided to let it go. He obviously wasn't going to tell her why he was here until he was good and ready. She turned sideways and crossed her legs. Let her hands rest on her thighs. Much more relaxed now she knew he wasn't here about her father.

'Okay.' She took a moment to realign her thoughts. 'Dad was working in Geneva when Mum rang him to tell him his mother had fallen and broken her hip. He flew straight home. After visiting her, CCTV footage showed him filling up his car at the Shell petrol station in Headington on 29th November 2009. This was the last time he was seen.'

'What was he doing in Geneva?'

'He worked at CERN.'

At the detective's blank expression, she added, 'It's one of the world's largest centres for scientific research. He was on a three-year tenure.'

He'd been thrilled when he got the contract. She could still remember him dancing around the house, playing Jimi Hendrix full blast, pulling both her and her mother along with his crazy gambolling. Sid had been excited for him at the time, but had had to hide her disappointment at him being away from home four days a week. At least they had weekends together, and she got to visit Switzerland.

'And he's still missing,' the detective mused with a frown.

'Yes.'

A small silence fell.

'Please,' Sid said, 'tell me why you're here.'

He considered his notebook for a second or two, then lifted his pale gaze to hers. She uncrossed her legs. Rested her forearms on the desk. Waited.

'I'm afraid there's been a... well, an unfortunate incident.'

'What incident?'

'A man has been killed.'

She thought she felt the earth tilt a little. 'What man?'

'His name is Owen Evans.'

For a second, she was ready to be shocked – Dear God, not Owen! – but she'd never heard the name before. Relief flooded her, making the tips of her fingers tingle.

'I don't know any Owen Evans.'

'Can I show you his photograph?'

'Of course.'

He reached into his backpack and withdrew a beige file. Extracted a picture and put it in front of her. A round-faced man with ruddy cheeks and soft brown hair streaked with grey smiled up at her. Snub nose, bow-shaped mouth. A neatly trimmed, greying goatee. Early fifties or so. He looked happy.

'Sorry,' she said. 'I don't recognise him.'

The detective didn't take the photograph away. By leaving it there, it was as though he was saying, *are you sure?*

'How did he die?'

'There was a… ah, traffic incident.'

She still didn't get it but without him elucidating, she had no option but to go along with him.

'He had some tattoos…' Kelly hesitated. 'I want to show you, but they were taken post mortem.'

He was, she realised, asking if she was squeamish. She had no idea. 'Try me.'

Another photograph, a close-up of what could have been a forearm but it was hard to tell. The skin was dead white, the tattoo ink blue. His hairs were soft brown. Her stomach didn't roll, she didn't feel sick. It was just a photograph of an equilateral cross within a circle containing four bold dots.

'It's the Hopi people earth symbol,' she said. 'They're a Native American tribe.'

He peered at the photograph. 'How do you know that?'

'I recognise the symbol because in my line of work I come across a lot of symbolism.'

'In what way?'

'It's all tied into belief systems. Jesus on the cross, for example. The ankh being a symbol of eternal life. The eye of Ra for protection. I'm interested in what makes people believe in them.'

'The science of the supernatural.'

He'd repeated the heading on her website. 'Paranormal phenomena do not exist,' she said calmly. 'It's been proven time and again, not just by me, but by a multitude of scientists. Still, people claim to experience them.'

'My mother gets her tarot cards read every once in a while.'

Sid felt a glimmer of a smile. 'She's not the only one. As long as her reader does no harm, I hope your mother gets something positive out of it.'

Kelly nodded. Brought out another picture of a tattoo, this one of a coat-of-arms with what could have been a lion rampant in one corner but it was terribly blurred. She peered closer, thinking of her father's old college cufflinks. 'Is it a college emblem?'

'How on earth...?' He looked nonplussed and she felt absurdly pleased she'd guessed correctly.

'Which college?' she asked.

'St John's.'

'He went to Oxford university?'

He hesitated briefly, which she took meant *yes*, before bringing out another picture. This one was of a goat-headed Baphomet image that she knew had been adopted by modern occultists after the Knights Templar were accused of worshipping it. The official insignia of the Church of Satan.

'Who *was* Owen Evans?' she murmured, but Kelly didn't

19

answer, just kept producing more photographs of symbols. Owen appeared to have tattoos over most of his body. Some were fuzzy with age, others sharp and new. Some she recognised, and those she didn't, she decided to memorise. Just in case. The one thing any half-decent psychic or paranormal sceptic needed was a good memory, and now she invented a mnemonic for each, briefly closing her eyes and reimagining them. Fast and simple and, usually, pretty accurate.

'Last one,' Kelly told her. She could see why. It was a tattoo of interlaced rings that she recognised immediately because it showed a simplified representation of the accelerator chain and the particle tracks.

She touched it with her fingertip. 'CERN,' she whispered. She looked across at the detective. 'Was he a scientist? Did Owen work at CERN too?'

'No. He was an academician who lived near Glastonbury.'

Before she could ask in what, he said, 'We found this in his car.' Reaching down to his backpack he brought out a clear plastic folder, inside which was a postcard. It was marked where it had been folded in half and was yellow with age. The picture showed a village of traditional alpine houses topped with steeply pitched roofs buried in snow. White-capped mountains rose on all sides.

Kelly turned it over so she could see the other side. He'd covered the message part of the card. Just the address was visible, handwritten in black ballpoint.

*Miss Sidney Scott,*
*55 Juxon Street,*
*Oxford OX2 6DR*

No. No, no, no, no.

The handwriting was small and cramped, slightly back-sloped. Messy, barely legible. It looked as though it had been written while astride a galloping horse but that's how it always looked.

It was her father's handwriting. No question.

4

D etective Kelly removed the paper covering the
message.

*Racing in the wild wind.*

A jumble of numbers followed.

*11, 5, 10. 2, 3, 23. 8, 19, 1. 5, 18, 3. 102,
20, 9. 87, 12, 7.*

A whistling started in Sid's ears as she stared at her
father's message.

'What does it mean?' the policeman asked.

'I have no idea.' Which was technically true but could
also be considered a lie. Her mind began to record the
numbers. Fast.

The detective leaned forward. 'Is it a code?'

*Yes,* she thought. *But do I share it with you?*

She continued staring at the numbers, her memory working at top speed.

'What's the reference to racing in the wild wind?'

*Nearly there*, she thought: *87, 12, 7.*

When he made to put the postcard away, she held up a hand, pausing him. She ran through the numbers once more, then again, backwards: *10, 5, 11.*

She had them all.

Her whole body was trembling but she wasn't sure if it was from distress or excitement.

'Whose handwriting is it?' Kelly was watching her.

She didn't say anything. She kept staring at the postcard. There was no stamp on it but he'd dated it, like he always did.

*29th November 2009.*

The day he'd disappeared.

Where had he written it? In Geneva, or England? On the aeroplane as he'd flown to the UK? After he'd vanished? Where was his copy of the book? She had no idea.

'Miz Scott?' As he watched her, the detective's water-grey eyes narrowed.

She didn't speak because she was scared she might start shouting or burst into tears.

When Kelly next spoke, his voice turned oddly formal. 'I need to tell you now that Owen Evans's death was not an accident.'

Her gaze snapped to his.

'This is a murder investigation.'

She opened and closed her mouth. 'Shit,' she managed. She felt a wave of dizziness wash over her. Did this mean Dad had been murdered as well?

'You recognise the handwriting.' It was a statement, not a question.

Sid nodded. 'It's my father's.' Her voice sounded rusty. 'Racing in the Wild Wind is a book.'

She'd borrowed it from Tenby Library while on holiday in Wales. It was about a wild black stallion – she'd snap up any book that featured a horse on the cover – and she'd barely finished it when a neighbour, a boy a year older than her, introduced her to the art of spying.

Noah, skinny as a rake, tow-haired, had become Sid's best friend that summer. Where she was horse mad, he was spy mad. He taught her about secret codes, spy rings, dead drops, disguises, shadowing, decoding signals. It had been Sid's father who'd shown them how to use Racing in the Wild Wind as a code breaker by giving them each a copy. Noah would leave her a whole bunch of numbers to decode, and then she'd give him another list of numbers in response.

The first number would be the page number, the second the sentence number from the top of the page, the third would indicate which word in that sentence was the one to be used, reading right to left. Luckily, the horse book had fairly large print and only twenty-three sentences on each page, or their messages could have taken days to decipher.

Whenever she thought of Noah, she smiled inside. The memories of that holiday were filled with nothing but her and Noah running around, swimming, mackerel fishing, beachcombing and eating ice creams. They'd come home for supper each night exhausted and sunburnt. Idyllic childhood days.

'Who wrote the book, can you remember?'

'Mavis Mitchell.' She watched as the detective made a

note. She had a copy of the book at home but she wasn't going to tell him. He could track down his own copy.

'Can you remember the last message your father sent you?'

'Yes.' She still had it tucked in the book. 'It asked me to make sure we had enough chocolate cake for him when he got home.' Dad loved chocolate of any sort. Dark, light, white, mint, caramel, strawberry. He had the sweetest tooth imaginable and was never happier than when opening a brand-new box of chocolates. 'It was just a bit of fun.'

A corkscrew appeared between Kelly's brows as he appeared to think. She wondered if he was aware of it.

'Where did Owen Evans die?' she asked.

Once again, Kelly ignored her question to ask a shedload of his own, most relating to her father and his disappearance. Some she could answer, some she couldn't. A lot of them she simply answered saying, 'Mum would have known,' which made her feel immeasurably sad. She still missed Mum *so much*.

Eventually, Kelly began to wind down, putting away his notebook and pen, gathering the folders to slip into his backpack.

'Why did Owen have my dad's postcard?'

'I don't think I can even hazard a guess. Not yet, anyway.'

'Where was it found?'

He didn't answer. A couple of photographs of Owen's tattoos slipped out of his folder and before he could catch them, Sid spotted the Baphomet image once again, but she didn't recognise the other tattoo, of a sunrise set in a triangle, with a red cross on top. She pointed at it. 'You didn't show me that one.'

'You're right. I may not have.' He spoke casually, making

her realise he hadn't shown her all the symbols. Why not? Or had he been testing her?

'It's the Hermetic Order of the Golden Dawn,' he said. 'Know them?'

'No.'

She accompanied him outside. The temperature had dropped and an icy wind was whipping sleet across the ground. Sid pulled her jacket collar up around her neck.

'Thanks for your time.' He was polite.

She walked to her car, half-watching him as he loped away, his narrow figure and long legs reminding her of the grey heron that she sometimes saw on her walks with Tank. She was desperate for a cigarette but since the whole of the university was smoke-free, she'd have to wait. Instead, she brought out her phone and looked up recent traffic incidents in Gloucestershire. Aside from the M50 link road blocked earlier due to an overturned lorry, there was only one other event of note.

B4425 closed east of Aldsworth after a serious crash overnight left a man dead. The road remains CLOSED whilst forensic collision investigation work takes place.

This was from Gloucestershire Police Specialist Operations, dated yesterday, so Sid put Aldsworth in her satnav, and headed there. Her father's last message could wait until she'd seen the site. She couldn't say why she needed to see it. She just did.

She smoked two cigarettes on the journey, and when she arrived the road was open but there was no crashed car, no police, no forensic officers. Streams of blue-and-white police tape were strung between an ash tree and a farm gatepost. She pulled into the muddy space next to the gate. Set the handbrake and climbed out.

A biting wind greeted her. The road was shiny with rain and the verges dotted with pockets of frozen sleet. Christ, it was cold. Cars shushed past, headlights on even though it was mid-afternoon. Arms wrapped around herself, Sid stepped to the area marked by police tape, looked around. She couldn't see any skid marks but she could see tyre tracks gouged into the verge. To her inexperienced eye, a vehicle had veered off the road onto the verge and buried itself in the ditch. She could see where branches and twigs in the hedge had been snapped. There was no broken glass or bits of metal in the grass or on the bitumen that she could see. She wondered what had made the police believe it was a murder case.

Sleet clung to her shoulders and hair as she climbed back inside her car. Set the heating to high. Rather than drive home via Cirencester, she decided to take an alternative route via Quenington. Windscreen wipers on, eyes on the farm tractor ahead, she didn't take in the discreet sign for the Hermetic Order of the Golden Dawn on her left, let alone the young lad at the top of the drive with a rifle in his hand. She was absorbed in wondering what message her father had left her.

# 5

Gabriel hefted the .22 rifle in his hand. It was ostensibly for rabbiting but he liked the feeling of power it gave him. There were PRIVATE PROPERTY and KEEP OUT signs at the gate along with cameras and an electrified deer fence, but it didn't always put people off. They'd had a couple of hikers walk across the cattle grid last year, rambling through the old deer park, and Father Luke had given them short shrift. They hadn't seen any Strangers since.

He was gazing down the drive thinking about nothing more than what soup might be for lunch when a car came into view. He saw it was a big black four-wheel drive but not who was driving. He brought out his binoculars. Just one man inside. He was in his shirtsleeves.

He called over Brothers Isaac and Saul. Pointed out the car. A flutter of excitement rose in his belly. Nothing ever happened here; every day was the same. The Guards unlocked the dormitory doors at daybreak and let them head for a breakfast of hard-boiled eggs and rice before putting them to work on the Estate. Some days he'd be mending fences, others helping move the cattle or drench sheep. The women, including his little sister Hannah and his mother, worked in the vegetable and fruit gardens. Supper was at sundown. Vegetables and more rice. The animals were sold Outside, the profits channelled back to keep the commune running.

Gabriel couldn't remember when he'd last eaten meat or even if he liked it. Both he and Hannah were permanently hungry, but apparently this was a Good Thing because obesity was a Sin.

He gave a shiver. A thin layer of ice pellets lay on the ground. Puddles were frozen. He hated winter. He never seemed to get warm. He envied the man in the car who was obviously nice and cosy since he wasn't wearing a jumper.

When Isaac snatched his binoculars from him, Gabriel felt a surge of anger. Swallowed it. Isaac was twenty-three, ten years older than him, and part of Father's hallowed Inner Circle. If you stepped out of line with any of them, you could find yourself locked inside the Shed for a week of solitary, no light, no food, just water. Gabriel's mother had been locked in there once, for stealing an egg. She'd been seventeen and pregnant with him at the time, but she hadn't been given any quarter.

'I know stealing's bad,' she told him when he'd asked her about it, 'but I wanted the protein to make you grow up big and strong.'

After three days, she'd thought she was going to die in there and was petrified that if she did survive, the experience would have damaged her unborn baby.

'But then a man came and saved us. He broke down the door to the Shed and let us out.'

When Gabriel asked her who the man was, she shook her head. 'I don't know, but I call him our Angel and pray for him every day.' She would always end the story by pulling him close and kissing him, telling him how much she loved him before making him vow *never to steal*, but sometimes he couldn't resist nicking the odd handful of extra rice for him and Hannah.

'Praise be the Lord,' Isaac murmured. 'It's him.'

'Who?' Gabriel asked. He was itching to snatch back his binoculars but didn't dare.

'Get Father Luke.' Isaac held out his other hand, flicking his fingers at Gabriel, a command to make him hand over his rifle. 'Tell him our beloved leader has come.'

Gabriel hadn't heard of a beloved leader but knew better than to ask any questions. When he showed his reluctance to give him the rifle, Isaac seized it. 'Get a move on!' he yelled.

Gabriel turned and ran for the Manor House. It felt good to run. Normally it wasn't allowed. You were supposed to walk everywhere. Running was undignified and indecorous, whatever that meant.

He ran past the dorms, the vegetable gardens, the stable blocks, chickens scattering, geese honking, waggling their tails and stretching their necks. Brothers and Sisters spun around, startled, as he tore past. Raced to the back of the house, to what in the old days used to be the servants' entrance. Bowling inside, he slowed his pace. He wanted to take it all in so he could tell Hannah about it later. He'd only been inside once before, when he was ten, and he couldn't believe how warm it felt.

The corridor smelled of cooking vegetables and something rich and delicious. He couldn't imagine what it might be. He ducked his head around the first door he came to: a cavernous kitchen. A team of women were chopping, cooking, washing up. Pots bubbled on a range, their daily soup, no doubt, but his eye was drawn to a golden-brown bird being basted in a roasting tin. A chicken. His mouth immediately watered.

'Gabriel?' one of the women asked, surprised. 'Whatever are you doing here?'

'I have a message for Father Luke from Brother Isaac.'

'He's upstairs, in his study.' She pointed at the ceiling. 'You know where it is, right?'

He'd never been further than the kitchen before but he nodded.

'Knock before you enter, okay?'

Senses filled with roasting aromas, stomach growling, he trotted back into the corridor. Swiftly popped his head into a variety of rooms including a laundry, a storeroom filled with cleaning equipment, and an enormous walk-in larder. He gazed longingly at the fresh fruit and tins of fish but didn't dare touch anything. At the end of the corridor, he opened the door into a huge hall. Rich rugs lay across a polished wooden floor. A massive fireplace was flanked by two enormous armchairs. It felt like a space for giants. Nobody was about.

He knew he shouldn't dawdle, but he couldn't resist going to the vast bookcase at the far end. There were leather-bound volumes of Shakespeare, T. S. Eliot and Tolstoy. He felt a bump of recognition when he saw the row of Agatha Christies. Now he knew where his mother got the books from. He ran his fingers reverently over the titles. *Robinson Crusoe* was one of his favourites along with *Boy Scouting*, which he could recite backwards if he had to.

Camp Fire Yarn. No. 20

A Knight (or Scout) is at all times a gentleman. A gentleman is anyone who carries out the rules of chivalry.

Secretly, Gabriel wanted to be a Knight when he grew

up, being *always ready with your armour on, defending the poor*, and *dying honestly*.

He loved Charles Dickens too. He'd lost count of the times he'd read *A Christmas Carol* and right now, he was on his fourth reread of *Great Expectations*. Mum called him a bookworm, but it was a compliment because it had been Mum who'd taught him to love books.

'You can travel the world in a book,' she said. 'Plus, you learn new things. Reading expands your horizon from this–' she'd twirl her hand to indicate the commune, '–to the Outside.'

He'd never been Outside, and whenever he thought about the world beyond the fence, he felt a weird slippery sensation in his stomach.

Reluctantly, Gabriel turned his back on the books and pattered up a grand staircase, past the enormous tapestry hanging there. He remembered Mum stitching it with the other women over several winters; the blazing sunrise set in a triangle, the red cross on top.

The upstairs landing was filled with lots of dull paintings of old people and moth-eaten-looking carpets. He'd heard Father Luke's bedroom was up here, and that the other seven were kept free for guests who visited. Several times a week, however, he asked for one of the Sisters to join him, but nobody talked about where, exactly, she slept.

Gabriel didn't linger but headed to where he thought the study was. He knocked on the door.

'Enter,' Father Luke called.

Cautiously, Gabriel twisted the brass door handle and pushed the door open. Stepped inside.

As soon as Father Luke saw Gabriel his face filled with fury. 'How dare you come in here,' he hissed.

Gabriel quailed. Hauled his courage up from his boots.

'S-sorry, F-Father, but B-Brother Isaac told me to b-bring a message.'

Immediately, the rage vanished to be replaced by a radiant expression. 'Ah. Brother Isaac.' A beatific smile filled his face. His voice became as smooth and soft as honey. 'Well, speak up, boy.'

'It's our b-beloved leader,' he stammered. 'He has come.'

# 6

When Sid turned into the farmyard, Tank came trotting over, ears pricked up and tail waving.

'He knows when you're coming,' Toby told her for the umpteenth time, and for the umpteenth time she said, 'No, he doesn't. He just heard my engine.'

'He knew, trust me.'

Sid rolled her eyes but didn't press it any further. She'd had Tank continuously filmed several times at Toby's so she'd have a record of his behaviour. The data she collected showed that whatever the dog did was completely random, and totally unrelated to the timings of her leaving wherever she was to come and pick him up, but Toby refused to be persuaded. He was convinced Tank had a psychic bond with her and that was that.

'Thanks for looking after him.'

'Officially he's still ours, remember.' He smiled as he gave Tank a pat. Slender and wiry, the farmer had fawn hair almost the same colour as his Jersey cows. His wife, a small woman with a broad face and prominent eyes, bred bullmastiffs on the farm. A nice little earner at over a thousand pounds a pup, but they were incredibly fussy who they sold to, with Toby vetting the buyers as closely as any parent giving away their child.

She opened the passenger door of her three-door Jimny and shifted the seat forward so Tank could scramble inside. She'd owned a sexy little Mazda MX-5 when she'd moved out here, which Toby had looked at with eyebrows raised.

'I take it you're not planning on going anywhere in winter,' he'd remarked.

She didn't think much of it until it rained for three days running and the track turned to mush. She'd had to walk to his farm in order to ring for a taxi to take her to her morning's appointment. It had been Toby who'd helped her trade in her sports car for the four-by-four Suzuki Jimny, to stop her from being 'ripped off', and Toby who'd seen her flinching at unfamiliar country sounds the day she'd moved in. She'd jumped at a deer's bark, then flinched when a pheasant cackled. She'd almost had a heart attack when a screech owl let rip in the wood opposite.

'Sorry, I'm a bit of a townie,' she'd said, feeling stupid but also slightly scared.

He'd dropped Tank off the same afternoon.

She bounced and jolted the Jimny to the cottage. Normally, she'd light the wood burner and put the kettle on but she couldn't wait. She stalked into the sitting room and picked *Racing in the Wild Wind* from her bookshelf. Looked up her father's message. It wasn't long.

*Dearest, darling daughter,*
*It's snowing here today! I wish you were here*
*with me to share a real Swiss-style hot chocolate*

*and throw some snowballs. I love you so very much.*
*Keep a KitKat for me!*
    *Lots of love,*
    *Dad x*

The message about the KitKat referred to their phone conversation the previous evening. The last time she'd talked to him, KitKat had been running a competition and she'd told him she'd bought several chocolate bars in order to collect their wrappers and enter. She couldn't remember what the prize might have been. A music speaker, maybe? She'd been obsessed with Sonos back then.

She'd been too old, really, for the messaging game, and it was only because she didn't want to hurt him that she'd kept doing it. She'd done it out of love for him, as he had, no doubt, for her.

Her legs weakened. She sank onto the sofa, clutching the book to her chest. His message was benign, entirely normal, written on the day he'd flown home and probably before he'd heard about his mother's fall. Tears ran down her cheeks. She hadn't thought she could cry for her parents anymore, but there they were, running into the corners of her mouth, dripping onto her shirt.

After a while, she wiped her eyes and blew her nose. As she regained some equanimity, questions began to rise.

Where had Owen got the postcard from? Why had it surfaced now, after fourteen years? Who had killed Owen? A drift of cold dread began to sweep aside her fantasies about her father being alive. She reminded herself that his car had never been found. No hospital had admitted anyone with memory loss when he'd vanished. Deep down, she'd always suspected he'd died, his body never found, but now she wondered if he had, like Owen Evans, been murdered. If so, why?

Sid sat for a long time, ruminating, only coming to when Tank nudged her, wanting his dinner. She was, she realised, very cold. She moved to the kitchen and lit the wood burner. Put the kettle on. She stood gazing outside at a wintry, steely sky.

One thing became clear. If she found answers to her questions, she might find out what had happened to her father.

---

Sid spent a couple of hours on the internet before heading for bed. She didn't sleep much. Nor had she been able to eat supper either. She'd had a glass of wine but it had tasted strangely sour so she'd poured it away. Stress playing its part, she assumed.

Not long after dawn, she switched on the bedside lamp. Gazed at the photo of her father on her dressing table, taken on her parents' honeymoon. He wore shorts and a huge smile. He looked enormously happy. His leather coin tray sat on her chest of drawers. Her mother's crystals were lined up on the windowsill.

When they were told the chemo wasn't working anymore, Sid hadn't dared bring up the subject of what Mum would like her to do with her body after she died, but her mother hadn't had any such reticence.

Although she'd been pretty ill at the time, she'd insisted they went to Rhossili Bay for a weekend. It was one of the places they used to take the camper-van as a family, and even though she struggled to get over the sand dunes, when they sank into the sand on the other side, waves crashing, seagulls wheeling and mewing, Sid didn't think she'd seen her mother as happy since she'd been diagnosed.

They shared their picnic, then she said, 'I'd like you to scatter my ashes here. And on the point,' she added with a twinkle. 'Make sure if it's windy, you'll keep your mouth shut.'

'It's always windy.'

She drew Sid close and kissed her hair and told her how much she loved her, how proud she was of her, and that she must never forget that.

One Sunday, Sid took the urn and tipped the ashes into a plastic bag. She was surprised how coarse they were and rubbed them between her fingers thinking of Mum's bones, her skull, her long fingers, all reduced to sepia-grey gravel. It was blowing a gale on the beach and she stood with her back to the wind while she trickled the ashes through her fingers. The wind was even stronger on the point, and when she finally upended the bag and shook it, a fine mist of grey dust snatched away in an instant, she surprised herself by smiling.

That night she'd curled in her mother's spot in her parents' bed, and when she decided to turn a new page and move to the country, she'd brought the bed with her. Even today, sometimes the kid in her still needed the comfort.

The next morning, Sid popped Tank out for his morning pee, and sipped her tea at the kitchen window, listening to the news. More dissent throughout the country over the continuing government cuts. Demonstrations in London, Manchester, Liverpool and Leicester. People shouting 'cutting respite care is not right!' and 'care, not cuts!' The trouble was, it wasn't just people ranting against the government's severity in reducing the UK's deficit because they were also fuming over the energy crisis, fracking, the rise in taxes, VAT, child poverty, and everything in between. There was mounting chaos in the country, and the commentator said, depressingly, that it looked like another Winter of Discontent.

*Great,* thought Sid, sighing. *The age of austerity and anxiety continues.*

Rinsing out her mug, she headed for the shower. Padded back into the bedroom in bare feet to stand in front of her wardrobe. She was going to Oxford today and since she didn't know who she might meet, she would dress a little better than usual. Black jeans, boots, a skinny-rib top. Silver bangles and hooped earrings. Wrapping a scarf around her neck, she scooped up her coat and a pair of gloves. Tank looked at her expectantly.

'It's back to the farm today,' she told him.

After she'd dropped him off, she took the A350 to the M4. Her week was flexible since she'd planned to spend it at home writing a series of articles for *Psychologies* and the *Grain of Salt.* She had a column in the *Skeptic Query* which gave her a regular income and covered the rent, but her earnings were incredibly erratic. Because she couldn't run to the bank of Mum and Dad when she fell on hard times, she'd worked her socks off to build up enough savings to support her if she couldn't work for a year or so. She had no intention of getting a full-time job. She liked her freedom too much.

Oxford was glittery with Christmas decorations, their cheer very much at odds with the crowds walking down the high street waving placards. As she drove, she was startled to see several enormous hoardings covered in photographs of an absurdly good-looking man in a sharply cut suit. With his tanned, chiselled features, full lips and perfectly straight nose, he was so handsome she found him faintly disturbing. Behind him floated a Union Jack. In his right hand he held a crucifix.

Marc Strong. Britain Above Everything, God Above Everyone.

Security Minister and a Conservative MP for Oxford West and Abingdon, he was well-known for his outspoken criticism of the current Conservative government, which he considered 'yellow-bellied' and 'soft' against the never-ending erosion of what he considered to be British. She'd received a fistful of junk mail last week, including a flyer from Marc Strong, telling her that her ambition should be a stay-at-home mother supporting her husband and children. Men, on the other hand, who had been lost and confused, abused by women for so long, should enjoy a 'traditional' life once again.

Her soul had shivered. She didn't want to be an outcast if she didn't get married, have kids, and put a Sunday roast on the table every weekend. She'd put all the junk mail in the recycling pile except Marc Strong's, which she'd put in the bin.

After she'd parked around the corner from Juxon Street, she walked to St Giles'. Stopped at the porter's lodge at the Front Quad of St John's College, which had been beautifully refurbished with four-centred arch openings and lined in stone and oak. She was greeted by the receptionist, a snappy grey-haired man with sharp eyes. Etched into the desk plate set before him were the words John Tatlow, Head Porter.

'Mr Tatlow,' Sid said. 'My name is Sidney Scott.' She was rewarded with a flicker of his eyes at her good manners in introducing herself properly. 'I wanted to talk to someone about a former student.' Sid had done as much research as she could online, and when she'd discovered Owen Evans was sixty, the same age as her father would be, she decided to do the next bit of research in person. She wanted to get a feel for the college as well as the student Owen might have been.

'He was here in 1982,' she added. 'He read Classics. He wrote a book in 2010 called *The Underworld: Folklore and Fact.*'

Another flicker. He recognised the name. He didn't, however, say anything. Just waited.

'You've heard what happened to Owen,' Sid stated.

The man gave a slow blink. 'The police were here yesterday.'

Sid heard several footsteps on stone, felt the presence of maybe two people taking their place to queue behind her, but she didn't turn around.

'Did you know him?' she asked.

Something in him tightened. He straightened his desk plate. 'Did you?' he responded. Not the sort of reply she'd expected.

'Not exactly. He had a note for me from my father. I want to know how he got it.'

'Who is your father?'

'Michael Scott.'

At that, the man stared. She had, for some reason, shaken him. His gaze went to the counter, then to the space behind her. 'Excuse me a moment.' He turned and stepped away. Sid craned her neck to see him go to a computer and bring up a bluey-grey coloured page. He then made a phone call. It was obvious he was talking about her because his gaze kept flicking her way. He then tucked the phone under his chin and made a note on a pad on the desk. After he'd hung up, he came over with the pad, tore off the top page and handed it to her. She was surprised to see it was a landline number. She didn't think anyone used them anymore.

'If you could ring Winstone Fairchild. I'm sure he'll be able to help you.'

'But I wanted to–'

'Ring him.' It was an order.

Sid was going to protest further but his gaze had focused over her shoulder. 'Can I help you?' he asked the person behind her.

Sid had been dismissed.

## 7

Standing on St Giles', Sid tightened her scarf against
the cold. With her back to the college wall, she rang
the number the head porter had given her. A young
woman – a girl? – answered almost immediately with a
brisk hello.

'Please can I speak to Winstone Fairchild?'

'I'm sorry, he's not here. Who's calling?'

'Sidney Scott.'

'Oh,' said the girl-woman. 'I've a note here telling me to
make sure (a) I get your number and (b) make an
appointment for him to see you.'

'My number will have come up, hopefully.'

'Yes.' She was bright. 'It's registered right here. Where
are you?'

'Central Oxford.'

'That's handy, since we're also in Oxford. For a moment
I was worried you might be in Outer Mongolia. But then
the line probably wouldn't be as clear. Sorry, I'm
rambling... He can come to see you, or you could come
here, and see him at his home?'

'His home, please.' She'd get a better idea of the man by meeting him on his own turf, as well as potentially meeting the young woman she was speaking to. His wife? His girlfriend?

'He won't get back until after four. Is that okay?'

After they'd hung up, Sid put the details in her contacts. Checked the time. Just after 1pm. She still had an hour before her meeting with the FLO – Family Liaison Officer – at Thames Valley Police. The original FLO, who'd looked after her and her mother when Dad disappeared, had long gone, replaced by another woman who Sid didn't know. Sid had wanted to speak to an investigating officer but she'd been told that FLO's weren't just there to make cups of tea and pass over packs of tissues; they had an investigating role too. The FLO, she was told firmly, should be her first port of call, and would make herself cognisant with the case before Sid dropped by.

Sid had also contacted Missing People, who still had her father listed on their books, and still looked out for him. They never gave up, and had a phenomenal success rate, thanks to having a policy that if you'd disappeared, you could get in touch with them and they weren't beholden to let your loved ones know.

Sid had been shocked at how many people who went missing didn't want to be found, and she'd found it heart-breaking to learn that even when the organisation had managed to track down a woman's missing husband – now living with another woman in Dubai – he'd insisted they couldn't even let his wife know he was alive and well. So, while he swanned around in the sunshine with his new partner, his wife was left to live in anguished limbo in the UK. Sid had thought this unbearably cruel.

*You wouldn't do that to me, would you, Dad?* she asked.

*Of course not.* He looked shocked.

*I spoke to Missing People this morning. They knew nothing about Owen Evans, and had no news of you either.*

His face grew sad, and then, as usual, his image blurred and he was gone.

Sid wandered through town, past museums and ancient colleges, through the Covered Market, Christmas lights and decorations sparkling and glimmering. She walked past her mother's old shop, which used to have its window full of crystals and quartz, butter candles and Tibetan pillar lamps. Now it was an arts supply store. Boring. She could remember the scent of incense that drifted along the street and felt the familiar ache as she cried inside. Mum used to love her incense sticks.

Finally, Sid made her way to St Aldate's, where the FLO greeted Sid with a brisk handshake – 'Hi, I'm Tina'– and ushered her through the bowels of the police station to a small untidy office with two desks and a window overlooking a courtyard car park. The air smelled of mints.

'I haven't got long, I'm afraid.' Tina was curt. Not a note of apology or regret which immediately got Sid's back up.

'You did warn me.' She managed to keep her voice neutral. 'And whatever time you can give me, I'm grateful.'

Tina glanced at her watch. Sat down behind the desk and clicked on a mouse, looking at her screen. Tight blonde curls, fake tan. Dramatic, painted-on, thick black eyebrows and eyelashes like twin spiders made her eyes look wide and unnaturally alert.

'So,' said Tina. 'Your father's been missing for fourteen years.'

Sitting opposite, leaning forward, Sid reiterated the story of Owen Evans and her father's postcard. 'The investigating officer is Detective Kelly. He's with the Gloucestershire Police.'

'Don't know him.' Tina squinted at the screen. 'Last time you saw Sandi, the previous FLO, was five years ago.'

That long? Sid was surprised. She'd thought only a couple of years had passed, probably because they'd mostly communicated by phone or email. Sandi had regularly checked for updates of John Does that would match her father's age and description, comparing his fourteen-year-old photograph with pictures from morgues. Whenever Sandi rang, it would stop her heart. Every time she said she hadn't found Dad, Sid felt a bitter rush of relief that he wasn't dead and fear at the thought he might be alive, and couldn't get in touch.

'So, what does Owen Evans having this postcard mean?' Tina nibbled at a hangnail. 'You say it's old. Dated the day your father vanished. Did they know one another, do you think?'

'No idea. Is there anything on his file? Any mention of something that might connect Dad and Owen?'

Tina shook her head. 'I'll make a note of the postcard, though.' She tapped briefly on her keyboard.

'Where did Owen find it?' Sid wondered out loud. 'If I can find that out, then I might find what happened to my father.'

'You might,' Tina agreed. 'But don't go turning detective, will you. That's my job.' She looked at her watch. 'Shit. I've got to go.'

As she rose, she grabbed a flyer from a pile of papers on her desk. It was, Sid recognised, one of Marc Strong's leaflets. Sid also rose. She gestured at the leaflet.

'Oh,' Tina said. 'I've got an appointment at his surgery with a client.'

'Do you know him?'

'I do, actually.' She smiled as she flipped the leaflet over to look at Marc Strong's picture. 'Not bad-looking, eh?'

'He advocates women to stay at home, not to work.'

'He means working professionally.'

'Like having a career?' *Like me and you*, she wanted to say, but held her tongue.

'I think it's shit that families aren't a priority anymore. Kids are dumped in crèches, others turned into latchkey kids... Trust me, if you saw even half what I saw...'

'You like what he says?' There was no judgement in Sid's tone, no edge to make Tina feel defensive.

'Totally.' Tina closed the office door behind them and continued to talk as they walked down the corridor. 'I mean I'm not a fan that he's a total Christian, a bit religious for me, but his God's credit system? What's not to like? If you're caught dropping litter on the street then you have to litter pick the M4 for a week. If you play your music too loudly on the train, you can't take a train for another month...

'Take the demonstrations around the country...' Tina pushed through a swing door at the end of the corridor. 'Instead of being mollycoddled by the state, we, as police officers, would have the right to take a miscreant and lock them up overnight. No exceptions. That would make those people marching in the streets think twice, trust me.'

'Overnight,' Sid repeated musingly. 'Are there enough cells?'

'He's already said he'd build loads more if he gets into power. Like we built those Nightingale Hospitals virtually overnight...' Tina opened another door, this time into reception. Sid followed her. 'He makes sense to me, you know. His idea is that everyone starts with say, a thousand credits, and if you fuck up by running a red light or causing a disturbance, you lose some, but if you do good, like donating to charity, you get credits. Simple. Even the stupidest criminal should be able to get it.'

'What happens when you run out of credits?'

'Then you're an idiot.'

Outside, it had started to rain. Tina lifted her face to the sky. 'Crap. I forgot my umbrella.'

---

Jack Straw's Lane was a mix of residential homes set on either side of a narrow road. Lots of trees and hedges. The air was rich with the smell of rotting leaves and wood smoke. She could have been in the middle of the countryside it felt so rural. Turning into a drive with moss down its centre she saw an ancient-looking stone farmhouse ahead. An old Vauxhall was parked outside a garage, along with two bicycles chained to a set of metal posts. She parked behind the Vauxhall.

Sid pressed the doorbell. Seconds later, the door was flung open.

'Hey, that was quick!'

Fourteen or fifteen years old, she wore ripped jeans and a happy expression.

Sid blinked.

'Shit,' the girl said. 'Wrong person. Sorry. I thought you were Win.'

She'd said, *Win*. Probably not her father, then.

'I'm Sidney Scott.'

The girl's eyebrows rose. She studied Sid in silence, then suddenly smiled.

'I'm Flick.' She opened the door wide. 'Win had an emergency but he won't be long. You're welcome to come in and wait.'

'How long will he be?'

Flick brought out her phone and punched some buttons. Almost immediately the phone pinged in return.

'He's on his way,' she said brightly. 'He says I'm to make you a coffee.'

'If you're sure...'

Sid followed Flick as she bounced down a corridor into a country-style kitchen. Natural oak cupboards and drawers, wide floorboards, a bookshelf crammed with cookery books, herbs and plants on the windowsills. More books were on the kitchen table along with coffee mugs, a half-full bottle of wine and a wine glass. A Christmas tree twinkled merrily in one corner. It was messy and lived-in and reminded her of her childhood home, except it smelled of buttered toast and not scented candles.

'Coffee okay or would you prefer tea?' Flick was already pulling open cupboards and bringing out mugs. Then she paused. 'Or would you like a lesbian tea? That's what Granny calls herbal tea. She's a terror.'

Sid made a neutral sound to cover any response Flick might be looking for.

'She likes her tea strong enough to strip an engine,' Flick went on. 'She used to fly Spitfires, you know.'

'Impressive,' Sid remarked. 'I'd love a coffee, please.' She didn't particularly want one, but since she couldn't smoke, at least she'd have something to do with her hands.

A Nespresso machine was prepped and coffee made. Flick pulled out a couple of kitchen chairs and invited Sid to sit. Propping her chin in her hands, she fixed Sid with a beady black gaze. 'Now. Tell me what you do. You look as though you'd do something really interesting.'

Sid gave the girl top marks for her social skills which, whether she'd planned it or not, would make Sid feel valued as well as put her at ease. 'You're very kind,' she said wryly, 'but it goes both ways. You first.'

'Absolutely not.' Flick lifted her chin. 'This is my house, I get to do the interview.'

Sid smiled. She couldn't help it. She liked her. 'I'm a supernatural scientist.'

'Wow.' Flick's eyes widened. 'I knew it. Fascinating. Fill me in.'

Twenty minutes later Sid was showing Flick how to convince strangers that she could read palms when a door slammed and footsteps sounded along the corridor. Flick's hands were upturned in Sid's, and they both turned their heads as a man walked into the kitchen. Tall and broad, his jeans were scuffed, his work boots dusty. His face was sheened with sweat and energy buzzed from him, like a boxer who'd just stepped out of the ring. Then she took in his hands, thick and strong, bunched at his sides. The knuckles were bruised and bleeding. She stared. Had he been in a fight?

'What the fuck are you doing?' He stared at Sid.

Flick pulled her hands from Sid's and got to her feet. 'She's showing me how to read–'

'I asked her, not you.' His gaze didn't move from Sid.

'Win, she's–'

'Shut it, Flick,' he snapped.

Flick rolled her eyes but didn't say any more.

'I'm Sidney Scott.' Sid rose to her full height.

A small silence fell as he stared at Sid and she gazed calmly back. Flick moved to the sink and ran some water. Came back with a cloth and handed it to Win. Sid could see the similarity immediately in their dark hair, the narrow length of their noses, the same tan colouring of their skin. There had to be fifteen years between them, which made them siblings? Cousins?

Win wiped his knuckles cursorily, his eyes never leaving Sid. Flick took the cloth back to the sink, sighing noisily, probably to make a point at being told to 'shut it'.

'My study,' Win told Sid. 'Now.'

Flick stuck her tongue out at him as he turned and marched outside, making Sid laugh and reminding her how little she laughed these days. In the corridor, Win stood waiting for her by an open door. He stood with his shoulders back, almost imperiously, and for a second, she thought he might salute. The laughter remained with her.

Inside the study, she looked around curiously. One wall was covered in books. *The Art of Statistics; The Psychology of Persuasion; Speed & Power; Jupiter's Travels, Etiquette in Japan.* It was an eclectic collection and if books revealed a personality then she'd be hard pushed to pigeonhole him. The opposite wall was as diverse. A framed photo of him as a boy deeply engrossed in a game of chess with a man who Sid guessed was his father. Another photograph depicted a student protest and, there at the front of the march, was yours truly.

He stood behind his desk with his arms folded. He was shaking his head. 'You people.'

Immediately, she bristled inside. If there was one characteristic she disliked most, it was prejudging others, but she wasn't here to defend herself. It would take too long, for a start, and she wanted to get home and pick up Tank.

'You knew Owen Evans?' she prompted.

His jaw flexed. He looked as though he was having trouble changing his thought trajectory.

'No.' He shook his head.

'But you knew of him.'

'Yes.'

Sid waited without saying anything. Silence was the best way to get information and she was hoping he'd expound.

But Win simply fixed Sid with his deep, dark-brown gaze. His jaw was still tight, his hands flexed. Neither spoke for several seconds. A car door slammed somewhere and outside, a blackbird chattered.

Sid caved in first. 'Why did you get the head porter at St John's to put us in touch?'

He hesitated before saying, 'Not just you. Anyone who came asking about Owen Evans.'

'Why?'

Picking up a pen, he spun it on the desk in front of him.

'What was Owen to you?' she pressed.

'He wasn't, until he died.'

What the hell did that mean?

The sharp, intent way he was looking at her made her stomach turn slightly greasy. 'Owen Evans had a postcard addressed to me, from my father.'

No response.

Did this mean he already knew this? Or was he just very good at keeping his sentiments concealed?

Sid ploughed on. 'Dad went missing fourteen years ago. He was last seen filling up his car in Headington.' She told him the same old story about her parents. She'd done it so often it didn't take long. He may be an opinionated jerk but at least he listened without interruption or offering banal sympathy. She finished by asking again, how he knew of her father, but he didn't answer.

Sid nibbled her lip before asking if Win knew how Owen might have come by her father's postcard. He opened his mouth as if to answer and for a moment she was stunned – he *knew*? – but then he sat at his desk and switched on a computer. He didn't offer her a seat, so she remained standing. Watched as he tapped on a keyboard.

'Your father went to Christchurch?' he asked.

'Reading physics.1985.'

'And Owen was at St John's at the same time.'

'It appears so.'

Win checked his computer. Tapped some more. For a long moment Win stared hard at her.

'What is it?' she asked.

He looked as though he was going to say something, then decided against it.

'Please,' she said. 'I'm trying to find out what happened to my father.' She was surprised at the pleading in her tone and he finally turned the computer screen around to show her a photograph.

Four students. Four young men with their arms across one another's shoulders. Three wore dark trousers and shirts, skinny ties. The fourth wore a tatty Def Leppard T-shirt and a denim Levi's jacket with fleece lining, which, although it was threadbare, the lining almost gone, still hung in her wardrobe.

'Dad,' she whispered.

# 8

Sid stared at the picture of her father, smiling with what she took to be his friends. She recognised the younger Owen, his soft, round face, and Marc Strong's angular good looks, but not the slightly built man with a luxuriant mop of sun-streaked hair.

'Who is he?' She pointed him out.

'Luke Goddard.' Win's expression was intense. 'With your father, are Owen Evans and Marc Strong.'

'I know Marc Strong,' Sid said. 'Well, know *of* him, but not Luke Goddard. Who is he?'

Win turned his head to look outside, but he didn't seem to be surveying the view of sleet falling on a wintry garden. His earlier animosity seemed to have fallen away, leaving him ruminative. 'Didn't your father ever introduce you?'

'Never.'

'Not to Marc Strong?'

'No.'

Silence fell.

'Why did your father befriend them, do you think?'

'I have absolutely no idea.'

'Hmmm.' He stroked his chin.

'Where did you get that photograph?' she asked. When he didn't respond, she added, 'Can I have a copy? Please?'

At that, he swivelled back to his keyboard, moved his mouse around. 'Your phone number?'

She gave it to him and after some more mouse manoeuvring, her phone pinged. The picture was now on her phone.

'Do you think they have anything to do with Owen's death?' she asked. When he didn't reply, she went on. 'What about Dad? Do you think they might know what happened to him?'

Instead of answering, he got to his feet and started checking his phone. 'I'm sorry, I have to be somewhere.'

From his lack of eye contact and haste, she knew it was a lie. He'd got what he wanted from her, whatever it was, and had no intention of giving her anything in return. Wanting to delay him, she swiftly scanned the objects on his desk, which included a miniature resin block with two figures wrestling. 'What dan are you?'

He looked startled for a moment, and then his eyes narrowed. 'Don't you dare start.' His tone was acid.

Wow, he certainly didn't like psychics. Not that she was a fan of them either, but not to the point of rudeness. It hadn't crossed his mind she might have clocked the resin award or seen the man-sized sweatshirt with the logo *The Judo Studio* hanging in the hallway. Guessing he was into martial arts wasn't exactly rocket science, but his mind had been clouded by his presumption of her.

'What did you tell Flick?' he sneered. 'That she'll find the love of her life next week?'

'Who says she hasn't already?' Sid smiled sweetly. 'And what about you? How's the divorce coming along?'

The skin around his lips turned white.

Nothing he didn't deserve. She'd seen the pale band on his third finger where his wedding ring used to be, and taken in the sheafs of legal papers on his desk, but the clincher had been the envelope in the bin addressed to him and franked by Lansdown Law, which she knew was one of Oxford's top specialist divorce lawyers.

He stalked to the door. 'You may be able to manipulate Flick, but not me.'

'Are you sure you wouldn't like a reading?' She widened her eyes innocently. 'I'm getting a really strong feeling you're emotionally stressed when in general you're normally relaxed and laid-back.'

Win pushed the door open so hard it smacked into the wall, but he didn't seem to be aware of it. He stood well back as if he couldn't bear to be close to her.

'Out.'

Feeling not unlike Tank when he'd done something naughty, like pinch a biscuit from her plate when she wasn't looking, she scooted along the corridor. As she approached the front door, Flick appeared. 'Stay for supper?' she asked Sid brightly.

'I don't think–'

'Please, pretty please,' she added, holding up her hands in a praying position. 'We're having spag bol. You can't say no to that.'

'That's very kind,' she said, flicking a look at Win, who looked aghast. 'But I'm afraid I have to be elsewhere.'

She could have laughed at the relief that flashed across his face.

'What about the weekend?' Flick brought out her phone as if to check her calendar.

Win looked at Sid, jaw locked. Sid had to resist the temptation to say yes and watch him squirm. 'I don't think so,' she said quietly. 'But thanks anyway.'

Silently, she walked out of the house and climbed into her car without looking at Win again.

---

Sid got home just as it was getting dark. She'd texted Toby so she didn't have to disturb anyone at the farmhouse and Tank trotted over the second she pulled into the yard. Her mail was in its usual place just inside the farmhouse porch; a council tax bill and a flyer for a new pizza restaurant that had opened in Melksham. She switched on the headlights as she drove down the track.

When she let Tank out of the car he immediately made for the back door, tail up, ready for his dinner. He'd just pushed his way past the leggy hydrangea – she really must prune it before spring – when he suddenly stopped. All his hackles rose.

Sid felt a moment's sheer fright. 'What is it, boy?' Her voice came out squeaky with adrenaline.

He stepped forward, stiff-legged, his tail held low.

Her fingers felt clumsy as she brought out her phone, ready to dial 999. She watched as the dog snuffed the ground and began to walk towards the cottage. He was growling softly, a low rumble deep in his chest.

Sid didn't follow him. She backed up to her car, ready to jump in and lock the doors, call the police. As she watched, the dog stepped to the back door and shouldered it open, walked inside.

She was sure she'd locked it.

Absolutely positive.

She could hear a jet flying overhead, the distant hum of a lorry from Bath Road, and then Tank arrived in a rush, all excitement and eagerness and wanting his dinner.

'What was it, then?'

He trotted towards the cottage, tail up, no hackles, body relaxed. When she didn't follow him fast enough, he returned to chivvy her along by butting her thighs with his head. The back door, she saw, had been jimmied open. Cautiously, she peeked inside to see Tank standing ahead in the kitchen, waiting for her. If there'd been a burglar, they wouldn't have wanted to hang around with a hundred pounds of angry guard dog prowling about.

Sid reached around the door-jamb and switched on the lights. Nobody shouted. Nobody rushed at her. Still, she didn't relax until she'd checked each room and every cupboard, Tank padding alongside, looking puzzled.

A couple of things had been moved but nothing stolen. Her laptop was still there, along with her credit cards and jewellery, and an original Salvador Dali sketch that Dad had bought years ago, when he'd visited Bruges, and which was now worth a hundred times what he'd bought it for. It showed a strange-limbed horse with clocks for eyes, and although her mother hadn't liked it, Sid, like her father, found it intriguing.

She fed Tank and while he rattled his metal bowl against the skirting board, she called Toby and filled him in.

'I didn't see anyone,' he told her, 'but I've been out at High Clay most of the day, fencing.'

Sid listened as he asked his wife, who said she hadn't seen anyone either.

'Never had any trouble before,' Toby told her. 'Not with kids, travellers or anyone. Most people don't even realise there's a cottage down the track. I'm sorry, love. Are you okay? Is that mutt looking after you?'

After reassuring the farmer she was fine, she took down the number he gave her of a locksmith he knew.

Toby added she could install any alarm she liked but at her own cost, 'if that was all right, love?'

The locksmith quoted an astronomical fee but said yes, he could come out within the hour. He recommended an alarm specialist who said he'd come out the next morning and install an alarm system, no problem. Meanwhile, she kept Tank next to her. He'd been a panacea for her nerves when she'd first got here, and right now, she'd never been more grateful for his protection.

Who might have broken into her cottage? Why? She took a shaky breath as she considered whether it might have anything to do with her enquiries. As she ran over the day's events, she couldn't see how she'd ruffled anyone's feathers. She'd only been to Owen's old college and dropped by to see the FLO afterwards. What about Win? He'd have had to have teleported himself here before she returned home.

Had the head porter called someone else as well as Win? Or was she being ridiculous? After dithering for a while, Sid called the Gloucestershire Police. Asked for Detective Kelly. He was, apparently, unavailable, so she left a message to tell him that she'd called.

She was too jumpy to eat, so after the locksmith had come and gone, she lit the wood burner and distracted herself by studying the photograph of the four students. Her father was definitely the odd one out, and not just because of his rock band T-shirt. The other three were preppy-looking lads who exuded a carefree air that for some reason, her father lacked. Sid zoomed in on their faces. Three pairs of eyes were creased at the corners in a seemingly genuine smile, but Dad's? His mouth was in a wide grin, but his bear-brown eyes were steady and serious, unsmiling. The more she looked at the foursome, the more she wondered what her father was doing with the other three. What linked them? And where had the photo been taken? When? Before she was born, she guessed.

Sid settled at the kitchen table with a glass of wine and started researching the four university students on her laptop.

While Owen had read Classics at St John's College, Oxford, her father had read science at Christchurch. Marc Strong, she learned, had read Philosophy, Politics and Economics in Oxford, at Balliol. Same timings.

Luke Goddard had read Theology and Religion, also in Oxford. Same timings again.

Four university students smiling into the camera together. Had they known one another before then?

Her fingers flew across her keyboard.

It took a while, but she finally pulled the information free.

All four boys had been at the same school.

# 9

While the alarm system was being installed the next morning, Sid made some phone calls. Checked out Google Maps. Her brain felt as slow as a slug after a rough night's sleep. Every sound the cottage made, every creak, every scratch of a branch against a windowpane had made her eyelids snap open and her heart rate accelerate, convinced the intruder had returned. She'd ended up bringing Tank, along with his bedding, to sleep on the landing outside her bedroom, but she still slept badly.

'You want a panic button installed?'

She glanced up at the engineer, a man in his fifties with a long, thin face.

'I'm not sure.'

'It can be connected to our monitoring centre via a silent alarm. We can then request emergency assistance from local security or the police.' He sucked on his teeth. 'It's not cheap, though.'

'How much?'

When he gave her the numbers, she blinked. 'Crikey. I could go to the Caribbean on that.'

'I know.' He was watching her, his eyes cautious. She thought she read anxiety there. 'Who broke in, love? Do you know?'

'I have absolutely no idea. They didn't take anything. Just looked around, I think.'

'A stalker?' he suggested.

She leaned back, folding her arms. 'Nobody knows where I live.' She told him she was uber-cautious about sharing her personal details; her website only offered an email address and she kept where she lived as secret as humanly possible.

The engineer just looked at her, slightly pityingly.

'Okay,' she conceded. 'So anyone could find out, if they worked hard enough.' She rubbed the space between her brows. 'But I can't think of anyone, not really.'

'Kids?' he suggested.

'Wouldn't they have made more mess? Or eaten my supply of chocolate, smoked my cigarettes?'

'Good point.' The engineer glanced at Tank. 'He's as good as any alarm system, if you ask me. But if you decide you want a panic alarm...' He reached into his breast pocket and withdrew a good old-fashioned business card. 'Call me.'

She set the alarm, feeling a weird sense of relief leaving her cottage which in turn made her angry. How dare someone unsettle her enough to make her glad to leave her own home? After she'd dropped Tank at the farm, she headed south, for Bruton. She still couldn't imagine who might have broken into her cottage and she spent the journey imagining on the one hand some weird stalker from Bath uni fingering her things, and on the other, Owen Evans's killer doing the same. Both concepts made her shudder inside and she wondered if she should have installed a panic alarm even if it was just for her peace of mind.

It took barely an hour to get there, along a winding country road that cut through ancient woodland and medieval stone villages, and she wasn't sure why she was surprised when she pulled through the school gates, because she already knew her dad had gone to a private school, but what a school! *Bloody hell,* she thought. *It must cost a fortune to send your kid here.*

She'd already checked its website and knew Stonehouse School was big, male only, and that it was old – founded in 1551 – and was in the top ten of the most expensive private boarding schools in the UK. But on seeing the huge baronial-style house she had trouble picturing her father here, at a school for super-rich posh boys.

Had Dad's parents really been that wealthy? Her grandfather had been a plumber and heating engineer, her grandmother a sales assistant for John Lewis. Not poor but not rich either. Both had died before their daughter-in-law – Sid's mother – got cancer, which was shit for Sid as both her maternal grandparents were dead and she would have loved some support at the time.

The head's secretary appeared at a clip, a bright-eyed twenty-something in a sharp little trouser suit who led her through great echoing spaces, a marble hallway, and up a massive oak staircase decorated with fake holly and ivy twists. Festive red ribbons and gold baubles hung everywhere. Along a wood-panelled corridor, Sid was shown a variety of portraits of headmasters past, cricket heroes, champion swimmers.

'We're all deeply shocked by events.' She turned to look at Sid with a sombre expression. 'To think an Old Stonehouser would be murdered...' She trailed off expectantly, inviting Sid to be indiscreet.

'Shocking,' Sid said neutrally, earning her a tiny pout.

The headmaster's study wasn't lined with dusty old books as Sid had imagined, but was a light and airy space of blues and greens. Even the little Christmas tree sparkling on the window ledge was decorated vividly in blue and silver. The headmaster was also a surprise, being relatively young, in his early forties, even if he was as bald as an egg.

It didn't take long to ascertain that he wasn't the person Sid should be talking to.

'Elizabeth Whitlock,' he told her. 'Liz knows every boy, every teacher that's passed through this school since 1975. She's a living encyclopaedia of Stonehouse. Extraordinary memory. Eidetic, in fact. Shall I call for her?'

'She's still here?'

'She's only in her seventies.' His tone was slightly scolding, as though she'd committed an ageist faux pas.

'I'd love to talk to her.'

While he called for Liz Whitlock and asked for tea for three, and yes to biscuits too, she stepped to the window and looked out. Acres of lawns, ancient trees, tennis courts, and a smartly painted cricket pavilion. It reeked of privilege and money, and she tried to imagine her father as a kid like those boys below, dressed in a smart blue uniform and joshing one another, but struggled.

God, how she wished Mum was still alive, so she could ask her what Dad had thought of the place – whether he was happy or not – ask her grandparents, a cousin, *anyone*, but there was nobody. Everyone was dead. She was, she thought gloomily, the last in the Scott line.

Tea came in pretty white china mugs accompanied by M&S chocolate biscuits. Liz came in a slimline, embroidered, knee-length purple velvet cardigan over a long velvet dress and chic black suede boots. Neatly cropped silver-grey hair, vivid blue eyes. Sexy seventies, Sid surmised, hoping she'd look half as good at that age.

'Poor Evans,' Liz said, taking a biscuit and munching. 'Who killed him, do we know?'

Sid shook her head. 'Owen had a postcard from my father, addressed to me. You know my father disappeared?'

'Yes.' Liz sighed. 'He came here thanks to our scholarship system.'

That explained *that*, then.

'He was very bright, your father. A nice boy too, but very taken up with his studies.'

'Not sporty?'

'He could have been, he just wasn't interested.'

'And Owen?'

Liz shot a look at the headmaster who gave a slight nod. There had to be confidentiality issues here, and Sid just had to hope she could glean something to set her on a path to find out what happened to her father.

'Dear Owen wasn't built for sport. He was–' she searched for the right word, '–not the sporty type. He liked his food a little too much, I think.'

'He was overweight?'

Liz gave a chuckle. 'Nobody was really heavy here, back then. No chocolates or biscuits on tap, or fizzy drinks. But yes, he was on the chubby side.'

'What about Marc Strong and Luke Goddard?'

Something sharp rose in her eyes. 'What about them?'

Sid showed her the photograph of the four students with their arms across one another's shoulders. 'I wondered about their relationship, if they'd been best friends at school, that kind of thing.'

'Relationship,' Liz repeated, gazing at the photograph. 'Hmmm.' She shot the headmaster another look. Again, a nod of the head. 'Well, I can tell you a story if you like.'

'Sure.'

'Those three boys, Owen, Marc and Luke, started boarding here when they were eight.'

'Eight?' Sid exclaimed. It seemed exceptionally young.

'A lot of children thrive away from the parents,' she said drily. 'Trust me.'

'What about Dad?' Sid felt alarmed on his behalf. She'd thought he'd adored his parents.

'He didn't come here until he was eleven.'

Sid was glad. She hated the thought of him leaving home at such a tender age.

A small silence fell, during which the headmaster topped up their tea and offered biscuits. Liz spoke as she sipped and nibbled.

'Anyway, there they were, three eight-year-old boys in their first term. I came across Luke lording it over some of the other boys in the common room. He'd ordered them to take off their clothes and stand barefoot in their underpants while he paraded in front of them with a white sheet wrapped around him, like a toga. He'd taken the cross from the housemaster's desk and was going around blessing them.

'"Call me Your Holiness", he demanded. Gosh, he was imperious. The kids were really cowed by him, but then he came across Marc, who said, "If I call you Holiness, you'll have to call me Archbishop".

'Then little Owen piped up. "Can I be a Bishop too?"

'"No", Luke declared. "You can be our warden".'

Liz put her mug down with a little click. 'I broke it up, of course, but it didn't stop the rot. It was only later that I learned Marc and Luke had run the class on a quasi-religious basis for ages. They held poor little Owen in their thrall. He followed them around like a lapdog.'

The two women looked at one another.

'Precocious,' Sidney remarked.

'Arrogant,' Liz said.

'Marc Strong appears to be going places,' the headmaster offered. He was choosing another biscuit as he spoke and missed the way Liz's expression changed. Sid studied the woman with interest, unable to work it out. Though Liz was presenting as blank, there was something in her demeanour that oozed antipathy.

Sid decided to confront this head-on. 'I'm curious, how do you feel about those boys today?'

Liz said nothing, lips pressed together as if to prevent herself speaking. Sid's curiosity increased, and she was aware of wanting to dig further. 'You don't like them.'

She looked taken aback.

'Was it the bullying?' Sid pressed.

'Nobody likes a bully,' she agreed, albeit tentatively.

Sid refused to let it drop. 'There's something else, isn't there?'

'Absolutely not.' She shook her head vehemently. 'I don't know what you mean.'

Liz's back was up, so Sid decided to let it go. She swallowed the last of her tea. 'What about my father? How did he fit into the trio?'

Liz took a breath, as though resettling her thoughts.

'He didn't, as far as I know. Yes, he was in the same classes, but I'd never say they were friends. I have to admit I was surprised when you showed me that photograph. I wouldn't have thought he'd fraternise with them.'

'Perhaps it was a one-off,' Sid mused.

'Perhaps.'

But somehow, Sid didn't think so. During her research last night, she'd found a handful more photographs online of the four students. A couple had been taken at what appeared to be a summer ball, all four young men dressed in black tie. Where Owen, Luke Goddard and Marc Strong appeared comfortable and urbane in their formal attire, her father looked unbelievably uncomfortable, like a brown bear muzzled and stuffed into a suit. A further picture showed them in a pub garden, drinking beer. The fact Dad hadn't mentioned them, or Mum either, Sid took to mean they were no longer friends. Or they were friends at uni only. Or they weren't friends as much as acquaintances. Or they'd fallen out. Or, or, or…

When the headmaster wound up the meeting, Sid thanked him, getting to her feet at the same time as Liz. He said he'd get his secretary to show her to her car – the place is like a warren – but Sid said she'd be fine, if Liz could point her in the right direction. As they walked down various corridors, the two women talked a bit about Owen, and it was only as they reached the cavernous hall entrance that Sid paused.

'There's something about those boys that you're not sharing,' Sid remarked.

Liz stared at her.

'Look,' Sid lowered her voice, 'I won't tell anyone if you don't want me to, but if it could be relevant, it might help me find my father.'

The woman continued to stare at Sid.

'Please,' Sid added.

Liz's expression turned fierce. 'If I tell you, and you use it in any way, I'll deny it.'

'I promise.' Sid solemnly crossed her heart for good measure.

Her blue eyes intense, Liz leaned forward. 'It wasn't Owen as much as Marc and Luke. They were just so… *awful*. Today, we'd say they lacked the empathy gene, or were on the sociopathic spectrum, but back then, we called them the little Hitlers.

'We had a school fair that summer. Splat the Rat, Dunk a Teacher, Apple Bobbing, all the usual games...' Her gaze grew distant as she spoke. 'Every year I dressed up as Psychic Ceres and pretended to read the boys' futures through my tarot cards. I was a drama teacher, so I made it pretty convincing... I wore a set of pointed false teeth, and false pointy fingernails. A grey wig beneath a silk scarf, big hooped earrings, lots of black. Inside the Fortune-Teller's tent, it was dark, just two candles alight. The boys never recognised me. They were, in fact, scared of me – the Wicked Witch – and used to dare each other to visit me.

'So it wasn't a surprise when those two swaggered in – dragging little Owen behind them – and crossed my palm with silver. I almost turned them away, but then I wondered if I could teach them a lesson. So, I read their fortunes, lots of hocus-pocus, that sort of thing. They were rapt. I told Luke he'd be head of the church one day, Marc that he'd be prime minister, and Owen king of the Otherworld. They absolutely fell for every word, excited, *thrilled* that they'd be "rulers".

'But then I said none of this would come true unless they conducted a magic ceremony with me and let their blood into my bowl.'

She glanced sideways at Sid, who concentrated on keeping her face perfectly impartial. She did, however, give a nod to encourage Liz to continue.

'They didn't like the sound of that very much, so I looked at my tarot cards and said, "What a shame, because without a real, heartfelt commitment to the cosmos, none of this is going to come true".

'Needless to say, Marc and Luke both held out their hands for me to cut. Owen needed some persuading but eventually he caved in. I brought out a silver dish and lit incense, intoned magical words, and cut their palms, let their blood drip into the dish and at the same time, I rubbed my fingers, which I'd already treated with Magic Smoke ointment. Clouds of white smoke appeared from my fingertips and, seconds later, I lit some flash paper which really got their attention.

'Then... well, things, er...' She cleared her throat and gazed into the distance as though wondering how to proceed. 'I then... well, I deepened my voice dramatically, trembling head to toe and pretending I'd been taken over by a dark entity who saw everything the boys did. This entity told them that bullies were weak, spineless creatures, and that anyone who was truly strong didn't need to put others down.

'"Be truly strong", the entity told them and at the same time, I threw some flash powder into the bowl creating a huge streak of flame. They actually screamed, can you believe it? And they ran like hell out of the tent.' Liz was gazing past Sid, her expression distant.

Something wasn't quite right about the story, but Sid couldn't put her finger on it. She could see why Liz wouldn't want the story made public. Cutting children's palms in a magic ceremony? She'd have lost a lot more than just her job.

Sid said, 'Did they stop their bullying?'

Liz refocused her gaze on Sid. 'No,' she said.

Was it her imagination or was Liz's expression fearful? Whatever it was, Sid found it unsettling. 'Did they come back for a reading another year?'

'Never.'

'Did you ever read my father's future?'

'No.'

'He would have enjoyed your show.'

A handful of boys strode past, chatting. One of them said, 'Hi, Miss Whitlock,' and she gave him a wave.

'What psychological effect do you think your reading had?' asked Sid. 'I mean, for example, Marc Strong is now a politician.'

Liz Whitlock looked discomforted. 'I do wonder sometimes, because Owen Evans immersed himself in Welsh mythology. In particular, searching for Annwn.'

What felt like an ice cube slid down Sid's spine. 'The Otherworld?'

'Yes.'

'And Luke Goddard?'

Liz swallowed. Turned her head away. 'He now has his own church. It's called the Hermetic Order of the Golden Dawn.'

## 10

Gabriel listened to the Beloved Leader with increasing excitement. Some of them were going to be chosen to go Outside! He'd nearly visited the local town once, when he and Mum had been tasked with collecting the groceries. Usually one of the Guards undertook the weekly run, but for some reason that day, it was the three of them cruising along the drive in the Estate's ancient Land Rover.

Initially, Mum had put Hannah on the bench seat between them – his little sister had been almost sick with excitement about the trip – but when they reached the cattle grid at the end of the drive, Father Luke was standing there, legs apart and arms crossed, blocking their way. When Mum stopped, he came over and opened the passenger door and beckoned Hannah out.

His mother had begged to take Hannah with them, she'd started crying which Gabriel had found a bit weird and over the top, but Father Luke had picked Hannah up, looking at her as he rocked her in his arms. 'We want Mummy to come back, don't we, little one?'

When he looked back at Gabriel and his mother, his eyes were cold.

'Because if Mummy doesn't return, who knows what might happen?'

Mum had climbed out of the Land Rover and handed Father Luke the keys. In return he handed over Hannah. They never did go and get the groceries.

Now, Hannah leaned close, whispering, 'You've been really good, let's hope they choose you. Then you can go and say hello to Grandma and Grandpa.'

His memory of his grandparents was hazy. He had a vague recollection of nice faces, kind faces. They'd only visited once, just after Hannah was born, but never came again. His mother had already sewn their address into the hem of his djellaba, in case he got the chance to go there. She'd also sewn her precious ring in there – a simple gold band with an inscription so tiny he could barely read it – swearing him to secrecy, which terrified him because if they were found he'd be shut in the Shed not just for a few days but two weeks, perhaps a month, and he'd *die*.

He was excited, he was petrified.

What if he was chosen? What if he wasn't?

What would Mum think? She was currently in the sanatorium, suffering from a bout of what Father Luke called, 'Soul Sickness'. Apparently, Mum had done something wrong in God's eyes, which had made her ill.

'God sees everything you do,' Father Luke said whenever one of them fell sick. 'And he punishes you accordingly.'

Gabriel had been allowed to visit his mother in the morning. He'd been shocked to find her pasty-faced and sweaty. He'd never seen her sick before. She had a bucket next to her bed into which she'd already thrown up. She'd told him not to hug her in case it was catching but then added, 'You won't get ill if you're good,' which kind of rubbed out what she'd said. He'd left her a small bunch of wild grasses he and Hannah had picked from the water meadows, which made her smile.

'ONLY THE PERFECT SERVANTS CAN BE TRUSTED WITH THE MISSION OF OUR LORD!' bellowed Father Luke. Today he'd ditched his usual brown djellaba for a long red robe with a black cross stitched across its front. Candles glowed beside the rough stone altar, casting flickering shadows over the black-robed Brothers and Sisters gathered in the church.

'We are commending them with the future of our world, our planet! It will take immense courage! Fortitude! And your bravery will be rewarded by the Lord on Earth as well as in Heaven!'

Gabriel felt Hannah's hand slip into his and snatched it away. Physical contact was Forbidden. *Please God, nobody had noticed.*

'WHO WANTS TO DO THE LORD'S WORK?' Father Luke thundered.

*Me, me, me!* He wanted to jump up and down to gain Father Luke's attention but held back. He knew he had to remain dignified, calm, or he'd never be chosen.

Brother Saul stepped forward. He brought out a folder. Started reading names.

'Aaron, Barnabas, Abigail, Claudia...'

He was announcing them alphabetically. No surnames. They didn't use them here.

'Dinah, Ephraim, Esther...'

*Please, please, please, please...*

'Ezekiel, Gabriel...'

At the sound of his name, he nearly fell to his knees. It had happened. He'd been chosen.

*Thank you, God.*

## 11

Thanks to a breakdown in Bradford-on-Avon, the return journey took Sid twice as long, and by the time she managed to find the entrance to the Hermetic Order of the Golden Dawn, it was dark. She dithered briefly before deciding to drive up and have a quick look. That's all she wanted, a peek of the place, and then she'd come back tomorrow.

There were no gates, just a cattle grid flanked by two stone pillars bristling with security cameras. A deer fence stretched into the distance on either side. A small red light at the bottom of the fence indicated it was electrified. One of the pillars sported a large sign with white letters against red: PRIVATE, *no public access or right of way*. It didn't worry her. She had a legitimate excuse to be here. Luke Goddard and her father had known one another at school as well as university. Easy.

Slowly, she rattled over the grid. She'd barely gone ten yards when something large and white sprang in front of her car.

'Shit!' She rammed on the brakes.

The white shape materialised into a man dressed in a long pale robe that looked like a djellaba. He came to her car, gesturing for her to wind down her window. He was in his thirties, chunky build, bearded. He was holding something by his side but her eyes went to the wooden cross on a leather cord around his neck. She smiled. He didn't smile back.

'Hi,' she said.

'Are you with the police?'

'Er, no.'

'You're on private property.'

'Yes, I saw the sign but–'

'Unless you're here on official business, I have to ask you to leave.'

To her astonishment, he brought out a rifle.

'Are you *threatening* me?'

He didn't answer.

It was then that she took in the other two men, one of whom had moved to stand behind the man she was speaking to, the other next to her passenger door. They all had rifles.

'Do you have licences for those?' Her voice came out several pitches higher than normal.

Silence.

Her skin was springing with sweat but she refused to back down. 'I want to see Luke Goddard. My name is Sidney Scott, and my father went to Stonehouse School with–'

As if on some unspoken command, all three raised their rifles. To her horror, they pointed their guns straight at her.

'Okay, okay,' she gasped. 'I'm going, okay?'

None of them moved.

'I have to do a U-turn. Please put your guns down.' She

was terrified one of them might pull their trigger and shoot her by accident but they didn't waver.

Sid put the car into gear and bumped onto the grass, all three guns following her every move. As soon her car was fully on tarmac and facing down the drive, she floored it to the cattle grid and between the twin pillars. She was pouring with sweat, her heart pounding. Glancing right along the road she had to brake hard to let a vehicle sweep past, and then she barrelled after it.

She was trembling, her fingers clenched around the steering wheel so hard her knuckles shone like white buttons.

No normal church guarded its grounds with armed individuals. No normal church frightened people away with threats. What were they guarding? What were they protecting?

Sid took a corner too fast, making the car slip a little. Her adrenaline spiked again. Shit. She forced herself to slow down.

*Calm*, she told herself, taking a deep breath, then another.

*You don't want to run off the road and get killed.*

*Calm.*

She switched on BBC Radio 3. Classical music flooded the car.

*Calm.*

Gradually, her heart rate settled, her breathing levelled out.

Sid drove home extra carefully, and when she pulled up outside her cottage, she shoved Tank outside to check the area while she sat in the car with the engine running and headlights on, all the doors locked. He trotted to the cottage then back without any apparent unease, so she followed him in, disabling the alarm as she went.

No intruder. Everything in its place, but still, she checked every corner of her little cottage until she was sure she was alone. Finally, she kicked off her boots, donned her Uggs and a knee-length baggy cardigan the colour of pondweed. It looked hideous but who cared? It was as warm as a duvet; she practically lived in it during winter.

First, she rang Detective Kelly. When she was told once again he was, apparently, unavailable, she left a message asking him to call her back. She'd had a couple of 'interesting experiences' was how she put it, which included an intruder at her home and being threatened by men with guns when she'd visited a church. That should get his attention.

She fed Tank. Then she lit the wood burner, brewed tea, and was about to light a cigarette – she was if nothing, a creature of habit – when she was suddenly overcome with a ferocious urge to eat. It was like a wild animal coming out of a cave, roaring for steak, chips, pizza, sausages, a burger, *anything*. She didn't think she'd ever felt so hungry.

The fridge held a pathetic array of veg and soups, nothing that was going to sate her. She hit the freezer, uncertain what she'd find. Thank God, she had a couple of curries, naan breads and rice. She put two curries in the microwave as one didn't look enough. Switched on the oven for the bread. She paced the kitchen waiting for everything to cook and when it was ready, she wolfed it down.

Her appetite had no doubt been triggered by acute stress. She knew all about the psychology as well as the physical effect of being terrified – as people often were when they thought they were facing something supernatural – and when she'd fled the djellaba-clad, gun-wielding men, her appetite would have been blocked to ensure she had loads of energy to run away, but now she was safe, her cortisol level was through the roof, demanding she replace that energy by eating two curries, two naans and a bucket of rice. Not that she actually ate it all, which made Tank's day. She decided not to feed him the curry – she was pretty sure it wouldn't be good for him – but he seemed to enjoy the rice and bread and when he'd finished, looked at her hopefully.

'Sorry, pal,' she told him. 'But that's all you get.'

He came over and put his head in her lap. Absently, she stroked his warm, silky fur.

What a day.

After a while, Tank ambled to sprawl on his bed while Sid cleared the dishes away. She put a Spotify jazz mix on low – music was a great mood leveller – and returned to the kitchen table and her laptop, where she started making notes, from Owen's tattoo of a sunrise set in a triangle – the symbol of the Hermetic Order of the Golden Dawn – to how three young, impressionable boys may have been so affected by Liz's made-up prophesies they were following them as grown men. She thought of herself at eight years old, falling in love with magic. She hadn't thought of magic as any sort of career until she'd turned fifteen, when she'd come across Carson Crucefix, a famous medium who used to tour the world giving live tarot readings to help find missing people as well as communicate with the dead.

The year after Dad went missing, her mother had received a call from Carson Crucefix's press office saying he was coming to Oxford. He was aware of their tragic situation and apparently, he had a message for them from Dad. He was going to give Mum and Sid free tickets to the event.

'Can't he give the message to us over the phone?' Sid

had asked. She'd been a kid but already she was a huge sceptic in all things psychic.

'No, he can't,' Mum told her. 'He's asked if we can wear something yellow, so he can spot us in the audience.'

Sid hadn't wanted to go, but seeing the hope in her mother's eyes, she dutifully wore a sunflower-yellow blouse while Mum wore a bright-yellow silk scarf that usually only came out in the summer. They listened and watched as Carson Crucefix did his readings and then he was pointing at Mum and saying, 'That lady, there, the one with the yellow scarf. I'm getting a man wanting to contact her. He's your husband, and he's missing, am I right?'

Mum stood up. 'Yes,' she said. 'That's right.'

The audience gasped.

'He disappeared in… I'm getting a summer month… no, it was approaching winter. Late November.'

'Yes,' said Mum. 'November 29th.'

'His name, he says is…' He closed his eyes. 'Speak a little louder, please… thank you. His name is Mike.'

Mum nodded. 'Michael.'

Another gasp from the audience.

Sid could see Mum was trembling and she put out her hand. Her mother gripped it like a drowning woman.

'He's telling me he's okay and not to worry. He says he loves you very much and that he'll be back home soon, he promises. Thank you so much, you can sit back down.'

The audience applauded. Mum burst into tears. Sid never knew if she'd cried because she believed that horrible man or whether it was because she'd been so appallingly exploited. Sid didn't ask. She just held her mum's hand. Afterwards she never said a word about what had happened because if she'd opened her mouth, it would have emitted a never-ending shriek of rage.

Six months after her mother died, it came out that

Carson Crucefix's press team would go through local papers looking for stories like theirs. They'd scout around for desperate people and inveigle them to attend his event where they'd be publicly used. Sid had watched Crucefix's fall from grace with satisfaction underlaid with an intense sorrow not just for herself and her mother, but all those people who'd put their trust in a heartless charlatan.

Little wonder when her mother died, Sid had swapped thoughts of becoming a lawyer to study the psychology of magic. Not that it happened overnight. She'd lost control for a while, lost her boundaries, overcome with recklessness in her grief, but she didn't want to think about that right now. She wanted to think about Dad, and why he'd disappeared.

She continued making notes, accompanied by a glass of Malbec. She was getting up to refill her glass when her phone rang.

*Number unknown.*

She answered, but didn't say anything.

'Miz Scott?'

'Detective Kelly.'

'I got your message. What's going on?'

Sid told him about her break-in, then the three men threatening her with their rifles that evening.

'The Golden Dawn?' He sounded stunned. 'Are you serious?'

'One hundred per cent.'

'I found them perfectly peaceful when I saw them earlier.'

That could well explain why they'd asked if she was with the police.

'I'll check their firearms certificates. You said they were all rifles, could you say what sort?'

'Sorry, no.'

'And you've now got an alarm.'

'Yes.'

'What made you go to the Golden Dawn?'

When she told him about her visiting the boys' school, he said, 'Hmmm,' but nothing else.

Sid leaned back, playing with the stem of her wine glass. 'How do you know Owen was murdered? And where was my father's postcard found?'

Another hmm-ing sound, then he said, 'Can I come and see you tomorrow morning? Or shall I meet you at the university?'

She picked up her phone to check her calendar, and saw a weather warning pop up. Torrential rain all morning, clearing mid-afternoon.

'Tomorrow morning is fine, at my place. You go past the farm and take the track on the right, through a patch of woodland. My cottage is at the end. If you don't have a four-wheel-drive, you might find a pair of wellies useful.'

'Righto. Make sure you set the burglar alarm tonight. Oh, and you'd better have my mobile number.'

She punched it in as he spoke.

She'd barely ended the call when her phone rang again. This time a mobile number appeared but not a name. Once again, she answered but didn't say anything.

'Is that Sidney Scott?' The man's voice was smooth and deep, making her think of blackstrap molasses.

She remained silent.

'I know this is out of the blue, and that we don't know one another at all, but I didn't want to send an email or a letter. I wanted to do this personally, so that you know I am totally genuine.'

*What the hell?*

'My name is Father Luke. I heard what happened tonight, and I'm calling to offer a massive apology.'

Sid's mouth dropped open. It was the last thing she'd expected.

'The Brothers are only allowed weapons to shoot for the pot on the estate – rabbits and pheasants and the like – and *not* to frighten members of the general public. I cannot apologise enough and hope that you haven't been overly distressed by what might possibly have been quite a traumatic event.'

'How did you get my phone number?'

'You're Michael's daughter. I found your website. Very intriguing it is too. I think you're doing some really valuable work. I would simply *love* to sit down with you and talk about what we both do. I think we're both extremely driven individuals and have a lot to offer one another, don't you think? Which is why I would like to invite you to my Sunday service. It's a really special event, this one, and with your talents, you may find it especially interesting.'

Sid listened with a mixture of appalled horror at his arrogant assumptions of her, and absolute fascination.

'I'm holding a healing assembly, followed by a prophesy sent directly from God. I'm inviting the media. BBC Points West are attending, for example, so it will be quite an event. Shall I send you an invitation? I can email it across if you like.'

'I'll certainly have a look.' She was cool. 'But I can't promise anything.'

'I do hope you'll come,' he urged. 'I really do want to apologise in person.'

Sid didn't respond but let him close the call himself, without her saying a word.

It was only after she'd let Tank out and climbed into bed that she realised Father Luke had never answered her question about how he'd got her phone number.

# 12

I t was blowing a hoolie the next morning, rain lashing
the windows and making the back door rattle. Sid was
outlining her article – *Are all psychics and mediums fakes?* –
when a double knock came from the back door and at the
same time Tank bolted upright and flung himself across
the kitchen for the utility room, toenails scrabbling and
barking fit to burst.

'Fucksake.' Her heart felt as though it had leapt from
her chest. 'Give me some warning next time.'

Hand on Tank's collar, Sid opened the door to find a
sodden Detective Kelly standing in the pouring rain. He
wore a Barbour and wellies, and his hair was plastered
against his skull as though he'd just stepped out of the
shower.

Tank didn't stop growling. 'He's a policeman,' she told
the dog, giving him a little shake. 'Please don't bite him.'

'Yes, please don't,' Kelly said, eyeing the bullmastiff
warily.

She pushed Tank aside as she said, 'Come in. You can

park your wellies...' She indicated her own sitting next to the washing machine, watched him sling his jacket over the side of the sink to drip onto the flagstone floor.

'Coffee?'

'Love one.'

He stepped into the kitchen, looking around with interest. 'Cosy,' he remarked. 'Remote.' His eyebrows lifted, inviting her to tell him why she lived somewhere so isolated.

'I like it,' she said. She'd meant it as a throwaway comment but then she realised it was true. She couldn't explain it, but she'd become used to counting the blue tits at her feeder, hearing the woodpeckers drum with their beaks, the owls hunting at night. It felt more visceral than living in town and now she wondered if she'd ever return.

He ran his hands over his wet hair, brought out a handkerchief to wipe the water from his specs. She suddenly felt mean having made him walk and went and fetched him a towel.

'That's kind, but I'm fine.' He smiled. Stepped to her Dali picture, had a look at the horse with clocks for eyes. 'Weird,' he remarked.

She didn't comment.

The kitchen seemed even smaller with him there and with a little shock, she realised he was the first visitor she'd had since her old school friend Aero had dropped by six weeks ago. She really had become a hermit.

They both stood as they drank their coffee and Sid ran him through her going to St John's College, then meeting Winstone Fairchild.

'Fairchild?' he repeated and at the same time, a strange rigidity seemed to drop over him. She tried to read his expression but the signals were mixed. His mouth was narrowed. She saw tension. She thought she saw apprehension, but couldn't be sure.

'You know him?' she asked.

For a moment she thought he wasn't going to answer, but then he said, 'We've met.'

'What, like professionally? Or socially?'

He took a studied sip of coffee, adding, 'All I can say is that he's not all that he seems.'

'What does that mean?'

He surveyed her steadily. 'Just be careful.'

Unnerved, she said, 'I don't understand. Why should–'

'Please,' he cut over her. 'If you could describe the men you saw with the rifles?' He brought out a notebook and a pen and looked at her expectantly.

She did her best, but thanks to being petrified and it being dark as well, she doubted if she could identify them at a line-up if she was asked. She went on to tell him what she'd found at Stonehouse School. She didn't mention Liz's scaring the boys with her Psychic Ceres impersonation.

'You're quite the sleuth.'

She wasn't sure of his tone, and bridled. 'Are you saying you wouldn't try and find out what happened to your father if he vanished without explanation?'

'My father died when I was three.'

'Hypothetically, then.' She refused to be derailed from her point, nor feel sorry for him.

He gazed at the windows, dribbling with rain. 'I guess I would, yes.'

'Well then.' She was brisk. 'I'd like to know how you knew Owen was murdered.'

'He'd been stabbed in the throat.'

*Fuck.* She put her hand on the kitchen counter to steady herself.

'That,' he added hastily, 'is something that isn't in the public domain, so please keep it to yourself.' He took a breath. 'We believe he'd been run off the road and, while he was still strapped inside his vehicle, he was murdered.'

*Bloody hell*, she thought. She ran a hand over her forehead and Tank seemed to sense her unease because he came over and stood next to her, where she could touch his shoulders.

'Where was my father's postcard found?'

'Tucked into the waistband of Owen's trousers, beneath his shirt.'

Sid stared. 'He'd *hidden it?*'

'It appears that way.'

'But it doesn't say anything. There's no hidden message there. It was just us playing around.'

'So you said.'

'How did Owen get it? Did he find it? If so, where?' A sudden surge of excitement. 'Or did my father give it to him?'

Kelly put his mug down. 'I'm afraid I don't know.'

Sid began to pace, Tank's eyes following her back and forth. 'What if he's alive? Maybe he's incarcerated somewhere. Locked up...' She trailed off, unable to think where, or why anyone would imprison him. She returned to her original hypothesis, that something bad had happened to him, preventing him from mailing his postcard, and coming home.

'Do you know who killed Owen?'

Kelly shook his head.

'Any ideas?'

'We always have ideas.' His voice was dry.

'Care to share them?'

'Sorry.'

'What about the Golden Dawn? Are their firearms legitimate?'

'They have half a dozen certificates as well as a gun cabinet. Father Luke insists the men you saw were out rabbiting and that you got the wrong impression.'

'Absolutely not!' She was incensed. 'Father Luke even rang me to apologise last night!'

'He did?' Kelly looked startled.

'He's invited me to some big church event on Sunday. He's going to take a message from God. Apparently, the BBC are going along. He's really excited about it.'

'You're not thinking of going.' It was a statement, not a question.

'I totally am. Fake psychics are right up my street, remember?'

His nostrils flared. 'That's not the point. I don't think you should go.'

'Why, because they have rifles for rabbiting?' She knew she was baiting him but couldn't seem to help herself. She hated being told what to do.

'No, because I think there's something dangerous about the place.'

'It's a cult. Of course it's dangerous.'

'If you go…' He suddenly looked uncomfortable. 'Will you go alone or with someone?' He looked around as though waiting for another person to materialise.

Sid folded her arms. 'I don't need a chaperone.'

'I'm sure you don't, but I'm beginning to wonder if your investigations aren't rattling someone's cage.'

An oily sensation began to ooze through her stomach, like a snake uncurling. 'You think my break-in was to do with my looking for Dad?'

'He disappeared. And you yourself concluded

something bad had happened to him. I wouldn't want the same to happen to you.'

She stared at him. He stared back.

'Was that a threat?'

'Absolutely not.' He looked shocked.

Sid narrowed her eyes. 'You know something about Dad, don't you?'

He shook his head. 'I only know what everyone else does, I promise. And I'm really sorry you haven't been able to find closure, but turning into a private eye isn't going to help.'

*That's what you think,* she thought mutinously, but she slowly pasted on a thoughtful expression to disarm him. 'You're probably right.' She gave a helpless sigh.

He nodded, seemingly satisfied at her surrender. 'In that case, I'll get back to my murder investigation if you get on with... well, whatever you're getting on with.'

'An article on fake psychics,' she told him brightly.

'I wish you could meet my mother and put her straight.'

'She wouldn't want any interference, trust me.'

Sid saw him into the utility room. His socks had *Jason's lucky fishing socks* stitched on their sides. As he shook out his Barbour, Sid pulled open the door to see it was still pissing down. Hastily she shrugged on her weatherproof jacket and shoved her feet into a pair of wellies. 'I'll drive you.'

He gave a rueful smile. 'I won't say no.'

She turned to Tank. 'You, stay.'

Her Jimny traversed the slippery, rutted track with ease. When she pulled up next to his car, he said lightly, 'Have a good weekend, then. Don't work too hard.'

She looked him in the eyes. 'You too, Jason. Hope the fishing's fun.'

His eyes widened. 'How the hell...?'

She gave a snort. 'Your socks. They're a bit of a giveaway.'

He burst out laughing. He looked nice when he laughed. Carefree. As he climbed outside he turned to give her a long look. 'Be careful on Sunday, won't you?'

She felt a little shock. She hadn't managed to fool him after all.

# 13

Sunday morning, Sid turned her head upside down to blast it with a hairdryer. The good thing about having short-cropped hair was that it took a nanosecond to dry itself into hedgehog bristles. She considered what to wear, what Father Luke might expect of her, and what she sought to achieve. She wanted to distract him and any of his followers to look at X while she was doing Y. Magicians called it misdirecting. Which meant she had to forgo her usual comforting, characterless uniform and pull out some stops.

She pulled on a high-necked plaid bodycon dress that stopped well above her knees. Sheer tights, sparkling earrings, and her favourite pair of Robin Hood boots with wide tops. A lick of mascara, some lip gloss, and a squirt of perfume... She paused. When had she last worn a scent? She'd sprayed it on automatically, just as she used to. She looked at herself in the mirror. This was how she used to dress. Sexy, confident, fun, *young*. She sighed, feeling a hundred years old inside. Would she ever be carefree again?

Not wanting to think about it, she chose one of her favourite coats, found a matching pair of gloves, and left the cottage.

When she dropped Tank off at the farm, Toby stared. 'Holy crap,' he said.

'What?' For a moment, she was baffled.

'Sorry.' He looked embarrassed. 'I've just never seen you… well, you know…'

'I'm going to church,' she told him cheerfully.

'Great.' He smiled weakly. 'Have a nice time.'

When she arrived at Golden Dawn's gateway, two pretty young women in nut-brown djellabas checked her invitation as well as her ID before giving her instructions and waving her on. Three men, also in djellabas stood to one side, chatting, keeping an eye on things. No rifles. No threats, just lots of smiles.

The drive wound though ancient parkland dotted with hundred-year-old oaks, beeches and majestic cypress trees. The ground was frosty, any puddles frozen. She saw some brown cattle grazing on clumps of hay and there were lots of crows pecking the ground for whatever crows pecked for. Grubs? Insects? She hadn't a clue. She hadn't absorbed much about the countryside despite living in it for so long, and she promised herself she'd do better, like read the bird book Aero had given her for her birthday, at least.

She breasted the brow of a hill to see an impressive manor house tucked in the bottom of a valley, like a conker in a soup bowl and well hidden away. From her birds-eye view she took in the formal ha-has and box-hedge gardens at the front of the house, the mammoth kitchen gardens at the back. There were orchards and stables, chicken houses and cobbled yards, a lake, and what looked like a tithe barn set on the other side of a tilled field. Dozens of single-storey brick buildings were lined in rows – dormitories,

Sid assumed. They were utilitarian, crammed together with wooden boards between them. It resembled a refugee camp rather than a religious community. On the other side of an ancient-looking church was an enormous, newish-looking building. It looked like it could be a concert hall or auditorium.

Apparently, before he became a cult leader (not that he saw himself that way, apparently, he was convinced he was a simple Man of God) Father Luke used to be a small-time preacher. He began gathering followers, holding meetings in his small house in Oxford. From the beginning, he cultivated the sons and daughters of wealthy families. They didn't see themselves as a cult – more as a tightly-knit group of like-minded people.

After five or six years, he'd moved here, inspired by the original Hermetic Order of the Golden Dawn which had been founded by three Freemasons in the nineteenth century. He then dropped out of view until one of his members fled. Her name was Julia Pemberton and her mother had posted her story online as a warning to other parents. Julia was nineteen and in her first term at university when a group of friends drew her in. She had no idea they were cult members.

*Father Luke represented a new way of looking at things – a progressive and exciting way of looking at Christianity. I was thrilled they were interested in me, they were so fun, so cool.*

The 'friends' told Julia she was special, that she was different.

*I became dependent on their praise, their love. Slowly, they separated me from my ordinary life, isolating me.*

She was so brainwashed, she gave her entire trust fund to the cult. Four and a half million pounds.

Although the cult had forced Julia to break contact with her family, she'd managed to escape over a decade ago. She was now thirty-eight.

Sid dropped Julia's mother an email via Focus on the Family, where she'd posted her daughter's story. Sid would love to talk to Julia, but she hadn't heard back.

Easing to the front of the manor house, she wound down her window to another djellaba-wearing follower who smiled, and told her where to park. There weren't many visitors that she could see, but there was a van with a BBC Points West sticker in its window, so all kudos to Father Luke. Most cults wouldn't countenance anyone from outside anywhere near them, let alone the media, and once again, she considered what his motivation was.

Publicity, obviously. But why? To attract more followers?

Sid climbed outside. The air was still and cold, refreshing. She looked around. Oxford's city centre was barely fifty minutes away, but the commune felt much more remote. Countryside all around, the smell of wet earth and leaves in the air. No neighbours. Just fields, cows and crows.

She headed to the canteen where, she'd been told, she would find snacks and beverages. She wasn't particularly hungry, but a strong black coffee would be good. The sun had come out and Sid unbuttoned her coat, briefly raising her face to the sky, relishing the warmth. It made her think of spring, even though it was months away. Walking to the back of the manor house, she joined the snakes of people converging on a long, glass-fronted building: Quartz Canteen.

As she walked, people stared, some openly, others with

sidelong glances. She had, she knew, dressed provocatively. Her dress was a vivid plaid of black and pink, her coat the colour of sapphires. She stuck out like a parrot amongst a flock of pigeons.

Grabbing a takeaway coffee, she took it outside for a smoke. There was nowhere to sit that wasn't covered in frost, so she propped herself against the canteen wall. Gazed at the stables, the handful of pretty bantams pecking between the cobbles.

She talked to her father in her head. *Are you alive, Dad? Or are you dead?*

*What do you think?*

*I think if you were alive, you would have let me know.*

*Correct.*

*What happened to you? How can I find out?*

Her father surveys her steadily through his button-brown eyes. She knows he's telling her to work it out for herself.

*Do you know Mum's dead?*

He doesn't believe her but when she insists it's true, it's like watching a sand sculpture erode in the wind.

'What are you doing?'

Sid turned to see a young girl aged around six or so, staring at her. She had fine blonde hair scraped into a ponytail. Her djellaba was the colour of a hazelnut.

Sid raised her cigarette. 'Smoking. It's very bad for you.'

Her brow furrowed. 'Why do you do it then?'

'It makes me feel good.'

'You're from Outside,' she said.

'Yes. I'm from Neston. It's in the West Country. Near Corsham. Not far from Bath.'

At that, her grey eyes lit up. 'Granny and Grandpa live in Bath. Do you know them? They live in Bear...' She screwed up her face. 'Bear-something.'

'Bear Flat?'

Again, those grey eyes shone. 'Yes!'

'What are their names?'

'Oh.' She thought long and hard. 'I don't know.'

'How long have you been here?'

'I was born here.'

What felt like a skein of cobwebs brushed over Sid's skin.

'Have you ever been...' Sid waved her cigarette towards the surrounding hills. 'Out there?'

She shook her head. 'Mummy wanted to, but–'

'Hannah.'

One word and the girl stilled. All her animation vanished. Turning around, she ran away.

Sid already knew who'd spoken. Still smoking, opting for an exaggeratedly casual stance, she waited until he stepped into view.

Father Luke.

He'd be the same age as her father if he was around, sixty or so, and he seemed to have aged well. His luxuriantly coiffed mane had a sprinkling of grey throughout and there were lines around his mouth and eyes, but otherwise he looked in good shape. He wore a silver cross at his throat, and another hung from a rope around his waist. His bare feet were brown and shoved into a pair of deck shoes. He was surprisingly small. She'd built him up to be a bigger man but she was five foot eight, and they were looking at one another eye to eye.

'Sid!' he exclaimed. His tone was delighted and he was beaming as though he was greeting an old friend. His charisma flowed over her like molten honey.

'Sidney,' she corrected. Only her best buddies called her Sid.

He looked as though he'd bitten on a lemon.

'Luke,' she said cheerfully.

'Father Luke.' His tone was stiff.

Neither of them offered to shake hands. He tried to smile, exude his previous bonhomie, and she was surprised to see it was strained. She would have thought he'd be more confident. She took a long drag on her cigarette as she studied him. No wonder so many women flocked his way. Easy prey in the face of a spiritual hot-link to a God who promised to relieve their burdens, be they illness, mental health problems, substance abuse, marital abuse, or, in some cases, simple loneliness.

He cleared his throat. 'I had no idea how like your mother you'd look.'

She felt the shock of his words against her breastbone. 'You knew Mum?'

'Knew?' he repeated, frowning.

'She died ten years ago.'

'I'm sorry. You must have been, what–'

'Eighteen.'

He sucked in a breath. 'That must have been dreadful, especially after losing your father.' His expression turned to ooze sympathy.

'When did you last see Dad?'

He looked taken aback. 'I can't honestly remember. But I did speak to the police at the time. I'm sure they have a record of my statement.'

'You were both at the same school, right?'

'Yes.' He looked away, then back. 'Look, can we discuss this after the service?'

She flicked her cigarette to the ground. Stepped on the stub.

He opened his mouth to object, thought better of it.

She'd usually pop the stub into a little bag she kept with her, and although it was pretty disgusting, it made her feel better that she wasn't littering. She still wasn't sure why she smoked. She thought she started because she could, because her parents weren't there to nag her, but as we all know, nicotine is horrendously addictive, just behind cocaine and heroin, and once she'd started, she was buggered if she couldn't stop.

'You're quite stubborn, aren't you?' He tried to look amused, but his eyes turned hard and shiny, like a pair of her mother's brown stone crystals.

Sid lit another cigarette. Lifted her chin and blew smoke skywards.

'Will you write about what you see here today?' He fiddled absently with the rope at his waist.

'I might.'

'People will find it interesting.'

'They might,' she repeated agreeably.

'My prophesy will go viral. You'll see.'

Sid studied the end of her cigarette. 'I'm sure there's something in the Bible that says priests shouldn't seek power or influence by deceit.'

He sighed, a small, exasperated sound. 'The prophesy will save lives. Hundreds, *thousands* of lives.'

She stared at him. 'You already know what you're going to say?'

'I saw it in a dream.'

*How convenient.*

'I have the BBC here.'

'Points West.' Her tone was dismissive. 'Local news. Not national.'

His eyes flared. 'I only need one report, you'll see.'

Again, she wondered what his game was.

He drew in a breath, exhaled. 'Shall I get someone to escort you to the church when the time comes?'

The emailed invitation had already primed her for an

11am service and she checked her watch to see it was just after ten thirty. 'How long will the service be?'

'Fifty minutes.'

'And I'll see you afterwards. Privately. Perhaps in your office?'

'My study.' He smiled, a slow sweet smile that was utterly beguiling. 'We can have a private chat.'

'Great.'

A look of satisfaction filled Father Luke's face. 'I'll arrange to have someone fetch you in fifteen minutes.'

## 14

Gabriel was trying not to stare at Sidney Scott. Hannah had told him she was amazing, beautiful, like a princess, but he hadn't really taken it in. His sister was six years old. She thought any woman who didn't wear a djellaba was like a princess.

'Hello.' Sidney Scott gave him a warm smile that creased the corners of her eyes. What colour were they? Blue? Purple? He'd never seen anything like them before. Nor anyone with hair like hers. Short and spiky like a pixie's. Her clothes were the most amazing colours, and she wore jewellery too. She was how he imagined someone would look if they'd come from another planet.

'Hi.' He was horrified to hear his voice squeak. He sounded like a mouse. Luckily, before she could see the flush that seared his face, she'd turned to Hannah. 'Hello again.'

'We're to take you to the service,' Hannah said importantly. 'We mustn't be late.'

'Absolutely.' Sidney Scott nodded. 'Now, I know your name is Hannah, but who is your friend?'

'He's my brother.'

'Does your brother have a name?'

'Gabriel,' Hannah said before he could open his mouth.

'I'm Sidney, but you can call me Sid if you like.'

'Sid,' Gabriel said, testing it out. It was a strange name, but it kind of suited her.

'Your names,' Sid said musingly. 'They're biblical, aren't they?'

Something in her voice made him prickle. 'I wasn't always going to be Gabriel,' he said. 'Mum told me–'

'Stop it!' Hannah looked shocked. 'You know we're not allowed!'

Gabriel snapped his mouth shut but he could see Sid was looking at him with interest. 'What did your mum tell you?'

'She would have called me–' he ignored Hannah's furious stare, '– James Tiberius, but Father Luke said I had to be called Gabriel.'

'I've always been Hannah.' His sister looked proud.

'Mum said that if she could have chosen Hannah's name, it would have been–' Gabriel started but Hannah swung round, stamping her foot. 'Don't!'

'Nyota,' he said.

Hannah looked as though she might hit him but Sid stepped between them. 'Why James Tiberius?'

'She named me after the captain of the starship *USS Enterprise*.' Gabriel pulled his shoulders back. 'Captain James T. Kirk.' He flicked a look at Hannah who was glowering. 'Nyota Uhura was a Starfleet officer.'

'Have you watched *Star Trek*?' asked Sid.

Both kids shook their heads. 'TV isn't allowed,' Gabriel admitted.

'But still your mum named you after two really strong, adventurous characters.'

Gabriel could feel his cheeks heat with pleasure. Even Hannah relented and nodded.

'I like the sound of your mum,' Sid said with a smile. 'Where is she?'

'In the san. She's sick.'

'I'm sorry to hear that,' Sid said gently, 'I would have liked to have met her.'

He nodded glumly.

'Next time.' She sounded optimistic, which was nice, as Mum was still really ill. Normally, anyone who had Soul Sickness got better in a day or two, but she'd been in the san for nearly a week. He and Hannah had seen her yesterday and she'd looked awful, pale and sweaty and gaunt. She'd been asleep, and although Gabriel had wanted to wake her, he hadn't been allowed. They'd left their home-made cards for her on her bedside table, along with a blackbird's eggshell he'd found in the summer. She loved anything to do with nature.

Father Luke had assured them she would get better soon. 'She was really naughty, you see. So she has to suffer for her transgression. She'll be up and about by next weekend. Trust me.'

Gabriel hoped Father Luke was right. He missed his mum more than he'd thought possible. Her smile, the way she'd press a kiss against his head, the stories she'd tell them before bed.

As she shifted her cross-body handbag, Sid's coat collar rose and dipped. He thought he saw something on her neck. Mindful it might be an insect, he said, 'You've got something...' while at the same time, touching his own neck.

'Oh, that.' Another smile. 'It's just a tattoo, but thanks.'

He could feel his eyes almost pop from his head. A tattoo? One of the Newcomers had a tattoo across his chest and Father Luke had forced him to stand in front of the congregation and take off his shirt.

*You shall not make any cuttings in your flesh, no tattoo or any marks on you: I am the Lord.*

'You want to see?'

Before Gabriel could say anything, she'd ducked down and pulled her collar aside to show a delicate swirl of deep-blue stars starting from a tiny point and expanding to the edge of what looked like a planet.

'It goes all the way down here.' She touched the base of her spine. 'It's in remembrance of my mum and dad.'

'They're dead?' Hannah said.

Sid hesitated. Then she said, 'Yes.'

Hannah reached out and took Sid's hand. Gabriel took the other. They held them for a moment. Her skin was cool and smooth, like milk.

'Sorry,' he said.

'Me too,' said Hannah.

'You're…' Sid cleared her throat. 'Very sweet.'

He and Hannah held Sid's hands as they walked through the farmyard and past the small, old church to the big new church. Gabriel felt a rush of excitement. He hadn't felt this alive since he could remember. As he and Hannah walked into the church on either side of Sid, every Brother and Sister turned to watch them. He didn't think he'd ever been so proud.

# 15

When one of the brethren asked Sid for her phone, she dutifully handed her little Nokia over to join five other phones resting in a leather tray. She was about to step away when a burly man barred her exit.

'I have to search you.'

'I beg your pardon?'

'It's the rules for all Outsiders.'

She looked shocked but this was exactly what she'd expected. Being filmed or photographed while he was performing would be anathema to Father Luke. She wondered how he was going to play the BBC. Perhaps they'd have an exclusive?

Shaking off her coat she made to hand it to Gabriel but the man grabbed it and checked its pockets. Then he took her little handbag and rummaged around in there as well.

Slowly, Sid stretched out her arms on either side of her. Her dress was skintight and short enough to show she couldn't possibly hide even a one-pound coin without it showing.

'Go ahead,' she purred. 'But don't enjoy yourself *too* much.' Her tone was insolent. Mocking.

He flushed and snapped his fingers at Gabriel. 'Go.'

Coat over her arm, handbag across her body once again, they made their way inside. The church – the auditorium – was huge. There had to be nearly a thousand people there and the air was buzzing with conversation, alive with anticipation, but it quietened as they walked inside. Everyone stared.

Sid was delighted when the kids walked her right through the church to the front row. Best seat in the house. She smiled at Father Luke – butter wasn't going to melt in her mouth right now – who smiled back. *Little does he know.*

A few people in suits sat in the same row, and further along she spotted a small group of people in casual clothes. She recognised the news anchor, a stunning blonde in a vivid blue dress, but nobody else. Had the anchor suffered a search? Had anyone else smuggled in a phone? And what about filming the service? Wasn't that what Father Luke wanted?

*I only need one report, you'll see.*

Then she spotted a man to one side of the stage with a camera and another a microphone. Both wore djellabas. Father Luke's men. Not a single BBC camera. Which meant Father Luke was controlling what was being filmed. Sid bet Points West wouldn't have liked that and was surprised they hadn't buggered off but then how many times were the media invited into the heart of a cult?

The service started with Father Luke asking for anyone suffering an illness to make their way to him. A man on crutches hobbled up to the stage where Father Luke anointed him with oil.

'HEAL ME, OH LORD, AND I WILL BE HEALED!' he roared.

Sid could practically feel the hair parting on her head from the power of his voice. It was fearsome, almost frightening, but absolutely enthralling. Everyone was rapt. He was a great showman.

After a couple of hymns and some more of Father Luke's bellowing about healing their physical bodies, they were asked to pray for the unfortunate man who was still standing in front of the stage.

'Who is he?' she whispered to Gabriel.

The boy glanced around fearfully before whispering back. 'Brother Peter.'

'How did he hurt himself?'

'He fell down the stairs.'

'Who saw him fall?'

Gabriel frowned. 'I don't know if anyone did. Why?'

It was her guess that Brother Peter was one of Father Luke's highly devoted followers, pretending he couldn't walk without crutches.

'Praise the Lord who heals all your diseases,' Father Luke boomed.

'Praise the Lord,' echoed the congregation.

Father Luke laid his hands upon Brother Peter's shoulders and bellowed, 'I WILL RESTORE YOU TO HEALTH!'

At which point – predictably – Brother Peter threw his crutches away and walked back to his seat, unaided.

The congregation went wild.

Next came Father Luke's prophesy. A lot of doom and gloom and talk of terrorists and the threat they were apparently bringing.

'Children!' he thundered. 'They will bring their bombs and kill us in our thousands!'

Sid glanced around to see everyone's eyes gazing at him adoringly.

'Our cities are in grave danger from innocents. They will come without knowing what they do and commit murder... We will die because we want the latest Xbox. We will die because we want a new phone. We will die because we want, want, want material things. We will die because one day, as we go Christmas shopping for our trite and selfish wants, we will be torn apart just days before the day of our Lord's birth for being so greedy and self-centred.

'From Glasgow to London, Birmingham and Manchester, God will rain down his punishment, hear ye, hear ye!'

She struggled not to tune out during his claptrap, perking up only when a woman who had recently been diagnosed with cancer rocked up. Spotting Father Luke fiddling with his sleeves, Sid reached into the top of her boot and brought out her smartphone. Started filming him.

'You can't do that!' Gabriel looked horrified. 'Filming's not allowed!'

'Oh?' she said, all innocence. 'Nobody said.'

Both Hannah and Gabriel watched her wide-eyed as Sid happily filmed Father Luke carrying out a classic scam.

With the woman on her knees before him, Father Luke reached down into her mouth and dramatically pulled out a rancid, dripping and bloody mess. He raised it high for everyone to see.

'Here is her cancerous tissue!'

She'd zoomed in and the film she now saved on the iCloud showed the cancerous mass as something off a butcher's block – perhaps the guts from a chicken? – that had been concealed in Father Luke's hand prior to supposedly pulling it from the poor woman's mouth. She didn't think she'd had such a clear example of a live trick like this, and she couldn't help smiling at the irony it was thanks to Father Luke himself.

*Serves him right.*

She would post the video once she'd left the cult. She had no idea how Father Luke would react and didn't want to be around when he saw his big exposé online. Two years ago, she'd unmasked a supposed professional fortune-teller and ended up with a hand-shaped bruise on her cheek. She wouldn't put it past Father Luke not to have a similar temper.

As soon as he'd given his final blessing and swept up the aisle to the main door, no doubt to bask in his congregation's adoration as they filed past, Sid was on her feet, slipping her smartphone into her handbag. She'd pick up her Nokia later – it was defunct but made a useful decoy – because while Father Luke was busy she wanted to take the opportunity to be a little nosy.

'Hannah.' She screwed up her face. 'I'm desperate for a pee. Is there a ladies' through there?' She pointed at the door to the side of the stage. She didn't need the loo, but it was the only excuse she could think of to exit through the rear of the auditorium and, hopefully, without Father Luke seeing.

Hannah looked anxiously over her shoulder then back. Bit her lip.

'There's one in the healing centre,' Gabriel piped up. 'Follow me.'

'No!' Hannah cried. 'We mustn't. It's against the rules.'

'Stay here, then.' Gabriel's tone wasn't unkind. 'I'll see you at lunch.'

Hannah's chin wobbled.

'Lead on,' Sid told Gabriel. Just before they disappeared through the door, she looked back to see little Hannah standing there looking after them with tears trickling down her face.

'*Sorry, love,*' Sid mouthed to her. She blew her a kiss.

Gabriel showed her to the healing centre. 'I shouldn't go inside without a Brother or Sister, but you'll be okay.'

Wanting to keep up the pretence, Sid stepped into a cool room that smelled of herbs. She flushed the loo and washed her hands. Carbolic soap. No mirrors. On the back of the door hung a dark-grey djellaba. Sid folded it as small as she could and tucked it under her arm.

Outside, Gabriel stood waiting. He didn't seem to notice the djellaba. She said, 'I have to go to Father Luke's study now. He said he'd meet me there.'

Gabriel blinked. 'He did?'

'Yup. Can you lead the way?' Then she realised if Gabriel was caught helping her, he could be punished, so she said, 'Don't worry, I'll find it myself.'

He frowned. 'Are you sure?'

'I'm sure.'

His shoulders slumped.

She touched his arm lightly. 'Come and say goodbye to me out the front of the house say, in about half an hour or so. My car is a small blue four-by-four. A Suzuki Jimny.'

Gabriel beamed.

Sid stalked past the original church, around the lake and past the stables back to the rear of the manor house. Glancing around, she saw djellabas spilling from the auditorium, the breeze catching their hems and making them resemble a cloud of brown and grey moths. She took in the guards standing at each entrance of the manor house and, slipping behind a sturdy oak tree, pulled the djellaba over her head, hiding her and her handbag, which was slung across her chest. The robe was long, probably a man's, and its hem touched the ground. With the hood up and her hands tucked into the folds of the wide sleeves, she lifted the hem a little so she could walk without tripping. Headed for the main rear entrance.

Two guards stood at the top of the steps, chatting. Keeping her gaze down, Sid headed for them decisively. Her heartbeat was up, her palms sweaty. She refused to consider what might happen if she was caught.

*You belong here,* she told herself. *You are one of them.*

Holding her breath, she pattered up the steps. The men were talking about the BBC presenter. Neither stopped her. The next second, she was in a corridor. A quick glance over her shoulder showed the men were still talking. It was as though she'd been invisible. Exhaling in relief, she kept going. She could smell roasting meat and hear the clattering of pans, women chattering. She glanced in rooms as she passed until she came to the end of the corridor, where a door opened into a vast hallway. A fire had been lit in a massive fireplace, roaring, but made little impact on the chill air.

Finding the hood a hindrance, she flipped it back before having a quick scout around. Cautiously pushing open various doors, she saw four reception rooms, an orangery, a billiard room, three toilets, a library and a rather magnificent ballroom with a ceiling covered in Sistine Chapel-style frescoes. All were empty.

Bunching the djellaba to her knees, she trotted upstairs, past a massive tapestry of a sunrise set in a triangle. At the landing, she strode right. Peeked into a variety of bedrooms, some with four-posters, some without. Bathrooms, dressing rooms, all sumptuous. A gent's lavatory had a stuffed, fully grown black bear – does a bear shit in the woods? – and the ladies' boasted pink onyx sinks and a ceiling of silk flowers.

This may be a religious commune where its residents

shared huge long dormitories and were fed in an industrial-sized canteen, but there was no expense spared for visitors and guests. She wondered if this was how Father Luke roped in new members: by lavishing them with luxury and telling them this was what God wanted for them.

At the far end of the wing was a set of stairs, linoleum; easy access to and from the laundry, she guessed. Back in the day, the landed gentry wouldn't have wanted to see dirty laundry being lugged through their splendid hall. Sid retraced her steps to head to the west wing. Here, she found the offices.

In the first room, she had a quick look at a computer, tapped the keyboard but the screen demanded a code. She went to the filing cabinet to find animal medicine logbooks, details of feed, crops and fertilisers, vehicle maintenance, repairs to buildings and machinery. Another cabinet held details and invoices for groceries, bedding, laundry, internet and phone, software maintenance, buildings insurance.

Everything needed to run a farm as well as a commune.

She slipped to the next room. The door was ajar and as she pushed it open she didn't have time to duck back because the man behind the desk was already looking at her.

He was tall and broad-shouldered with dark hair. He wore jeans and a flannel shirt that wouldn't look out of place in a farmyard.

He said, 'What the hell are you doing here?'

# 16

Win came around the desk, the breadth and energy of him making Sid take a step back. She wasn't sure if she was scared or if it was something else, and her muscles tightened.

'For God's sakes, take that thing off.' He gestured angrily at her djellaba. 'He'll hang you if he sees you in it.'

Since he was probably right, Sid wriggled out of the robe. Snatching it from her, Win tossed it over the back of the office chair before coming to her and putting a hand beneath her elbow.

'Downstairs. Now.' He propelled her into the corridor.

When she began to resist he swung her around to face him. His eyes were as hard and cold as basalt.

'You really want to be found up here, snooping?'

'I'm not snooping,' she said, pretending annoyance. 'I was—'

'Snooping.'

He firmed his grip on her and since she had no doubt he had every intention of strong-arming her down the stairs, she snatched her arm free, saying, 'I get the message, okay?'

'Go,' he snapped.

Sid spun on her heel and stalked back down the corridor, down to the hall, Winstone Fairchild behind her. At the bottom, he swept her to stand in front of the fireplace, crackling and spitting and warming her backside.

'What are you doing here?' she asked. 'Are you–'

'There's something I want to say,' he cut over her.

'But what do you have to do with the Golden–'

'Just listen, will you?'

She flung up her hands. 'Okay, okay. Keep your hair on.'

'This from a trespasser, a potential burglar?' His eyebrows shot into his hairline.

She lifted her chin. 'I was heading to meet Father Luke in his study, as arranged earlier.'

He gazed at her steadily. 'You lie incredibly well.'

She gazed back, refusing to show her discomfort.

'Look,' he said. He lowered his voice. 'I know you're trying to find your father, but some rocks you don't turn over.'

'Is that a threat?'

'No.' He fixed her with his level brown intense stare. 'It's a warning.'

She widened her eyes, inviting him to continue.

'There's something dangerous going on. I don't want you caught up in it.'

'Like what?' Her mind whirled.

His lips tightened into a line indicating he wasn't going to say.

'Does it have anything to do with my father?'

He took a breath. 'I don't know.'

A door banged somewhere making him turn his head and listen. Once again, she found Win a dichotomy. His clothes screamed *manual worker, builder*, but there was an odd sophistication about him in the way he spoke and held himself. And then there were his knuckles, bruised and scabbed.

'What do you do?' she asked.

'What?' He looked disconcerted.

'I mean professionally. For a job.'

'I'm an investment broker.'

'Really?' She looked pointedly at his hands which he promptly put behind his back.

'Yes, really.'

Why was she surprised? Investment brokers could get into brawls like anyone else, she supposed. Was it because of the diverse display of books in his office that she'd thought he'd do something more exciting? Erroneously, she noticed that although his eyes were deep brown, they had faint flecks of gold radiating from their irises.

'Individual investors,' he added, 'can't buy shares directly from the stock market, they need a stockbroker.'

'You buy and sell the stocks Father Luke wants to invest in?'

'Yup.'

'Do you work for a firm, or yourself?'

'I work for Clan Capital. The Golden Dawn is one of our major clients, and–'

He stopped suddenly at the sound of a door opening and pointed at a toned female sculpture on the mantelpiece, an angel with her hands raised to heaven as her gold-painted wings lifted her into the sky. Diamonds were cupped in her palms. 'Damien Hirst,' he told her in a loud voice. 'A gift from a grateful follower who suffered from bulimia, and who he cured.'

Win's gaze moved to fix on something over her

shoulder. 'I was just telling Miz Scott about the generosity of some of your congregation.'

Sid turned to see Father Luke sweeping across the parquet floor. 'I've been looking for you.' His eyes were on Sid.

'And here I am,' she replied affably.

'She got lost,' Win said. 'She was trying to find the loo and, well, I rescued her. I showed her the downstairs ladies'. Hope that's okay.'

Father Luke didn't even glance at Win. 'Follow me,' he commanded Sid. 'We can talk privately in my study.'

As Sid made to join him, Win stopped her. Bending his head to hers, he whispered in her ear. His lips were so close she could feel the little hairs tremble. Goose bumps rose along her arm.

'You owe me,' he hissed.

No time to think as Father Luke was ushering her upstairs and into his office where three men stood, arms folded and facing her. He was closing the door and, to her horror, locking it behind him and pocketing the key.

# 17

'Your phone.' Father Luke clicked his fingers at her.

'Why do you want my phone?' Her pulse was pounding and she was glad she sounded genuinely baffled. The three men stood there, as unmoved as tombstones. Were they the same three who'd threatened her with their rifles?

'You were seen filming me.'

Sid frowned. 'Nobody said I couldn't. There were no signs, either.'

'You're being disingenuous.' His face was set like stone. 'Give it to me.'

'I'm sorry, but no.' She kept her voice calm and polite despite her panic rising. *He'd locked the door.* 'It's my property, and since nobody told me I couldn't take photographs or video...' She trailed off as Father Luke clicked his fingers and the three men stepped forward, two of them gripping her arms while the third started to unbuckle her handbag strap.

'Hey, you can't do that!' She tried to pull free but they were incredibly strong and held her fast.

The third man pulled her handbag free. Passed it to Father Luke. Still the men held Sid. Father Luke opened the zip.

'Don't you *dare*,' she hissed.

He delved inside. Brought out her phone. He then went to the door and unlocked it. 'Bring her,' he commanded.

On either side of her, still grasping her arms, the men walked her downstairs. In the hall, Father Luke took her phone to the fireplace. Grabbing a poker, he put her phone on the stone hearth and started smashing it.

Sid was trembling from a combination of fright and fury.

'I will report you to the police,' she told him. 'And I will sue you for damage to my property.'

'Report…' Smash. 'All you…' Smash. 'Like.'

Bits of plastic and metal were strewn everywhere. Every time she tried to free herself, the two men gripped her arms even more firmly. She could feel the bruises forming. Helpless, she watched Father Luke scoop up the detritus of her phone and throw it on the fire.

Finally, he turned to face her. 'The Guards will see you out.'

'But I want to talk about my father. You and he were–'

'You forewent my goodwill the minute you pointed your phone at me in church.' His face was pale and pinched.

'You went to school together, Oxford uni together–'

'Take her to her car,' he commanded the Guards. 'Make sure she leaves.'

No point in asking for her defunct Nokia. She'd buy another on eBay if she needed one.

With two Guards on either side of her, the other at her back, Sid walked to her car.

Gabriel stood next to the driver's door. When he saw her, his face lit up into a smile.

'Hey,' she greeted him.

'Hi.'

She gestured at the three men. 'Who are these guys?'

'Brothers Isaac, Saul and Jeremiah.'

'Which one is which?'

The three men glowered as Gabriel pointed at each, saying their name. The swarthy one was Saul, the fair-haired one Isaac, and Jeremiah had a mole at the side of his mouth the size of a walnut.

'Nice to meet you,' she told them. Sarcasm laced her tone.

'Go,' growled Brother Saul. 'Now.'

Sid unlocked her car. Looked at Gabriel.

'Will you come back?' he asked. His voice trembled a little.

'No, she won't,' snapped Brother Saul. 'She's not welcome anymore.'

Gabriel crumpled. She didn't think she'd seen a more miserable kid. She went to him and gave him a hug. With her lips against his ear, she whispered, 'If you could, would you come with me?'

'Yes,' he whispered back, 'but I can't leave Hannah.'

'Enough!' barked Brother Isaac. 'You go now!'

She desperately wanted to tell Gabriel she'd come back for him, rescue him and his sister, but she didn't dare give him false hope. 'I hope I'll see you again.' She touched his cheek with her fingers. 'It would be nice to hang out together.'

He managed to raise a smile. 'Yes, it would.'

As she drove away, she saw Brother Isaac bring out a walkie-talkie and speak into it. His eyes were on her car as he spoke.

When Sid breasted the top of the hill she looked down to the manor house to see the tiny dot that was Gabriel still standing there, watching her go.

Her heart turned over. Literally. She was rocked with such an intense and powerful emotion it made her feel dizzy and close to tears. It was, she realised with a shock, the first time she'd truly felt something for someone else since her mother had died.

*Shit*, she thought, it hurt like hell.

---

Gabriel stood in front of Father Luke trying not to quail. He wanted to be brave and not show his fear because he'd learned over the years if you looked scared, it just made Father Luke worse.

*Camp Fire Yarn. No. 21*

*Very few men are born brave, but any man can make himself brave if he tries – and especially if he begins trying when he is a boy.*

Father Luke's eyes burned like lasers. 'You accompanied her from the church?'

'She said she was going to see you in your study.'

'What else did she say?'

Gabriel screwed up his face as he thought. 'She said I could come and say goodbye to her out the front of the house. Her car is called a Suzuki Jimny.'

'Did you see her filming me?' Father Luke's voice was silky.

Pure terror shot through Gabriel. He knew he mustn't lie, but he didn't want to be put in the Shed.

'No.' His voice shook. 'I was w-watching you. It was amazing, you curing Brother Peter.'

Father Luke's eyes took on a glassy look that made Gabriel's bladder soften.

'You're not lying, are you?'

'No.' He tried not to whimper. He wasn't a kid anymore and he wished he didn't feel so scared. 'Promise.'

'Because if you are, it won't be you put in the Shed. It will be little Hannah who suffers for your sins.'

Although he knew he'd burn in Hell for the lie, Gabriel felt his spine stiffen. He held Father Luke's gaze. His trembling stopped. 'I swear I'm telling the truth.'

Father Luke's gaze deepened as though he was probing, questioning Gabriel's soul.

Gabriel held his breath.

'What else?'

*Sid asked if I could, would I come with her.*

'Nothing.'

'Brother Jeremiah said you liked her.' His eyes narrowed to slits. 'He said you were besotted.'

To his horror, heat rushed from his neck to his cheeks. Frantically he shook his head.

'She didn't try to seduce you into running away?'

Gabriel shook his head again. 'No.' It was a whisper.

'I bet if you could, you would. She's a very beautiful woman.'

Gabriel didn't dare speak for fear of giving himself away.

The seconds ticked past. Gabriel's heart was drumming as fast as a rabbit's and when Father Luke turned his head away, Gabriel exhaled in a rush.

'You may go.'

It was all Gabriel could do not to run from the room.

# 18

S id drove straight to Oxford, the closest town. She had to force herself to concentrate on driving and not replaying what had just happened. She could hardly believe Father Luke had destroyed her phone let alone used the Brothers to restrain her. It was unbelievable, shocking, and showed how far Father Luke had gone along the road to hubris.

*Report all you like.*

He thought he was untouchable. Well, she'd see about that.

As she neared the city centre, she was frustrated when she found the road ahead blocked thanks to a demonstration, forcing her to undertake a fifteen-minute detour. She'd watched the news this morning to see Marc Strong demanding the prime minister deal with these *miscreants, disruptors of normal people's lives.* He'd been commanding and powerful, very much the strong leader, and she thought of Liz's story of Father Luke and Marc Strong as boys, dressing up in togas and bullying the rest of the class into treating them as their leaders. Both men were now in positions of power which psychologically Sid found fascinating. Where had their arrogance come from? Were they born that way, or encouraged by their parents? She supposed Liz's 'prophesy' wouldn't have held much water without other influences, and Sid suspected it had simply compounded their own egotistical beliefs of themselves.

Marc Strong showed no sympathy for the demonstrators. This morning, she'd felt sorry for the protesters who were feeling the squeeze of inflation and the cost of living, but right now, as she was forced into another city zone and had to pay an extra fee, her sympathy turned to annoyance.

After she'd parked, she headed for a computer store she knew near the Ashmolean Museum that sold mobile phones. She couldn't afford to wait until she got paid for her latest articles to buy a replacement iPhone, so she used some of her savings. She didn't have a landline and not having a phone where she lived was unacceptable. Tank was a huge comfort, but if she needed the police or, God forbid, an ambulance, Tank was as much use as a banana.

Thanks to the in-store salesman it didn't take long to block her original SIM and insert a replacement into her new phone before reactivating her number. Over the next hour she worked on reinstating all her information and when complete, her phone, thank God, was good to go.

The first person she called was Detective Kelly. As she described Father Luke smashing her phone, the way his henchmen had practically carried her downstairs, she felt herself start to tremble.

'You want to make a formal complaint?'

'Yes.'

'It's best done in person. You could come to the station

but how about I come to you? I can take down your statement.'

'Isn't it your day off?'

'It won't be a hardship.' There was a smile in his voice.

'I'm in Oxford at the moment.'

He made a hmm-ing sound. 'I'll actually pass the Golden Dawn on my way across. How about if I stop and have a chat to Father Luke?'

'And say what?'

'That he's committed an offence, for starters.'

Sid wasn't sure. Was that how it worked? The police talking to the offender as well as the offended?

'I'll give him a warning,' Kelly added. 'It's not a conviction but it'll stay on his criminal record for twelve months.'

'Hey, that's great.' She felt surprised. Was it really that easy?

'See you in a couple of hours. Where shall we meet?'

'How about the Old Bookbinders Ale House,' she said on impulse. It used to be her local and although it could be said she was biased, it really was one of the best pubs in town. Cosy, atmospheric, with wooden beams, rough brick floor, wood-burning stove, mismatched chairs and tables and a collection of vinyl records and beer badges on the walls. Sid used to know all the bar staff, and going there was like being at home but with top food and an endless supply of alcohol. It was the one place she'd missed like mad when she'd first moved and she'd be only too happy to wait there for as long as it took for Kelly to arrive.

'Sounds good,' Kelly agreed.

To kill time as well as regain a sense of equilibrium, Sid wandered through the Covered Market which glittered and gleamed with Christmas lights. She was glad to see Sasi Thai was still there, buzzing as usual, along with

Chocology and the Oxford Cheese Company. She always felt weird and slightly disconnected whenever she returned to her old haunts, as though they'd been in a dream she'd once had.

She paused to admire a beautiful display of wild berries in deep shades of red and blue outside Jemini Flowers, wondering if she should relent this year and buy a Christmas flower arrangement. No, she decided. It would just make her sad.

The Bookbinders Ale House, when she arrived, was packed to the rafters with people finishing Sunday lunch.

'Hey, look what the cat's dragged in!' Nora's face was alight. Love your outfit. Sexy boots and all.'

Sid looked at Nora's sweatshirt with the Milky Way swirling across its front and a small arrow pointing at one edge saying, *you are here*. At the other end of the Milky Way was another arrow: *the restrooms are here*.

Sid chuckled. 'Love yours too.'

To Sid's surprise, Nora ducked down to fetch a Riedel glass from behind the bar.

'You still keep it?'

'Always lived in hope, Sid. One day you were here, the next you vanished.' She pulled a face. 'We missed you.'

'Awww.' Sid went and gave her a hug. 'You're sweet.'

'What's it going to be?'

'I'm driving, so a white wine spritzer would be great.'

Nora popped her at a table by the window that had just been vacated, letting Sid settle down with her phone. When Detective Kelly arrived forty minutes later, he had sprinkles of snow on his shoulders and hair. She'd been so absorbed in reading up on common assault, police cautions, warnings and penalty notices that she hadn't realised it was snowing. He stood just inside the pub door, a satchel over one shoulder, looking across the crowd. His gaze travelled over her then snapped back. He stared at her for a second, looking oddly nonplussed before he walked across the room.

'Sorry, I'm later than I thought.' He put his satchel on the floor, next to the empty chair opposite her.

'The protests.'

'Nightmare,' he said. 'I don't envy our boys and girls out there. I've a friend in the Met who says it's turning nasty.'

'They said the same on the news this morning.'

Apparently, protests were now gaining traction in most cities. In London, the John Lewis store had been damaged by rioters throwing smoke bombs and rocks while anarchists graffitied buildings and vandalised shops and banks along Oxford Street. It was the biggest public backlash against the government's spending cuts since it came to power.

Kelly pulled a face. 'God alone knows where it's going to end.'

Sid began to get up, saying, 'What can I get you?' but he waved her back down.

'I'll get it. How about you?'

She'd barely touched her spritzer. 'I'm fine. But thanks.'

At the bar, Nora's eyes travelled purposely between Sid and the detective. Surreptitiously, she sent Sid a thumbs up. *Go, girl.* Sid grimaced. Nora had been a witness to her shameful past. She hoped Nora wouldn't let anything slip to Kelly, or hint at the woman she used to be. Next time, Sid decided, she'd go someplace where she wasn't known.

Kelly returned to the table with a pint and a packet of crisps. Settled next to her. 'Nice place.'

'Yeah, I used to like it.'

'Don't you miss being in town?'

'No.'

'Why did you move? I mean, where you live is very nice, don't get me wrong, but don't you find it–'

'Did you see Father Luke?' she interrupted. She didn't want to make small talk, let alone discuss her motivations for moving somewhere so isolated.

'Yup.' He took a gulp of beer. 'He denies everything. He says you're making it all up, that you're a sad person, lonely, and are seeking attention.'

She just looked at Kelly.

'Don't worry, I cautioned him.'

'Doesn't he have to admit the offence and agree to be cautioned in order for it to be official?'

When the detective didn't say anything, she added, 'If he refuses to admit guilt, which he obviously does, he can be arrested and charged. Am I right?'

'Don't tell me you're a lawyer in your spare time.' His tone was light but she'd obviously hit a nerve.

'I don't want him to get off scot-free.' She leaned forward, her tone fierce. 'He needs to know he can't bully people like that.'

'I gave him a verbal warning, okay? And I'll update the forces control room so his name will appear on a computer record by the Gloucestershire Police. It's not a criminal record, but it'll show up on DBS checks. That should be enough, shouldn't it?'

DBS, she'd learned, was an acronym for the Disclosure and Barring Service, responsible for the processing and issuing of checks that allowed recruiters to vet potential employees.

'It's not even a slap on the wrist!' She scowled. 'It's not like he's going to be going for a job or anything. He should suffer some kind of consequence, shouldn't he? He got his men to manhandle me, for Pete's sake. He destroyed my phone, forcing me to come to Oxford when I had other things I wanted to do.'

He began to look alarmed. 'You're not thinking of reporting him seriously, are you? Taking him to court?'

'I'm tempted, believe me.'

Kelly turned his beer glass around and around. 'What if he refunded the cost of your phone? Your travel expenses. Made a monetary reparation.'

It took a second for his words to sink in. 'You're talking about bribing me to keep quiet.'

'Hardly.' He looked offended. 'He's already been cautioned by me. Isn't it enough?'

She thought about it. 'No.'

'Even if I told you he's got some seriously powerful lawyers?'

'The court will spot his type a mile away. Taking a sledgehammer to crack a nut. I'll walk it.' She smiled at the thought.

Kelly considered her for a long while. Then he reached down to his satchel and withdrew a pad of A4, along with a pen.

'Tell me exactly what happened. I'll log this at the police station and get you a crime reference number.' He looked gloomy, no doubt at the extra work she was giving him.

By the time Sid had given her statement, he'd nearly finished his pint. She downed what remained of her spritzer. 'I wanted to talk to Father Luke about my dad, but I kind of scuppered my chances. Have you learned anything about my father during your investigations into Owen's murder? Like why he had my father's postcard hidden on him?'

The detective shook his head. 'All we've gleaned is that Owen was extremely troubled before he died. His wife said he had mental issues.'

'What kind of mental issues?'

'Bizarre delusions and fantasies. He wasn't psychotic, but he was so preoccupied with his delusions, his marriage was on the rocks.'

'He was hallucinating?'

'You could say so. He believed he was going to be king of the Otherworld. Nuts, eh?' He smiled as though he found it amusing but Sid didn't smile back. She was thinking of those three eight-year-old boys in their togas.

'Grandiose delusions,' she murmured.

He looked startled. 'That's what Harriet said. His wife. I saw her yesterday. Her house looks up at Glastonbury Tor. It's pretty amazing, actually.' He tilted his head on one side. 'What do you think of the Tor, with your paranormality hat on. Do you think the Holy Grail is buried beneath it?'

'Put it this way, I won't be taking my spade with me when I next visit.'

'She said Owen insisted on buying the house because a black stream below ground connected it to the Tor.'

It wasn't the first time Sid had heard this. According to geomancers, black streams were usually known as lines of underground toxic energy, in contrast with white streams that carried healthy regenerative energy. More twaddle that had, as far as she knew, absolutely no science behind it.

'Did Harriet believe him?'

He shook his head. 'She's a teacher. Very feet-on-the-ground, which is why Owen's behaviour drove her so crazy.'

Sid played with her glass. 'I'd like to see her. She might help shed some light on what happened to my dad.'

'Please don't.'

Sid raised her eyebrows.

'Her husband has just been murdered, remember?' Kelly

put his hands on the table, expression intent. 'She's in a really bad place. She's also dosed up on tranquillisers. I doubt you'll get much sense out of her.'

A ball of frustration rose in her throat and Kelly seemed to sense this because he leaned back, considering her. 'How about if I ask her if she'll see you? I know she's a mess but I suppose you never know...'

'Hey,' she said, surprised. 'That would be great. Thanks.'

In the conversational lull, Sid stretched a little. 'I saw Winstone Fairchild at the Golden Dawn today.'

Immediately, Kelly's gaze sharpened. 'What was he doing there?'

She frowned. 'He's Golden Dawn's stockbroker. I assume he was there to talk investments.'

Kelly took off his specs, looked at them briefly before putting them back on. 'Did he say anything to you?'

*Some rocks you don't turn over.*

The detective was affecting casualness, pretending he wasn't really interested, which made her say, 'No. He just showed me to the ladies.' She hoped she wouldn't come to regret lying to him, but what had Win said? He'd warned her. Just as Kelly had done.

Sid picked up her handbag, her mind turning to the drive home, collecting Tank. She indicated her witness statement, still lying on the table between them. 'I'll have to go to court, but when I win, he'll have a police record.'

Kelly grimaced. 'You like a fight, don't you?'

She stared at him, momentarily floored. Did she? She used to love a scrap, which was why she'd wanted to be a lawyer all those years ago, but now? Suddenly discomfited, she got to her feet, wrapped her scarf around her neck and pulled on her coat.

The detective downed the remainder of his pint, rising

to join her outside. 'I was going to ask if you'd like to stay for something to eat, but–'

'Sorry,' she cut across him, walking away without looking back. She could feel him watching her, probably confused at her abrupt departure, but what could she say? I'm sorry but I don't want Nora giving anything away?

The first time had been three months after her mother had died. She'd been eighteen years old and smashed with grief; unstable, volatile, a walking unexploded bomb waiting to be detonated, when she'd bumped into a guy in the Covered Market.

She could remember the way their eyes met, and how she'd felt real for the first time since Mum died. He'd been in his late twenties. Brown curly hair. Biker leathers.

'I've never been on a motorbike,' she said.

He smiled. 'We can remedy that, no problem. I have a spare helmet in my pannier.'

The ride was wild, exhilarating. He took her to Wales, along sweeping roads edged with heather, gorse and bracken. When he opened the throttle, she clutched his waist and screamed at him to *go faster*!

He called her a crazy woman and she laughed from deep in her belly, carefree and wild for what felt like the first time since her father disappeared. They ended up at his place, somewhere past the A40, she had no idea where. They took their helmets off. He led her into his house, into his bedroom. They didn't say anything. His eyes were as brown and calm as a slow-moving river. She felt as though she was drowning but she also felt elated, every nerve-ending thrillingly aware. It was like being reborn.

'I love the way you growl.' He nuzzled her neck afterwards, scooping her close. 'Like a little tiger.'

When it came for her to leave, he offered to ride her home but she didn't want him to know where she lived.

She asked for a taxi. He didn't ask for her number but stood in his driveway and blew her a kiss as she left.

When she told Aero about it, he'd been horrified. 'But he could have been anybody!'

'What, like a serial killer?' she'd snorted.

'Jesus, Sid.' His brow was creased with anxiety. 'You really should be more careful.'

His words had no effect because she'd had no intention of stopping what she'd discovered was her drug of choice. Because whenever she took it, it was as though Mum and Dad had never existed.

## 19

The first thing Sid did when she got home was download her video of Father Luke scamming his congregation from the iCloud and post it online.

*Mock or miracle?* Sid asked her followers.

To her satisfaction, it didn't take long before the video had gained traction, being shared across social media platforms from Neston to New York.

Wood burner lit, tea and ciggy on the go, Tank in his bed, she searched online for Harriet Evans, teacher, Glastonbury, and immediately found her through LinkedIn. She dithered briefly, wondering whether to drop her a note or not.

*She's in a really bad place. She's also dosed up on tranquillisers.*

Sid didn't want to cause the woman any more stress, but what could be the worst that could happen? That she'd ignore Sid? Report her to Kelly? The detective would be annoyed, no doubt, but when would he ask Harriet if Sid could see her? It might be days, *weeks*. Sid had never been particularly patient and decided she couldn't wait.

She worded her note carefully, saying how sorry she was about Owen, how she was trying to find her missing father, and that a postcard to her from her father had been found hidden in Owen's clothing on the day he died. She used simple language, straightforward. No shirking realities. Nothing ambiguous that could be misunderstood.

She hesitated before she posted her message, but when she thought of her father's bear-brown eyes, the way she'd tug his beard in her fists when she was a toddler, his laughter, she clicked send.

The second it had gone, she immediately felt better.

'Supper,' she announced to Tank, 'to celebrate.'

She ate a Charlie Bigham macaroni cheese on her lap while half-watching *Countryfile*. Christmas was looming and today's show was all about discovering Christmas in Lincolnshire. Merry street markets, cosy inns, beautiful churches. A segment on how to create your own festive displays had Sid looking at Tank. 'It's just you and me again. I think we'll have roast beef. I know it's your favourite and we can eat yummy beef sandwiches for ever.'

As usual, when Aero had invited her to join him and his family for Christmas, she'd lied.

'I'm staying with a cousin in the Lake District.'

'The same cousin you spent Easter with?' He'd looked sceptical.

'The same.'

He'd sighed, but if she was honest and said she wanted to be alone, she knew he'd badger her relentlessly until she caved in and she absolutely didn't want to spend Christmas with another family. She would much rather ignore it, and keep her sorrow and loneliness to herself.

Before she headed to bed, Sid watched BBC Points West. Massive anti-austerity, anti-authority demonstrations not just in London but Birmingham and

Cardiff. Over a hundred people arrested, and twenty-one injured including fifteen police. Then Marc Strong's face filled her screen with his creepy good looks and shiny white teeth.

'Mindless yobs are hiding under the pretence of these legitimate marches. We need to crack down on them, hard. We've been too wet, too liberal for too long. It's time to stand up to these bullies and keep our streets safe for our law-abiding citizens.'

Next up, in full technicolour, was Father Luke, bellowing about cities being in danger, and bombs killing everyone in their thousands. There was no footage of any other part of his Sunday service. Just ten seconds or so of his bombastic 'prophesy' and the news anchor saying carefully neutral things about the 'commune'. She guessed the djellaba-clad film crew she'd seen on stage with Father Luke had clipped the footage to just show his prophesy, and not his scams. It was a snapshot, something few people would remember and again, Sid wondered what Father Luke's game was.

Checking her social media feeds, she was delighted to see her video of Father Luke gushing with likes and loves, the odd angry face, and even more delighted to see it was being shared and quoted at speed, gaining traction as more and more people joined in to talk. The comments ranged from fury, *how dare he manipulate his congregation like that!* to the unconvinced, *of course a paranormal disbeliever has their mind closed to any kind of miracle.*

Her messages were still amplifying when she headed to bed. *Job done,* she thought in satisfaction.

Once again, Sid slept with Tank outside her bedroom door, only waking when her phone alarm clock went off. Monday morning: kettle on, Tank outside, give Tank his breakfast, tea, ciggy, shower, walk Tank before finishing her latest article and sending it off. Her usual routine, unless she was called to deal with a haunted house or demonic possession, neither of which were on the cards today.

To her surprise, late afternoon, she was pinged by LinkedIn. She just about fell over when she saw the message was from Harriet, who'd left Sid her phone number. Sid immediately called her.

Harriet sounded surprisingly together considering her husband had been murdered, making Sid wonder if she was in denial or so deeply shocked she'd blocked her emotions. Was she really on tranquillisers? She didn't sound as though she was. After saying how sorry she was about Owen's death, Sid reiterated her reason for contacting Harriet. 'Dad was at school with Owen, as well as in the same univer–'

'Oxford.' Harriet cut over her. 'Yes, I know all that. They were good friends, back in the day. And you want to see me to help you find Mike?'

'Yes.'

Small silence. 'How about tomorrow. I'm working from home after four.' She rattled off her address.

'Thank you so–'

Harriet hung up.

'Much,' Sid added into empty air.

―――――――

It was raining when Sid drove south the following day. There were few cars about, and behind her she could see a motorbike. Something large and powerful. She wouldn't have noticed it if she hadn't been surprised that it didn't overtake her. She kept waiting for it to pull out and charge past, but somewhere around Shepton Mallet, it vanished.

Sid parked outside Harriet Evans's home, a pretty brick cottage at the end of a narrow lane bordered by towering hazel and blackthorn hedges. Straight ahead rose the Tor, topped by the stone tower.

Her heart squeezed.

There was a brief period when they thought Mum had beaten cancer. It wasn't long – just a few months during the summer – but she dived into life like a kingfisher diving for its last meal. She wouldn't sit still. She walked everywhere, her face raised to the sun, gulping in sights and sounds, hugging trees, stroking the leaves of plants. It was as though she knew the cancer was going to return.

One Thursday in June she started packing the camper. Sid asked her where she was going.

'We,' she announced with a flourish, 'are going to Glastonbury.'

It transpired she had, miracle of miracles, managed to purloin tickets for them through one of her customers. Five days of hedonistic, glorious musical madness on a farm over the summer solstice. Sheer heaven.

On the second evening they walked out into the humming sunset and stood at a crossroads in an improvised street beneath an oak, watching thousands upon thousands of people walking past. Everyone was completely shit-faced, glassy-eyed from alcohol or some substance or other. Not that they were particularly sober, having been on the rosé for most of the afternoon, but they'd cracked up.

Mum headed to the alternative health field, dragging Sid in her wake. Sid tried not to scoff and open her mind to the petals of an angelic visitation, and how to immerse herself in a Water Circle in order to find her inner serenity, but she struggled. When Mum sat her down with a supposedly renowned psychic called Angela Aires, real name Patricia Jones (Sid looked her up later), to see where Dad was, it took all her self-control not to scream.

Angela billed herself as a clairvoyant, harnessing her mind's eye to channel information about a person, object, location or event. She 'guided' Mum by apparently talking to her spirit guides who stood just behind her, ready to give her advice on where Mum was to look for her missing husband.

'He's waiting to be found,' Angela said earnestly. 'Trust me.'

Sid wouldn't have minded if psychics actually helped her mother. Mum went to psychics because she was desperate, but she wasn't talking to a counsellor who could give her tools to help her cope with her husband's disappearance. She was talking to some fuckwit stranger who merely gave advice. Today's fuckwit stranger told them that they should look for Dad near the Chalice Well at the bottom of Glastonbury Tor.

And sure enough, when they left Glastonbury, Mum insisted they drive to the Well and have a look. Just in case.

It was the only time they fought.

'Let's hope the next psychic doesn't tell you Dad's in New Zealand!' Sid yelled.

'And let's hope one day that you'll open your self-righteous, obstinately closed mind!' her mother yelled back.

Now, Sid smoked a cigarette while she gazed at the Tor, thinking not just of her mother, but the legends of King Arthur that swirled in the area. As Detective Kelly had mentioned, the Holy Grail was said to be buried beneath the Tor, and King Arthur buried in Glastonbury Abbey. The nearby fort at South Cadbury had long been suggested as the location for Camelot. Had King Arthur existed? She loved the romance of it but was, to put it mildly, sceptical.

Turning away, she saw Harriet Evans had opened her front door and was watching her through narrowed eyes. Fifties, average height, average weight. Mousy hair brushed her shoulders. She wasn't good-looking but nor was she ugly. She was, simply, one of the plain Janes of the world. She looked Sid up and down.

'Well, well. If it isn't the supernatural scientist herself.'

Her gaze flashed with malice.

# 20

'Hi,' Sid responded to Harriet Evans mildly, thinking *what the...?*

'You know Owen was murdered?'

Sid took a breath. 'I'm sorry.'

'What do you know about it?'

'Nothing. But Owen had a postcard of Dad's, written to me, hidden on him.' She explained about the code game they used to play. 'He'd dated it the same day he vanished.'

'How is it possible that Owen had it?'

The malice remained. Sid couldn't think why.

'Either he found it, or... I don't know,' she finished lamely.

Harriet's lips thinned. 'It's unbelievable. My husband killed by God alone knows who... and for what? Why?'

She didn't appear at all upset over Owen's death. People's grief could come in many different guises. There was no right or wrong way and there was, she guessed, a Harriet way.

'I was hoping you might know something.' Harriet chewed her lip. 'But it seems you know less than nothing.'

'Sorry.'

Harriet put her hand on the door and for a moment Sid thought she was going to close it in her face, but then she hesitated. 'The police have been less than useless...'

Sid waited quietly while Harriet dithered. Finally, she seemed to come to a decision and opened the door wide. 'Come in, then. I suppose you'd like some tea or coffee.'

Refusing to be put off, Sid said, 'A coffee would be lovely,' and followed her into a hall. Her eyes went to a collection of family photographs displayed behind Perspex. Harriet and a small man with soft brown hair and a big smile. Owen Evans, looking very much alive and, it had to be said, like someone you wouldn't mind getting to know.

'You're welcome to his study,' Harriet said. 'The police have had a look and taken his laptop. If you can make any sense of anything, let me know.'

She was relieved when Harriet told her to help herself to the cafetière; she was going to do some marking in the kitchen. She was an English teacher and had a lot to get through. Owen may be dead, but that was no excuse. She couldn't let the kids down.

Sid was torn between disliking Harriet or admiring her practical nature in getting on with things. She opted for the latter and said, 'Lucky kids,' which earned her an acknowledging nod.

Owen's study was a mess. Notebooks, box files, cardboard files, pens, stacks of paper, books everywhere, piles of magazines. She rummaged around. Lots of stuff on English mythologies, copies of medieval Welsh manuscripts, stacks of notebooks filled with copious transcriptions and observations on Annwn, the Otherworld in Welsh mythology. There were notes on ley lines, geometric alignments running across ancient landscapes, and archaeoastronomy. Papers on equinoxes, megaliths and the Metonic cycle. A whole box on black holes.

She rummaged through the mess to find more books, this time on Satan and Satanism, the Underworld, Hell, evil souls and eternal punishment. She frowned as she remembered one of Owen's tattoos, showing a goat-headed Baphomet image; the official insignia of the Church of Satan.

Shuffling through some maps, she saw Owen had scribbled on an Ordnance Survey map of the area. There was a cross marked on Glastonbury Tor, and others around Chalice Well and the White Spring. Chalice Well was where Angela Aires had told Sid and her mother to look for Dad.

*It means nothing*, she told herself. It's just a well. She looked up the White Spring on her phone to see it was a temple and pilgrimage site.

She drank her coffee. Went through everything again.

It was a jumble of disparate information that she didn't know what to do with. Was any of it connected to Dad's disappearance? She went to stand in the doorway.

'Harriet?' she called.

'Yes?'

'Can I ask a question?'

'Sure.'

Harriet appeared, a pair of vivid pink spectacles perched on her head. Her eyes were red, her mouth swollen. She'd been crying, but from the way her shoulders were back, her chin thrust forward, she wouldn't appreciate Sid mentioning it.

'Did the police take anything else apart from his laptop?'

'Not that I know of.'

Long silence where the two women gazed at one

another. Then Harriet looked away. 'It was your father's disappearance that tipped Owen over the edge.'

Something inside Sid tightened. 'In what way?'

'Since Mike worked at CERN, with people who worked on the large Hadron Collider, Owen believed that your father had found a space wormhole or some such, and travelled to another world. A parallel universe.'

'But Dad didn't disappear in Geneva. He was in the UK. There's CCTV footage to prove it.'

'I know!' Harriet almost shouted. 'But Owen didn't believe it! He said it would have been tampered with. That there were hugely wealthy and powerful people who wanted to stop him from finding the wormhole. That the Bill and Melinda Gates Foundation engineered it to keep the truth from the world; that they were travelling between the two worlds to amass even more money; and that CERN is under their control.' She took a breath. 'Owen spent the last decade trying to find the Otherworld, convinced your father was already there.'

'But even if Dad had found a gateway like that, he would have come back and told us.'

'I wasn't dealing with someone sane,' Harriet snapped. 'He was living in a fantasy. And those tattoos... He said he'd need them in the Otherworld because you can lose a piece of paper, but you can't lose your skin.'

She gave a harsh laugh. 'He'd gone quite mad, you know, so much so, that I told him I was going to get a divorce. I blame your father. If it hadn't been for him, Owen would never have lost his mind.'

Ah. Now she knew where the malice came from.

'I'm sorry.'

'I'm sorry too.' She gave a weak smile.

Sid leaned against the door-jamb. 'What do you know

about his friendship with Marc Strong and Luke Goddard?'

'They were at school together. Then they rattled around Oxford together.'

'Would you say they were good friends?'

Something jagged rose in Harriet's eyes. 'Put it this way, he was a better friend to them than they were to him.'

'In what way?'

Harriet looked into the distance. 'It wasn't something you could put your finger on. No single event to use as an example. They'd call Owen up and he'd jump to do whatever they asked.'

'Did they spend much time together?'

'They weren't in each other's pockets, if that's what you mean. I think the last time they saw one another was two or three years ago, at some reunion or other.'

Small pause.

'I don't suppose you know someone called Winstone Fairchild?'

Harriet shook her head.

'When did you last hear from Owen?'

'I...' Harriet's lips wobbled. Real grief began to rise.

'I'm sorry.' Sid's heart twisted.

Harriet dabbed furiously at her eyes. 'H-he called me the day h-he died. It was incredibly garbled...' She gulped in a big breath and went on. 'I could barely understand a word. He'd used Siri, and was obviously driving. He was shouting at the phone. He sounded hysterical.'

Sid stared. 'When was this?'

'Last Monday. 10.20pm. He was on his way home to me. He never normally calls me from the car. Says it's too distracting.'

The traffic report had stated the B4425 had been closed

after a *serious crash overnight left a man dead*. Had Owen called his wife just before he'd been murdered?

'He was yelling the name Leah, over and over. Something about the John Radcliffe Hospital and another woman's name. Amelia. I tried to calm him down, talk to him properly but he wouldn't stop shouting. And then the line went dead.'

Sid's nerves were quivering. 'How long was the call, do you think?'

Harriet brought out a tissue and blew her nose loudly. 'Half a minute? Less? I can't be sure. He was absolutely hysterical.'

'What other words did you hear?' Sid asked.

'Like what?' A vestige of her former antagonism flitted across her face.

'Anything at all.'

She thought for a moment. 'It was all about saving Leah. He kept screaming, Leah...'

Sid waited.

'I had no idea it would be the last time I heard his voice. Amelia. Leah...' Her eyes suddenly widened. 'Oh my God. I didn't realise. Mike. He said your father's name.'

Sid felt as though a bolt of electricity had gone through her, but she kept her face neutral, not wanting to disturb Harriet's thoughts.

'Mike...' Harriet faltered as she said his name. 'I can't believe I forgot.'

Sid assured her that it was normal in a stressful situation not to remember absolutely everything. Harriet stared at the floor for a while, then looked up at Sid. 'I told the police all this. But not that he said your father's name. I shall let Detective Kelly know.'

Sid thought of Detective Kelly and how little he'd shared with her. She guessed that was normal in a murder investigation, but she found it incredibly frustrating. Owen had had her father's postcard. He'd hidden it. He'd potentially been driving, hysterical, away from his murderer.

Had Owen discovered what had happened to her father?

'Who do you think Leah and Amelia are?' Sid asked.

Harriet nibbled her thumbnail. 'I've never heard either name before.'

They both stood quietly for a moment or two.

'I don't want to be insensitive,' Sid said carefully, 'but do you have any idea who might have killed Owen?'

Harriet tilted her head, glancing up at the ceiling. 'On a bad day, I think he was having an affair and the husband went after him. On a good day, I wonder if it was a case of mistaken identity.'

'If he was having an affair, who might it have been with?'

Harriet closed her eyes, pain etched in every feature. 'I honestly don't think he was, but he spent so much time at Chalice Well, he may as well have been.'

## 21

Sid's mind was a whirl as she slipped into her car. What if Owen had discovered what had happened to her father? And he'd tried to tell Harriet as he drove away from his killer? Had Owen's killer killed Dad?

A gust of wind shook the car. Grey clouds scudded past the Tor as Sid picked up her phone, dialled.

'Sidney Scott,' Detective Kelly answered his phone warily.

'Detective Kelly. I have just seen Harriet Evans and–'

'I thought I told you,' he snapped, 'not to contact Harriet Evans directly.'

'She was fine,' Sid said airily. 'I mean, not hugely fine knowing her husband had been murdered, but she was pretty together.'

'You obviously caught her at a good time.'

*Obviously.*

'Look, she told me about Owen calling her as he was driving. That he was shouting at her, hysterically, the names Leah and Amelia.'

'Yes.' The word was cautious.

'She forgot to mention that he also said my father's name. Mike.'

'He did?' He suddenly sounded interested. 'In what context?'

'Harriet couldn't really remember. She could barely make sense of what he was saying but she remembered he'd said those three names. Amelia, Leah and Mike.'

'Anything else?'

'She mentioned the John Radcliffe Hospital.'

A grunt which she took to be an affirmation.

'Which is where Dad was last seen, when he visited his mother. Aside from when he filled up his car in Headington, of course.'

This time, silence.

'I think all this is tied into my father.'

More silence, during which she hoped he was thinking, and connecting some investigative dots. She watched a couple of rooks flapping wildly in the wind. 'Harriet told me Owen called her at 10.20pm. Was that just before he died, do you think?'

'Just because I told you *how* he died doesn't mean I'm going to divulge any further details of my murder investigation...' His voice faded briefly, became muffled. She heard him talking to someone else. 'Yes, I'll be there in a sec... No, don't wait for me...'

He came back saying, 'Where is *your* investigation–' he weighted the words 'your' with heavy irony, '– taking you now?'

'Well, since you ask, I'm off to Chalice Well since that's where Owen spent a lot of time, apparently.'

'Who are you seeing there?' His tone was polite, as though asking who she was having tea with.

'I don't know yet,' she said brightly. 'Why? Who did you see?'

'Please.' His tone was serious. 'Be careful. This isn't some paranormal jaunt. There's a real killer out there.'

Immediately, she sobered. 'I'll be careful.'

He hung up without saying anything else.

*Thanks a bunch,* she thought. *You're nothing but a one-way street hoovering information from me and giving me fuck-all in return. And what about the crime reference number for my complaint against Father Luke?* Sid kicked herself for forgetting to ask him.

As she headed out of town for Chalice Well, she became aware of a motorbike behind her. For some reason it unsettled her and she was relieved that when she indicated left and slowed a little, it swept past. A monster gunmetal-grey bike with panniers on either side. She forgot all about it as she turned her mind to Owen and her father.

*They were good friends back in the day.*

Owen had been obsessed with mythology, her father, science. The two didn't mix, or so she'd thought, but then her everything-has-an-explanation father had married her woo-woo mother, which was an anomaly in itself.

Sid parked on the road and walked to Chalice Well, billed as a *sanctuary of healing, sanctity and peace.* Mum had loved it here and Sid had too, especially since its peaceful environment helped heal her outburst at the festival. She'd apologised, then Mum did too, and they'd left arm-in-arm, talking about nothing but the butterflies they'd seen, the number of frogs.

Sid walked up the path, planning on following the course of the waters to their source, but she stopped at the outer gate, staring at the sacred Well's symbol which adorned not just the gate, but the entrance sign and the two benches alongside.

She walked to the gate and ran her fingers gently over the ironwork. Based on the *vesica piscis,* the symbol was a mathematical shape formed by the intersection of two congruent discs, each centred on the perimeter of the other. Owen had had the same symbol tattooed on his arm. Poor, deluded Owen, and his poor, long-suffering wife.

Inside, it didn't take long to find someone to talk to. Apparently one of the Chalice Well Essences Practitioners had just finished a healing session and was happy to see her.

When a tall woman with an erect bearing, silver-grey hair and piercing blue eyes appeared, Sid did a classic double-take.

'Liz?'

The women stared at one another.

'I thought you were a school trustee,' said Sid. She was finding it difficult not to stare. No slimline embroidered velvet or chic black suede boots today. Instead Liz wore flowing robes and sandals. Her feet were long and brown, her toenails clear and smooth. She looked ageless and gleamed with good health.

'I am.' Liz glanced around as though to check nobody was nearby. 'But confidentially, I also work here.'

'The school doesn't know?'

Liz surveyed her at length as though weighing up what she was going to say next.

Sid waited.

'Come and sit with me,' Liz said. 'And I'll explain.'

She led Sid to a pergola. They settled on a pretty wooden bench just as the sun broke through a cloud to light the cobbled, artfully mossy path ahead.

'Something materialised when I read those boys' futures.' Her voice was soft. 'Something I couldn't explain. It happened when their blood mixed in the bowl. I told you that I threw a powder into the bowl to create a huge flash, but I did no such thing. The flash happened spontaneously. It had nothing to do with me.'

'Perhaps some flash powder settled there.' Sid's tone was mild. 'Or some dust from the flash paper you used.'

'Don't worry, Sidney... may I call you Sidney?'

'Sid, please.'

'Well, Sid. I tried to explain to myself what happened logically, trust me. I didn't believe in ghosts or demons, the paranormal, but I couldn't explain away the fact my eidetic memory started at the same time. Nor could I rationalise the sensation of a spirit slipping inside me. A male spirit, who spoke through me to those boys. I didn't have to put on a man's voice. It was Him.'

She closed her eyes. 'I said I terrified the boys but it was me who was terrified.'

'I can imagine.' Sid was gentle.

'The spirit wasn't benign. It was malevolent and mean. It didn't tell the boys to stop their bullying. It told them they were destined for great things and to have faith, everything was in place and that they'd fulfil their potential if they kept strong.' Her hands twisted together. 'When the spirit left me, I was physically sick. I saw a psychologist privately, who told me the spirit was really me, and that I had to have more compassion for that part of me that was trying to avoid some painful feelings that would surface by punishing the boys.

'The therapist wanted to see me further, to delve into my childhood.' Liz's expression hardened. 'But I didn't need therapy. I just needed that evil spirit never to return.'

'Did it?'

'Never.' A flash of relief crossed her face. 'Instead, a calm and tender life-force came to me to give me faith.'

'Faith?'

'If you tell anyone this, I will deny it.'

'I won't tell a soul, I promise.'

Long silence.

Then Liz smiled. 'I don't know why I trust you, but I do.'

Sid smiled back. 'I don't know why I like you, but I do.'

In spite of the heavy atmosphere, they both laughed.

Liz said, quite seriously, 'I belong to Wicca.'

When Sid didn't fling up her hands in horror or run away, she added, 'My name is Litha, meaning midsummer festival, summer solstice.'

Wicca, Sid already knew, was a way of life based upon the reconstruction of pre-Christian traditions. Wicca was a deep appreciation of earth and nature, being moved by a sunrise, moonlight shimmering on a clear river, the petals of a beautiful flower, the song of birds, and was a recognised religion.

'It's a peaceful belief system,' Sid said. 'Harmonious.'

'I am also a White Witch.'

'I see.' Sid could also see why Liz wouldn't want her religion being made public. If the parents at Stonehouse knew one of the school trustees was a witch, there would be hell to pay. The headmaster, on the other hand, would probably simply have a heart attack and die on the spot.

'Our basic tenet is "Harm None".'

'I like it,' said Sid.

They sat in companionable silence for a while. Then Sid said, 'You know what I do, right?'

'You try and disabuse people like me.'

'Yes and no. I try and find a rational explanation for inexplicable things.'

'You don't believe in demons?' Liz arched her eyebrows.

Sid gave a wry smile. 'No.'

'You haven't met one yet.'

'And your malevolent spirit?' Sid asked. 'The one who appeared when you made the prophesy to the boys?'

'He came to them for a reason. He used me.'

'And your calm and tender spirit?'

'He just is. He's wiser than I am, kinder too.'

'He could be the best part of you, shining through.'

'He could be,' she said agreeably, 'but I know differently.'

She tilted her head, considering Sid. 'He's here now. He says he wishes he had a human form as he'd like to hold you, and heal you.'

Sid stared. 'I don't need healing.'

Liz put her hand on top of Sid's. It was warm and soft. 'Yes, you do, darling girl. You need to forgive yourself so you can start to live again.'

Sid snatched back her hand. She was surprised at how unnerved she felt.

'Self-forgiveness means letting go of what went wrong. Accept the past and show yourself compassion. You're living in limbo. It's time to move forward, leaving shame and guilt behind so you can step into your future.'

Sid knew most psychics used cold-reading techniques without realising it. They had 'true believer syndrome', where they had no paranormal abilities but believed they did. She'd heard them referred to as 'shut-eyes' in her business, which gave her the creeps. Liz was a shut-eye and right now, Sid wished she wasn't quite so good.

'I didn't know I was so easy to read,' Sid said lightly. 'What tipped you off?'

'Nothing.' Liz frowned. 'Cyfrin just knows these things.'

Cyfrin? Hastily, Sid decided to change the subject. 'Harriet said Owen came here a lot. What was he like?'

She took a moment before responding.

'Passionate. Interested. I could say anything and he'd

take it seriously. Nothing was out of bounds. I liked his enthusiasm for everything. He also made me laugh.'

He sounded like her father. She could picture Dad sitting between them on the bench, listening to Liz, respecting her beliefs, his expression kind, his shiny brown eyes alight with humour.

*I don't believe in angels and demons, but I'd quite like to.*

'What do you think happened to Owen?' Sid asked.

'He fell ill, did you know?'

'His wife mentioned it.'

'He was obsessed with finding Annwn.' Liz closed her eyes. 'I actually told him that it was me playing Psychic Ceres at school, but although he said he believed me, I could tell he didn't.'

'Did you see him often?'

'He didn't just see me. We all knew him. He'd come here to "rest", was how he put it. He used to get manic, you see, so we'd pop him in the crystal room and play gentle music, calm him down. He'd come even when we were closed. We ended up changing the lock codes to his birth-date so he could always have access. We were–' her mouth twisted, '– actually very fond of him.'

'When was the last time you saw him?'

'The day before he died.'

What felt like a spider scurried down Sid's spine.

'He asked if any of us could undertake an exorcism, get rid of the demon that he believed had taken him over. He was terrified his wife was going to divorce him and he wanted it driven out. When we told him none of us were priests, he said not to worry. He knew a man of God who'd help.'

Sid closed her eyes. She knew what Liz was going to say next.

'Father Luke.'

# 22

Gabriel helped Hannah pack. It didn't take long as they didn't have much. Just their djellabas, socks and underwear, a comb and a hairbrush. Hannah took her doll, which Mum had made for her second birthday, and a woollen hat, which she'd also made. Gabriel packed his paper aeroplane and one of the pine cones from his collection. Everything between them went into a single plastic carrier bag.

He hadn't expected Hannah to be chosen for the holy mission as well as him, and although part of him was relieved they wouldn't be separated, the other was infuriated because he'd have to look after her.

'You have to be really good,' he told her. 'You mustn't annoy anyone. You must do as you're told and not answer back.'

She nodded but the pout on her lips told him she would probably rebel at some point. He couldn't think what might happen if she had one of her tantrums Outside. They'd been told people didn't tolerate badly behaved children and that if they stepped out of line, the police would come and take them away, put them in a youth detention centre. He didn't know what this was, exactly, but it was obviously a threat, and didn't sound like anywhere fun. Somehow, he'd have to make sure Hannah was a model of perfection, but how he was going to accomplish this, he didn't know.

'Come on.' He held out his hand and together they walked to the assembly area. Nearly all the children were there along with five minibuses. They were, they'd been told, going to various cities across the country. He'd seen Mum this morning, who'd awakened when they walked into the san. She didn't have the strength to sit up, but managed to say she hoped they were going to Bath, where Grandma and Grandpa lived.

'They've got a tree-house,' she whispered. 'And a cat called Tinsel. She'll be pretty old by now but she'll love you.'

She hadn't said much more. She'd been too weak and when he'd said goodbye, she'd fallen asleep. He left a pretty brown-and-white-striped snail shell for her on her bedside table so she'd see it when she woke up.

At the front of the house, he ran his eyes over the minibuses. Three silver, one white, one black. None of them knew what their mission was yet. Apparently, they had to wait until everyone was in place, and then they'd be told. He had, however, caught the words London and Glasgow as well as Birmingham and Manchester.

When they climbed on board the silver minibus, he saw Brother Saul in the driver's seat, Brother Isaac behind him. He did a double-take. Neither man wore their usual grey djellaba but trousers and white shirts. As Gabriel gaped, Saul laughed.

'Your clothes are on your seats.'

Gabriel wondered if he was dreaming. Jeans, T-shirts,

fleeces and trainers. Clothes that Outsiders wore. But what made his eyes widen further were the juice cartons laid on top, along with a packet of crisps and a bar of chocolate. They were only ever allowed chocolate at Easter time, and even then, they had to share their egg or chocolate bar with four other children. Father Luke said eating chocolate, or any sweets for that matter, was *tempting gluttony.*

Hannah squealed with delight, falling on her chocolate in rapture. She gobbled hers down before Saul had even started the engine, but Gabriel saved his bar for later, knowing he'd break it into tiny pieces, eking it out to try and make the treat last for the journey.

He didn't know it, but he was grinning as they trundled through the commune gates and along the road, his eyes alight, his whole body tingling with excitement.

He could hardly believe it.

They were going on an adventure.

# 23

As she drove home, Sid's mind was crowded with thoughts of Owen's hysterical phone call to his wife. The names Amelia, Leah and Mike reverberated around her mind. Then there was Liz, the White Witch and shut-eye. Was she right? That Sid was living in limbo? And all that twaddle about forgiving herself... really?

The scales had fallen from her eyes a year or so after her mother had died. She'd had to sell the family home to pay inheritance tax and was sharing a house with Aero. She wasn't working. She was spending what remained of her parents' money on whatever she chose. Nineteen, still unable to face her grief, she'd been going crazy through summer, partying, clubbing, shopping, going to endless festivals. She went through the money like water.

There'd been an incredible heatwave that particular week, turning the streets into saunas, and she'd joined a group of friends in a beer garden overlooking the river.

She could still remember the snorting laughter, all the more obvious for being stifled. She'd been returning from the loo inside the pub, and caught their sniggers as she passed the open window where the gang were sitting in the sunshine.

'It's Sid, one hundred per cent!'

The guys were huddled over a phone.

'Look! She's even got Sid's hair!'

Aero appeared, looked over their shoulders. 'Jesus Christ. Get rid of it.' He sounded furious. 'And give me back my phone, you dickheads.'

'Hey,' protested one of them. 'It was just a bit of fun.'

More sniggering at the word 'fun'.

'You're just jealous she hasn't done you.'

'She hasn't done you either.'

'I wouldn't want to go there. Jesus, can you imagine the STDs? She fucks pretty much anyone who buys her a drink.'

Heat burning her cheeks, Sid returned to the table, head held high, pretending she hadn't overheard anything. Later, she grabbed Aero's phone – she knew his passcode as he knew hers – and had a look.

It was a porn site. It showed a pretty girl-woman with sheets of waist-length hair – yes, like Sid's – in a bar and having sex with a group of men.

Sid went to bed that night as usual, but she didn't sleep. She saw herself clearly for the first time. How shallow, selfish and irresponsible she'd been. She found she couldn't look anyone in the eye the next day.

She went house-hunting the next morning and moved into her cottage the day after that, telling Aero she'd fallen in love with the countryside.

*She fucks pretty much anyone who buys her a drink.*

She was so ashamed.

Sid didn't sleep much that night; her mind writhed like an agitated nest of worms. Flashes of some of the men she'd been with were overlaid with images of Owen's tattoos imprinted on his dead flesh. She saw Father Luke smashing her phone all over again. Marc Strong's smug, good-looking face loomed at her out of the TV. She saw Gabriel and Hannah. Hannah's face crumpling as she and Gabriel left her behind. Gabriel's misery when she left the commune.

*If you could, would you come with me?*

*Yes, but I can't leave Hannah.*

Her mind jumbled Win with Detective Kelly and her father, and by the time dawn broke she felt ineffably weary. Tank seemed to sense her exhaustion and when he came into her room he rested his head on her bed, blinking at her until she stroked him, making his tail wave gently.

She struggled up. She couldn't lie in bed anymore. She had places to go, people to see. After getting home from Harriet's yesterday, she'd hit the internet, and then the phone. She'd called Tina, the FLO, who'd rung back once she'd brought up Sid's father's file.

'The police spoke to everyone on your grandmother's ward at the time,' Tina told her. 'Patients, doctors and nurses. Nobody could help, really. Except there's a note here... it says one of the nurses saw your father leave the ward at around 3pm. Paul Mo stated that he looked very angry.'

'What?' Sid didn't remember this. 'Dad was angry?'

'Apparently.'

'What was Dad angry about?'

'It doesn't say.'

'What else?'

'Apparently, when his mother fell asleep, your father spoke to the patient in the bed opposite.' Sid heard a tapping sound. Tina's fingers on her keyboard. 'She was there for an appendectomy.'

'Do you have her name?'

'Sorry. Patient confidentiality issues.'

'What else did Paul Mo say?'

'That's it, I'm afraid.'

'What about anyone else on the ward? Any statements from them?'

'There's two saying your father sat with his mother for an hour or so.'

'Until she fell asleep, when he spoke to the patient in the bed opposite.'

'Yes.'

'What made him angry? Did he look at his phone, maybe? Who pissed him off?'

'I'm afraid there's nothing here.'

*And Granny was dead, so we can't ask her*, Sid thought.

'Do you have Paul Mo's details?'

'I can't give those to you, but if I were you, I'd try the hospital directly and see if they can track him down. He might still be there, but if not, they might know where he could have gone.'

'If he's moved, they won't necessarily give me his details.'

To Sid's surprise, Tina said, 'Leave it with me,' and barely two hours later, Tina had arranged for Paul Mo to ring Sid.

'I can't tell you anything more,' he said. 'Your father was angry. He left.'

There would be more, Sid thought. There always was.

'I know it's been a long time, but would you mind if we met? We've never spoken, and it would really help me with some sort of closure.'

'Well… I'm not sure…' he prevaricated briefly, 'but if you need to… okay. Let's meet, if you want.'

Apparently, he'd moved to Bristol's Nuffield Hospital. 'I can nip out for a coffee, if you can come here?'

'Of course. Where would suit you?'

He suggested a café on Park Street. 'Eleven o'clock okay?'

'Perfect.'

After a breakfast of porridge and toast – her appetite was still firing at full capacity – she dropped Tank at the farm.

'I'll try and collect him before it gets dark.'

'No problem,' Toby's wife Rachel said with a smile.

Tank gazed at her morosely. 'Don't try and make me feel guilty,' she told him. 'You'll do nothing but happily suck the heat out of Rachel's Aga all day.'

Tank looked mournfully at Rachel, which made them both laugh.

Sid headed to Bristol, the centre of which was crammed with demonstrators. Dear God, when was it going to end? There were two mounted police officers at one end of the street and several more police officers walking along the edge of the crowd.

Sid slipped past College Green which was thronging with people and made her way to the café. She thought she'd arrive first but Paul Mo was already there, his narrow form perched on a stool at the coffee bar. He gave her a tentative wave, mouthing, 'Sidney?' and she waved back. She took the stool next to him, and they ordered. Flat white for him, black coffee for her.

When their coffee arrived, she fiddled with her cup, trying to quell the urge for a cigarette. 'Thanks for seeing me.'

'I can't see how I can help, I'm afraid. But I'll do my best.'

She smiled. 'Thanks. If you could tell me what you remember, that would be great.'

He recounted what Tina, the FLO, had already told Sid. That Mike Scott came to see his mother in hospital, sat with her for an hour, and when she fell asleep, chatted to the woman in the bed opposite.

'Who was in for an appendectomy.'

'That's right.'

'What did they talk about?'

'I have no idea.'

'Was it the woman who made him angry, do you think?'

'No idea. But it could have been. He'd been talking to her and then he stormed out. He nearly flattened me, you know, barrelling down the corridor like that. He was a big bloke and... well, I pressed my back against the wall to let him pass. It was like he couldn't see me. His face was actually white with rage. It's not often you see that. Normally people go puce, but in extremis, the blood leaves their face.'

Her ears hummed. *Dad was white with rage.*

'Tell me about the patient he spoke to.'

'She was in her late twenties. Very quiet. Subdued. She'd come in with a burst appendix, but luckily, we caught her in time. She'd had an operation and was on antibiotics. She went home after a couple of days.'

'Where was home?'

'Even if I knew, I couldn't give you her details.'

'I understand.'

They fell quiet as a young couple took a table behind them, chatting excitedly about the protests. Paul Mo pushed aside his coffee and began to shrug on his coat. Desperately, Sid tried to think of something else to ask him but nothing came immediately to mind, so she thanked him and let him go. Settling the bill, she headed outside.

Head down, walking slowly along College Green, she was checking her emails when the crowd surged across the green towards her. She'd been aware of it but not that it had been closing in, or how fast. She didn't have time to get out of the way and the next instant she found herself swept along.

'Hey,' she protested. 'Wait up a minute...'

She tried to step sideways, but a man with a bullhorn elbowed her aside. 'Public spending cuts don't heal!' he thundered. 'We will fight these savage cuts and not let them destroy peoples' services and lives!'

'Bastards!' someone shouted behind her.

'Banker wankers!' yelled another.

'Please, let me through...' Sid's heart was pounding as the crowd marched her relentlessly forward, jostling her from side to side. Panic rising, Sid attempted to shoulder her way free but a woman lurched into her, knocking Sid off-balance. 'Hey,' she yelped and the next second, her feet tangled, and she was falling, about to get trampled, when an arm went around her waist and scooped her upright.

Sid was gasping, heart pounding as the arm tightened, bringing her to her rescuer's side. 'Want to get out of here?' he asked.

# 24

To Sid's shock, she realised her rescuer was Win. 'Yes, please,' she managed.

He began to push their way through the crowd. It was like being anchored to a walking fridge-freezer and when a man cursed them, trying to square up, fists bunched, Win said calmly, 'I wouldn't, if I were you.'

Sid couldn't see Win's face but whatever expression he wore, had the desired effect. The man backed off.

Win headed for a gap that had opened on the right. He shouldered them through it, slipping them into the opening of an alleyway to stand in a space of relative safety. Her heart was still pounding as the crowd streamed past, shouting slogans. When the bulk of people had moved down the street, Win looked down at Sid.

'Are you always in trouble?'

'Not intentionally.'

She wondered at the coincidence of him being here at the right place, the right time to help her but before she could say anything, he said, 'Glad I was passing?' prompting her to say in return, 'Yes, very. Thank you.'

'No problem.'

Was that a glimmer of a smile at the back of his eyes?

Today he wore another pair of jeans and a leather jacket, the same work boots. Didn't investment brokers wear suits? Perhaps all his business was done online.

'Sid,' he said gravely. 'May I call you Sid?'

She hesitated briefly but considering he'd just rescued her, she thought it would be churlish to say no. Besides, since she thought of him as Win, and not Winstone, it was only fair.

'Sure,' she said.

'Sid. Why didn't you tell me you were a paranormal sceptic?'

'You'd already made up your mind what I was.'

'Yes,' he admitted. 'I saw you and Flick and assumed the worst.'

'Which was?'

He rolled his eyes to the sky. 'Look, I got you wrong, okay?'

She folded her arms, waiting.

'You want to watch me squirm?'

'It would be nice.'

He dropped his gaze to meet hers. 'I'm sorry. Okay?'

'There,' she said sweetly. 'That wasn't so hard, was it?' She struggled to contain her smile.

'It's no excuse, but let's just say I have a healthy dislike of soothsayers.'

She tilted her head to one side, encouraging him to go on.

He sighed. 'My sister had cancer. Not Flick, but Zara. She forewent treatment thanks to a "healer" who cited conspiracies of big pharma and hidden cures. He had Zara doing yoga and tai chi, drinking Chinese herbs...'

'Things like that can improve comfort and quality of life,' Sid remarked.

'But they don't *cure* cancer.' His jaw pushed forward. 'Her so-called healer told her that amygdalin, which comes from apricot kernel extract, can kill cancer cells. But what she didn't know is that it can cause cyanide poisoning.'

'Zara was poisoned?'

'Which actually was a blessing in disguise because that's when she finally realised what a crock of crap she was being fed.'

She glanced down the street to see the crowd thronging down St Augustine's Parade, still shouting.

'What are you doing in Bristol?' she asked.

'I work here.'

'Clan Capital.'

'That's right.'

Something guarded rose in his eyes. Why?

'Don't you feel at all accountable working with the Golden Dawn? After all, most of their money comes from people coerced into handing it over.'

He shrugged. 'Money is money. It has no emotions or attachments.'

'But the people who have money do.'

He surveyed her cautiously through watchful, intelligent eyes. 'What if I told you I was there for another reason.'

'Like, what?'

'They're hatching a plan. I want to know what it is.'

She blinked. 'What plan?'

'If I knew, I wouldn't be wanting to know what it is.'

*Pedantic as well as judgemental.*

'While you're searching for your father,' he went on, 'if you hear of anything, any rumour of any plan, will you let me know?'

'Is it connected to Dad?'

'Yes. No.' He glanced away. 'It's complicated.'

She glanced pointedly at her watch. 'I've lots of time.'

He dropped his gaze for a moment, as though arranging his thoughts. 'Okay. Marc Strong was at university in Oxford.'

*Along with Owen Evans, Dad and Father Luke.*

'Uni is usually a place where students build their self-confidence, make new friends from different countries and backgrounds, exchange ideas, expand their knowledge. Marc Strong used it simply as one big, long political rally, raising support for his own ends. He registered the BPL, the British Patriotic League, as a political party, in his second year.'

She'd heard of the BPL, a far-right, fascist political party that had, rather frighteningly, been gaining traction recently.

'He's with the Conservatives now,' she pointed out.

'Because it suits him.' He glanced up and down the street. 'There's a group of MPs who are backing Marc Strong in a political endeavour, but quite what, we're not sure.'

'We?'

Win looked back at her. 'Ask another.'

'You think this plan involves Marc Strong and Father Luke?' Her tone was disbelieving.

'Oh, yes. They've been planning this for years, trust me.'

Anyone who used the words *trust me*, invariably made Sid mistrust whatever they went on to say, but she made sure she pasted an open expression on her face to keep him talking.

'Things are coming to a head, politically. Nationalism is the biggest political force in the world today. Whether it's Putin with his invasion of Ukraine or China's attitude to

Taiwan, or America withdrawing from Afghanistan and moving back into its "America first" position, nationalism is the dominant ideology.' He gestured down the street at the receding crowd. 'Just look at that. The protests around the country. The discontent, the violence.'

'What are you saying?'

'The time is ripe for Marc Strong to make his move.'

'If he's a nationalist, and the people want nationalism, then what's the problem?'

'Patriotism is the love of your country. Nationalism is an us-versus-them ideology. You find enemies where they don't exist and build your views around pre-existing aversions.' Win gave her a long look. 'More worryingly, however, is that he wants to bring in God's social credit system.'

She immediately thought of Tina, the FLO saying, *What's not to like? Even the stupidest criminal should be able to get it.*

'But we're secular.'

'We won't be if he ever gets into power. His vision is to make everyone go to church every Sunday, and if they don't, they get fined.'

'That'll never work,' she snorted.

Win gave her a sharp look. 'Nobody thought Hitler would become a dictator.'

'We have a democratic system which–'

'He just needs a single break, and he'll turn our country upside down.'

He was being melodramatic, she decided. Paranoid.

'He's already written his "Blue Book" setting out his political philosophy. Society will be run by carrot-and-stick regulations. We will be controlled by data and AI, the police – compliant instruments to enforce the rules.'

It sounded like a dystopian movie, and Sid said so.

His gaze was so piercing she felt as though she'd been run through by a rapier. 'You won't be laughing when he's in power and you, as a woman, have no rights. You'll be–'

His head snapped around at a shattering, splintering sound.

The crowd roared.

More crashing and, with horror, she realised a shop window had been smashed. Then someone let off a smoke bomb and everything went to hell. Win grabbed Sid's wrist and they ran.

# 25

When they reached the safety of a side street, the sounds of chanting and smashing were drowned by the police sirens. A police car swept past, hotly followed by two riot vans, bristling with cops wearing helmets and Kevlar vests.

Win watched them go. 'Where are you planning to go now?' His eyes remained on the police cars. She got the strange impression he was itching to join them.

'Home. My car's in the NCP.' She pointed over her shoulder.

He gave a nod and at the same time, she remembered Detective Kelly's tension when she mentioned Win's name. 'Do you know a Detective Kelly?'

His gaze swung back to her. His expression was unreadable.

'Yes.'

'You don't like him,' she said.

He blinked. 'Not true. It's just that sometimes he suffers from a conflict of interest.'

'What do you mean?'

'Best if he tells you himself, I think.'

In the silence that fell between them, he glanced down the road, after the police vehicles. 'Will you be okay if I leave you?'

'Yes. And thanks for—'

'You be careful.' His gaze was earnest. 'Because believe me, something wicked this way comes.'

He'd quoted a couplet from *Macbeth*, which had been spoken by the second of the three witches, and at that moment, a chill breeze drifted across the nape of her neck, cooling the sweat gathered there. She shivered, a momentary and involuntary reaction.

He touched her arm briefly, a surprisingly intimate gesture of farewell, and then he was jogging away, in the direction of the police cars. She gazed after him until his broad form disappeared, glad she was heading in the opposite direction.

---

Sid drove home running over everything Win had told her, struggling to get her head around everything from her father storming out of the hospital, *white with rage*, to Owen's murder and then some secret political plot coming to fruition that sounded outlandish, crazy, *ridiculous*.

The news had nothing but reports on the countrywide demonstrations. Peter Jones, the department store in London, had been under attack while anarchists got to work on Sloane Street.

Win's voice came to her. *The time is ripe for Marc Strong to make his move.*

Thank God Win had been there to help free her from the crowd. It was odd, him materialising seemingly out of nowhere, but she couldn't help but feel grateful. She wondered what he was doing now. Punching someone on the nose?

The sun was sinking over the horizon as she pulled up outside her cottage, lengthening the shadows. The air smelled of frosted leaves and she could hear a pair of tawny owls calling to one another; 'too-wit' from the female and 'too-woo' from the male. Or at least that's what Toby told her. He'd given her a small pile of mail which she now put on the kitchen table before filling up the kettle for a cuppa and lighting the wood-burning stove. It was going to be cold tonight. Minus three, her weather app told her.

Cigarette and tea to hand, Tank at her feet, Sid flipped through her mail. Two magazines, a food delivery flyer and a small padded envelope with no stamp, no address. Just her name. She opened the envelope and shook out the contents.

A small, soft grey object slipped onto her kitchen table.

A dead mouse.

It appeared to have had its neck broken.

A plain white tag had been tied around its little grey foot.

Capital letters, bold.

*THIS IS WHAT WILL HAPPEN TO YOU IF YOU KEEP MEDDLING.*

Sid stared at the mouse for a long time.

---

Detective Kelly arrived at eight thirty the following morning to collect the mouse, the note, and the envelope.

Sid had already decided not to mention her experience with the crowd demonstrating in Bristol yesterday, or Win's rescue; she didn't want him distracted.

'I'll get it checked for fingerprints.' He was brisk. 'Any idea who it might be from?'

Sid had thought long and hard about this and now she said, 'The only person with access to mice that I can think of, is Father Luke. There'd be loads of them in the farmyard.'

Kelly gave her a disbelieving stare.

'Check his handwriting,' she told him.

Kelly did everything but roll his eyes. 'And nobody saw anyone deliver it.'

'No.' She'd already asked Toby and Rachel.

They were standing on her doorstep and although it had started to drizzle, she wasn't feeling friendly enough to ask him inside.

'You know that Owen visited the Chalice Well the day before he died.'

A nod.

'He told one of the practitioners there that he was going to see Father Luke, to get exorcised. Did he go to Golden Dawn, do you know?'

'Father Luke says not.'

*Yeah, right.*

'So, where did he go?' she pressed.

He glanced over his shoulder at his car, then back. 'We can't say for certain.'

It was like wringing cement from a cloth and Sid had to swallow her impatience. God, how she wanted to kick his shins! 'Any luck with Amelia or Leah?' she pressed on. 'They're biblical names. Are they members of Golden Dawn?'

His lips tightened a little but he didn't say anything, so she told him about Paul Mo seeing her father storm out of the hospital, white with rage. At that, Kelly nodded. 'I spoke to Tina, the FLO, yesterday.'

She blinked. *Hallelujah,* she thought. Finally, the detective was connecting some dots to her father.

'Anything else, Miss Marple?' he asked.

'I don't think so, Detective. How about you?'

'Nothing I can share, I'm afraid.'

She raised her eyes to the sky in an exaggerated gesture of despair, which caused a spark of amusement but she didn't return it. She was beginning to find him and his reticence extremely annoying.

She folded her arms. 'Do you have a crime reference number for me?'

He winced. 'Sorry. I'll try and get it to you later.'

Sid decided there was no point in holding her breath. Going after Father Luke for smashing her phone probably wasn't at the top of his detective's list when he had a murder to solve.

'Where to next?' he asked, sounding genuinely interested.

'Oxford.'

'Seeing who?'

If he'd shared even some of his investigation with her, she would have told him, but as it was, she was feeling bolshie and pissed off, so she said, 'I just need to get some Christmas shopping done.'

From the expression that settled on his face he didn't believe her, but he didn't say anything. She began to close the door. He put out a hand to stop it shutting. Gave her a long look. 'Try to keep out of trouble, okay?'

She gave him her sweetest smile. 'I'll do my best.'

# 26

For security, many MPs no longer offered drop-in advice surgeries, but Marc Strong was old school and kept old-fashioned rules.

*My door is always open*, stated his website. *I want to hear your concerns, and I want to help.*

Sid had checked with Marc Strong's office before turning up, to be briskly told that as she wasn't a constituent, she'd have to make an appointment. But Sid must be warned, the woman went on imperiously – she sounded like a right battle-axe – that he was extremely busy and the first appointment that could be offered was over a month away.

'What time does surgery end?'

'Eleven thirty.'

'I shall be there at eleven thirty. Please tell Marc Strong it's about him and his old school friends Michael Scott, Luke Goddard, and Owen Evans. Owen Evans has just been murdered, so I think Mr Strong may well be interested in what I have to say.'

'I'm sorry?' The woman sounded taken aback.

'I shall be there at eleven thirty.' Sid was firm, and hung up just as the woman began to squawk. Only time would tell whether she'd let her boss know about Sid or not, and if not, she'd have to doorstep him.

His surgery today was being held in a village just east of Abingdon, in a village hall that resembled a cross between a Nissen hut and a public toilet. Inside, however, it looked like village halls everywhere, with linoleum flooring and plasterboard walls. A Christmas tree stood on the stage at the far end. Behind the makeshift reception desk, sat a sharply attractive woman with a shiny helmet of blonde hair and an honest-to-God twinset and pearls. She looked as though she'd stepped out of the pages of 1950s *Vogue*. Stuck on the wall behind her was a poster of Marc Strong holding a Union Jack in one hand and a crucifix in the other.

**Strong by name and strong by nature.**

'Can I help you?' the woman asked.

'I'm Sidney Scott.'

The woman's cherry-red lips pursed. She looked Sid up and down before her eyes fixed to the top of Sid's tattoo. Until Sid had her hair shorn it used to be relatively hidden and sometimes, she forgot she had it until someone – like this snotty gatekeeper – stared at it as though Sid had a pile of dog crap smeared on her neck. 'You're early.' The woman looked pointedly at the small, ostentatiously positioned clock that stood on her desk.

*So, bite me*, Sid thought.

'He won't have time to talk to you,' she told Sid archly. 'He has to leave for London directly after his last surgery for a meeting with the security services.'

'I'll make it quick, then.'

'That's not the point.' She made a small huffing sound between her perfectly painted lips. 'He just doesn't have *the time.*'

Sid didn't think it worth responding and moved aside to prop herself against the wall. She brought out her phone, tapped for a bit and ta-da, there the woman was, arm-in-arm with Marc Strong at some black tie do. His wife, Audrey, was the only family member amongst Marc Strong's parliamentary staff, paid with taxpayers' money. Audrey liked hard work and looking after her family. She had three children all at university, a degree in home economics, and was a *whizz at budgeting and sewing on stray buttons.* She liked nothing more than housekeeping and cooking, and prided herself on supporting her husband in his *very important work* in parliament.

> We have a traditional marriage. Christian. We like things that way, as it used to be with our parents. You knew where you stood then. The children go to school, the woman looks after the home. The husband works all day to come home to a hot dinner on the table. Where have those values gone?

*Yawn,* thought Sid, glancing up when two people left, then a bit later, two more. The ostentatious little clock ticked busily. At eleven fifty, two men appeared. Big men, muscular and strong-looking, both wearing jackets and ties. She took in their earpieces. They resembled the type of close-protection officers you'd see flanking film stars.

And then there he was. Tall and broad-shouldered, as classically handsome as a movie star, but it wasn't his stature or good looks that gave off the aura of power. It was his wide-legged stance, the way he held his hands with the knuckles forward like some kind of prizefighter. Only people with influence and money possessed that kind of physical arrogance.

Marc Strong.

His eyes clicked to Sid, then he walked to Audrey who was already on her feet. 'Darling,' he said. His wife raised her face for him to carefully peck her lips without smudging her lipstick. Her eyes never left Sid's. It was as though she was saying, *he's mine, hands off.*

'Sorry to leave you all the clearing up,' he told his wife.

'You know I love to help.'

He smiled down at her. 'I don't know what I'd do without you.'

'Nor do I,' she teased. She began to reach out a hand to grasp his in what Sid guessed was designed to be a bonding gesture, but he was already moving away from her, forcing her hand to drop back to her side. She immediately began busying herself with some papers on the desk to cover the miniature humiliation while at the same time Marc Strong stepped towards Sid.

'Sidney Scott, how nice to meet you,' he said smoothly, hand outstretched. His grip was firm and cool. 'I was so sorry when your father went missing. And poor Evans. Did you know Evans?'

She shook her head. 'No, but he had a–'

'Walk with me.' It was a command.

As they stepped outside, Sid glanced over her shoulder to see Audrey watching them. Sid gave her a little finger wave which earned her a poisonous look. They walked down the path and into a biting wind, one security guard ahead of them, the other behind.

'Do you have any idea what happened to your father?' Marc Strong turned his head, his eyes sharp on hers.

'That's what I'm trying to find out.'

'Why are you here? I can't see how I'll be of any help. It wasn't as though Michael was a close friend of mine.'

'It was Owen Evans,' she told him. 'He had a postcard from my father on him.'

She could have said it was going to rain later for all the reaction on Marc Strong's face. Had he already known? Or was he such a consummate politician you couldn't tell what he was thinking?

'And you think because Owen was my friend, that his death links your father's disappearance to us?'

*Yes.*

'I don't know.'

'My car.' He pointed at a black Range Rover four cars along from her Jimny. She kept pace with him as he headed that way. Rain started to fall. Marc Strong flung his head back and raised his face to the sky, seemingly unaffected. Not like the security guard ahead who increased his pace while ducking his head low between his shoulders as though the smaller he made himself, the less wet he'd get.

'I love my surgeries. I always feel so united with the people, to God, so *connected*.' He turned his head to look at her, a strange light rising in his eyes. 'Are you religious?'

'Not particularly.'

'Why not?'

'I believe in science, not a belief system that rests on nothing but stories.'

'You might think differently if you were introduced to Christianity properly.'

Sid decided not to tangle with him over religion and concentrated on stepping around a set of puddles.

'Why aren't you married yet?' he asked.

She could have gone for the less combative option and said she hadn't met the right man, but she decided to face him head-on with this particular subject. 'Because I like my independence.'

'Have you ever thought how very selfish that is?'

She stared at him for a moment, taken aback by his rudeness. 'What, you mean not cooking for my man every day, slaving over a hot stove, foregoing my own life for his? Us women worked hard to get the vote, you know, and I don't think we're going to give up our liberty easily.'

He made a tsk-tsking sound. 'You should talk to some of my constituents. I'm incredibly popular with women. They tell me all the time how they want to be released from the tyranny of trying to "have it all" and have time to concentrate properly on their family. My mailbox is full of messages from women telling me how they're ashamed to say they're a housewife. They want to be proud to be married, looking after their family. When I become prime minister, they will be *so happy.*'

'Sounds like the new Stepford.'

'You make it sound like that's a bad thing.' He looked amused.

*Dear God,* she thought, *I'd rather kill myself than be a Stepford wife.* Sid took a deep breath and told herself to *calm down.* She wasn't here for a political discussion. She was here to ask questions. 'When was the last time you saw Owen?'

'Two years ago, at a college reunion.'

'What about my father?'

'I honestly can't remember. But it was years rather than months before he went missing.'

They'd reached the Range Rover which had been beeped open. One guy was already in the driver's seat while the other stood next to the open rear door, waiting for his boss to climb inside.

'And Father Luke?' she said, more as a shot in the dark

than expecting anything helpful. 'When did you last see him?'

He stopped walking to look at her. 'On Sunday. At his prophesy. Rather splendid, wasn't it? I saw you, Sidney, in the front row. Looking every inch the paranormal sceptic I have to say.' He smiled, like a wolf surprising its prey.

She tried not to react, but she felt creeped out at the thought of him seeing her, and knowing who she was without her knowledge. When she spoke, she made sure her tone was level. 'I thought it was disgraceful, scamming his congregation like that.'

'Oh, come now, Sidney. Don't tell me you don't believe in miracles?' He made to climb into the car. Sid stepped closer, ignoring the security guard who raised a meaty hand against her.

'Have you seen Detective Kelly?'

The muscles on his face tightened fractionally. 'Yes. I saw him yesterday. I couldn't help him either.'

'Do you know someone called Leah?'

His expression turned blank. 'Who?'

'How about Amelia? Or Julia Pemberton?'

Still, the same expression. He genuinely didn't recognise the women's names. At last, she was beginning to read him.

'Do you know a Winstone Fairchild?'

She spotted a definite tightening at the corners of his eyes. He knew Win.

'No,' he said. 'Why? Who is he?' He spoke casually as he climbed into his car, flicking a finger at his guard. He didn't seem to notice that she didn't answer.

Sid returned to the village hall to find Audrey helping two ageing men stack chairs into one corner.

'What do you want?' Audrey scrutinised Sid for a long moment.

'Did you know my father, Michael Scott?'

To Sid's surprise, the woman softened. 'Marc told me earlier that he's a missing person. That must be awful. But no, I didn't know him. Marc said he was at the same school, but that they weren't close friends. He told me your father was–' she looked sideways as she tried to find the right words, '–part of the same crowd, but not part of his group. Does that make sense?'

'And Owen Evans?'

'Marc saw him from time to time but personally, I didn't know Owen. He certainly never came to the house.' She took a breath. 'I can't believe he was murdered.' She shook her head and Sid was amazed at how not a single hair in the blonde helmet moved. She must have sprayed it with Superglue. 'I think Marc last saw him at a reunion over two years ago.'

Nothing Sid didn't already know, but not wanting to give up, she threw in the women's names; Leah, Julia Pemberton, and Amelia.

Zilch.

'What do you think of Father Luke and his commune?'

'We have nothing to do with it.' She drew herself tall.

'You weren't at the Sunday service?'

'Certainly not.' She looked appalled at the prospect.

'Your husband was there.'

A frown. 'No, he wasn't. He was in the car, coming back from London.'

'Well.' Sid spread her hands. 'That's what he told me just now. He saw me there, witnessing Father Luke's prophesy.'

'You're lying.'

'I'm not.' Sid looked at her curiously. 'What intrigues me, is that he's obviously lied to *you*. Why?'

'And what intrigues me–' Audrey stepped so close to Sid she could smell her perfume, something summery and light, '–is what your game is. If it's to come between me and my husband then you've got another thing coming. Now, get out, before I call the police.'

---

Sid spent the rest of the day at home, busying herself with ordinary things. She tried to concentrate on writing her article, but ended up staring through the window, words and phrases galloping around her head.

*Owen spent the last decade trying to find the Otherworld, convinced your father was already there.*

*The prophesy will save lives. Hundreds, thousands of lives.*

*Why aren't you married yet?*

*You need to forgive yourself so you can start to live again.*

Sid was so absorbed in her thoughts she was shocked when Tank started nudging her for his afternoon walk. Hours had passed without her realising it.

She took Tank out, and when she returned, checked her messages. One was from the university, wanting her to give another talk, another from someone wanting a haunting investigated, but it was the third that made her jump to her feet, saying 'Yessss!' and making Tank jump.

It was from Julia Pemberton, the woman who'd run away from the Golden Dawn.

```
I'm sorry but I can't talk to you.
```

Sid took that to mean *won't* talk, but what the hell, at

least the woman had got in touch. The rest of the message, however, had her punching the air with her fist.

```
If you can get to talk to Leah at the
Golden Dawn, she might be able to
help. Good luck.
```

She'd found Leah! She was a cult member!

Hastily, Sid messaged back, trying to assure Julia she would never divulge any information about her to anybody – she was obviously scared of sharing her history at the cult – but there was no response.

Ridiculously energised, Sid rang Detective Kelly, but got his messaging service.

'I've got a lead to my father. Call me.'

Sid began pacing. She wanted to see Leah. She wanted to see Father Luke. She wanted to go to the Golden Dawn and rip it apart at the seams and *find her father*.

When Kelly finally called her back, it was the end of the day and her nerves were shredded.

'I want to go to the Golden Dawn tomorrow. Can you come with me?'

'I'm sorry, but I'm with the chief super all day, and I'm–'

'Owen was shouting the name Leah at his wife just before he was killed and I've just had it confirmed that Leah is a cult member at the Golden Dawn.'

She'd barely finished speaking when he said, 'How soon can you get here?'

## 27

Gabriel was watching *The Lion King* on TV with Hannah. Babies' stuff, but despite his outward contempt, he was riveted. Watching TV was, Brother Isaac had told them sternly, a special treat, and although he hadn't said they ought to keep it a secret, somehow Gabriel knew he shouldn't tell anyone.

They wore mufti and although Gabriel loved being in normal clothes, he found them strangely constraining and not as comfortable as his djellaba. Hannah, on the other hand, didn't care about comfort. She'd fallen in love with her little red-and-white sweater which had a snowflake on the front, and she'd refused to take off her sparkly pink trainers with blue ponies on their laces, even at night. He had to wait until she was asleep before he could slip them from her feet.

Brothers Isaac and Saul were playing with their phones. Nobody except the Guards and senior Brothers were allowed phones and to his amazement, Saul allowed him a look. Gabriel had been awestruck. You could watch movies, send messages, take photos and videos and play games. Saul laughed at Gabriel's incredulity when he showed him *League of Legends.* It almost made becoming a senior Brother worth all the hard work required.

They were staying in a house somewhere in London. Four bedrooms, three bathrooms. He was sharing a room with Hannah but the Brothers had their own rooms. The house had carpets and pictures on the walls, and a huge kitchen and a fridge full of food. He'd stuffed himself the first night, which had made him sick. Brother Saul had laughed.

The rest of the group had travelled elsewhere. Apparently, they had to wait until everyone was in place wherever they were, and then they'd be told their mission. In the meantime, Gabriel was happy to be somewhere warm, where he could eat as much as he liked.

As Simba, the young lion, was set to challenge Scar to end his tyranny on the TV, Gabriel fingered the outline of Mum's special ring where it lay tucked into his front jeans pocket along with the tiny piece of paper with his grandparents' address: No. 1, Bloomfield Avenue, Bath.

# 28

Detective Kelly greeted her with a grunt when she hopped into the passenger seat of his car. 'Miss Marple.'

'Detective.'

As he pulled out of the station she spotted a motorbike at the end of the street. Gunmetal-grey with panniers on either side. Her stomach clenched. Was it the same bike she'd seen en route to Harriet and the Chalice Well? As she stared, she saw a man in leathers and helmet appear. He walked to the bike and climbed on board, pushing it off its stand. She felt oddly relieved when he rode off.

Kelly drove fast, overtaking when he could and making Sid flinch each time.

'You're quite safe,' he told her as he barrelled past yet another vehicle. 'I've done several high-speed training courses.'

'Great,' she said weakly.

He barely slowed down for the cattle grid, and when two djellaba-wearing men stepped into view to wave him down, he simply buzzed down his window, calling, 'You know me already.'

Both men waved and nodded.

'Nice one,' said Sid.

'So,' Kelly said, as he parked outside the front of the manor house, next to a shiny black Range Rover. 'We've ten minutes before we're due to meet Father Luke...'

But Sid was already striding to the rear entrance of the house, Kelly hot on her heels, saying, 'Hey, wait a second... for fuck's sake...' Sid ignored him, kept going.

The place was busy with people lugging groceries. One woman was carrying a tray of eggs, another a box filled with Brussels sprouts. There were great bunches of herbs, plucked chickens, sides of beef, sacks of potatoes. Sid marvelled. She felt as though she'd been transported back in time where an old-fashioned feast was being prepared.

The kitchen was in full swing with women chopping, grating, rolling pastry, lining tins. It was noisy and frenetic, with a large woman striding back and forth barking orders as she gestured with arms the shape and colour of giant sausages.

'What's all this in aid of?' Sid asked a young woman squeezing lemon juice into a pan.

The woman stared at her, then at the detective. She didn't say anything, went back to her juicing.

Sid drew Kelly aside. 'How about you leave me here for a couple of minutes.'

He looked between the young woman and Sid. Gave a nod.

After he'd gone, Sid tried again. 'Looks like a big dinner's being prepared.'

The young woman ignored her. It was as though Sid hadn't spoken.

'Do you know where I can find Leah?'

At that, the woman looked up. 'Leah?'

'Yes. I'd like to see her.'

The young woman looked around as though Leah was going to appear, then dropped her gaze. 'You're from Outside. I'm not allowed to talk to you.'

'I don't want to talk to you,' Sid said patiently. 'I want to talk to Leah.'

The young woman put down her lemon and walked away.

Sid tried an older woman with a tired, lined face. 'Where can I find Leah?'

The woman looked at her warily. 'Who's asking?'

'I'm a friend.'

The woman looked at Sid for a long time. 'Why Leah?'

'I'm hoping she might help me find my father. He went missing fourteen years ago.'

'Your father?' The woman's voice was faint.

A pan dropped with a clang into the sink. The woman jumped.

'Where's Leah?' Sid looked around the busy kitchen. 'Is she here?'

The woman made to answer but abruptly, her mouth snapped shut.

'Rebekah!' The word was like a whip-crack across the kitchen. The woman looked as though she might faint. 'Desist!'

Sid watched the woman scurry away to the sink, head bowed.

One of the Brothers crossed the kitchen to Sid.

'Brother Jeremiah,' she said, recognising his walnut-sized mole.

'You're trespassing. Please, go to your car.'

She surveyed his steely expression and said, 'Of course.'

He looked surprised that she'd relented so easily.

As Sid left the manor house by its rear door, she spotted Detective Kelly on one side, talking to a pretty young woman with long white-blonde hair plaited to her waist. She was holding an oversized box filled with vegetables, carrot fronds hanging over the side. Sid walked past them, but a few paces further, something made her look back. They weren't talking as much as arguing. Kelly appeared to be trying to take the box off the woman while she attempted to sidestep him. Her face was angry, her cheeks flushed, and Kelly didn't look in any better temper with a glowering expression. His attempt at trying to help a pretty woman with her load obviously wasn't going down well.

Sid strode out towards the old church, pleased that the detective was distracted and that Brother Jeremiah hadn't followed her. She wanted a scout around and when better to do it than with the legitimate cover of accompanying a police officer?

As she walked, she kept her eyes open for Gabriel and Hannah, but she couldn't see any kids. Perhaps they were having lessons? Passing the auditorium, she caught the sickly-sweet stench of pigs. She couldn't see any pigs, so she headed to a barn nestled beside a copse of ancient beech trees. It was open on one side, and she could see several animal pens along with stacks of hay bales. A tractor stood to one side.

Opening the gate, she peered inside the first pen to see two large pink-and-grey pigs lying on their sides, seemingly asleep on a deep bed of straw.

'Pinky and Perky,' a woman's cheerful voice said.

Sid looked up to see a rosy-cheeked woman approaching. Her dark hair was tied in a ponytail and she wore a dull-brown djellaba and rubber boots.

'They're sweet,' Sid said.

'You're from Outside.' The woman's gaze was assessing. 'Are you a police officer?'

'I came with the police,' Sid prevaricated.

Immediately, a guarded expression rose.

'I want to talk to Leah.'

The woman shook her head. 'Impossible.'

'Why?'

She didn't answer but when a stubborn look settled on her face, Sid decided to change tack.

'I'm trying to find out what happened to Owen Evans, along with a friend of his, who went missing a while ago.' On impulse, Sid brought out her phone, showed her a picture of her father.

The woman's face lost colour so fast, Sid put out a hand in case she fell.

'You recognise him?' Her voice cracked with excitement.

The woman was fixated on the photograph.

'He's my father. Michael Scott. He went missing fourteen years ago. I'm trying to find him. I'm Sidney Scott.'

The woman's colour didn't improve. She remained ashen.

'When did you see him?'

The woman looked up at Sid, eyes filled with fear, and then she bolted.

# 29

'Hey!' Sid broke into a run behind her. 'Wait!'

The woman vanished around the corner of the barn. Sid pelted after her, saw her tearing towards the church. Sid set off in pursuit but when the woman disappeared behind a clump of trees, she lost her. She jogged around the area but not knowing the estate, she had no idea where the woman might have gone.

Her heart rate settled back to normal as she returned to the farmyard, striding up the rear steps and into the gloom of the manor house. She couldn't wait to grab Kelly and confront Father Luke with the fact one of his followers recognised her father's picture. No sooner had she stepped through the door when she heard raised voices coming from the kitchen.

'Well, where is she?!'

A man's voice. Not Father Luke's. For some reason, the tone was familiar, if not the anger.

'I'm s-sorry, Beloved Leader, I don't know.' Sid recognised the frail voice of the elderly woman she'd spoken to earlier. Rebekah.

*Beloved Leader?*

'What did she ask you? Tell me her *exact* words.'

'She w-wanted to know what we were c-cooking for.'

'What did you say?' The voice turned silky.

'That it was f-for a special d-dinner. That's all.'

Footsteps beat against flagstones. Sid guessed it was the man, pacing. 'And you!' He sounded incensed. 'How could you let her out of your sight?'

'She won't have gone far.' This man's tone was steady, controlled. With a shock, she realised it was Detective Kelly.

'She'd better not have seen our technicians working.'

'What do you mean?' Kelly's voice sharpened.

'Just keep her away from the basement, that's all I ask,' the man snapped.

'I don't understand,' Kelly tried again. 'Why do you need tech–'

'None. Of. Your. Business.' The man's voice turned low and vicious.

'Don't forget I'm here as an investigating police officer,' Kelly warned.

'And Mariam?'

Silence.

Holding her breath, Sid inched her head around the door-jamb.

'I can't trust anyone to stick to a simple script. We're on the brink of history and I'm surrounded by idiots…' The man continued to rant.

Sid saw Rebekah, the elderly woman, cowering next to the sinks. The young woman stood next to her, head bowed. All the other women were frozen, gazes glued to the floor. Kelly stood with his back to the window. His little round specs seemed affixed to her and her heart hopped. She thought he'd seen her but then he turned his head away to look at the man who'd stopped pacing and had put his hands on the huge, central wooden table.

Marc Strong.

'Just *find her*,' he hissed.

What was he doing here? His wife had said he had a meeting with the security services in London. Why was he lying to Audrey? He'd also lied to her about being here on Sunday. What else had he lied about?

'And when I do?' asked Detective Kelly.

'Get her out of here.'

As Kelly stepped forward, Sid ducked back and out of sight, started scampering down the corridor. But she wasn't quick enough. She'd barely touched the door at the end of the corridor when Kelly's hand landed on her shoulder.

She swung around. 'Please,' she started to say, but he put a finger to his lips. Glanced over his shoulder then back.

'The basement,' he whispered. 'Go and find what's in the basement. I'll stall him. When you're done, go to the car. I've left the keys in the ignition.'

She could feel her eyes round in dismay. 'No way.'

'Look...' He scrubbed a hand over his hair. 'In a perfect world I'd like to get a search warrant but I don't think we have time. There's something coming to a head, and I want to know what it is before I go to the judge. Father Luke's lawyers are worse than a pack of attack dogs, and whatever is in the basement will be long gone by the time I come back with a warrant.' His voice lowered urgently. 'I want to know what's there.'

Win's voice. *They're hatching a plan... they've been planning this for years...*

'See you at my car.' He didn't wait for her to acknowledge him but strode away.

*Fuck.*

She wasn't a police officer. Shouldn't Kelly go to the basement himself? Why her?

*Because I'm expendable.*

She didn't know where the thought came from, but she realised it was probably true. Kelly could deny all knowledge of her, if she was caught.

*Shit.*

Dare she go to the basement? Did it have something to do with her father? Had Dad seen whatever was there, and been killed for it?

Sid dithered. She wasn't a hero but she couldn't turn her back. Not now one of the followers had recognised her father's picture. Dad had been *here*, at the Golden Dawn. A strange urgency dropped over her. She began inching her way down the corridor. Could she access the basement by using the rear stairs?

She crept into the gigantic hallway and up the staircase. Moved along the corridor to the east wing, heading for the linoleum stairs. As quietly as she could, she pattered down. When she reached the ground floor, she peered downwards at the next section of steps. What was the worst that could happen?

Sweating, Sid wavered.

And then, just as she was about to turn tail and head back up the stairs, she heard her mother's voice, cutting through all her doubts and fears.

*Do it, Sid. Be bold. Go and see what's there.*

Before she could change her mind, she tiptoed down the stairs. At the bottom was a wooden door, painted blue. Cautiously, silently, she turned the doorknob. Pushed the door open a crack. She was greeted by a blast of cool air. She paused, listening. She thought she heard the crackle of paper, then the sound of Sellotape being pulled. As carefully as she could, Sid eased the door open a little more, inching her head around the door-jamb.

Bare stone walls were lined with shelves filled with supplies. Loo paper, kitchen towels, industrial-sized cans of tomatoes, baked beans, chickpeas. There were tins of peaches, bins of flour and sugar. Just two people were there. Two men, but they weren't dressed as cult members. They wore boiler suits and stood in front of a worktop.

She saw a variety of tools – pliers, wire cutters, pincers – but her gaze was drawn to the stack of Christmas presents to one side. Brightly coloured, lots of gold and red ribbon, images of Santa and his sleigh, reindeer and snow.

Another *zzzzz-iiip* as Sellotape was pulled.

Sid stared. They were wrapping Christmas presents?

Then she took in a set of what looked like sticks strapped together with a mobile phone. Wires ran between the sticks into the phone.

She stared and stared, unable to believe what she was seeing. She could feel the blood drain from her head.

*No, no, no, no, no.*

She closed her eyes. Opened them again but the sticks of dynamite were still there.

*FUUUUCK.* Her mind became a howl of horror.

They were making bombs.

As she watched, one man put the bomb into a shoebox and packed it with bubble wrap before putting the lid on and passing it to the second man to wrap.

She was rooted in place, terror wrapped around her heart. She'd thought she was in danger poking around a cult, but this? It was incredible, horrifying, unbelievable.

Sid forced herself to move, to bring out her phone. She had to record this. Send it to Detective Kelly. He wouldn't believe her otherwise. Nobody would. They'd think she was mad.

Heart pounding, moving infinitely slowly so as not to alert the men, she inched up her phone and videoed the two men, the bombs, the Christmas presents.

When she was done, she edged backwards, out of sight. Sweat poured down her spine. Her mouth was dry, as though it had been packed with sand. Her mind was one continual shriek: *Shit, shit, shit.*

Gently, she pulled the door to. Her insides were knotted. Everything seemed unreal but she knew she wasn't mistaken. They were sticks of dynamite. They were bombs.

With trembling fingers, she put her phone back into her bag. Made her feet move for the staircase, began to climb. She didn't think she'd made a sound, but to her horror, a man spoke behind her.

'What are you doing here?'

She turned and looked down to see both men standing at the bottom of the staircase. In their forties, one with brown hair, the other red. No other particular identifying features. They were clean-shaven, their hair short-cropped. It was difficult to gauge through their boiler suits but she got the impression they were muscular. For some reason, probably prompted by their silence and focus making the bombs, she thought: *military.*

'I'm looking for Gabriel and Hannah,' she said, with more confidence than she felt.

'You're not wearing a djellaba,' the redhead said.

'That's because I've been especially good. Father Luke only allows one of us to wear our own clothes on any one day. It feels odd, but in a nice way. I guess it reminds us of our previous life, before we connected our hearts to Father Luke, and to God...' She prattled on, taking the risk that they wouldn't know the finer details about the cult and realise she didn't know what the fuck she was talking about.

Brown hair cut off her flow with a raised hand. Indicated the blue door. 'Did you look in there?' He held her gaze, eyes boring into her.

She shook her head. 'We're not allowed in the store cupboard. It's forbidden. The children wouldn't dare either.' Sid frowned. 'You didn't hear them, did you? They're usually quite noisy.'

The men glanced at one another, seeming to come to a decision. They began to move back to the blue door.

Sid sighed. 'They'll have gone to the music room, right at the other end of the house. Typical.' She didn't look at them as she walked up the stairs but when she heard the door to the store room close, the catch clicking shut, she could feel the muscles across her shoulders relax.

Sid walked back along the corridor on legs as soft as grass. She was trembling and felt sick. She brought out her phone, looked at the video. Part of her hoped she'd imagined the bombs but no, there they were, in full technicolour. She considered Father Luke. She still didn't know how he'd reacted to her video of him scamming his congregation, but she bet it hadn't been pretty. He'd do more than smash her phone if he had an inkling of what she'd just recorded, She was better off without it and, once she'd sent the video to Kelly, she could download it from the iCloud as she'd done before.

She opened the first door she came to. A sumptuous bedroom drenched in red velvet and gold. Quickly, she forwarded the video to the detective before saving it on the iCloud. She crept across the room to the chest of drawers standing between two windows. Switched off her phone. Pulled out the bottom drawer and slipped it into the space below. Replaced the drawer. It wasn't foolproof but it was better than nothing.

She tiptoed down the main stairs, through the hallway and into the kitchen corridor. She had to get to Kelly's car and get out of here, but in the meantime, she had to appear normal, as though nothing had happened. She had to pretend she was still searching for her father. She had to pretend to be the woman she'd been this morning. Putting her shoulders back, lifting her chin, she took several deep breaths and strode through the house, for the front door.

Outside, her spirits sank to see Marc Strong and Kelly standing beside the detective's car. Behind them stood Brother Jeremiah.

'Hey.' She walked towards them, expression bright as she looked at Detective Kelly. 'I lost you.'

She then looked at Marc Strong.

'Hello,' she said breezily. 'What a coincidence seeing you this morning, and here you are again.'

'Here I am again,' he agreed smoothly.

'Well.' She gave a little laugh, a nervous one. Looked at Kelly. 'I'm done here, if you are?'

Kelly gave a nod. 'Sure.'

From his casual demeanour she guessed he hadn't seen her video. Her mind began shouting, *let's go!*

'What's the rush?' Marc Strong was looking at Sid.

'No rush, not really,' she gushed, 'but I have a dog. I have to get home because I can't leave him on his own for more than a couple of hours, it's too unkind. They're pack animals, you know, they're not meant to be alone, they're social creatures who crave human company and leaving him on his own is really cruel...'

'A dog,' he repeated. 'I see.'

'Don't say it–' she rolled her eyes, '–that because I'm a

single woman, my dog is a child substitute. I get it all the time.'

'I'm sure you do.' His eyes didn't leave hers. They were searching, penetrating, seeming to strip away her lie.

'Right.' She looked at Kelly. 'Good to go?'

'The detective has someone he needs to say goodbye to first, don't you, Detective? Why don't you go and see Mariam and come back here in say–' Marc Strong checked his watch, '–fifteen minutes.'

'I really need to collect Tank,' Sid said desperately.

'Fifteen minutes,' Marc Strong repeated.

Kelly hesitated, looking between Sid and Marc Strong.

*Don't leave me!* she shouted at him in her mind. *I've got to get out of here!*

But Kelly wasn't clairvoyant. He didn't hear her, or see the urgent pleading on her face. He walked away.

# 30

'Come with me,' Marc Strong told Sid. It was an order, not a request.

'But I really need to get–'

'Jeremiah,' he said. 'Please escort Miz Scott inside.'

When the Brother came over and made to grip her arm, Sid snapped, 'Don't touch me.'

'Then please...' Marc Strong gestured ahead of him.

Terror crept into her heart. She forced herself to move, to walk back into the house. As they passed the kitchen, Marc Strong ducked his head inside. Called across the kitchen. 'Rebekah. Bring tea and cake into the blue room. And tell Father Luke to join us. Make the tea with his special Earl Grey. As he likes it.'

Marc Strong signalled that Sid walk ahead of him along the corridor.

*You can do this.* Her mother's voice. *Keep calm, and he won't notice a thing.*

Sid concentrated on her breathing, keeping it deep and slow.

*Kelly will come and find me. We'll be in his car in no time.*

'This way.' Marc Strong led her across the hallway and down another corridor. He moved very quietly for such a big man. He opened a door on the right and ushered her into a reception room, decorated from ceiling to floor in varying shades of blue. The only other colours came from the antique furniture along with an assortment of religious paintings. Jesus on the Cross, the Holy Trinity, The Annunciation.

'Very blue,' she remarked. She was glad her tone was even and didn't betray her fear.

'It's soothing, don't you think?'

'Hospitals use it to calm patients,' she said. *It's just tea,* she told herself. *Drink it, and leave.*

'Please, have a seat.' He indicated two matching vintage armchairs covered in turquoise velvet upholstery. An antique tea table was set between them. Sid sat down, tried to look relaxed, putting her handbag on the floor beside her, spreading her hands on her thighs. Her palms were damp, her pulse thumping.

'The detective told me you're looking for someone called Leah.'

'Yes.'

'Why?'

'I think she might know something about my father.'

'Your father came here, to the commune?' Genuine bafflement rose.

'I don't know. That's why I want to talk to Leah.'

'How very odd.'

A gentle tap-tap on the door made him turn his head. 'Enter!'

Rebekah carried a tray laden with teapot, three cups and saucers and what looked like a lemon drizzle cake to the table. She poured the tea and cut the cake, popped the slices on three miniature cake plates and scurried away.

Sid looked at the cake. She'd never felt less like eating, but she didn't want to give away her nerves, so she picked up the plate and said, 'Looks delicious.'

'Everything is home-made. I do love it here. It's like a second home.'

'Did Owen come here?' Sid asked then sipped her tea.

Instead of answering, he said, 'Tell me, will you remain a spinster all your life?'

She had to concentrate hard to arrange her thoughts against the way her pulse was jumping. 'If it means retaining my independence and freedom of thought, then yes. Not every woman wants to be subjugated by their husbands. We're not living in the 1950s any longer. Not that Audrey realises that.'

A flash of anger sparked in Marc Strong's eyes. 'The husband provides and protects. The wife nurtures and nourishes.'

Sid's father sprang into her mind. His passion for equality. 'It's a shame you'll lose perhaps twenty-five per cent of the best brains in science.'

Marc Strong raised his eyebrows in mock surprise. 'But we won't lose any women scientists. They just have to be single.'

For a moment, Sid's mind froze in disbelief. 'You'd make that law?'

'Everyone wants a patriarchal society.' He spread his hands wide as if to say it wasn't his fault. 'It's well overdue.'

'What about educating girls? Will you stop that too?'

'Of course not.' He looked shocked. 'I'll just tweak it a bit. More emphasis on domestic science and sewing, for example.'

'I'm afraid you won't be getting my vote.'

'I won't need it.' He smiled.

The arrogance of the man made her want to chuck her

tea at him. Instead, she raised her cup to her lips, drank the rest of her tea. Put her cup down with a little click.

She made to get up but he waved her down. 'Father Luke won't be long.' He shot his cuffs, checked his watch.

'I'm sorry,' she insisted. 'But I really must be going…'

'To get your dog.' His tone was mocking, making it clear he thought she was pathetic, but she refused to react. Picking up her handbag, she rose and started to walk out of the room. Her legs felt as though they were far away from the rest of her and her head seemed to be disconnected, floating above her shoulders. She prayed Detective Kelly's keys were still in the ignition. She wouldn't wait for him. She'd drive away on her own. Get out, get to safety. Raise the alarm. As she stepped across the huge hallway, a wave of dizziness washed over her, making her knees soften.

She went cold all over.

Another wave of dizziness and she nearly fell. Dear God, they'd put something in her tea. Something really strong if it was having this kind of effect after just one cup.

Desperately, Sid tried to keep walking, but her legs refused to move. Slowly, she collapsed to the floor. She tried to crawl but her limbs wouldn't do as she asked.

Marc Strong came to stand over her.

'You know your mistake?'

She couldn't move her mouth to speak.

'It was the mention of children to my engineers. You see, there are no children at the Golden Dawn anymore. Not a single one.'

When a pool of black ink started to encroach at the corners of her vision she tried to shout, NO! but it didn't stop.

The last thing she remembered was thinking, *fuck*.

# 31

Sid awoke in a double bed in a room set in the roof of what she took to be the attic of the manor house. Wooden beams arched above her, antique rugs dotted the floor. Edged with red and green curtains were two tiny windows showing a bright blue sky. Her handbag rested on a chest of drawers. Her coat hung from a hook on the back of the door.

Cautiously, she rolled out of bed. She was fully dressed, aside from her boots which had been neatly placed by the door. Her mouth felt furred, her mind slow. She was incredibly thirsty. Stepping to the door, she tried the handle. Although she wasn't surprised to find it was locked from the outside, she still felt a surge of fear. An oak door, it was as sturdy and solid as concrete.

'Hello?' she called, banging loudly with the edge of her fist. 'Is anyone there? Help!' Her voice turned into a shout. 'HELP ME!'

Nothing.

She shouted again and again.

Silence.

*Where is Detective Kelly?*

Nerves humming, she turned around and surveyed the room. Walked to pick up a chair set in the corner and placed it below the windows. She climbed up and peered outside. The view, she had to admit, was spectacular. The formal garden – lots of box hedges, arbours, a couple of fountains – ended with a ha-ha to preserve an uninterrupted view of fields rising to a sea of rolling hills. She could hear nothing but the chirp of a small bird that might have been a sparrow.

She tried to open the window. Locked. She considered smashing the glass – she might just squeeze through – but she'd probably break a leg or worse if she jumped.

Carefully, Sid inched around the room. She found nothing in the chest of drawers, nor the cupboard. There was a plastic wastepaper basket next to the bed, a single light switch that turned on the central light in the ceiling. One book written by Father Luke, *Stop Whining and Get on with Your Life*, and the Bible. She picked up a small blue book that had been propped on her pillow.

*Marc Strong's Little Blue Book.*
   *The Solution to Our Modern World*

She opened it roughly in the middle.

*It is important to note that people's social credit scores may decrease based on the behaviour of their relatives.*

She opened another page.

*The score may prevent students from attending certain universities or schools if their parents have a poor social credit rating.*

Another page.

*You may gain credits by visiting your parents on a frequent basis.*

*Win,* she thought, despair in her heart. *You were right. Something wicked this way comes.*

Sid shoved the book aside. Prowled around the room. No en suite or basin, but there was a portable loo in one corner, two rolls of loo paper. She checked a small cabinet doubling up as a bedside table to find it contained a six-pack of bottled water and some chocolate, packets of nuts. She cracked open one of the bottles and drank. Almost immediately, she felt better.

She went through her handbag to find everything as she'd left it. She considered the water and food, the loo, and tried not to panic. It seemed she wouldn't be going anywhere for a while. *Detective Kelly!* she yelled in her mind. *Where the fuck are you?* Her stomach tightened when her next thought hit. *Is he captive too? No. They wouldn't abduct a police officer. They aren't that stupid.*

She paced back and forth. Marc Strong had told her his engineers had seen her. Whatever plan he was hatching with his bombs, he couldn't afford to have her shouting about it, which was why she was incarcerated. How long would she be here? And what did he mean about there being no children? Where had they gone? Was the manor house going to be blown up? Was Father Luke planning a mass murder-suicide?

She looked outside again. Paced the room some more.

After a while, a surge of weariness pressed over her. Fully dressed, she climbed under the bed covers and closed her eyes.

It felt as though she'd only been asleep for a few

minutes when a wave of nausea gripped her stomach. Her eyes snapped open. At first it began like an earth tremor and then increased in pressure until her stomach cramped and hot, acid vomit rushed up her throat. She only just had time to grab the wastepaper basket before she threw up. Again, she vomited, kept vomiting until she hung over the bucket with strings of saliva hanging from her mouth.

Then the diarrhoea came.

She was sitting on the portable loo when what felt like iced water flowed through her veins and she was shuddering and shaking, freezing cold but sweating. Eventually, she staggered back to bed. Her stomach was aching and the nausea continued to ride her, but she'd stopped being sick. She had a fever, she knew, and her head ached. Where had this illness come from? Then the cool voice spoke up. *If they drugged your tea, why wouldn't they drug the water?*

Sid carefully wormed her way to the bedside cabinet and pulled out the water bottles. They were all sealed. On weakened legs, she took one of the bottles to a shaft of sunlight to inspect it. It didn't appear to have been tampered with, but what if they'd used a syringe with a fine needle?

She staggered back to bed, pulling the covers over her, and lay there shivering, freezing cold but with sweat pouring off her. She didn't think she'd ever felt so dreadful.

She'd fallen into a light doze when the door opened and a young woman slipped inside. She wore a cinnamon-coloured djellaba and a pair of soft-looking moccasins. She was carrying a tray with glasses and a jug of water.

'Hello,' she said. 'I'm Illa.'

Sid managed to heave herself upright but before she could put her feet on the floor, let alone make a rush for it, the door had been closed. She heard someone turn a key in the lock on the other side.

Illa put the tray on the chest of drawers. Came and sat on the bed next to Sid. She was short and rather dumpy, with curly brown hair and a sweet smile. She looked at the wastepaper basket and pulled a face. 'Oh, dear. You're not very well, are you?'

'Put shum-thing in the water.' Her words were slurred, her voice gravelly.

'Whatever do you mean?' A frown marred her forehead.

'I drank a bottle...' She pointed at the bottle of empty water standing on the bedside cabinet.

Illa picked it up. Peered at it. Then she went to the bedside cabinet and brought out the remaining five bottles. Looked at those as well. 'I don't understand.' She was still frowning.

'Poisoned.'

Her face cleared. 'Don't be silly. Look, I was told you were in a pub in Oxford yesterday. You probably picked up some horrid bug there. I was going to take you for a shower but I think you should stay here until you're better.'

'No.' Sid forced herself up. 'Love a shower.'

'Tomorrow.' Illa was firm. 'I'll come back tomorrow.'

# 32

Gabriel and Hannah were watching another movie on the TV, *Home Alone*. He and Hannah couldn't stop laughing, cracking up when the booby traps caught the burglars out. Brother Isaac had gone to pick someone up from the railway station, and the movie was in its final stages. Hannah and Gabriel were on the edges of their seats, totally gripped, when a terrifyingly familiar voice sounded.

'Children?'

Gabriel lunged for the remote control. Punched the off switch. The TV fell silent. No picture, no sound. *Would he know?*

'Pray with me,' he hissed at Hannah.

They both slipped off the sofa and fell to their knees. Closed their eyes.

'Dear Lord,' Gabriel murmured. 'Forgive us our sins...'

He heard the front door close. Footsteps started along the corridor. Had he heard the TV? A sick feeling entered his stomach.

'Hannah. Gabriel.'

Gabriel looked up. Father Luke stood there, filling the doorframe. His face was puce with rage.

'Television is the work of the DEVIL!' he roared.

Gabriel didn't know where it came from. He spoke without thought. 'But we were listening to the wireless. They had a service on the BBC. Hymns.'

Hannah's mouth opened.

'Hannah sang along to them, didn't you?'

For a long, empty second, Hannah stared at Gabriel. *Please follow my lead*, he begged. *Please, please.* Tremors of fear rolled down his spine.

'Yes,' she said, quite clearly. 'I sang along.'

The crimson rage vanished as Father Luke gave them a radiant smile. 'My children. I should never have doubted you. You are a credit to the Lord Jesus.'

'Thank you, Father,' Gabriel whispered, his heart filling, desperate to please him but petrified that he'd lied.

'You're a good boy,' he said, still smiling. 'And you're a good, lovely girl.'

'Thank you, Father,' Hannah piped up.

'Blessed be the Lord.'

'Blessed be the Lord,' Gabriel and Hannah parroted.

'My little missionaries.'

He turned and said, 'Bring them here.'

Isaac appeared with two large Christmas presents, one wrapped in red and white with sparkly polar bears all over it, the other red and gold with angels.

'Presents for Santa,' he told them. 'He will be so pleased with them.'

Hannah's eyes rounded. She adored Santa and his elves, and could recite every one of his reindeer's names.

'Which one would you like to carry?' Father Luke asked Hannah.

Shyly, she pointed at the one with the bears.

'And you?' He looked at Gabriel. 'Are you happy to carry the angels?'

He nodded.

'They're quite heavy, but you won't have to carry them far. Brother Isaac will carry them for you until you get close to Santa.' Father Luke smiled. 'Santa will be so pleased with his presents.'

# 33

Come the morning, Sid could barely drag herself out of bed she was so weak. Illa put Sid's arm around her shoulders and helped her stumble to a bathroom with a walk-in shower. Outside stood two burly men in striped djellabas. Even though she still felt dreadful – she'd been dry-retching a lot of the night – Sid was impressed. She could barely lift a finger against a butterfly and she'd been assigned two guards?

She was a threat, there was no doubt.

She couldn't stop wondering where Detective Kelly was. Would he have driven away without her? Or had something happened to him too? She had to trust he would come for her. And what about Toby, her landlord? Wouldn't he have missed her when she didn't turn up to collect Tank as planned?

In the bathroom she took in the luxury of the huge fluffy towels, the underfloor heating and indulgent bathroom products. Bright green palm fronds contrasted against the pale-grey marble and chrome fittings.

Everything was high-end, with fresh crisp linen on the bed and cashmere throws.

She hadn't dared drink any more water and was now incredibly dehydrated. When she saw the drinking glasses set on the sink below the mirror, she filled one to the brim with water from the tap. Drank it down then poured another. Illa pulled a face. 'Tap water here's horrible. You have bottled water in your room.'

'It's poisoned,' she whispered.

Illa gave her a look that mingled concern with wariness, much like someone would look at a vagrant ranting on the street. Sid didn't have the energy to argue.

Once she'd showered, Illa wrapped her in one of the fluffy towels and helped pat her dry.

'Do you know Leah?' Sid asked.

'Of course.'

'Can I see her?'

Illa shook her head. 'She won't be allowed to see you, an Outsider. Besides, she's in the san.'

'What's wrong with her?'

'She's got Soul Sickness.'

'What's that?'

'It's what we get if we've done something wrong. God sees everything we do and punishes us when we stray.'

'God has made her sick?'

'Yes.'

'How sick?'

Illa glanced away, biting her lip.

'Like me?' Sid suggested. 'Vomiting, diarrhoea?'

Illa wouldn't meet Sid's eye.

'What did she do?'

'I don't know.' It was a whisper. 'But she's really sick.'

*What a way of keeping control of your followers,* Sid thought. *Step out of line, you get poisoned, and after you've*

214

*recovered, you live in terror of transgressing again in case the all-seeing eye of God spots you.*

'Father Luke will make you better, just you wait and see.' Illa smiled sweetly as she helped Sid into a pair of pretty rose-dotted pyjamas.

'Did you ever see a man here, an Outsider, around the same age as Father Luke, but with a big bushy brown beard?'

Illa shook her head. 'You're the only Outsider I've seen. Aside from our Beloved Leader, of course.'

'You're talking about Marc Strong.'

'Who?'

'The dark-haired man who's here from Outside.'

'He's our Beloved Leader,' she said stoutly.

Sid let it rest for a bit. God, she was drained.

'Father Luke asked me to ask you something,' Illa ventured.

'What?'

'He wanted to know where your mobile phone is.'

'Tell him I didn't bring one. I didn't want him to destroy it like he did last time.'

Illa mouthed silently, obviously memorising Sid's exact words.

'When did you...' Sid rallied her strength to talk further. She was already tired out. 'Come here?'

Illa's face lit up. 'Five years ago. My parents went crazy but it's the best thing I've done and–'

'Why... crazy?'

At this, Illa looked at the floor. 'To join the Order, you have to give up worldly goods. I donated all mine to the Order. My parents didn't understand.'

*I'll bet,* Sid thought, but she didn't say any more. No point. Little Illa was a true believer and probably wouldn't take to being challenged.

Sid tried to detangle her hair but the effort was too much and she dropped her hands to the marble top and bent her head, exhausted.

'Here,' Illa said gently. 'Let me.'

Sid allowed herself to be led to a stool in the corner and, like a child, let Illa comb her hair. When Illa opened the bathroom door, Sid ignored Illa's gentle glance of exasperation and filled two glasses with tap water. As she stepped outside, Sid had braced herself to throw the glasses down and try and make a break for it, but as she'd expected, the two burly men were still there, arms crossed, waiting.

Meekly, she let Illa take her to her room, where she put the two glasses of water on her bedside cabinet. With a little huff, Illa walked to the cabinet and withdrew a bottle of water, cracked it open, and steadily drank the entire contents.

'There,' she said on an exhale. 'It's not poisoned, okay? You picked up something in town.'

Sid said, 'If you really believe that, would you mind taking the tops off each bottle and having a swig?'

Her eyes widened as the implications of what Sid had said sank in. 'You don't trust me?'

'It's not you per se.' Sid wearily sat on the edge of the bed.

'Well, if it makes you feel better...' Illa did as Sid asked, and cracked open each bottle, taking a lengthy swig from each. Recapping them, she left them in a neat row on the cabinet top. 'Now, you get some rest. And for goodness' sake, rehydrate yourself. I'll come in later.'

But Sid didn't see Illa again, and later, when her thirst began to rage, she resisted drinking from the bottles.

She clung on to the rule of threes.

*Three minutes without air. Three days without water. Three weeks without food.*

She could last for three days, she told herself, but as her tongue thickened and her throat swelled, her mind kept returning to Illa tasting each of the bottles.

*For goodness' sake, rehydrate yourself.*

In the middle of the night, Sid cracked and drank from one of the bottles.

Half an hour later she wished she hadn't. She became so ill she thought she might die.

# 34

Gabriel held tightly onto his sister's hand, terrified they'd be separated. He'd never been in such a crowd before, one that shifted and pulsed like a living creature.

'Ow.' Hannah tried to wriggle free of his grip. 'You're hurting me.'

'Sorry.' He relaxed his fingers slightly. 'I don't want to lose you, that's all.'

'I'll hold onto your jacket instead,' she told him.

But her grip was too tiny, too slight, and he knew it would slip, so he said no, they had to hold hands. Hannah started to sulk.

'Look!' He tried to distract her by pointing at an enormous poster of a woman with smoky eyes who was painting her lips bright red.

**Beauty is an attitude.**

He thought she looked amazing, even if totally unreal. He couldn't imagine any of the women at the commune using make-up even if they were allowed to. Beauty came from inside.

'Shall I buy you some lipstick?'

Hannah dissolved into giggles.

Disaster averted. He continued to follow Brother Isaac, trying to memorise the route. If they got separated, he wanted to know how to get back to the house.

*Camp Fire Yarn. No. 5*

    *Exploration*

    *You should notice everything as you go along the roads, and remember, as far as possible, all your journey.*

Isaac was just ahead. He was carrying their Christmas presents and would, he said, give them to him and Hannah when they got to the Christmas market.

Hannah began to skip at his side. A woman glanced at her, smiling. Another nodded, eyes warm. Father Luke had warned them that everyone in the city was Evil, with underlying motivations of cruelty and greed, but he hadn't seen anyone being mean. Perhaps it was a cover and underneath their nice smiles lay Satan?

Gabriel gave a shudder.

He followed Isaac as he approached an escalator. Gabriel made a mental note of the arrows. Circle and District Line. Piccadilly. Mum had told him all about the Underground but he'd never thought he'd see it. It was loud and noisy, smelly and chaotic, but he didn't think he'd felt so alive. He had to help Hannah onto the escalator. She hung onto his hand, mouth pursed. Concentrating.

When they began to walk up the stairs – WAY OUT, REGENT STREET SOUTH – the air turned cold and although it wasn't fresh and reeked of fumes and fat, it smelled much better than it had down in the tunnels.

At the top, he took two steps and stopped. His jaw dropped. Hannah stopped too. He could hardly take it in. The sparkling lights, huge glittering snowflakes, strings of fairy lights, giant screens showing videos, neon signs, baubles. He'd never seen anything so beautiful. People were everywhere. Traffic, taxis, red buses, traffic lights blinking, pedestrian lights beeping. It was incredible, awesome, overwhelming.

'Stop gawking and get a move on,' hissed Isaac. He'd returned and was pushing them forward.

'This isn't it?' Gabriel was amazed. He couldn't imagine anywhere busier than Piccadilly Circus.

'No. The Christmas market's at Leicester Square. Just over there.' He pointed past a beautiful statue of a boy with wings, balanced on one foot as he released an arrow from his bow.

As they walked, Gabriel marvelled. He'd thought the world Outside was going to be scary, filled with horrible people. Terrifying. Instead, it was simply marvellous.

He could live here forever.

# 35

Sid awoke in the middle of the night to find her mother sitting on the side of the bed.

'Oh, sweetheart,' she said.

She put a cool hand to Sid's heated forehead. Her smile was soft, her turquoise eyes filled with love.

'Where... how are you here?'

'Shhh. Don't talk. Rest.'

'I'm so thirsty.'

Her mother brought a cup with a straw to Sid's lips. She gently supported Sid's head as she drank. 'There. That's better, isn't it.'

Sid lay back. Closed her eyes.

When she opened them again, her mother was still there, but this time, her father stood beside the bed. He wore his gardening jeans and the bright-red sweater she and Mum had given him years ago – with a ridiculous cartoon-style reindeer on the front – and which he wore religiously every Christmas.

Sid started to weep. 'I've missed you so much.'

'We've missed you too, love.'

'I've done some awful things.' She told them about her spending their money without thought, her extravagance, her recklessness. She described the brown-eyed boy, the other men, what the gang thought of her.

*She fucks pretty much anyone who buys her a drink.*

She couldn't stop crying.

She talked about how she'd used sex as a quick fix for emotional, physical and intimate comfort. That she'd wanted sex to check that she was still alive. She talked about alcohol, how it helped to dampen her emotions, but how it lowered her inhibitions, making her dangerously confident, *stupidly* carefree.

For the first time, she clearly saw she'd used sex as a coping mechanism.

'Grieving can be complex,' her mother said softly. 'Sex can be an escape, or it might provide the moment of tenderness and comfort you needed when we'd gone.' She picked up Sid's hand and held it. Her father put his hand on top.

'It's not your fault. You were hurting. You did what you had to do to survive. We love you. We always will.'

Sid's weeping receded and as her parents continued to speak loving words of forgiveness and understanding, she fell back to sleep.

## 36

The Christmas market sparkled and shone. People bustled and jostled, smiling, laughing. There were red-roofed stalls selling candles, Christmas tree decorations, cards and pictures, biscuits, hot wine. Gabriel's mouth watered when he saw the hot dogs.

'Later,' snapped Isaac.

They were in the centre of the market when Isaac handed them their Christmas gifts. As he'd warned, they were heavy and both he and Hannah had to use both hands to hold them. Hannah was squeaking with excitement. 'Where's Santa?'

Isaac looked around. 'Oh, dear. He's not here.'

Hannah stared. 'He has to be. I've got his present.'

Isaac looked around again. He said, 'I think you should give your present to those police officers over there.' He pointed through the crowd where a male and female officer stood side by side, watching the crowd. 'They'll give it to Santa.'

'No.' Hannah scowled. 'I want to give it to Santa.'

'Gabriel?' Isaac looked at him. His expression was

fierce, and Gabriel's stomach swooped. It was the same look he got just before he slapped or punched him. 'Take your sister and deliver your presents to those police officers.'

Mouth dry, Gabriel nodded. 'Come on, Hannah,' he said. 'Let's do as Isaac says.'

'No.'

'I know what...' He ducked down to look at her straight. 'Let's go to the officers and ask where Santa is. They'll tell us and we can then go and give Santa his presents.'

Slightly mollified, Hannah began walking with him through the crowd but she was muttering, which was never a good sign. As they neared the officers, Gabriel turned around to check on Isaac, but he'd vanished. Gabriel felt a surge of fright. Where had he gone? On tiptoe, he stretched as high as he could but he couldn't see the Brother anywhere. He would, he decided, deliver the presents to the officers and then run back and try and find him. He didn't dare not complete his task but he was also terrified of getting lost.

As they approached, Hannah began to dig her heels in. 'I want to give it to Santa.'

'You will.' He tried to cajole her. 'We just have to ask them where he is.'

'No.' She stamped her foot. 'I want to go and find him NOW.'

To Gabriel's horror, she turned and as fast as a rabbit, darted away.

'Hannah!' he yelled.

She didn't stop. Clutching her present to her chest, she simply ran faster.

Still yelling, he broke into a run after her. Although the

present was hampering him he didn't dare put it aside and ran as fast as he could.

For a horrifying second, he lost sight of her but then a woman pointed to his left and he hared that way. He was still shouting her name when he spotted her bright blonde hair bobbing past a tree. How had she got so far ahead of him?

Gabriel was tearing past a stall selling hot wine when a man stepped out, right into his path. His present went flying.

'Sorry, son.' The man looked mortified. 'You shouldn't be running like that, you–'

Gabriel glanced at the present, then back at Hannah who was about to vanish again. Abandoning the present, he tore after his sister, ducking and weaving, occasionally hitting someone, hearing startled voices, '*Hey, slow down.' 'What's the rush?' 'Cool it, man.*'

He lost her.

Gabriel stood in the centre of the Christmas market. He was about to open his mouth and scream her name when there was an almighty explosion and a punch of air hit him, lifting him off his feet and slamming him onto the ground. His ears were ringing and his body felt numb. Dust floated all around. He struggled to his knees. People were sprawled on the ground. Some were moving, some lay still.

Gabriel staggered upright.

'Hannah,' he choked.

Another explosion, another blast wave.

This time, Gabriel lay there for a while. He was trembling, his vision wavering. He couldn't hear anything through the ringing in his ears. What about Hannah? She'd be terrified. He had to find her.

Blinking, trying to clear his eyes, Gabriel inched

himself to all fours. He felt dizzy and slightly sick. He forced himself to his feet. Stood there swaying. He tasted blood. He raised his hand to his face. His fingers came away bloody. He didn't immediately know what had happened. All he knew was that the Christmas market had vanished and in its place was bloody devastation.

Part of the market had been flattened. He turned around to see the tree he'd run around had a huge chunk in its trunk missing and that it had toppled over, pinning people to the ground.

His mind was a single shriek: *HANNAH!*

He stumbled past people trying to help others. Some stalls were still standing but others had been ripped to pieces. Bits of wood lay everywhere, broken glass. He saw a man with his leg blown off, blood pumping. Another had no face. Gabriel tried not to look. He was whimpering.

More blood, more torn limbs, more ripped bodies.

And then he saw it. A single pink trainer with blue ponies on their laces. It was covered in blood, with red-and-white sticky fronds hanging from it. He picked it up to see his sister's foot was still inside. He made a moaning sound as he dropped it. He was trembling head to toe.

He began looking for her, but it was all a mess of blood and bone and hair. Scraps of red-and-white material clung to torn flesh. He recognised it as Hannah's snowflake sweater. There was nothing left of her. She'd been obliterated, along with everyone around her.

Gabriel sank to his knees.

He was groaning.

He stayed there, rocking back and forth, fixed on the remains of Hannah's little red-and-white sweater. He heard sirens, became aware of police cars and ambulances disgorging dozens of uniformed people but he still didn't move.

When a woman asked if he was all right, wanting to help him to his feet, he shook his head and rocked even harder. He didn't want to leave the warm wreckage that was Hannah.

Gabriel knelt on the bomb-blasted ground until darkness began to fall. Only then did he allow a man in a fluorescent yellow jacket to lead him away.

---

'He's not said a word.' The man had shucked off his fluorescent jacket to show a fleece which had *First Responder* stitched on its breast pocket. He was talking to a blowsy woman with shiny skin. She wore a shirt with *Hospital Volunteer* on it. The man looked at Gabriel. 'My guess is it's shock.'

'Poor lad.' She squeezed her face up in sympathy. 'Let's see what we can do to help.' She held out a hand but Gabriel didn't take it.

'Come on, lad. You need something to eat.'

When she moved off, the man turned away to talk intently to another man in uniform. Not knowing what else to do, Gabriel followed the woman down a corridor filled with people lying on trolleys, people rushing past, machines beeping, the odd shout. The woman pushed her way through a pair of swing doors, down another corridor, then she turned right before opening a door and into a café. Turning around, she said, 'I'm Maureen.' Then she pointed at the food counters. 'What would you like?'

He didn't think he'd felt less like eating in his life. He shook his head.

When he hesitated, she added, 'You can have anything you want. I'll pay. Go on, just have a look. It won't do any harm to look.'

Obediently, he stepped across and as he took in the extraordinary array of sandwiches, pastries and cakes – he'd never seen such a selection of food – he experienced a wild rush of exhilaration. He was alive. He could feel his breath in his mouth and lungs, the ground beneath his feet. He staggered a little and Maureen put out a hand to help steady him. This time, he let her grip his arm.

'All right, love?'

He gave a nod. She looked pleased. 'What'll it be, then?'

Gabriel chose an egg sandwich, a chocolate brownie and a chocolate-chip cookie.

'And to drink?'

He pointed at the chocolate milkshake.

'You like chocolate by any chance?'

Unlike Father Luke, who thought chocolate was the Devil's nectar and would already be flushing with rage, Maureen was smiling. 'I love a bit of chocolate myself, I do.'

While Maureen chatted on, Gabriel ate every scrap of his food and drained his milkshake dry. His brain, which had been suspended by shock, began functioning again, albeit as slowly and as stickily as a slug.

'Who were you with in the market?' Maureen asked. 'Your parents?'

*Hannah*, he thought. *My little sister.*

He expected tears to fall, for him to cry, but nothing came.

'Can I call anyone?' Maureen's wide shiny face was earnest and kind.

Gabriel reached into his front jeans pocket and pulled out the tiny piece of paper, passed it over.

'Number one, Bloomfield Avenue, Bath.' Maureen's face cleared. 'This is where you live?'

Gabriel nodded.

# 37

S id had no sense of time passing, whether it was day or night. She was aware of people coming and going, and at one point a vigorous man with a mop of floppy red hair came and took her temperature and examined her. Desperately she tried not to drink anything she was given but she had little choice when one of the burly men came in and pinched her nose while the other held her mouth open.

Her life became a blur of diarrhoea and vomiting, being rolled over in bed as her sheets were changed, being bed-washed, falling unconscious, waking to be forced to drink more poison.

She thought she was going to die here, but then the two burly men came in one day and picked her up, put her arms around their shoulders, and, between them, lugged her out of her room. She couldn't raise her head or use her limbs at all and her feet dragged on the ground. Saliva ran from her open mouth and down her pyjamas.

At some point she lost consciousness and came to in

the auditorium. It was packed. Thousands of people were creating a steady murmuring buzz of excited chatter. The men hauled her onto the stage. The crowd fell silent.

'We are here today to HEAL!' Father Luke roared.

The crowd roared back. 'Praise the Lord!'

'This young woman came to us terribly sick, suffering from dengue haemorrhagic fever. She is in the grip of this terrible disease at its most severe. She has immense joint pain and cannot get rid of a severe headache. Right now, she is threatened with organ failure, severe bleeding, dehydration and, if I don't intervene, death.'

The crowd oooh'd and aaah'd.

'With you at my side,' he boomed, 'we can cure her!'

The crowd went wild.

Father Luke came to Sid and placed both his hands on her head. She tried to raise her gaze, couldn't. She continued to dribble.

'The prayer of faith will save the one who is sick,' he thundered, 'and the Lord will raise him up. And if he has committed sins, he will be forgiven.'

'Praise be the Lord,' the crowd chanted.

'The Spirit of the Lord is upon me,' Father Luke's voice resounded around the auditorium, 'because he has anointed me to heal this poor woman and restore her to full health.'

He paused. Gradually, the crowd fell silent.

'LORD! Heal this woman!'

Sid could do nothing but hang between the two men and watch her drool drip onto the floor.

'Now, we must let her rest. She will recover in God's own time.'

She felt something press against the top of her head and at the same time, the congregation sighed. Had he kissed her hair?

Using the main aisle so everyone could get a good look at her, she was carted out of the auditorium. She saw a row of TV cameras following them like silent, unblinking eyes. Sid managed to swing her head to look at the congregation's faces. Young mothers with babies, elderly people, backpackers. Asian faces, African, Chinese. White skins, black and brown. They didn't wear djellabas, but normal clothing.

She tried to form the word *help*, and although her mouth was numb, she kept trying. And then she saw someone she recognised. Illa. She was looking at her in horror. Sid screamed *help* with her eyes but she was past the girl in seconds.

Back in her room, the men deposited her on her bed and left. Sid closed her eyes and sank into oblivion.

When she came to, sunlight was streaming through the windows. She hadn't a clue what day it was but from the height of the sun, she guessed it was mid-morning. To her surprise, she felt a little better. As weak as a newborn lamb, and as tottery, but the nausea and fever seemed to have left her. She raised herself up on her elbows to see a huge bowl of fruit on a table that had been set beneath the window. Apples, oranges, apricots, pears, grapes, a watermelon already sliced.

Slowly, she padded over to see there was also a carton of soya milk and some muesli. Fresh bread and jams. Hard-boiled eggs, slices of cheese and ham.

Her mouth flooded with saliva.

Dare she eat? Or was the whole lot poisoned?

Sid looked at the bread. *Seriously,* she thought. *Is it possible to poison a slice of sourdough?*

Not if Father Luke wanted to 'heal' her.

Sid had a grape. She groaned aloud as the sweet juice exploded in her mouth. Part of her told her to be careful and not overeat but she couldn't help it. She didn't think she'd ever been so hungry.

It didn't take long before she was full, making her realise she'd been here for longer than she thought. Her stomach seemed to have shrunk to the size of a walnut. Looking at her detritus, she hid the watermelon skin and wiped out the muesli bowl so it looked as though she'd hardly eaten anything. Then she climbed back into bed and closed her eyes.

She didn't stir when she heard someone come inside and remove the food. Nor did she open them when lunch and dinner arrived and was taken away.

The next morning, after her breakfast had been removed, Father Luke came in. He took her temperature, checked her pulse.

'You're feeling better, yes?'

'Not really.' She made her tone soft. 'I mean I'm not being sick anymore but I still feel dreadful and terribly weak.'

He frowned.

'Well, eat as much as you can. We need to restore your strength.'

She gave a wobbly smile. 'I'll try.'

'You do that. You've been terribly ill but you'll be better in no time, thanks to the Lord.'

Sid sank back on the pillows and closed her eyes.

She could feel him studying her but she didn't move. Just let her breathing even out and deepen, as though she was falling asleep. When she heard him leave, she headed to the table and ate as heartily as she could while trying to hide the fact she was ingesting as many calories as possible.

The following day, Father Luke returned. Ran through the same checks: temperature, pulse. 'You look quite a bit better, Sid.'

'I'm feeling a little better.' She gave a wan smile. 'The nausea is still there, though.'

He looked at her for a long time. She tried her best to look pitiful.

'Do you think you can walk to the auditorium later this morning?'

'Not yet, I don't think.'

He looked across at the food. 'Try and eat something.'

She didn't answer, but curled on her side away from him. 'Promise,' she murmured.

Father Luke didn't return the next day. Instead, a sturdy middle-aged woman arrived to help Sid shower. The woman didn't introduce herself or talk at all, so Sid didn't either. She continued to pretend she was enfeebled when in actual fact, her energy levels had returned. She'd started doing exercises in her room, star jumps and squats, running on the spot, wanting to remind her body it would be called on very soon to *run*.

She had another look at *Marc Strong's Little Blue Book*, the list of rules. Attend church every Sunday, volunteer at the local hospital, you received credits, but if you didn't, you were fined. If you dropped litter in a shopping centre, you wouldn't be allowed to return for the next month. If you didn't stop fully at a stop sign in your car, your car would be impounded. Watch the wrong thing on the internet, you'd have to relinquish your computer.

He promised CCTV cameras on every street corner, down every lane, ostensibly to protect the people from crime but then, in horror, Sid remembered what Win had said.

*Society will be run by carrot-and-stick regulations. We will be controlled by data and AI, the police – compliant instruments to enforce the rules.*

If he was right, she had to hope Marc Strong never

came into power. Talk about a nightmare coming true.

# 38

Not long after breakfast the following day, the sturdy woman appeared to help Sid dress. No djellaba today but Sid's own clothes. Her jeans and stretchy top felt strangely constricting after the freedom of a single robe.

'You're going to the morning service.'

'What's the date today?'

'Why, it's Christmas Eve.'

*Dear God*, she thought. She'd been here for over ten days. Ten days

of her life spent being horrendously ill then desperately trying to recover.

Her clothes had been washed and ironed, but she was required to wear a nut-coloured djellaba over the top. When Sid questioned why, the woman replied: 'So we are all equal. No vanity.'

Not long later, Father Luke returned with the same two burly men who'd lugged her about before, and a wheelchair. The men helped her into the wheelchair while Father Luke watched silently. Nobody spoke.

Outside, Sid raised her face to the sun. She felt as

though she'd been imprisoned for months and to breathe fresh air, feel the winter chill against her skin, was bliss.

The service was much the same as the last, except the congregation had increased. A third appeared to be members of the general public. Everyone witnessed Sid's 'healing' with rapturous applause while she scanned the auditorium, planning her escape. In the front row she saw a man with a mop of floppy red hair staring at her as though he couldn't believe his eyes. Was it the same man who'd been in her room, examining her?

As she was wheeled outside, she was surprised when the Brothers diverted to the car park at the front of the house. To her disbelief, Detective Kelly stood next to a mud-spattered Ford sedan, watching her approach. She couldn't help it. She sprang out of the wheelchair and raced across.

'Get me out of here.'

'Jump in.'

Sid dived onto the passenger seat and buckled up, trembling with a combination of terror that the Brothers would haul her outside and incarcerate her again, and anticipation that she was going to be freed. As soon as Kelly was inside the car, she shouted, 'Drive!'

Kelly put his foot down and roared away, up out of the valley and for the gates.

'Faster!'

He increased his speed, barely slowing for the cattle grid and gunning the car onto the main road in front of a lorry, forcing it to brake. It blared its horn at them.

'What the fuck!' she said, gasping as adrenaline continued to flow. She twisted in her seat to look at the side of his face. Rage poured out of her now, unstoppable, ferocious. 'I've been in there for ten days! Where the fuck HAVE YOU BEEN?!' She never thought of herself as violent but the next second, she'd punched him.

'Shit!' Detective Kelly yelled as the car swerved. 'Just wait a minute, will you?'

Kelly hauled the car to the side of the road. Bumped along the verge briefly before coming to rest outside a farm entrance. The lorry behind them gave a furious blast of its horn as it swept past.

'Where the fuck...' To her frustration, tears rose, of relief mixed with anger. 'I waited for you. They poisoned me and you left me there... I thought I was *going to die.*'

She sobbed as she raged. She ignored the tissue he offered and raised a fist, wanting to punch him again and he flinched back, hands raised. He didn't say anything. Just let her rant. Finally, she ran down. Took a shaky breath.

'You got my video?'

He stared straight ahead through the windscreen.

'They've got my sister.'

'What do you mean?'

'She's with the Golden Dawn.' He brought out his phone, showed her a photograph of the pretty young woman he'd been arguing with outside the kitchen.

In a rush, Sid remembered what Marc Strong had said to Kelly before he'd forced her to the blue room to have tea.

*The detective has someone he needs to say goodbye to first, don't you, Detective?*

'Mariam,' Sid said. Dismay descended.

'Her real name is Alice.'

'You ignored the video.'

He spun in his seat, skin pale. 'No, I did not. I took it to my superior.'

'So, why isn't Father Luke behind bars?' She leaned towards him, her tone a single long hiss. 'He was making *bombs* for Chrissake.'

He took off his spectacles, closed his eyes and massaged his eyelids with his forefinger. 'There's more going on than you realise.'

She stared at him. When he remained silent, she said, 'Well, come on, then. Tell me what's going on.'

He put his glasses back on and stared at her. His eyes were red-rimmed with exhaustion. 'You'll soon find out.'

'What do you mean?'

He didn't answer. He put the car into gear and pulled out. 'I know what you're thinking.'

She didn't take her eyes off him.

'That I'm weak. Self-serving and gutless–'

'That's just for starters,' she snapped.

'If you go to the authorities, then I'll never see Alice again.'

'I can't be held responsible for your family difficulties.'

'I'll never see you again either.'

The words sent a chill through her. 'Another threat, I take it.'

He didn't answer, which for some reason, made his words even more disturbing. When he turned south, away from Gloucester, she said, 'Hey, you're not taking me to the police station.'

'I'm taking you home.'

'But I want to pick up my car.' She'd left it in the visitor's car park at the Gloucestershire police station.

'It's at your cottage.'

She blinked. 'Whatever did you do, hotwire it?'

'We got it towed.'

'We?'

He didn't respond.

Sid gritted her teeth. 'I still want to go to the police station. I want to make a report.'

'I wouldn't, if I were you.'

She felt a cape of disbelief drop over her. 'I've been kidnapped, poisoned, and held up as being miraculously cured of something Father Luke actually gave me and you want him to get away with it? He's making bombs in his basement and you're doing nothing about it?' She took a breath. 'And what about my father? A woman at the Golden Dawn recognised his photograph. *He'd been there.*'

Still, the detective remained silent.

Sid stared at the road ahead as a variety of memories crashed through.

Win's voice: *It's just that sometimes he suffers from a conflict of interest.* Kelly's sister being at the Golden Dawn would definitely be considered that.

She said, 'You didn't lodge my original report over Father Luke destroying my phone, did you?'

More silence.

'And it was you who gave Father Luke my phone number.'

When they crossed the M4, the heavens opened. Rain poured over the windscreen so fast the wipers had trouble keeping up.

'You tried to stop me from seeing Harriet, Owen's wife.'

Sid took a breath.

'Was it you who put the dead mouse in my mail?'

He glanced across at her, shocked. 'No. Absolutely not.'

'Then who did it?'

His lips tightened into a thin line.

'Do you know?'

He shook his head. 'Not for certain.'

'So, you have an idea.'

'I always have ideas.' He sighed.

'Which you're not going to share.'

'Correct.'

She remembered the first time they'd met at Bath uni, and him showing her pictures of Owen's tattoos. He'd purposely withheld the tattoo of the Golden Dawn; she'd only seen it thanks to it accidentally slipping out of his folder. He had, she realised, undermined her with Father Luke every step of the way.

Sid let a silence stretch before she said very quietly, 'You're a snake.'

They spent the rest of the journey without speaking. When they arrived outside the farmhouse it was to see several cars parked in the yard. Christmas lights twinkled from every window, reminding her it was Christmas Eve.

As Kelly made to drive on to her cottage, she said, 'Let me out here.'

'Your car is at your cottage.'

'But not the dog.' She climbed outside into the rain. It was icy cold but it felt invigorating after her internment. She didn't look at Kelly as he executed a three-point turn and drove away.

Tank, predictably, went berserk when she walked inside the farmhouse. 'Hey, boy.' She knelt down to hug him but he was too excited to stand still, dancing around her, groaning deep in his throat. 'You miss me?'

'He cried.' Toby watched them with a half-smile. 'He went off his food. It was awful, to be honest. I'm glad you're back.'

'Me too.' She buried her face in Tank's neck. 'Ewww.' She pulled back. 'Where's he been? He stinks.'

'He smells like he usually does.' Toby looked offended. 'It's your sense of smell that needs recalibrating. Where have you been anyway? Someone called Saul came by to say you'd been taken ill. Were you in hospital?'

She looked up at him, his round, open face, and decided the less she involved him, the better. 'Something like that. I'm better now.'

'Do you need some basics?' Toby's wife Rachel appeared with a couple of kids in tow who smiled and said hello.

'Hi.' Sid recognised them as Toby's nephew and niece from last Christmas.

'Milk and bread?' Toby offered. 'What about tomorrow? Where are you spending the day?'

'With friends.' Her stock reply.

Toby looked at her askance. 'The same ones you stayed with last year? And the year before that?'

When she looked away, he said, 'You're really welcome to join us, if you–'

She shook her head.

'How about if we drop a bit of turkey round later, that be okay?'

'You don't have to–'

'Grunt will do it, won't you, Grunt?'

Grunt turned out to be a teenager called Grant who said yes, of course he'd drop a food parcel to her tomorrow but only if they stopped calling him Grunt.

'Of course, Grunt,' Toby said, which earned him a mock punch that ended with the two men wrestling good-naturedly across the floor.

When they learned her car was at the cottage and that it was still chucking down outside, Toby and Grant piled her and Tank, and an assortment of carrier bags from Rachel, into a Land Rover. At the other end, they disgorged everything into the utility room, wished her a happy Christmas, and rattled off.

Sid went through the cottage, switching on all the lights. It was bitterly cold, so she switched on the heating as well as lighting the wood-burning stove. She couldn't stop touching things. Her mother's crystals, her father's desk clock, a bowl of shells collected over the years, another of pretty stones. Nothing seemed to have been moved. She checked all the locks and told herself there was no one out there. She told herself that since Father Luke had let her go, she was safe.

She unpacked the carrier bags from the farmhouse, and was immeasurably touched to see not just milk, bread, butter and eggs, but a huge multi-layered box of chocolates (Dad would have loved that!), some home-made mince pies, a carton of clotted cream and two Christmas gifts. Carefully wrapped at the bottom of the last bag was a little Christmas tree that lit up when its battery was switched on.

Gifts on the windowsill, Christmas tree on the kitchen table twinkling merrily, Sid made a conscious effort not to think about everything that had happened. She wanted to prolong the feeling of safety, celebrate that at least a chunk of yesterday's world had survived.

She was home.

She didn't think about the future or how fragile it might be. She simply made a mug of tea and booted up her laptop. Her phone was still hidden at the commune and since she had no intention of going back and collecting it, she'd have to get another phone when the shops opened... when? Boxing Day? The day after? She leaned back and stretched. It felt fantastic to be here. Tank settled beneath the kitchen table, his head on her foot as though he didn't trust her not to vanish on him.

'Softie,' she told him.

As she took a sip of tea, she suddenly thought of a cigarette. *Good God.* She hadn't had a ciggy in days. She hadn't even considered it. Sure, she'd been sick, but even when she'd been recovering, the thought of smoking hadn't crossed her mind. Inside, she gave a laugh. *How to stop smoking! Get kidnapped and poisoned!* Not exactly the punchiest of titles, she admitted.

Checking her social media feeds, she saw her last post, of Father Luke's scam supposedly curing a woman of cancer, had gone viral. Hundreds of thousands of shares were spreading faster than wildfire as people discussed her 'healing' at the commune. The vigorous man with floppy red hair who'd taken her temperature at the commune, was apparently an independent doctor who'd been invited to examine her, and endorse her illness as genuine. She considered posting a message with the truth behind what had happened, but when she saw the bots at work – she had no doubt that's what they were – undermining or scorning any sceptics, she decided she'd wait until she had a proper plan in place. No point in going off half-cocked and inviting nothing but animosity.

Sid began sorting through her emails, enjoying the sense of normality they brought. Several e-cards wished her a merry Christmas, including the university and the *Skeptic Query*. Three messages had come through her website. One wanted a malicious spirit dealt with, another asked for a poltergeist to be removed. The last was a cheery message from Flick, the girl she'd met at Win's what felt like a lifetime ago.

```
Hope you don't mind me contacting
you. I just wanted to wish you a
merry Christmas and a great New Year.
If you ever fancy that spag bol the
offer's still open. My stepbrother
agrees, by the way. He made a total
```

prat of himself and he knows it.
Love, Flick xxxx

Sid smiled. Shot back a message wishing Flick a merry Christmas too and that yes, that spag bol could be good come the New Year.

Finally, she poured herself some wine and settled to catch up on the news, but even in her wildest imaginings she'd never envisaged what might have happened in the time she'd been imprisoned.

Just over a week ago, the entire country had been put under a curfew for forty-eight hours after a wave of horrendous bomb attacks around the country.

In his position as MP, Marc Strong demanded that decisive measures be taken by the government. He wanted to bring in new laws regarding acts of political violence, with a penalty of lifetime imprisonment, and set up special courts to try these offences.

When the prime minister refused to comply, he was given a vote of no confidence and forced to resign.

Horror crawled through every vein as she continued to read.

The contest to succeed the PM had already started. Two candidates were going head-to-head to be named leader of the UK's Conservative Party and therefore become prime minister.

One, was David Reville, a regal-looking man who Sid barely recognised. The other, Marc Strong.

She clicked on the BBC video of Marc Strong within the report.

'The United Kingdom is a great country, but we have lost our way. That's why I am standing to be leader of the Conservative Party and your next prime minister. To bring us back to basics where good, decent people can rest easy, living their lives as they want to in safety, and those who do us harm are punished properly.'

A reporter stepped into view. 'The voting between the two candidates will begin in the New Year, with the successful candidate automatically becoming prime minister once they've been counted.'

Marc Strong beamed.

# 39

It wasn't the neat brick house on the street Gabriel imagined. It was much larger, with views of the city from the front windows. He'd been told he'd be taken into the city after the holidays, to go shopping, maybe see a movie. There was a tree house and as Mum had told him, an ageing cat called Tinsel, who came and purred around his ankles when he came downstairs in the morning.

His room had a night-light in the shape of a globe. It glowed like the moon and when he woke from a nightmare, it was the first thing he saw and immediately, he knew where he was.

No.1, Bloomfield Avenue, Bath.

His grandparents had collected him from the hospital and taken him home. When his grandmother – *call us Granny and Grandpa* – had asked him about his mother and Hannah, whether they'd been with him at the Christmas market, the memory of what happened came up and smothered him, squeezing the breath from his lungs and making him cover his head with his arms and open his mouth in a silent scream.

'They said to let him be.' Grandpa chided his grandmother. 'He will tell us in his own good time. He needs to feel safe first.'

'But what about Lucie?'

For a moment, Gabriel didn't know who she was talking about, but then remembered that's what his mother was called before she was reborn as Leah at the Golden Dawn.

'She'd never have let them go out on their own.'

'We'll find out, love. We just have to be patient and thank heaven that we have Gabriel.'

Granny's face was splotchy, her face swollen. He guessed she'd been crying. Grandpa on the other hand was solid and steady, even though he did have dark circles beneath his eyes. Gabriel wished he could tell them everything, but every time he opened his mouth to talk he felt a monstrous lurch that threatened to turn into a torrent of darkness so immense he would be swallowed whole.

There was talk about Christmas and roast turkey, whether he liked Christmas pudding or preferred chocolate log, innocent questions he could have answered but he couldn't trust himself to speak so he responded to them by using his hands and gesturing.

He spent a lot of time watching TV. Eating. He felt guilty as he tucked into pizza, toast, beef pie, apple crumble. How could food taste so good? He didn't think how Hannah would have loved it. He didn't think of his mother. He simply existed, walking from his bedroom to the bathroom, the kitchen to the living room, with his grandparents' eyes trying not to follow his every move.

On Christmas Eve, he was watching TV when the doorbell rang. He knew it was the postman who'd rang it, wanting a signature for a delivery, but it was late afternoon and the postman usually came in the morning. Bored with TV, Gabriel went to the window and looked out.

The sound that came out of him was something between a whimper and a scream.

Standing on the doorstep, dressed in a mushroom-coloured djellaba, his hands folded in front of him and looking as humble and deferential as one of his just-beaten followers, was Father Luke.

Gabriel ran. He didn't think, he just ran. He tore through the kitchen, ignoring Granny's startled exclamation, flung open the back door and pelted across the lawn. A shadow sprang out at him from behind the rhododendron bush.

'Gabriel,' the man snapped.

It was Brother Isaac.

Gabriel froze in terror. His bowels softened.

'Come here.'

Normally, Gabriel would scurry to a Brother who'd called, do his bidding, but nothing was normal anymore.

Gabriel hesitated. He could see another shadow detach itself from the tree trunk that held the tree house, and another further down the garden. Heart hammering so hard he felt sick, he walked to Brother Isaac.

'Good boy.'

He walked right up to Brother Isaac and as the Brother reached out to grab him, Gabriel ducked around him and pelted for the fence. As quick and nimble as a squirrel he was up and over and dropping into the garden next door, racing for a back gate between two shrubs, his ears filled with the Brothers yelling, screaming behind him, and he was pushing through the gate and then he was on a pavement, next to a road, and he was running, running, running for his life.

# 40

Sid found herself glued to the TV as it reran endless footage of the bomb attacks. Multiple explosions, screams, dust, brutal carnage through five cities. People fled to their homes in terror as armed police filled the streets, the curfew announced. The streets were empty until groups of vehement protestors appeared, throwing bottles and attacking police. Dozens of police were badly injured, one losing an eye, and two more were in intensive care fighting for their lives.

Marc Strong was, apparently, pushing for A Political Protestor Decree. Picking through the legal terminology, Sid felt a chill when she read this would give the incoming prime minister the power to arrest and jail anyone who stood against him.

A political commentator Sid followed said Marc Strong was following in the footsteps of Adolf Hitler, who'd introduced the Enabling Act of 1933, which gave him the power to override individual rights and seize control. In Germany – where the diversity of the German people called for democracy – the people thought it impossible that one could force a dictatorial regime, but look what happened there.

Rumours spread like wildfire, that Marc Strong wanted two huge new prisons built, *gulags!* screamed people on social media – along with rafts of new CCTV cameras installed countrywide. More rumours said he'd jail anyone who stood against him, and vanish not just them, but their families.

Just like Hitler.

Sid wasn't sure what was real and what wasn't, but whatever was going on was already dividing the country. Marc Strong promised the police new powers to arrest, and a massive recruiting drive put under way the day he'd take power. C of E churches would be given new funding, faith schools abolished. As many people praised him – *he's just what this country needs* – as were against him.

When she saw his social media campaign, sophisticated and clever, mixing humour with traditionalism, she had the unnerving sensation of seeing a well-oiled machine that had taken years to build, being wheeled out to do its purpose, and when Marc Strong appeared on TV holding his *Little Blue Book*, she felt a real frisson of fear. She couldn't imagine people rolling over to attend church, let alone give to charity by force, and if he did get into power and start to enforce his ideals, she could see insurrection looming.

She had to pray the Conservative Party saw sense, and voted for David Reville.

Sid had thought seeing Marc Strong all over the internet was bad enough until she turned on her TV to watch the news that night. Father Luke was there, in full technicolour.

'God told me we would be punished for our misdeeds. He said children, with all their innocence, would be sent to teach us a lesson, for us to return into God's fold. I warned everyone. I held a service, told as many people as I could, but nobody listened.'

The newsreader came into view. 'Here's a clip of Father Luke's prophesy, at his Sunday service two weeks ago...'

And there he was, thundering.

'Children! They will bring their bombs and kill us in our thousands! Our cities are in grave danger from innocents. They will come without knowing what they do and commit murder... From Glasgow to London, Birmingham and Manchester, God will rain down his punishment, hear ye, hear ye!'

The newsreader returned, saying, 'Nobody has taken responsibility for these shocking and appalling attacks. All we know is that dozens of children, aged six to sixteen, carried bombs disguised as Christmas presents and brought them into city centres where they were detonated. We still don't know where they got the bombs or what, exactly, their motivation was. Every child, the authorities have confirmed, has died in the attack.'

Sid was shaking, worse than when she'd been poisoned at the commune.

Marc Strong's voice: *There are no children at the Golden Dawn anymore. Not a single one.*

Father Luke and Marc Strong had used the children from the Golden Dawn to implement their hideous plan.

Win's voice in her head. *Something wicked this way comes.*

She had to keep swallowing to stop herself from being sick. It was inconceivable that Gabriel and Hannah were really gone. She felt a colossal lurch in her heart as she pictured Gabriel and Hannah holding her hands as they walked her to the auditorium, Gabriel's eagerness to join her, his refusal to leave his sister, and a rush of emotions rose like lava from a volcano and spilled, white hot. Grief and fear seared every vein, every nerve, but above all, rage roared in its deep red-black wrath.

She sprang up, began to pace. Tank lay in front of the TV, chin on his paws, watching her. What if she went to the police? But what about Kelly's warning?

*I'll never see you again...*

Was it because something would happen to her, or to him?

She didn't like the fact Father Luke had let her go. What did it mean? Did he think she wouldn't have the courage to report what she'd seen? Was it because her "cure" was filmed, and she could easily be discredited? But then he didn't know she'd filmed the bombs being made, and hidden her phone in his manor house.

What if she went to the Wiltshire Police? Even with the video, what chance would she have of being believed? With deepfake videos now almost the norm, who would believe her? The whole thing was wild, crazy, unimaginable, unbelievable.

But it was true.

She didn't want to be a hero. She was back in her cottage with her dog and all she wanted was to return to her little life, reading books, writing articles, doing the odd ghostbusting event.

A wave of exhaustion washed over her. She didn't think she'd ever felt so tired. She had no energy to do anything but get undressed and climb into bed. It was only when she was on the brink of sleep when she thought: *no way am I going to find what happened to Dad now.*

## 41

Christmas morning and it was tipping down. Sid forced Tank outside briefly before making a mug of tea and taking it back to bed with a stack of toast and marmalade. She lay gazing at the rain dribbling down the windows, feeling snug and secure, but no matter how she tried to arrest it, the horrifying wheel of what had happened never slowed.

It would get better, she knew. As time and distance grew from what she'd seen on the news, her experience at the Golden Dawn, they'd slip and blur until, eventually, she could think about things without her pulse shrieking in terror. In the meantime, however, she had to find a way to live.

Firmly, she directed her mind to the present and not to the past. *Don't look back, don't look back.* She repeated the phrase over and over and gradually, as the day passed, her mind took it on, accepted it, forming a carapace and enabling her to function.

She opened her Christmas gifts to find a smart new collar for Tank – padded red leather – and a personalised phone case. She hadn't thought she had it in her, but when she saw the picture on the back of the case, she gave a bark of laughter. It was of Tank, sitting in the farmyard not just looking as handsome as a dog could, but he was fully alert and watching the farm entrance, as though waiting for her.

Sid pottered through the morning, enjoying treats she wouldn't normally have. A hot bath with lots of smellies, mince pies for elevenses, a glass of Prosecco. The TV murmured in the background, Christmas carols, gentle things that soothed her.

Grunt – or rather, Grant – turned up with a plate piled high with turkey and all the trimmings, gravy and all, which she speedily reheated in the microwave before settling to eat it in front of the TV with a bottle of red wine.

She didn't feel sad about being on her own. She thought about her parents but didn't dwell on them. Her mind was taken up with the present, concentrating on the movie she was watching, the festive food on her lap.

When someone knocked on the back door, she assumed it was Grant with another food delivery, except for Tank's reaction. He launched himself at the door, barking loudly enough to be heard in Oxford.

'Settle down, boy,' she grumbled but as usual, he took no heed. Putting her hand on his collar, she opened the door.

To her amazement, a police officer stood on her doorstep. A lumpy woman half Sid's height with acne on her chin. She looked half Sid's age too. Behind her rested a patrol car with mud spattered up its sides and wheel arches. Another officer sat in the driver's seat. A man. He looked disgruntled.

'He afraid of getting his feet wet?' Sid asked.

The woman glanced behind her then back. She gave a

small smile of complicity. 'My name is Constable Norris. I'm sorry to disturb you, especially on Christmas Day, but I've been authorised to search your house.'

'I'm sorry?'

'We've been alerted you may have a minor staying here.'

'What?'

'Please, may I come inside?'

'But I don't have a minor–'

'It's just a simple check, that's all.'

'But I don't…' Sid trailed off when the woman's neutral expression began to fade into something sterner. Desperately, she tried to think through the alcohol fug in her brain. She couldn't think why she shouldn't let a police officer inside but what the hell?

Constable Norris looked down at Tank, who was still growling, a deep rumble in his chest. 'If you wouldn't mind putting him away – perhaps a crate or kennel? – while I come inside…'

'I would, actually.' A bolshiness entered Sid's tone.

'Are you saying you're refusing me entry into your home?'

Sid was opening her mouth to say no, not exactly, when the constable said, 'In that case I shall return with a warrant.' She looked at her watch. 'In about two hours. I'm sure the judge will be delighted to have her Christmas Day interrupted by you.'

Sid was so gobsmacked, she couldn't take in the words. 'I don't understand. Why on earth do you–'

'Just let me have a look, then I'll be out of your hair and you can carry on with your festivities.'

Still holding Tank by his new collar, Sid caved in. She stepped back, opening the door wide. 'Knock yourself out.'

Norris looked at Tank. For a moment Sid thought she

was going to be difficult, but then she said, 'Keep a hold of him, please.'

While the constable poked around upstairs, Sid downloaded the video she'd taken of the bomb-makers from the iCloud onto her laptop. Sweat began to spring as she watched it. Could she show it to the constable? Should she?

Sid heard the constable move into the bathroom, then she was trotting downstairs. Norris had a look in the sitting room and that was it.

'Can I show you this?' Sid asked, turning her laptop around.

The constable looked at it warily.

'It's something I filmed a couple of weeks ago. I was prevented from taking it to the police but since you're here...'

Sid pressed play. Norris watched, and then she took a step closer, eyes narrowed. 'Where did you film this?'

'In the basement at the Golden Dawn.'

She'd barely finished saying 'Dawn' when the constable stepped back, her face clearing. 'Ah. Yes, I was warned that you had a... ah, problem with Father Luke. Didn't you accuse him of stealing your phone? And now, even though he cured you of that awful disease, you still want to defame him?' Norris glanced at the laptop screen again. 'Clever, these deepfakes. I almost believed it for a second.'

'It's not a deepfake. It's real.'

Something in her tone made the constable pause. She looked at it again.

'Those bombs,' Sid said, 'went on to be distributed among the Golden Dawn's children.'

Norris looked at it again, frowning. She said, 'Send me a copy through the Thames Police website and I'll take it to my boss.'

'Who's your boss?'

It was as though Sid hadn't spoken. The constable was already through the utility and outside, calling over her shoulder, 'Have a good Christmas, now.'

---

Boxing Day dawned bright and sunny with a brisk wind that sent vivid white clouds scudding. Toby and family had turned up on her doorstep late morning in wellies and waterproofs and swept her and Tank out for a long country walk. It was convivial and fun, lots of jokes and storytelling, and for a couple of hours Sid was beautifully distracted into living for the moment.

She hadn't been able to work out what the constable had been doing at her cottage. *We've been alerted you may have a minor staying here.* What minor? Who had alerted the police? She'd searched for missing kids on the internet but hadn't found anything that stood out. She'd asked Toby and Harriet too, but they knew nothing about it. Peculiar, and disturbing, it was a mystery she couldn't fathom and she was glad to be out in the fresh air with nothing to think about but having a laugh and looking forward to a cuppa with a mince pie when she got home.

As they returned to her cottage, standing outside her back door and still chatting away, she thought she saw something move at the edge of the wood. A deer? There were loads of muntjac in the area, along with roe, but from its height and the way the figure moved, she thought it was human. She asked Toby if any farm workers were on the farm today.

'Nope. It's just me and the missus doing the milking.'

'Any shooting parties or anything?'

He shook his head. 'Not until next week. I'll be sure to let you know.'

Sid waved them off, went inside. She had her tea and mince pie and an hour later, headed outside with Tank again. This time, she headed straight towards the place where she thought she'd seen the figure. 'Come on, boy. Let's go find some squirrels.'

At the word squirrels, Tank trotted ahead expectantly and vanished in between the trees.

She was sure she'd imagined things, and didn't expect to find anything, so she just about leapt out of her skin when a branch snapped ahead of her.

'Tank?'

Stepping around a chestnut tree she saw Tank standing there, looking at something ahead of him, and then he moved away to sniff at a pile of dead wood. If Sid hadn't looked at precisely the same spot her dog had been looking she would have missed him. Motionless, half-hidden by shrubbery, the man was dressed head-to-toe in camouflage gear, his face smeared with brown and green. He was looking away from her, probably to avoid bringing attention to himself with any movement or the bright whites of his eyes.

Heart knocking, Sid moved aside, pretending she hadn't seen him. Self-preservation said she didn't want to tangle with whoever it might be.

'Tank,' she called, 'hurry up.'

But Tank had other ideas and to her dismay, after peeing on the stack of wood, ambled towards the figure to say hello. He was a fearsome attack dog in the home, but outside it? He loved meeting new people.

'Tank! Come!'

There was a flurry of leaves and then the man said, 'Fucking hell.'

Sid approached the pair cautiously to find the man with his back rammed against a tree trunk staring at a hundred pounds of bullmastiff while the bullmastiff looked back at his new friend in bafflement that he wasn't being given a friendly pat.

'Sorry,' Sid said. She stepped over and put the dog on a lead.

'I like dogs,' the man said. He wiped his face with a hand, smearing the green stripes into brown. 'But he gave me a bit of a start.'

'Understandably so,' Sid said agreeably. She took in the man's big army-style boots. Binoculars hung around his neck. A backpack lay at his feet. The area was trampled, leaves squashed and mud churned, showing he'd been there for a while.

'You look like you're on an exercise.' She looked around as though expecting to see more soldier-like people to appear.

'Nope,' he said, shaking his head. 'I'm birdwatching. I find this gear helps me get really close.'

'Good spot for it, these woods,' she said. 'Have you seen the Lesser Green Tit? It's such a pretty bird.'

'No. Not yet.' He raised his binoculars. 'Maybe before the sun sets.'

'Good luck.'

Sid turned around and retraced her steps. In four paces, between the trees, she could see her cottage clearly. *Lesser Green Tit my arse*, she thought. He wasn't a birdwatcher. He was watching *her*.

# 42

Gabriel slept rough the first night. Instinct had told him to go somewhere busy, so he'd pelted away from the Brothers, down the hill and into the city, where his grandparents had said they'd take him shopping. People had been everywhere. There were food stores and clothing stores, even a chocolate shop. He'd paused to listen to the carol singers beneath a huge fir tree decorated with lights and for a moment he thought of the carols they used to sing at the Golden Dawn, him and Mum and Hannah, and he was unaware of his sob, but a woman next to him said, 'Are you okay?' and he'd run away.

When darkness fell and the shops closed, the crowds dispersing, he'd walked and walked, until he found a park. There, he waited until there were no people or cars about before pushing through the bushes and shrubs. He'd found a patch of ground between a cluster of dense bushes and sat there for a while, trying not to cry but he couldn't help it. When he stopped, his face felt as fat and swollen as a pig's and he had to breathe through his mouth because his nose was so stuffy. After a while, an irresistible urge to sleep came to him. He lay down, resting his head on his arm. He didn't think he'd sleep but amazingly, the next he knew a dog was snuffling nearby.

'What have you got, girl?' a man asked.

The dog wriggled through the bushes and greeted Gabriel, tail wagging. It was still dark, but not as dark as it would be in the country because of all the streetlights.

'Go away,' Gabriel hissed.

The dog continued to wag. There was a crunching and scuffling sound and then an old man's face appeared, as wrinkled as a scrunched-up piece of paper.

'Good morning, lad.' He didn't appear surprised to see Gabriel there.

When Gabriel didn't say anything, he went on. 'Good spot you chose. Out of sight, nice and quiet. But be warned, the park's people will be here when the sun comes up. I suggest you move unless you want to be found.'

Gabriel clambered to his feet, his limbs feeling stiff and cold. The man's face withdrew, along with the dog, but when Gabriel pushed through the bushes, he and his dog were still there.

'I don't know your situation,' the man said, 'but may I suggest you go to the café at the drop-in centre for homeless kids? It's warm and does a cracking bacon roll. They're good people. They'll look after you.'

Gabriel turned away.

'It's free, and you get a hot cuppa too. They won't force you to stay. Walk with me and have a look. If you fancy some grub, then in you go, and if you don't, then no harm done.'

The man reminded Gabriel of Maureen, who'd been so kind to him, buying him all that food. He was hungry, but not as hungry as he sometimes could be at the Golden Dawn, but even so. He was tempted.

'Come on, then.'

Which is how Gabriel had ended up at the Wild Dog drop-in centre, which wasn't just for the homeless, but a place which kids used like a kind of youth club. It was warm, though the dirty yellow walls and faded blue and grey curtains that hung on the windows made the place look pretty miserable. There was a pool table, some computers, and a TV in the corner. A tatty Christmas tree stood at the end of the café counter, along with some fake holly and ivy.

The café manager was called Ros and it was Ros who'd persuaded him to stay for Christmas. Like Maureen, his grandparents, and the old man, she was really nice, and when she realised he couldn't speak, she didn't seem to turn a hair. 'Let's call you Mog, after Mowgli. That okay? We can't keep saying Oi You, can we? You've heard of Mowgli?'

He shook his head.

'Mowgli was a boy who was brought up by wolves until hunters found him.'

He wanted to ask what happened next but when he opened his mouth, all that wanted to come out was a red-black rush of terror as he screamed Hannah's name.

'It's okay, Mog,' Ros said kindly. 'You're among friends here.'

The more people he met, the more he realised how much Father Luke had lied. Or was it all the Devil's work, and these people were all making him trust them so they could… what?

Ros showed him where he'd sleep before giving him a towel and pointing him to the shower. Squeaky clean, he was then given beans on toast and a huge mug of hot chocolate before being introduced to the other kids, most of whom flapped a disinterested hand except for a boy around his age, with freckles and eyes the colour of hemp who came to talk to him.

'I'm Robin.'

Gabriel gave a nod.

When Robin realised Gabriel had never seen a computer before, let alone experienced the internet, he showed him how it worked.

'You can look anything up. Try it. Put something in the search box, like pretty girls, or judo fighting, and see what happens.'

Awestruck, Gabriel quickly learned how to see videos, play games, watch YouTube, TikTok.

'It's child-protected so it's a bit dumb, but you can have fun if you want.'

It was Robin who showed him around the centre. Kitchen, utility, storerooms, bathrooms, dormitories. There was an attic, with a drop-down ladder, and a damp basement that smelled of mould and mice and was filled with tatty pieces of furniture, kids toys and plastic bags of who-knew-what. Tour over, the boys returned to the common room. Both computers were now occupied, so Gabriel pulled a book from the shelf, by someone called Lee Child, and started reading. It didn't take long before he was completely absorbed and had to be roused for lunch.

Later that day, a female police officer ducked her head around the door. 'Anyone called Gabriel here?'

Gabriel went rigid. All the blood seemed to drain from his head.

'Anyone?'

'Nah,' said one kid as another said, 'Nope.'

'Where's the boy who arrived this morning?' She was looking at a piece of paper, then back into the room.

Collectively, everyone in the room gave a shrug.

'Thanks so much.' The officer was sarcastic as she left.

His adrenaline spiked when Robin made to follow her, but Robin put a finger to his lips and whispered, 'Stay here.'

Robin was back within minutes. 'It's not you,' he said. 'The picture they've got is a drawing of some little kid dressed in one of those long robes Arabs wear.'

A djellaba.

A drawing. He remembered Mum sketching him from time to time. She'd drawn Hannah too. She'd said if she had a camera, she'd be taking loads of pictures of them so she could remember them as children after they'd grown up. He couldn't remember when she'd last drawn them. Two years ago? Three?

'The copper's gone,' Robin added.

In relief, Gabriel slumped in his chair. Closed his eyes. *Thank you, God.*

# 43

'There's a man in the woods, watching me,' Sid told Detective Kelly.

Kelly made a sound in his throat that could have been frustration or disbelief.

'What are you going to do about it?' she insisted.

'I will pass the information on to the relevant department.' His voice was stiff and formal.

'Which department?'

'I assure you I will do it straight away and you will hear from them directly.'

'I showed a constable the video I took in the basement, she said–'

'If you will excuse me, I have pressing matters to attend to.'

To her shock, he hung up.

She'd suspected he might be difficult – he'd sabotaged her investigation into her father's disappearance pretty effectively – but she hadn't thought he'd blank her.

If Kelly wasn't any use, then who could she go to? Sid phoned Tina, the FLO, to be told she was on holiday until the thirtieth, could anyone else help? Sid weighed up the pros and cons of talking things through with someone new, and when she decided it was too complicated, she called the Wiltshire Police instead and reported she was being stalked.

When she saw who turned up, Sid wasn't sure whether to groan or not. It was none other than Constable Norris, but at least this time she had a more cheerful-looking companion. Another woman, with red hair and a big smile.

'You've a stalker? Any idea who it is?'

'Never seen him before, but he's in the woods over there, pretending to be a birdwatcher.'

The man wasn't there but that didn't stop both officers prowling around the area. 'Looks like he's been here a while,' Norris remarked. 'Hopefully, he saw us and has been scared off for good.'

'Hopefully,' Sid agreed.

They started to walk back to the cottage.

'Did you show my video to your boss?' Sid asked.

'Yes.'

'What did they think?'

Norris glanced at her companion. 'We're checking it out.'

'To see if it's a deepfake.' Sid sighed.

Norris looked slightly discomfited as she gave a nod.

Sid watched them go, thinking. Why was the man watching her? Why did anyone undertake surveillance of another: to see what they did, where they went. Feeling surprisingly bullish, she bundled Tank into the back of her Jimny and went for a drive. She had no destination in mind, she just wanted to see if she was followed. It being Boxing Day, the roads were relatively busy, but not as busy as usual, and she meandered her way to Bath and beyond, keeping an eye on her rear-view mirror. After forty minutes and with a sense of relief, she told herself she wasn't really under surveillance and took the next left turn intending to turn around and backtrack. The instant she saw the road was clear, she swung the car around in a U-turn and at the same time, a gunmetal motorbike appeared. A huge bike with two panniers.

As it passed, she turned her head, catching the last three numbers of its number-plate: FLL.

It roared up the road, taking the next right and disappeared from view.

Sid stared.

It had to be the same motorbike she'd seen when visiting Harriet and then Liz at the Chalice Well. With the motorbike and the watcher in her wood, her every movement was being noted. Why?

It wasn't until she checked the news later that things began to fall into place.

Gabriel.

He was all over the news and the internet.

A breath escaped her, an audible gasp, as she read the scrolling script.

**BOMBER SURVIVES. NOW ON THE RUN.**

A teenage boy was wanted for killing dozens of people at Leicester Square Christmas Market, London.

The teenager had set off a deadly bomb in a vicious attack.

He may only be thirteen or fourteen years old, but he was responsible for every one of the brutal murders.

He had to be caught before he killed again.

The commissioner of the Metropolitan Police came onto her screen. Tightly cropped pewter-grey hair, bulldog jaw, hard grey stare. 'We will not rest until we find him. And we will find him, with the help of the British people.'

The stare seemed to pierce her soul.

'We need to find this sick and twisted boy, and find who supplied the bombs, and who organised these terrible, appalling attacks.'

Sid watched the news over and over again, along with the CCTV footage that had been released. It was on a continuous loop on several stations with a variety of commentators trying to make sense of it all. She watched as Hannah slipped her hand free from her brother's and ran, as fast as a whippet, away from him. She saw Gabriel running after her, colliding with a man who sent his Christmas present flying. She saw him hesitating between his fleeing sister and his Christmas present, his abandoning the present. The bomb blast. The devastation.

She leaned back in her chair. Watched a pair of sparrows flutter to her bird feeder then flutter away. She hadn't filled it since she'd been back.

Her mind filled with Gabriel's narrow, intelligent face. Against all odds, the kid was alive. Was that why Father Luke had healed her? In case Gabriel ran to her? It was, she realised with a lurch, the reason why Constable Norris had been sent to check on her cottage. *She'd been checking for Gabriel.*

The boy was, after all, the only surviving witness who could blow the whistle on Father Luke, and prevent Marc Strong from seizing control of the government. She put her head in her hands as she pictured herself going to the authorities. She was simply one tiny voice in an ocean of misinformation and deceit and without Detective Kelly onside, what chance did she have?

Depressed, Sid made herself some supper but when she came to eat it, and to Tank's delight, she'd lost her appetite.

'That had better not happen too often,' she told him as she scraped her meal into his bowl. 'Can't have you running to fat.'

She didn't sleep much that night and when she awoke, she felt bleary-eyed and tired. While the kettle boiled, she looked outside to see frost lay on the ground and that the bird bath had frozen. Not a bird in sight. Still in her dressing gown, she pushed her feet into a pair of wellies and filled the bird feeder. Back inside, she sipped her tea. Two minutes later, two blue tits zipped into view, grabbing a seed each before zipping back into the beech tree.

She wondered if the man in the woods had returned after the police had gone. Had he stayed on watch, freezing cold? Was he out there now? She didn't want to go and find out in case he turned nasty so she decided to enlist Toby to have a look later in the day.

Unsure what to do next, whether to use social media to get her story out or not, she considered those she might be able to trust. There was her oldest friend Aero, a variety of acquaintances, but the one person who popped into her mind was Win.

*Something wicked this way comes.*

She decided to head to Bath to do some shopping, and from there, contact Win and maybe see him, form some kind of plan to expose Father Luke and Marc Strong, as well as save Gabriel. Slightly cheered by her decision, she showered and dressed and dropped Tank at the farm. When she told Rachel that she was being watched by a fake birdwatcher, Rachel was horrified. 'I'll get Tobes to have a look when he comes in for lunch. He'll take his shotgun. Give him a scare if he can.'

Alarmed, Sid said, 'Don't let him do anything daft. I don't want Toby in jail. The police have had a look, I just want to know if the man's returned or not.'

Sid left Rachel dragging Tank – looking over his shoulder at her soulfully – inside the farmhouse, while she headed into town. The next hour was then spent buying another phone, and going through the same palaver with the SIMs before downloading the information from her old phone and reactivating the new one. Afterwards, Sid wandered around the city centre eyeing the sales, ending up in Waitrose and buying food and wine before heading to her car on the next level down. She'd just put her shopping in the passenger footwell when her phone rang.

*Number unknown.*

As usual, she answered without speaking.

'Sidney?' a woman asked. Clipped, cut-glass accent. 'Sidney Scott?'

'Yes.'

'It's Audrey here. Audrey Strong.'

Sid blinked. 'Hello, Audrey.'

'I was wondering if we might meet.' Her voice dropped. 'Confidentially, I mean. Just you and me.'

Sid's curiosity just about went through the roof. Was this about her husband lying to her? Or something more? 'Of course,' she said. 'I'm in Bath at the moment but–'

'Can you come to Chiselhampton?' The words were hurried and almost whispered. 'I'm doing the flowers in St Katherine's Church. I'll be there for the next couple of hours, but then I must get home.'

Sid checked Google Maps. 'I'm on my way.'

Audrey gave her directions where to park, which door to use to the church.

'I'll see you soon.' The woman's voice was heavy with relief. 'Thank you.'

# 44

S id was glad the weather was cold enough to keep the veggies and chicken relatively chilled until she got home. Driving past Bath Racecourse, she switched on the radio. A chat show; lots of people praising Marc Strong for promising to take a firm hold of the country, but when his *Little Blue Book* was mentioned, it got fairly short shrift, which gave her hope until she listened further. It appeared that although the older generation didn't like being told what to do, the younger generation thought the credit system a good idea.

'If you throw a takeaway carton out of your car window,' said one woman, a young professional, apparently, 'then being banned from having takeaways for a month will certainly teach you a lesson. There should be consequences for people who don't know how to behave.'

The sun came out when she left the M4 for the A34, but the vista was gloomy. The frost had melted, leaving sodden fields and leafless trees, stark hedgerows. Spring seemed a long way away.

The church wasn't in a village but faced a country road

with a manor house behind it and a farm nearby. After parking outside, she walked along the gravel path to the west door. The church was tiny, with stuccoed walls and a cornflower-blue door. The clock looked recently refurbished and was in matching blue with a shiny gold dial and dated1762.

Inside, it was cold and smelled of wood polish and freesias. Audrey was arranging flowers near the altar. Today she wore a neat pink suit with a white Peter Pan collar. Kitten heels and tiny pearl earrings completed the ensemble.

She put down her secateurs and walked down the aisle to Sid. 'Have you been here before? No? Well, John Betjeman honoured it in verse in 1952 and made a personal appeal for funds to support it…'

She chatted on, making Sid realise she was nervous. Finally, she opened a waist-high wooden door and stepped inside to take a pew, upon which sat a buff A5 envelope. Sid settled next to Audrey.

'Does your husband know I'm here?'

'Yes.'

Sid was surprised. 'I thought our meeting was confidential.'

'It is.' Audrey looked baffled. 'Between the three of us.' She folded her hands in her lap, gazed ahead at the gold cross on the altar. 'Marc wants to know something. It's quite simple.' Although her voice was steady, she began wringing her hands, distressed and fretful.

Sid stared at the minister's wife. 'What's that?'

'Where Gabriel is.'

Sid continued to stare. 'Do you know who Gabriel is?'

Audrey's jaw clenched. Her hands continued to twist.

Sid brought out her phone. Brought up the video. Passed the phone over. 'Do you know where I took this?'

As Audrey watched, her lips clamped together as though to prevent a scream.

'In the basement of the Golden Dawn.'

Long silence.

'You know what happened,' Sid said softly. 'You know it all, don't you?'

Audrey shook her head. She'd lost colour and her skin had taken on a sickly sheen. 'I... I had n-no idea.'

'Not until the deed was done.'

Audrey closed her eyes. 'He has to find Gabriel.' It was a bleat.

'To stop him from telling the truth.'

The woman kept her eyes firmly shut, but she gave a tiny nod.

'How does it feel, doing his dirty work?'

'G-Gabriel hasn't contacted you?'

'No.'

Audrey opened her eyes. Her expression was stark. 'If he does, will you let my husband know?'

*Absolutely not*, thought Sid, but instead she said, 'Why would Gabriel contact me? It's not like we know one another particularly.'

'You're the only person he knows outside the commune.'

'But that doesn't mean–'

'Marc spoke to Father Luke who said the boy showed an attachment to you.' Audrey leaned forward, suddenly animated. 'He knows Gabriel inside out. He will come to you.' Audrey brought out her mobile phone. 'This is Marc's number.'

As she recited it, Sid tapped it into her phone. Not that she planned on ringing him, but it was prudent to have it.

'Only thirteen people have his number, of which you

273

are one.' Audrey's eyes sharpened as she began to regain her poise. 'Do you understand the importance of this?'

Sid nodded.

'You will call Marc the second Gabriel contacts you.'

This time, Sid didn't nod. Just looked at Audrey flatly.

The women stared at each other. Audrey's poise began to falter. 'Please, Sidney.'

Sid remained motionless.

'It's not just Marc's life. It's mine. And the children's...'

'And the people who died?' Sid's tone was disbelieving as she gestured around the church. 'How in heaven's name can you reconcile yourself? And do it here, in the house of God?!'

Audrey's gaze moved past Sid's shoulder. Her whole body stilled. Sid saw her eyes flickering as she thought. Then her shoulders went back and her chin lifted, showing she'd come to a decision.

'He said you might be awkward.' Audrey's demeanour was now steady and strong. 'He isn't normally pushed into doing something like this, but if you don't do as he wants... what *we* want...' Audrey picked up the envelope beside her and opened it. Brought out a handful of photographs and passed them over. To Sid's shock, she saw they were of Toby and Rachel, their children. Toby's grandparents were there too.

'What the–'

'They have rather a big loan, your farmer friends. What if AgriCredit Corp, their financiers, hear of rumours that DEFRA are investigating them for illegal practices? What if AgriCredit demand foreclosure of the loan? What if they couldn't meet the full repayment?'

'No way.' Sid's voice came out several notes higher.

'What would happen to their herd of Jerseys, their dog breeding, their home?' Audrey's voice became more and more fierce. 'He means it, Sidney. He's not a man to be trifled with.'

'He can't go around threatening people!' Sid gave a bark of shocked laughter that echoed in the cold space. 'We're not in Russia, for God's sake!'

'He knows a lot of people of influence.' She tilted her head. Her expression was like ice, the compassionate woman vanished beneath a cape of self-protective fervour for her and her family. 'Marc knows judges, surgeons, police chiefs, CEOs of banks and multinational corporations. You name a profession, he'll find someone of influence to help him.'

Another threat. Sid's mind raced. Did he really hold that much sway? Or was it all hot air?

'So...' Audrey rose. Her expression was cold. 'Soon Gabriel will be in safe hands, yes?'

Sid rose and pushed open the pew door, walked through the echoing church and outside. On the top step, she turned and looked Audrey in the eye.

'Tell your husband to go fuck himself.'

# 45

After lunch, to his horror, Gabriel saw his picture on the TV. It was a video taken from above of him and Hannah as they walked to the Christmas market. They were holding hands. The picture then flipped and he was alone, running through the crowds before he got knocked by that man, making him drop his present before he ran on. He'd just disappeared out of view, when a massive white flash filled the screen. The next shot showed the devastation, the torn-apart tree, the flattened stalls, people sprawled on the ground.

The sound was turned off but he could read the words at the bottom of the screen. He was wanted for murder. The authorities believed it was his fault all those people, and Hannah, had died.

At the same time as his picture filled the screen – a pencil drawing of his face, unmistakably him – he pushed his mug onto the floor so it smashed into pieces. Everyone was immediately diverted. As far as he could tell, nobody had seen him on TV.

Terrified, not knowing what to do, he cleaned up his broken mug then went outside, onto the street.

He tried to pray but he was too panicky. His mind darted frantically, like a hare jinking from the hunt. He wanted to go to his grandparents, they'd help him, but Father Luke might be there, or one of the Brothers. He wanted his mother, his bed in the dormitory, his pile of pine cones and stones on his little table. He wanted Mum to give him a hug and tell him it was all right. As he thought of his mother, an anguished howl lodged in his throat. What would she say when he told her he'd lost Hannah? That if only he'd held onto her hand more tightly, anchored her to him, she'd be here today. Then another thought slipped through.

*If he'd held onto Hannah and Hannah had done as she'd been told, he would be dead too.*

Was Mum okay? Was she still in the san? Had she been told about Hannah? As he thought of his mother, he fingered her special ring buried deep in his front pocket. He wished she was here, her arms around him, pressing a kiss against his head, and suddenly, his mind split away, remembering Sid coming to him outside the manor house and giving him a hug. How she'd put her lips against his ear and whispered, *If you could, would you come with me?*

Before he lost his nerve, Gabriel went back inside the drop-in centre and when the computer became free, settled himself there, typed into the search box: *Sidney Scott.*

A whole load of pictures popped up, men as well as women and there she was, two rows down, with cropped hair and a smiling face. He clicked on the box and her face filled his screen. *Supernatural scientist. Ghostbuster. Contact Sid through her website, she'd love to hear from you.*

Gabriel asked Robin to show him how to set up an email address. He didn't use his own name Gabriel, but another Sid would recognise. Then he sent her a message.

# 46

Sid headed to collect Tank, her mind squirrelling over her meeting with Audrey. Why hadn't Marc Strong met her himself? Was it to tie Audrey in tightly to him and his hideous scheme? Or was he just too busy campaigning? Then she realised he wouldn't want to be seen anywhere near her, so he could discredit her if needs be. She found it repulsive that he'd kept his grand plan from his wife, springing it on her only when the chips were down. She guessed if Gabriel had died in the bomb blast, Audrey would be none the wiser and could have taken on the role of premier's wife with impunity, smiling through diplomatic cocktail parties oblivious to what she'd married.

When Sid arrived at the farm, it was to find Toby waiting for her. 'I went into the wood. Someone was there, but he ran off. I fired a shot after him, to give him fair warning.'

'You didn't.' She was shocked.

'I aimed wide, he wasn't in any danger. I doubt if he'll be back.'

'Oh, Toby.' She stepped forward and gave him a hug. 'You're a star. You really are.'

He cleared his throat. Patted her on the shoulder. 'Anytime, Sid. Just holler.'

When Rachel came out with Tank, Sid did a double-take. Rachel's eyes were rimmed with red. She'd been crying.

'Is everything okay?' Sid asked.

'It's nothing.' Toby was brisk.

Rachel shot him a look. 'So says Mr Optimistic. It's just that our finance company just rang.'

Sid felt a spike of dismay. 'What about?'

'Don't,' Toby warned Rachel, but his wife ignored him. 'He said it involved our tenant as well, remember? And we had to let Sid know because–'

'I don't want to worry Sid, it's our problem and–'

'She needs to know!' It was a shout. 'Because if AgriCredit foreclose our loan, she'll be homeless too!'

'He said he's *thinking* about it.' Toby was robust. 'He hasn't decided.' He turned a kind eye on Sid. 'So don't you worry. I'm sure it'll be fine.'

Sid drove away feeling as though she'd been punched in the gut. Marc Strong had moved unbelievably fast. She'd barely left his wife two hours ago which made her think he'd probably primed his AgriCredit contact, and all it had taken was a final call to tell the financier to press the potential destruct button on the farm.

*Fucking hell.* She hadn't honestly thought Marc Strong held as much influence as he'd have his wife believe but she'd been dreadfully wrong. He was a supremely ambitious man who'd no doubt garnered the right people in the right places to help him to the top. She couldn't help it; she began to cry as she bounced down the oh-so familiar track, muddy water splashing up her wheel arches, Tank emitting smells only a farmyard bullmastiff can.

She didn't want to lose her home.

She loved her little cottage and loved having Toby and Harriet as her landlords. They were her *friends* goddammit.

After feeding Tank, Sid poured herself a massive glass of the strongest red she could find. A fifteen per cent Argentinian Malbec that Aero had given her last time he'd visited. She'd barely taken a sip when her phone rang.

'Sidney.'

All the hairs on the nape of her neck rose. Marc Strong.

'If you hear from Gabriel, you will ring me. Yes?'

She couldn't see she had an option.

'Yes.' Her voice was a croak.

'Good.' She could hear the satisfaction in his voice. 'Then AgriCredit will hold on the foreclosure for the time being, but if you step out of line in any way whatsoever, they will act swiftly.'

He hung up.

Sid chugged down her glass of wine like it was water. She didn't eat. On the news, the newsreader announced that Marc Strong was gaining votes across the party, and he was now pulling well ahead of David Reville. The commentators reckoned Marc Strong was now a shoo-in.

Sid drank the bottle of Malbec in front of the TV, unable to think what she could do in the face of Marc Strong's seemingly all-pervasive power.

It was midnight before she went to bed. She was exhausted and drunk, but couldn't sleep. How had it come to this? A potential dictator in the wings, waiting to take control of the government, and what about Father Luke? He now had a congregation of over twenty thousand, and hordes of people were signing up to join the Golden Dawn, convinced he had a hotline to God, and could save them from their sins, their torment, their death.

She tossed and turned until she finally gave up and went and made herself some Ovaltine. Sitting at the kitchen table, she checked her messages to see two had come in from her website. One was a man wanting his sister's cottage in Wales 'de-haunted', as he put it, while the other was from someone called James T. Kirk wanting to meet up with her.

She stared and stared, horror crawling.

*No, no, no. It couldn't be, could it?*

Gabriel had said his mother had named him after the captain of the starship *USS Enterprise*. Captain James T. Kirk.

Stomach clenched, she shot a message back.

Who recommended you to contact me?

She didn't expect a reply; it was the middle of the night. But the response was immediate.

Nyota.

This time, her stomach did a backflip. Nyota Uhura, the Starfleet officer Hannah would have been named after if she hadn't had to take on a religious name.

It was Gabriel, no doubt about it.

Sid abruptly pushed her laptop away. Her heart was beating hard, nausea rippling through her. She wanted to weep, she wanted to scream. Before she could change her mind, she pulled her laptop towards her and typed:

I'm sorry, I can't help.

Fear and guilt swamped her. She started to sweat.

*Don't look at his reply. You are not responsible for him. You must think of Toby and his family. Your cottage, you and Tank.*

Sid refused to think about Audrey and how her compassion had vanished beneath a cape of self-protective fervour for her and her family.

She closed the lid of her laptop.

She wouldn't tell Marc Strong she'd heard from Gabriel, but nor was she going to help the boy. It was a cop-out, but it was all she was able to manage.

# 47

G abriel stared at Sid's message for a long time. It was quiet in the hostel, with everyone asleep, but he could hear the occasional car driving past, reminding him what Mum had said once. *Cities never sleep.*

He sent another, longer message to Sid, but he didn't hear back. Crushed, bewildered and frightened, he wondered what to do. So he prayed. He'd prayed a lot over the years and even though God apparently heard every word, Gabriel had never heard from Him, or seen a sign. Not that he'd ever told anyone that. He wouldn't have dared. On his knees, eyes tightly shut, he prayed for help, for guidance. Then, not wanting to appear selfish or ungrateful, he prayed for the world and all its troubles, and thanked God for the drop-in centre and the food in the kitchen.

Amen.

He knelt there for a while, considering his options. He decided he would stay here until the morning, in the warm, and after breakfast, head back to the park. But when the time came for him to leave and he saw the rain pouring down, Gabriel came up with another plan.

## 48

Over the next few days, Sid tried to get on with her life, but she struggled. Gabriel continued to message her, so she stopped checking her emails. She felt unmoored, adrift, as though someone had just died. She vaguely supposed she'd lost herself, that she was grieving for the woman who'd wanted to save Gabriel, stand up against Marc Strong and Father Luke, but had been bullied into submission.

*It will get better, with time.*

But it didn't get better. Guilt continued to haunt her from the shadows, dogging her heels, whispering Gabriel's name. The weekend came and went. Tank moved around her carefully, seemingly aware of the demon gnawing at her soul, and making her realise dogs were incredibly insightful in reading moods.

Monday morning, she expected to feel a bit brighter. But who was she kidding? She had to drag herself out of bed and force herself to get dressed when all she wanted was to curl up and pull the covers over her head. She couldn't feel like this forever, could she?

Knock-knock-knock.

She didn't even jump when Tank tore to the door, barking. She'd become strangely desensitised.

Sid opened the door to find Win standing on her doorstep. He held a bag of what looked like pastries and had a startled expression.

'Gosh, he's big.'

'Friend,' she told Tank as she let the dog's collar go. Tank gave a polite wag when Win said, 'Hello, boy,' and gave him a pat.

Sid said, 'What are you doing here?'

'I thought you might like breakfast.'

'Not particularly.'

'I might like a coffee?' He looked hopeful.

'Whatever.' She opened the door for him, finding she didn't really care. Win kicked off his boots and followed her inside, looking around curiously.

'Nice place,' he said. He peered at her Dali picture but didn't say anything, just held up the bag. 'Plates?'

She pointed at a cupboard and watched as he put the pastries out. Without asking, he went to her coffee machine and prepped it. Made them both a coffee. Sid drank her coffee but didn't eat. Just watched Win polish off several croissants with an obviously robust appetite.

'Something's happened, hasn't it?' He surveyed her steadily.

She looked away. Gave a shrug.

'It wasn't Father Luke,' he went on, 'because even though he pulled that stunt about curing you, it didn't knock you flat. It's something more recent.' His eyes were shrewd as he studied her.

She shrugged.

'Tell me, Sid.' His expression turned earnest. 'I can help, but I need you to start communicating.'

Slowly, Sid rose to her feet. 'You should go now.'

Win didn't move, but looked up at her. 'You know Marc Strong orchestrated the terror attacks.'

She didn't move.

'And that when they find that boy Gabriel, they will make sure he never speaks out.'

Another silence.

'Do you really want democracy to founder?' He continued to look at her. 'Do you want him and Father Luke, to *win*?'

Slowly, he stood. Her tiny kitchen accentuated how tall and broad he was. For a moment, she remembered her grief for her mother and how she made herself feel alive. She looked into his eyes. Deep brown, as brown as peat, with thick lashes. She dropped her gaze to his mouth. A tiny curl of desire unfolded deep inside her. Could she? Should she? She'd do anything to kill the deadness, the pain inside, even if it was only for a fleeting moment.

Infinitely slowly, she brought up a hand and touched his cheek. She could feel the faintest brush of bristles under her fingers. She let her thumb rest against the corner of his mouth and purposely licked her lips.

'Sid…' His voice was husky.

She slipped both hands around the back of his neck, bringing her body to rest lightly against his. The curl of desire began to grow and heat, and at the same time, the sensation of guilt and shame that had been dogging her began to dissipate.

'Er…' Win gently rested his hands on her waist. 'Is this a good idea?'

She raised herself up on tiptoe to wind herself against his body.

His eyes darkened. He made a groaning sound deep in his throat. 'I think…'

'Don't think,' she whispered. Her lips were an inch from his. Their breath mingled. He smelled of coffee and sugar.

He brought his hands up to hold her wrists. Gently brought them back to her sides.

'You want to,' she said.

'Oh, yes, I want to,' he agreed. He brushed the tip of her tattoo on the side of her neck with his fingertips, making her shiver. 'I want to see where this leads. I want to kiss every inch of you. But not like this. Not when you're in whatever weird space you're in. I want you to be with me one hundred per cent when I make love to you.'

Sid didn't move until he'd gone.

---

That evening, Sid didn't bother making supper. She poured herself a glass of wine and picked at the croissant Win had left. If she had to give herself advice, she'd tell herself to snap out of it, but the longer she left it, the bigger the shame at abandoning Gabriel.

*Do you want him and Father Luke, to* win?

She was pushing the remainder of the croissant into Tank's bowl when her phone rang. She answered it without thinking.

'Has he contacted you yet?' Marc Strong asked.

'No.'

'Don't you have *any* idea where he might be?'

'No.'

'What did Winstone Fairchild want?'

She felt a little shock in her system. 'What do you mean?'

'He came and saw you earlier.'

Another shock. 'That man's still there?'

'What man?' He sounded genuinely startled.

Marc Strong wasn't watching her? If not, then who was the man? And how had Marc Strong known Win had been here? She looked around. Recalled the burglary where nothing had been taken. Had a listening device been planted?

She had to unglue her tongue from the roof of her mouth it was so dry. 'It must have been a hunter. Out shooting pheasants.'

Small pause.

'You haven't answered my question.' He sounded impatient. 'What was Win–'

'We just had breakfast together.'

'He's wrong about Gabriel, you know. We won't hurt him. We just want him back at the Golden Dawn, with his mother and where he's safe.'

A little voice of rebellion spoke up: *Yeah, like I believe that.*

'You do know that Win's father was my tutor, back in the day?' When she didn't respond, he gave a chuckle. 'He hasn't told you? I wonder why not. Anyone would think he was hiding something.'

With that, Marc Strong hung up.

If things had been normal, she'd have been enraged that Marc Strong had eavesdropped on her conversation with Win earlier, but as it was, she simply felt even more helpless. She walked around her cottage, looking for listening devices beneath lampshades, behind pictures, but found nothing. She would, she decided, ring the alarm installer in the morning and see if he could help or recommend anyone. He'd been nice.

She went to bed early. She lay there for a long time, gazing bleakly into the darkness. After a while, she saw the curtains moving a little in the chill night-breeze. She thought she heard her name being called. Slipping out of bed she went to the window. Opened the curtain to see Gabriel standing in her garden, looking up at her.

*Please*, he said.

And then she had his hand in hers and they were running through the streets of Oxford, the sound of gunfire behind them. The streets vanished and they were in her cottage, Gabriel sitting at the kitchen table with her laptop, Tank at his feet. She was making eggs and bacon.

Then she woke up.

As sleep cleared, her consciousness becoming fully awake, she realised she wasn't alone. Her mother was standing at the side of the bed, looking down at her. Her father was at her side.

'I'm dreaming,' Sid spoke out loud.

'If that's what you want to believe.' Her mother gave a small smile while her father rolled his eyes.

'It's the truth,' Sid insisted.

'Semantics,' Dad said. 'All that matters is that we're here, and want you to know we'll be with you when you fight the bastard.'

'Michael.' Mum's voice was chiding.

'She's got to fight! She can't let that man win.'

'Your father's right.' Mum was nodding. 'You've got to stand up to him, dearest Sid, no matter what the cost. You know you can do it. You have the courage and the wit.'

'But I'm scared,' Sid admitted.

'Of course you are! Who wouldn't be? But Gabriel needs you, and you need him too.'

Sid struggled up. 'What happened to you, Dad?'

'Ask Leah.'

She heard Tank wander in, felt him pushing his nose into her hand as though asking who she was talking to. She expected her parents to vanish but instead they smiled.

Her mother blew her kisses. 'We're always with you, darling.'

Then they were gone.

'Fuck.' She switched on her bedside lamp. Squinting in the sudden light, she looked around the room, then at Tank, who was blinking. 'Did you see them? No, because if you did, you would have barked, wouldn't you?' She pushed the covers back and put on her father's robe. It was, she saw, four o'clock in the morning but she felt wide awake and energised.

She'd had a waking dream, just as she'd had in her delirium at the Golden Dawn. Her psyche needed the love and protection of her parents, as well as approbation and encouragement, and so she'd, literally, called them up out of her subconscious.

'Just in case you're really there,' she said, 'thanks Mum, thanks, Dad. I needed a kick up the arse.'

## 49

The alarm installer found two listening devices in her cottage, one in the kitchen, the other in the sitting room. They were tiny, one tucked between a photograph and its frame, the other simply popped into the top of a bowl of feathers and shells on the windowsill.

Outside, the alarm guy said, 'You want me to disable them?'

'No.' Marc Strong would only replace them. 'I'll move them whenever I make any sensitive calls.'

With the bowl and photograph firmly outside, Sid started contacting everyone she knew in the media, including everyone who'd "liked" her video of Father Luke's healing scam, saying she had something far more damaging and far-reaching she wanted to share. She didn't use overly emotive words like emergency, crisis or catastrophe, or anything along those lines, because people had become desensitised. What she was hoping for, was that people who'd opened her initial video of Father Luke's scam would simply be curious enough to open her second video, and she'd take it from there. And, cross fingers, watch it go viral.

She planned on interviewing Gabriel and posting this third video across social media as well as sending it to every TV and radio station she could think of. All she needed was to secure one interview, and the whole world would want to see the boy and hear what he had to say.

Gabriel was the only surviving bomber.

Who wouldn't want to interview him?

But she had to get to him, and secure his safety first.

She'd considered asking Win for help, but she couldn't put aside Marc Strong's voice, his smug chuckle.

*You do know that Win's father was my tutor, back in the day? He hasn't told you? I wonder why not. Anyone would think he was hiding something.*

A Google search showed her that Win's father, Christopher Fairchild, eighty-one, was one of Marc Strong's most loyal supporters.

*Fuck.*

What did this mean? Was Win trustworthy or not?

As Sid ran over each conversation with Win, she realised how cagey he'd been with her, right from the start. She remembered the way something guarded had risen in his eyes when she'd asked him what he'd been doing in Bristol.

*I work here.*

*Clan Capital.*

*That's right.*

Anxious, apprehensive, she googled Clan Capital.

*A strong and leading wealth management team. Our clients enjoy the qualities of a large, friendly management firm while benefiting from our team's experience...* blah, blah. Sid checked where their offices were. London, obviously. Oxford, Birmingham, Manchester, Glasgow. Not Bristol.

Sid called Clan Capital's main number, asked to speak to Winstone Fairchild. 'He's also known as Win.'

'Winstone or Win Fairchild,' a brisk voice confirmed. 'Which office, please?'

'I can't remember, sorry. It's in the UK, though.'

'Please hold.'

Sid found herself holding her breath.

'I'm sorry, madam, we don't have anyone by that name on our records.'

Sid hung up. *Shit.* He didn't work for Clan Capital. He'd lied.

And then she remembered asking Marc Strong if he knew Win. Oh God. Marc Strong had said no, but he'd lied. The men knew one another.

Then there was Detective Kelly. *He's not all that he seems... be careful.*

She wanted to scream. She desperately wanted to call Win, lean on him – she didn't want to do this alone – but there were too many variables. She couldn't risk Gabriel's safety.

Dragging her courage up from the soles of her feet, she put the first part of her plan into place by going into Bath and withdrawing five thousand pounds. When she was asked what it was for, she had a moment of madness, wanting to reply, *I'm going on the run with the surviving London bomber.* Instead, she asked why the teller wanted to know.

'It's just to make sure you're not being coerced in any way.'

'Nope. I just need it to pay a couple of bills.'

The teller weighed the money and popped it in an envelope for her.

Sid then bought two phones, with cash. Pay-as-you-go, they were active immediately. In Urban Outfitters, she bought a handful of clothes for Gabriel. In Next, some underwear and socks, a sleep T-shirt and shorts. Finally, she went to Topping bookshop and bought two books.

Back in the cottage, she sat and brought together her plan. Looked it over several times. It was fraught with difficulty and danger, but it was the best she could come up with.

She then went to her laptop and logged into her emails. Read each of Gabriel's messages. They'd all been sent between midnight and 4am, so she waited until midnight and this time, she replied with a plan.

# 50

The first day Gabriel spent hidden in the basement scared him half to death. Every creak upstairs, every voice calling, every footstep had his heart leaping from his chest, convinced Father Luke and the Brothers were coming to get him.

The room was gloomy, the light leaching through a barred window filmed with grime. He put his hands round each bar and gave them a heave – he'd have liked an emergency exit – but they didn't move.

*Camp Fire Yarn. No. 3*
   *The Scout Law*
   *A Scout smiles and whistles under all difficulties.*

He didn't feel like smiling and he couldn't whistle in case he was heard, but he decided to keep busy by going through the piles of bin bags and tidying things up. Come the afternoon he was busting for a pee, and although he told himself he'd have to wait, he quickly realised he'd have to make do, and managed to unearth a kid's plastic bucket, which he peed into before sticking it in the far corner.

When darkness fell, and everything quietened, everyone asleep, he crept into the kitchen and grabbed some food. Then he tiptoed to the common room, and used the computer. When dawn broke, he took a couple of books to the basement and spent the day reading and sleeping. That became his routine. He didn't think beyond each segment of his self-imposed confinement. He simply existed day by day, night by night, and tried not to think about his mother, or Hannah, or Father Luke, who had given him and Hannah their Christmas presents – the bombs – because each time he did his skin felt as though it was burning, his heart about to explode.

He continued to pray, trying to be grateful to Him, that he had shelter and food. He blessed Maureen and Ros, and Robin the hemp-eyed boy, careful to show he was grateful so as not to cause God's wrath.

*Camp Fire Yarn. No.22*
  *In doing your duty to God always be grateful to Him.*

It was tipping down outside, not long before dawn one day, when Sid's message came in. He just about leapt from his chair and ran around the common room shouting with excitement.

She'd contacted him, at last!

It was a formal-sounding message about her costs for her business, what he might expect if he employed her, but in the last sentence, she asked what his favourite book was. He didn't know what she meant by it, and for a moment, he dithered. He was pretty sure it was *Boy Scouting*, but he didn't want her to think it was childish, so he chose something else.

*The Catcher in the Rye.*

He'd only read it twice because it had been confiscated as being 'inappropriate'. Brother Isaac had snatched it from him asking where he'd got it from, and he'd lied, saying he'd found it. No, he'd told the Brother, he couldn't remember where. No, he hadn't read it. He'd only read the first page. Brother Isaac had stared at him hard but Gabriel hadn't flinched. He hadn't wanted Mum to get into trouble.

*The Catcher in the Rye.*

Now, Sid said:

```
Good choice. Mine's Pat Barker's The
Silence of the Girls. Know it?
```

```
Sorry, no.
```

```
I like crime and mystery too. What
about The Grey Man? I love that book.
You can read the first few chapters
on Amazon. Let me know what you
think.
```

Baffled, but willing to go along, Gabriel looked it up. The novel resembled its title, dull and uninspiring, but once he'd started, he was gripped. It was a spy story, and in the third chapter, his breathing froze. The spy character detailed an easy message code, where two people had a copy of the same book and used it to message one another.

Excitement nipping his belly, he went back to Sid.

```
There's barely three chapters. Is it
long enough for me to know if I like
it or not?
```

```
Let's try another.
```

Sid gave him an alternative book title.

When he checked it out, he saw the free "look inside" for this particular book seemed to go on forever.

```
It looks interesting
```

*I know it's fantasy, but it's a great read. 23, 4, 3, 48, 22, 6.*

The numbers seemed to go on for ever, and then she said:

```
God, sorry, my dog jumped up onto my
keyboard and it ran away with me.
```

Gabriel decoded the numbers as fast as he could to see Sid's secret message.

```
Let's use this book to talk. If you
understand, respond with the word:
cockroach.
```

Gabriel typed back.

```
Good job it was a dog and not a giant
cockroach.
```

It took some time, sending coded messages back and forth, but thankfully dawn was still an hour away by the time they'd finally settled on a plan. She was going to meet him in the park, where he'd hidden originally and where the old man's dog had found him, in five hours.

9am.

Gabriel decided to go to the rendezvous early. He didn't want to risk not being there when Sid arrived. Besides, he guessed it was probably best if he went when it was dark. When the time came, he carefully crept through the centre. He plucked a waterproof jacket from the rack by the door, along with a woolly hat, and he was reaching for the upper bolt on the front door when a voice behind him said, 'What are you doing here?'

# 51

Sid had already packed. She hadn't used a suitcase or anything that might be construed to be an overnight bag, but put her things in a couple of cardboard boxes. She wouldn't need much. She was already cashed up, having been to the bank yesterday.

Now, she left the cottage. She purposely left her phone behind – she didn't want to be tracked – but put the two new pay-as-you-go phones into her handbag.

She dropped Tank with Toby, and asked Toby for a favour.

'Sure,' he said. 'You know I'll always help.'

'I know who's stalking me,' she said. 'Some guy I met through work. He's not just watching me, but following me too.'

'Jesus, Sid.' He looked horrified. 'What can I do?'

When she told him what she wanted, Toby agreed without hesitation. 'Happy to help.'

Cardboard boxes in the back of her Jimny, Sid drove to the SouthGate Shopping Centre car park in Bath. She parked before returning to wait out of sight, near the entry ramp. When Toby arrived ten minutes later, she stepped into his sight and he stopped, picked her up. He drove to her car, where she decanted her boxes into his Land Rover.

'Give me five minutes before you leave,' she said, passing him the Jimny's keys.

'Okey-dokey.'

Sid drove the Land Rover out of the car park and parked it on Brassmill Lane, where Toby would see it when he turned off the A4 in her Jimny. Donning a baseball cap, she walked to the Europcar offices and hired a Ford Focus. She used cash. She had to give them her driver's licence details, but at least if anyone was watching her credit card transactions, nothing would show. Going off-grid was practically impossible these days; all she could do was buy time.

Back in the city centre, with a spare cap in hand, Sid finally headed for Green Park. She was early, but then Gabriel might be early too. As she approached, it started to rain and she pulled up her waterproof hood. The park was empty when she arrived. It was small, barely three acres, its west side bordered by handsome Georgian houses. There was a play park and a sloping area that led to the river. She spotted the clump of shrubs at the far end that Gabriel had mentioned, and walked casually over.

A quick glance around showed just one man, walking his spaniel at the far end. She called, 'Gabriel,' a few times, but he didn't answer. Sid pushed her way through the bushes, rainwater dampening her jeans. She found the patch of ground he'd told her he'd slept on, but no sign of the boy.

Tucked in her waterproof, rain pattering all around, Sid settled in to wait.

# 52

'Mog,' Ros said. 'How on earth did you get in?'

He stood frozen. She was standing there in an enormous padded dressing gown the colour of raspberries. She had pink fluffy slippers on her feet.

'Is it you who's been eating the food?'

He wanted to say sorry, but although he opened his mouth, no words came out.

'Look, it's tipping down out there.' She moved back a little. 'Come into the kitchen and I'll make us tea and toast.'

He shook his head. Reached for the top bolt and pulled it free. Did the same with the lower, but when he turned the door handle and pulled, the door was locked.

'Looking for this?' Ros held up a large, brass key.

He felt like screaming. How could he have been so stupid?

Ros put the key in her pocket. Cocked her head. 'Marmalade on your toast? Or would you like an egg?'

Stomach writhing like a bag of eels, he affected nonchalance and shrugged.

'Egg, then. Let's make it two.'

Gabriel followed her into the kitchen. As soon as Ros opened the door at eight o'clock, he'd be gone. It was only ten minutes' walk to the park. He'd still be early for Sid. He watched Ros move around the kitchen, fetching bread and eggs, butter, a frying pan. She switched on the radio. A man was talking about the weather, how it was going to rain for the next few days.

Ros waved a spatula at Gabriel, indicating he should sit. He sat and watched her crack the eggs into a hot pan, put on the toast. She kept giving him sidelong glances. When she put the plate in front of him he wanted to thank her, but his throat wouldn't work.

'Tuck in,' she said brightly. 'I'll be back in a tick.'

Gabriel hadn't had anything hot to eat in an age and the eggs were delicious. He scraped his plate clean with a piece of bread, then buttered another two slices and ate them too. When Ros returned, he got to his feet to help her wash up.

'You don't have to do that.' She looked surprised.

He ignored her, washing the pan and his plate, the utensils. Ros dried. He was discomfited when she continued looking at him.

'Where are you from?'

He shrugged.

'Have you always been mute?'

At that, he paused and looked into her eyes. They were a soft hazel with green flecks. Really pretty. He thought of his screams and howls he'd bottled inside and shook his head.

'Oh, Mog.' Her face scrunched up. 'I'm so sorry.'

He looked at the clock above the cooker. It was already past eight but she'd made no move to unlock the door. Anxious, trying not to show it, he drank his tea. Watched Ros as she made herself a coffee.

They both jumped when someone banged on the front door.

'I'll get it.' Ros's voice turned funny as she walked outside. He couldn't say why, but he didn't trust it, so he followed her quietly. Saw her open the door and at the same time as she said, 'He's inside, in the kitchen,' he took in the uniformed policemen – two, no *four of them* – and then he was turning and running down the corridor, footsteps pounding after him. 'Stop!' a man yelled. 'Police!' shouted another.

Gabriel hared into the common room, heading for the window. He knew it was locked but still, he ran at the glass full tilt. There was nowhere else to go but through it.

*Camp Fire Yarn. No. 21*
  *Never say die till you're dead.*

He'd barely passed the computer table when he felt something slam into him from behind. He crashed onto the floor, all the wind knocked out of him. A man lay on top of him. He was saying over and over, 'Got you, you little fucker. You *fucker.*'

Gabriel closed his eyes, purposely slumping his body.

A woman said, 'You do not have to say anything, but it may harm your defence if you do not mention when questioned something which you later rely on in court...'

He heard more footsteps in the room, radios crackling, people saying, 'We got him,' and, 'Christ, it really *is* him, isn't it.'

He slowed his breathing. Felt his heartbeat begin to level out.

'Anything you do say may be given in evidence. Do you understand?'

Gabriel thought about Sid, her beautiful violet eyes.

She'd said if he was late, she'd wait for him. She'd said if he didn't turn up today, she'd wait every day at 9am until he came to her. He didn't want her to have to wait, though. The longer he was delayed, the more danger she might be in.

'Do you understand?' The woman's voice hardened.

Gabriel kept the vision of Sid in his mind.

'Hey, you.'

He felt the man's hands lift his shoulders and drop him back down. Gabriel's cheek smacked into the floor but he didn't make a sound, give any indication he'd felt it. He'd learned not to show pain from Father Luke. If you grimaced or whimpered, he just hit you harder.

'Fuck. I don't believe it. He's out fucking cold.'

Gabriel felt a woman's cool fingers on his cheek then against his neck, testing his pulse.

'You hit him bloody hard, Stew.'

He felt the man ease off his back. 'Shit. He's breathing, yes?'

'Yep. Pulse okay too.'

'Hey.' The man's face was near Gabriel's. He could smell coffee on his breath. 'Wake up, you sod.'

When Gabriel didn't respond the man said, 'Fucking wake up or I'll get my taser out and give you a shock so hard your heart will be juddering for the next week.'

'Stew…' The woman's voice was warning.

'He heard me,' the man hissed.

Gabriel didn't know what a taser was but the threat was real. Panic began to rise inside him like steam from a kettle. He forced his mind to his scout book. Recited the paragraph about courage.

*The thing is, when you are facing danger, don't stop and look at it but take the plunge, throw yourself boldly at it, and it won't be half so bad as it looked, once you are in it.*

'He should have come around by now.' The woman sounded worried.

'Fuck.'

'Should we call an ambulance?' A new voice spoke up. 'If we let anything happen to him, we'll be totally fucked.'

A short pause.

'Call it,' the man snapped. He got to his feet. 'Fuck, fuck, *fuuuuuuck.*'

Gabriel pictured the man clutching his head, expression infuriated but as he did so, he could feel his pulse begin to rise so he brought back the image of Sid, her smile, the way she'd whispered to him. Another part of him was aware of people moving about, the chink and clunk of belts and metal, but his mind was full of Sid.

Then he heard a siren closing in.

'Stand back,' the man said. 'Give the boys 'n' girls a clear run.'

A flurry of movement. The siren was silenced.

Carefully, slowly, Gabriel took a deep breath. Then another. Tensed his muscles. Nobody seemed to notice. He tensed them further, readying himself.

Urgent footsteps. Voices saying, 'He's breathing?' 'Yes.' 'You check his vitals and I'll…'

Gabriel brought his feet under him and sprang up. He didn't look left or right. He simply put his head down and accelerated straight for the window.

'Fuck!'

'Stop him!'

A uniform lunged at him but he was going too fast and was past them in a flash.

'STOP!'

Three more paces and he was using the sofa as a springboard. Right shoulder down, he squeezed his eyes shut, pursed his lips, and as he launched himself over the radiator for the window, he covered his head with both arms and brought his knees into his chest, doing his best to make himself as round and hard as possible.

Gabriel smashed through the window like a giant football. He plummeted onto the pavement, his right shoulder taking the brunt, and for a moment, couldn't move. He felt stunned and winded, but he forced himself up and began to stagger down the street. He was completely unaware of the cuts on the backs of his hands, his scalp and ears, his knees, and that blood was beginning to pour.

'STOP!' A scream behind him. Footsteps hammered. They were *so close*.

Adrenaline poured into his system seeming to give him wings. He didn't look behind him. He ran as fast and straight as an arrow for Green Park.

# 53

Sid heard a distant siren but decided not to show herself. Her pulse was up, her attention sharp as she listened but all she could hear was the rattle of rain on her hood. Gradually, however, she became aware of shouting and to her dismay, realised it was coming her way.

Then she heard more sirens.

Carefully, she edged her way out of the shrubbery and to her disbelief, saw Gabriel tearing through the park gates. Just outside the park were two police officers giving chase, chests out and legs pounding, and behind them, several more.

Two police cars stopped with a spray of water by the park railings, disgorging more police. Gabriel was running for her and she began to run for him, she couldn't think what else to do, and then she heard the roar of a motorbike. More shouts as a big grey motorbike muscled its way past the police vehicles and entered the park, slewing its way across the grass, spraying a rooster tail of mud.

Gabriel reached her, blood pouring down his face, his

eyes wild. Sid swung him behind her, wanting to protect him from the police pounding towards them, but the motorbike overtook the police and to her disbelief, slithered to a halt between her and the cops.

'Get on the bike!' the rider yelled. 'Sid first! Gabriel, hang on as best you can!'

Sid could barely believe it. It was Win. It was his voice, his dark eyes urgent behind his rain-streaked visor.

'Quick!' he shouted.

There didn't seem to be enough room for three but Sid threw a leg over the machine and felt Gabriel do the same, clinging to her back like a monkey. Win twisted the throttle and the motorbike skidded horrifyingly to the side, unbalanced, and Sid clutched Win's middle, thinking, *No! Please don't fall over!*

It was as though the motorbike heard her. The rear tyre dug into the earth, Win twisted the handlebars, and they were upright, surging around the police and powering for the gate. Police sirens blared, their blue lights twirling. Two officers stood in the gateway, hands raised in a STOP position but Win didn't slow down. Instead, he increased his speed, aiming straight for them. Sid was yelling, 'Get out of the way!' and at the last second they sprang aside, their faces white, mouths open in a shout she couldn't hear above the roar of the motorbike.

They swung left and past the police cars, who'd have to turn around to follow them, and roared north briefly, flashing through two red lights before swinging left onto the Upper Bristol Road and accelerating hard. She could feel the vibrations of the bike's engine in her body, her handbag against her hip, Win's leather jacket bunched in her hands, Gabriel's knees gripping her waist, his arms around her chest. She could hear the tyres heavy *shhh* through the spray, the sirens behind them. She saw the rain ahead and the spatter turned into heavy drops. She squinted as they roared down the middle of the road, oncoming traffic inches away.

*Fucking hell.* He was going fast. She moved her hands so her arms were around his waist as she clung on. Her hood had been flung back and her hair was plastered against her skull, her face stinging from the rain. They thundered past Victoria Park's children's playground and as they approached the next traffic lights, Win used his horn in a long, unbroken blast. Traffic scattered, and then they were through.

The rain came down harder as he dropped a gear, slowing to turn left into Locksbrook Road. Warehouses flashed past. Electrical and plumbing supplies, printers, cabinet makers. As they neared Brassmill Lane, Sid had the wild thought they were going to pick up her car, which Toby would have left there when he'd collected his Land Rover, but then Win braked hard, compressing Gabriel and Sid against him, and turned abruptly into a garage selling used cars.

Ahead, an elderly man in overalls stood beside an open garage door. He gave no indication he'd heard the sirens blazing and when they'd bounced inside the garage, he lowered the door behind them.

Win didn't turn off the engine. He turned his head. 'Off,' he said sharply. 'Quick as you can.'

Sid and Gabriel clambered to the ground. Her jeans were soaked and her legs felt soft. She was trembling all over.

'Bert–' he jerked his chin at the man in the boiler suit, '–will give you the necessaries. I'm going now. Let them give chase.'

Bert was already at the far side of the garage, raising a roller door. Win snapped his visor shut and rumbled his motorbike to the door, and then he was through. Bert quickly lowered the door behind him.

Sid turned to Gabriel. His mouth was open, his eyes blank with shock. He was soaking wet. Blood seeped from a variety of cuts. Like her, he was shaking from head to toe. Instinct made her step forward and wrap him in her arms. It was like hugging a surfboard but she held him close and murmured, 'Wow, Gabriel. You're amazing. I can't believe you can run so fast, or how brave you are.' She continued to hold him, crooning assurances until gradually, his muscles relaxed. Another minute or so and he raised his arms and put them around her waist, pressed his cheek against her breastbone.

She heard police sirens closing in, getting louder and louder. She found herself gripping Gabriel tighter as they approached, and then they were past, and fading into the distance.

She closed her eyes, shuddering. She could barely believe they'd got away.

'Sidney.' Bert's voice was soft.

Sid looked over Gabriel's sodden head at Bert. He was in his eighties, she guessed, with wide shoulders and eyes as beady and bright as a blackbird's.

'Sid,' she managed. 'My friends call me Sid.'

He smiled. 'Sid. We need to tend to Gabriel.'

'Yes.'

Bert walked to a set of shelves lining one side of the garage. Returned with a first aid kit and a bottle of mineral water. Dragged over a metal chair. 'Son, I have to see to your injuries. You need to take off your jeans and sit on the chair.'

Sid started to move away to give Gabriel some privacy, but Gabriel simply did as he was told. Together, Sid and Bert dabbed the boy's wounds clean before applying antiseptic, then plasters and bandages where needed. He didn't flinch, didn't say a word. When Gabriel was dressed once more, Bert handed Sid a set of car keys. 'The Porsche.' He pointed at a beefy matt-grey SUV-style vehicle facing away from them. He then passed her a set of house keys. 'Win's place. Meadow Barn. He says you've been there before but I've programmed it into the satnav.' Finally, he offered her a mobile phone.

'It's okay,' she said. 'I have a couple with me.'

'Can I give you Win's number?'

'Of course.'

'And mine. Just in case. I may be old, but I can still be useful.'

In a normal situation, she would have smiled and said something kind, but she simply gave a nod. She gave him the number of one of her phones. She didn't, however, give Bert the number of the second phone. She thought it prudent to remain cautious.

Briefly, Sid went online. Checked a couple of things before buckling Gabriel into the passenger seat of the Porsche. He still hadn't said a word, but she let him be. He'd been through too much for her to start badgering him. Sid started the engine. Smooth and powerful. Bert cranked open the garage door and she drove out. But instead of following the satnav's directions to Meadow Barn, which was seventy miles north-east of Bath, she headed in the opposite direction.

# 54

Sid arrived at the Chalice Well at 2.30pm. She would have loved to have gone to Win's place, but until she had answers to all her doubts over him, she thought it safer to keep a distance, especially with his father being such a loyal supporter of Marc Strong's. What if he found out she was at Meadow Barn with Gabriel and told Marc Strong? It didn't bear thinking about.

The garden was open every day, but nobody was there; it was still chucking it down. Telling Gabriel to stay in the car, Sid went to the healing centre which, being Sunday, was closed. She went to the front door and the keypad lock.

Liz's voice: *He'd come here to "rest"... even when we were closed. We ended up changing the lock codes to his birth-date so he could always have access.*

Owen Evans's date of birth had been easily found on the internet and now Sid punched in the code, and slipped inside. Silence all around. A faint aroma of incense drifted along with the patter of rain against the windows. Quietly, Sid padded across the sisal floor, taking in the twin sofas facing each other across a glass coffee table, the bronze buddha on the reception desk, the quotes on the walls.

Radiate boundless love towards the entire world.

Give, even if you only have a little.

She explored the centre, checking each room. There were massage tables and shiatsu mats, peace lilies, rubber and spider plants in every corner, no doubt breathing life into every room and adding a calming vibe to each space. She checked out the crystal room, where Owen had 'rested' to find a chaise longue, more plants, and a chrome shelving unit covered in crystals and gemstones. A pair of natural amethyst quartz crystals stood on either side of the window.

The kitchen boasted a kettle and a cupboard of herbal teas and groceries. There were packs of nuts and seeds, nut butters, flatbreads, soy milk, muesli. Enough for her and Gabriel to survive the day. She went and fetched him inside. They were both still soaked from their motorbike ride and she turned the heating up, suggesting they put what clothes they could on the radiators to dry. Then she headed to make them both tea. When she offered him sugar, he nodded.

'One spoon, or two?'

He put up two fingers.

She threw some food together, put it on the coffee table. Together, they sat on one of the sofas, eating and drinking their tea. Gabriel may not be talking at the moment, but at least he had an appetite. Afterwards, he curled up and, with a cushion under his head, fell asleep. Sid felt fatigue aching in every bone and muscle, but the dreadful wheel of her mind wouldn't let her rest. She had to get her timings right. First, she had to post the video of the bombs being made at the Golden Dawn. Second, secure an interview on the TV with Gabriel. Or should it be simultaneous? She leaned her head against the back of the sofa and closed her eyes. She didn't think she'd ever been so tired. She needed to sleep. Even if it was only for ten minutes, it would help.

Mercifully, she began to move toward sleep but just after she let go, her limbs jerked and adrenaline poured into her system at the memory of the police racing after Gabriel and straight towards her. She sat up, heart lurching, careful not to wake the boy.

How could she secure a TV interview if Gabriel wasn't speaking?

Once again, she closed her eyes. This time, she slipped into unconsciousness.

She felt as though she'd barely been asleep when she heard the bang of a door and a man say, 'What the... Hello? Hello?'

Sid sat bolt upright, blinking in the sudden light. Darkness had fallen outside and the man had switched on the lights. He had a sharp brown goatee and a whip-narrow build. He was staring at her and Gabriel, who was also sitting upright, hair in tufts, and blinking like a startled owl.

'Who are you?' the man demanded. 'What are you doing here?'

Sid swiftly rose and grabbed her jeans, tossed Gabriel his.

'Sorry,' said Sid, pulling on her jeans. 'We got caught in the rain.'

'So it seems.' The man was eyeing them suspiciously.

'We're friends of Liz.' Sid looked at her watch. 'We were

supposed to be meeting her at her home but...' She gave a self-conscious chuckle. 'We fell asleep.'

The man brought out a phone and dialled. His eyes roved over Gabriel and his array of plasters and bandages. 'Liz?' he said. 'I have two people here, kind of camping out in the centre, who say they know you...' He arched his eyebrows at Sid.

'Tell her it's Sid and Owen.'

He repeated their names into the phone. 'Oh. I see.' He blinked several times. 'Well, in that case, I'll see you soon.' He put the phone back into his pocket. 'She's on her way. I'm sorry I, er...'

'Doubted us. I can't say I blame you.' She gave him a rueful smile which he returned carefully. 'I'll tidy up. Wait for Liz.'

The man nodded but she didn't like the way he was studying Gabriel. 'Come on, Owen,' she said. 'Give me a hand, would you?'

Obediently, Gabriel began to help tidy away the plates and food detritus. The man watched them briefly, and then said, 'Well, then,' rather crossly, and walked out of reception and down the corridor.

Liz arrived half an hour later in a flurry of bangles and raindrops that clung to her shoulders and hair. 'Well,' she said brightly. 'You both. Whatever have you been up to? Let's get you into the treatment room, shall we?'

Liz sat Sid and Gabriel side by side on a massage table and stood before them, arms crossed. 'So,' she said.

'So,' Sid repeated. She was sweating lightly, unable to work out how much to tell Liz, how much to trust her.

'Oh,' Liz said, suddenly glancing aside and looking surprised. 'Oh, I see.' Liz turned back to look at Sid. 'Cyfrin says you must have complete faith in me.' Her gaze was earnest.

*Bloody Cyfrin*, Sid thought, and even though she felt stressed to the max, found herself mentally rolling her eyes.

'And he says that even though you don't believe in him, he believes in you and you *have to trust me.*'

Sid knew that Liz was using her cold-reading techniques to read her anxiety, but as she gazed into Liz's ardent blue gaze, she took a leap of faith.

'This is Gabriel. He's from the Golden Dawn.' Sid brought out her phone and showed Liz the video of the bombs being made. 'I took this when I was in the basement of the commune.' She went on to describe her incarceration and as she spoke, she could feel Gabriel's intense gaze on the side of her face. 'I thought I was going to die, but then they stopped force-feeding me whatever drug it was and let me recover. Father Luke then "healed" me. I went home to discover the world I knew had been turned upside down. That the prime minister had been forced to resign. That Marc Strong looks likely to become the next leader.'

Liz listened without interrupting, expression intent. 'You're saying the entire thing was planned by those two men.'

'Yes.'

Her gaze deepened. 'I wish I'd never given them that reading when they were boys.'

'You can't say you're responsible for what's happened. If it hadn't been you, it would have been something else that would have triggered them.'

'Even so.' Liz looked past Sid's shoulder. 'Come home with me now. You can organise yourselves from there.'

'I don't want to put you at risk.'

'I already did that when I tried to teach those boys a

lesson and it backfired.' Liz was robust. 'Time for me to make amends.'

---

Liz's home was a maisonette in a converted school. She shared a front door with four other flats, but also had a door that exited her home through her leafy courtyard and to the street behind. Two bedrooms, a study and bathroom upstairs, an open-plan area downstairs with a kitchen overlooking the courtyard. There were dreamcatchers and celestial suncatchers, shelves shaped like moons, lots of crystals, bells and essential oils.

Three cats greeted them when they arrived and immediately Gabriel was diverted, picking them up and stroking them, eyes shining.

'What are their names?' Sid asked.

'Luna, Lolly and Merlin.'

Liz showed Gabriel into the spare room, saying it was his and that Sid could have her room as she'd take the sofa.

'No way,' Sid protested.

'Yes way. You're both exhausted. I will make us some supper and then to bed. We can make plans in the morning. Meanwhile, both of you, help yourself to the bathroom.' Her gaze was meaningful, and Sid realised that she and Gabriel probably reeked of adrenaline, sweat and fear. 'I can wash your clothes. Have them dried by morning.'

Liz loaned them clothes, a long robe for Sid and jeans and sweatshirt for Gabriel from her grandson's wardrobe. He was, apparently, sixteen years old and wanted to become a doctor. Supper was spaghetti and pesto. Afterwards, Sid gave Gabriel her second phone. Showed him how it worked, where the video was stored. Shared her, Win and Bert's numbers, along with Liz's, all of which she spent some time memorising before double-checking them.

Gabriel put the phone carefully in his jeans back pocket before patting his front pocket as though checking for something inside – a habit she'd seen him repeat over and over and one which, one day, she'd ask him about. As she and Liz settled in the living area in front of the faux gas fire, flames flickering, she watched Gabriel pad around the flat looking, it seemed, into every cupboard, every corner.

'What are you doing?'

He shrugged. She let him be. Watched as he picked up a book and took it to his room. Later, she went to check he was okay to find him fast asleep, book on his bed. She switched out his light and blew him a kiss. 'Sweet dreams,' she whispered.

Sid and Liz turned on the TV and watched the news headlines. To their surprise, there was no mention of Sid or Gabriel, or the police chase in Bath.

'Well, that's weird.'

'I don't like it,' Liz said. 'It means that if you and Gabriel vanish, you will be out of sight, out of mind.'

To Sid's dismay, Liz then brought out a pack of tarot cards.

'Liz, please don't.'

'It's my house,' Liz stated calmly. 'And I intend to arm you with as much information as I can so that you have as much in your armoury as I can give you.'

Sid held her tongue as Liz dealt a series of cards and placed them into a Celtic Cross, which consisted of ten cards supposedly representing the past and future influences, personal hopes, and conflicting influences. In other words, pretty much everything so the reader could mix and match their questions to suit whichever route they wanted to take according to their subject's body language.

'When did Gabriel lose his speech?'

Sid sighed. 'I don't know, but I assume it was during the bombing.'

'Poor lad.' She studied the cards. 'He'll be okay, though, with you looking out for him.'

*Thanks.*

'You won't stay here for long.'

*Stating the bleeding obvious.*

'Do you have anywhere safe to go to when you leave?'

'Maybe.' Sid thought of Win's place, Meadow Barn. 'I'm not sure.'

'Why the hesitation?'

She didn't talk about Win or Bert, but spoke instead about her fear of trusting the wrong person or people.

'Use the barn.' Liz was definite. 'Wherever it is, it's safe, the people there are trustworthy.'

Sid stared. She hadn't told Liz about any barn.

'I thought tarot was more of a conversation,' Sid said, slightly unnerved. 'Not a prediction.'

'I'm just doing what comes to me.' Liz looked at some more cards. 'The name Greg is strong, really strong. I don't know why… And who is Lucie?' She gave Sid a searching look but Sid just shrugged. She didn't know any Lucie's. 'Are you sure?' Liz pressed. 'She's really important. Something to do with your father.'

'Leah?' Sid said. That was why she'd returned to the Golden Dawn, to see Leah. If she hadn't, she'd never have seen the bombs, never have been poisoned and incarcerated and for a wonderful moment, she fantasised how her life would be if she'd never gone to see Leah.

'Maybe.' Liz looked doubtful. 'But I don't think so.'

Again, Sid shrugged.

'Hmmm.' Liz went on. 'There are massive forces looming against you.'

*That'll be Marc Strong, then.*

'But we know about them. You have your champions, Sid. You have to trust them, when the time comes.'

For a while they talked about how impregnable Marc Strong was and how it might be possible to bring him down, which involved a lot of imagination and even more luck.

'Who are you contacting media-wise?'

They talked about Sid's plans for a while, agreeing she couldn't do much until Gabriel began talking.

'Should I take him to a psychologist of some sort?' Sid asked.

'Not yet. I'd let him settle down a bit first. He's been through a lot. He'll speak when he feels–'

Liz paused when Sid's phone rang. Only three people had the number: Bert, Liz and Gabriel.

'Hello?'

'Where are you?' The voice was dangerously low.

Win. Bert must have given her number to him.

'We're quite safe,' she told him.

'Fucksake!' he exploded. 'I've nearly killed myself three times, nearly totalled the bike on umpteen occasions, and you're not fucking here!'

She remained silent.

He made a sound as though he was being strangled.

'You still have the car?'

'Yes.' It was parked at the rear of the flat, along the street.

Win half-groaned, half-sighed.

'I can't protect you if you're not with me.'

'Sorry about that,' she said, and hung up.

# 55

Sid awoke from a deep sleep. For a nanosecond she thought she was in her cottage and that a screech owl had woken her but then she became aware that people were in the room.

'I'm sorry.' It was Liz. She was close to tears. A man stood behind her. He wore a balaclava and held a gun to her head. He was a big man, muscular and strong-looking.

'Where's the boy?' he asked.

Desperately, Sid tried to clear her head. 'What boy?' she managed.

Another man appeared. He also wore a balaclava. 'We were told you were with a boy.'

'Then someone told you wrong. He ran away in Bath. I haven't seen him since.'

'Shit.'

The man stomped away. Sid heard him moving around the maisonette. Her heart was jumping, her mind whirling. Where was Gabriel? Had he run away, or had he hidden somewhere?

'If you could get up and get dressed,' the first man told Sid, 'it would prevent me from doing this nice lady harm.'

'Sid...' Liz's voice was shaking. 'I'm s-sorry. It was Geoff, who you saw at the centre. He came here, wanting to see me. I let him in and these men were with him... Dear God, I am so stupid.'

Sid didn't say anything. There seemed no point.

'Liz, could I have my clothes?'

Liz looked at the man who snapped, 'Fetch them, lady.'

Liz scurried away, returned in a flash.

Sid clutched the clothes to her chest but let her sweater drop over her handbag which she'd put on the floor next to the bedside table. 'I have to use the bathroom.' She made it a bleat.

The man gave a grunt. 'If you have to. But leave the door open.'

'Pervert,' she mumbled, ducking down and lifting her handbag along with her sweater. She left the door open an inch as she got dressed. Opened her phone and swiftly messaged Liz. She left the phone and the Porsche keys in the bathroom cabinet before pattering down the spiral staircase, where the other man checked her handbag.

'Where's your phone?'

'It didn't survive the motorbike chase yesterday. Did you hear about that? For some strange reason it wasn't on the news and I–'

'Shut it.'

Obediently Sid shut it and allowed herself to be led to an ageing Volvo. One man drove while the other sat in the back with her.

'Where are we going?'

Nobody answered her.

'What's the sentence for kidnapping?'

No response.

Sid's hands were sweating and she spread her fingers on her lap to try to dry them as well as appear calm. Inside, a voice was wailing, *Shit, shit, shit.* She tried to quell it. Would Liz ring the police? It was hard to say, but if she had Gabriel with her, she'd probably keep quiet to keep him safe. She might, however, call Win. Sid had given Liz his phone number.

When the driver pulled off his balaclava, the man next to her did the same. She stared at them in disbelief. They were Marc Strong's close-protection officers.

'Seriously, guys, this is crazy! You can't go around kidnapping people! Don't you know that you can get life imprisonment for this?' She'd looked it up after Father Luke had incarcerated her. 'Do you really want to go to jail for the rest of your life?'

'We're not kidnapping you,' the one next to her said, irritated. He was broad-faced with a hard, tight mouth and a malformed nose which looked as though it had been broken not once, but several times. 'We're just... taking you to meet someone.'

'Marc Strong.'

'He just wants this kid, okay? Can't you give him over?'

'You know who "this kid" is?'

Broken-nose shrugged.

'He's the only surviving kid who set off those bombs.' When Sid went on to explain who Gabriel was, that Marc Strong and Father Luke orchestrated the entire attacks, the man turned a cold eye onto her.

'Who gives a shit. It's a means to an end, isn't it?'

'What?' She was incensed. 'You're condoning the preplanned murder of dozens–'

'This country's gone to the dogs because of you wet liberals,' he snapped. 'So shut the fuck up.'

So Sid shut the fuck up and decided to spend her time

planning. She planned what to say, what to do, how to do it, who she'd call upon. She had to be convincing. She had to use every ounce of her knowledge and experience to spin her web and entrap the fly.

Liz's voice: *You have your champions, Sid. You have to trust them, when the time comes.*

Eyes shut, palms resting on her knees, she thought of Win and Bert, Liz and Gabriel, Toby and his family. Then she thought of her mother and father. Detective Kelly. She remembered the aura of love surrounding her childhood home, the freedom they'd enjoyed. No social credit system looming. No *Little Blue Book* winging its way into everyone's homes.

They drove for an hour and forty minutes. She still had her handbag. Not much of a weapon but if she swung it over her head into someone's face, it could hurt.

They turned off at the Amesbury junction and turned left at the roundabout before switching immediately right, for a petrol station and Travelodge. They pulled into the Travelodge car park which had nine cars parked there, and no streetlights. The Shell garage opposite glowed bright yellow like a sun in the darkness. They cruised to the far corner and parked next to a black Range Rover. The same one she'd seen outside the village hall at Marc Strong's surgery. The driver switched off the engine. Broken-nose climbed out of the car and came around to her door, opened it.

'Out.'

She slipped into a damp and bitterly cold night. She could hear the faint *shushhh* of the A303 behind her. English roads never slept.

He pointed at the Range Rover, where the front passenger door had opened. 'In.'

She wondered if she shouldn't try and make a run for it,

but Broken-nose seemed to read her mind and quickly stepped forward, reaching out and clasping her upper arm with a grip that could have ruptured an oil pipe.

'Ow!' Sid tried to yank her arm free. 'That bloody hurts!'

'Get in the fucking car,' he hissed.

'Okay, okay.'

She walked to the car, rubbing her arm. Glanced inside to see Marc Strong in the driver's seat. 'Get in,' he told her.

She slid onto the passenger seat. Closed the door. It was warm and smelled of leather and the faintest aroma of woody aftershave. She looked straight ahead and took a deep breath to steady herself.

*Do it, Sid. Be bold.* Her mother's voice.

*You can do this.* Her father's.

She looked across at him. Now her sight had adjusted, she could see him quite clearly from the ambient light from the Shell garage. A tiny tick pulsed at the corner of his right eye.

Sid looked back coolly, with equanimity. No ticks. She was ready. She was calm, and filled with purpose.

# 56

'You didn't ring me when you found Gabriel.' Marc Strong's expression was tight.

'Correct.'

He looked surprised that she'd agreed. 'You were with Win Fairchild.'

'Correct.'

'Does he have the boy?'

'No.'

'Where is Gabriel?'

Sid leaned back and folded her arms. Gave him what she hoped was a pitying look. 'You really think I'll tell you, just like that?'

Marc Strong glanced at Broken-nose, who'd taken up position by her door to prevent her from opening it. 'If you don't, I'll do more than drop a dead mouse in your mail. I'll kill your dog. Maybe your farmer friend will suffer an accident. Perhaps lose an arm in his wood-chipping machine.'

'You don't get it, do you?' Her voice was cool.

He tilted his head and looked at her beadily, like a crow

studying a newborn lamb, choosing which eye to peck out. 'Get what?'

She felt a surge of elation. She'd hooked him. She'd turned the tables and was now running the conversation. She was amazed it had been so easy. Casually, Sid briefly studied her fingernails. 'You've got a brain, use it.'

His nostrils flared. He didn't like that.

'You're nothing but a bully,' she said. 'Always have been, and probably always will be. So much so, you go through life like this.' She put a hand over one eye. 'Half-blind.'

He stared.

'I know your *Little Blue Book* is about punishing bad behaviour, but what about rewarding good behaviour?'

Long silence while he looked at Sid, and Sid looked back.

'What do you mean?'

'God.' She gave a laugh. 'You really are thick, aren't you?'

Fury crossed his face.

'If you can't work out why I went to Win, rather than you, then God help this country with you in charge.'

A pulse began to throb at his temple.

Sid sat up straight. Put her shoulders back. Looked him in the eye. 'I will give you Gabriel, but I want something in return.'

Bafflement crossed his face. 'Like what?'

She rolled her eyes. 'I'll let you guess, but put it this way, I've been driving the same battered old Suzuki four-by-four for far too long.'

Another silence, and then he said, tentatively, 'Money?'

Sid began a slow clap. 'He got there, at last. Well done, Mr Strong, Minister of Security and MP for Oxford West and Abingdon and Conservative candidate seeking to become prime minister of the United Kingdom.'

He stared at her for a moment. 'I didn't have you down as money-driven.'

'So says a man born into money,' she sneered.

'I thought you were more altruistic.'

She gave him a look of exasperation. 'Altruism doesn't pay the bills. Nor does it pay for a holiday to St Lucia, or a decent bottle of Margaux.'

His eyes narrowed. 'How much money?'

She'd thought long and hard about this, and decided on an amount that wasn't small, but wasn't ridiculously large either. Something he could rustle up relatively easily, but that would still hurt.

'Three million. Pounds, that is,' she added. 'Not Thai baht. In cash. Used notes, please.'

'And you'll give me Gabriel.'

'Yes.'

He considered this. 'Do you really think I'm that stupid?'

Her stomach dipped.

'How do I know you won't trick me?'

'You don't.' She held his eyes in a challenge. 'But not only do I want my friends left alone, I want some luxuries in life. I want to buy my own cottage somewhere, travel the world for a bit. I don't, however, want you coming after me. I want a peaceful life, okay? I have no axe to grind here. I'm just a woman wanting to go home and have enough money to keep me comfortable.'

His eyes gleamed. 'How very unlike your father you are.'

'So my mother used to say.' She spoke without hesitation.

'You think he'd be proud of you? Doing what you're doing?'

'It doesn't matter what he might think since he's not

around. Besides, I really don't care, as long as I get the money.'

An interminable pause fell, in which she stared resolutely at Marc Strong and he stared back. Suspicion crawled into his eyes.

She felt a wave of panic.

Had she gone too far?

Finally, to her relief, he said, 'Where's the boy?'

She gave him another pitying look.

His face smoothed out, his features becoming as immobile as a bronze bust.

'Okay, so how do we do this?'

Something inside her thrilled when he said those words. She'd hooked him, one hundred per cent; rod, line, sinker and all.

'You get the money, and we will go together and get Gabriel.' She flicked a look at Broken-nose. 'But I'm not staying here.'

'Sorry.' Marc Strong climbed out of the car, taking his car keys with him. 'You don't get to dictate to me.' He locked the door behind him.

She watched him walk to his men and speak to them. She couldn't hear what they said but it didn't take long, because barely two minutes later, he was back. 'You will wait with my men until I return.'

'What about the police?' She tried to bluff. 'My friend will have called them. They will be searching for me.'

'No search has been started as nobody has been alerted.'

She gave a snort. 'Like I believe *that*.' She made her tone dismissive, contemptuous, hoping to bait his ego into showing off.

'Why do you think I'm the *Security Minister*,' he hissed. 'When Gabriel popped up, I had every lead sent to me. Dozens of sightings, none of which meant anything until I saw my old drama teacher's name, Elizabeth Whitlock. Her work colleague rang the police, reporting he'd seen a teenage boy who looked like the terrorist at his healing centre. I sent my men to talk to him. You know the rest.' His eyes gleamed. 'You can't move in this country without me seeing.'

From behind them came the sound of a lorry passing.

'Did you know,' Marc Strong went on, 'Elizabeth Whitlock dressed up as a witch and tried to scare us, as boys?'

'Yes. She mentioned that.'

'It turned on her, did you know that too?'

'She said something about making you believe you heard a real, live demon that scared you half to death.'

'Who says it wasn't real?' Something crawled from the back of his eyes and squatted there, watching her.

'I thought you were Christian.' Her voice was a notch higher, betraying her disquiet.

'You need a balance, don't you think? Yin and Yang? Dark and light?'

'I don't care for the dark.'

'But it can be so very rewarding.' He smiled a slow smile to reveal his shiny white teeth.

Sid put her hand on the door handle. 'Do me a favour?'

'You're not in a position to–'

'Bring a banknote counter with you.'

After Marc Strong had left, Broken-nose and his buddy ushered her to the Travelodge where they purloined a room with two single beds, a desk and an armchair. Broken-nose switched on the TV and sprawled on one of the beds. The other guy took the second bed while Sid took the chair. Her adrenaline began to ebb, leaving her shaky but elated. She'd succeeded in putting the first part of the plan into operation, but what about the rest?

She wondered how long it would take Marc Strong to get the money. Half a day? A whole day? Two days? She thought of Liz and Gabriel, and Win, who, because of his father's connection with Marc Strong, she hadn't trusted enough to help her. Why had he lied to her about working for Clan Capital? She remembered the broad strength of him, and how he'd felt when she'd wound her body around his.

Without realising, she fell asleep.

Sid awoke at 6am when Broken-nose announced he was starving, so they headed to the restaurant where both men tucked into the Ultimate Unlimited Breakfast. Great mounds of sausages, bacon, eggs, beans, hash browns. Sid stuck to black coffee and pancakes. They went back to the room. Watched more TV. According to the news, it now looked as though Marc Strong would be coronated as prime minister within the next day or so. She had to hope, to *pray* her plan would work.

She was given a BLT sandwich and a Snickers bar at lunchtime. A bottle of mineral water. The day crawled past. From time to time she considered asking one of her minders to buy her a packet of cigarettes, but when she actually visualised lighting up and dragging smoke into her lungs, she couldn't work out if it was the nicotine she wanted, or if she just wanted something to do with her hands. A bit of both, she realised, finally deciding that since she hadn't missed smoking much over the past couple of weeks, she could do without.

She jumped to her feet when Broken-nose's phone rang. He listened briefly, looked at her. 'Let's go.'

It was 7.10pm and night had fallen. Flanked by her minders, Sid stalked outside and to the Range Rover lurking at the far end of the car park, where Marc Strong stood at the rear. He beckoned her over. A medium-sized suitcase lay on the tailgate. He opened it. It was full of money. Her breathing stalled, a combination of disbelief and exhilaration. *She was going to do this.* The enormity of it made her fingers tremble as she picked up one of the bundles.

'Each one is worth ten thousand.'

She checked the currency strap to see that yes, each bundle was worth £10,000. She sifted through the suitcase, flicking a variety of bundles to check they weren't stuffed with newspaper.

'I brought a set of currency scales.'

'Let's use it.'

It took a while to work their way through the money, but Sid didn't stint on her checks. If she was genuinely money-driven, she'd want every note proven. She wouldn't want to be ripped off. When they were finished, she said, 'Great. Now, I need to phone Gabriel.'

Suspicion rose.

'I thought he was mute.'

'He can still listen, though. Take instructions. I need a phone, though.'

'Greg,' Marc Strong barked at Broken-nose. 'Give her yours.'

Greg didn't look best pleased, but did as his boss asked.

Sid dialled the number from memory. Marc Strong insisted she put it on speaker.

The instant it was answered she said, 'Gabriel? It's me, Sid. Look, I know you can't speak, but I need you to do something for me. I'd like you to go to that garage Win took us to that time. Remember it? I'll meet you there in... hang on. I need Google Maps...'

She looked up Locksbrook Road with Marc Strong peering over her shoulder.

'We'll be there in just over an hour. We'll be in a black

Range Rover.' She moved to the front of the car and read out the number-plate. 'Don't show yourself to anyone else, okay? Just me and my friends. See you soon, okay?'

She hung up. Gave back Greg's phone. They were about to climb into the car when his phone pinged. A message had just come in. Greg stared at it.

'What?' Sid demanded.

He turned the screen so she and Marc Strong could read it.

> It's not that I don't trust you, Sid. But I don't know your friends! I just want to go home. See Mum. Can Father Luke pick me up rather than your friends?

Sid looked at Marc Strong, who shook his head. 'Tell him we'll drop him off at the Golden Dawn.'

Greg typed the words.

The response came fast:

> I want Father Luke.

'Tell him, no.'

> I won't go with anyone else.

'No.'

This time, there was no response.

'Shit.' A muscle began to tick in Marc Strong's jaw. 'Let me type.'

> Gabriel. I'm not sure if we can get Father Luke to you tonight. Much better if we collect you, and take you there?

> No.

Sid took a breath. Faced Marc Strong squarely. 'Look, he's just a kid. Scared and on the run. I think we should get Father Luke to bring him in. He'll trust him. He might run a mile when he sees you and your thugs.'

'Hey,' protested Greg.

'Well, what else would you call yourselves?' She was tart.

'Close-protection,' he responded huffily.

She just looked at him. He glanced away.

Marc Strong had stepped aside and was now talking on his phone as he paced. His steps were angry, his body movements jerky. Finally, he returned. 'Father Luke's going to meet us there.'

'In that case,' Sid said brightly, 'let's get this show on the road.'

# 57

They arrived at the garage at 8.15pm. As they pulled between the gates and into the forecourt, Marc Strong said, 'Where the hell is Luke?' He was searching expectantly. 'He was meant to get here first.'

Security lights had come on, flooding the area. Several cars were parked at the far end, along with a panel van propped on bricks. Tarmac glistened with rain. They all climbed out of the car. There was no other sound or movement. If the gate hadn't been open, she'd assume nobody else was there.

As if on cue, another car rolled through the gates and parked alongside. Father Luke climbed out. As usual, he was dressed in his djellaba. He was on his own. When Marc Strong went to talk to him, Father Luke squared up to him, like a boxer might do before a fight. Sid slipped out of the car and walked quietly over. Nobody showed any interest in her. It was as though she didn't exist.

'I said we should never, *ever* be seen together after that day.' Father Luke had flushed a mottled red and his brow was creased as though he couldn't believe what was happening. 'Don't you realise the danger you're putting us in? People aren't stupid, they will talk, start to put things together... I've just set up another commune in California and you're–'

'If that boy starts to speak on the TV,' Marc Strong snapped, 'your Californian dream may as well be on the moon.'

A stark silence.

'You get the boy,' Marc Strong instructed, 'and I will deal with him.'

Father Luke stared at him as though he'd lost his senses. 'What do you mean, deal with him?'

'We can't have him running around, knowing what he knows.'

'He won't be running around. He'll be with me at the Golden Dawn.'

Marc Strong smiled thinly. 'What about when you're in California?'

'His mother will keep him in line. She's recovering from a nasty bout of Soul Sickness and won't want another. Trust me.'

'Your poisoning your followers to terrify them into submission is one thing, keeping a witness to what we did, alive, is quite another.'

Father Luke gaped at him. 'Are you saying what I think you're saying?'

'All those children died,' Marc Strong hissed, leaning in to Father Luke until their faces were only an inch apart. 'You knew every single one. You gave them their pretty Christmas presents and detonated them. You didn't turn a fucking hair. And now you're bleating about a boy who should have died that day, who will destroy us both if he isn't dealt with?'

Father Luke turned white. 'Yes, but don't you see? God

spared Gabriel. He wouldn't have done that without good reason.'

Silence.

'I take your point,' Marc Strong said grudgingly.

The breath seemed to go out of Father Luke. 'Thank God.' He raised a shaking hand to his forehead. 'I really thought you were serious.'

'You really think you can contain him?' Marc Strong looked thoughtful.

'Yes. Of course. He's a good boy. Obedient and biddable.'

'His sister died in the mission.'

'In a great cause. When Gabriel knows little Hannah sits at the right hand of God, bathed in the radiance of His glory, he will understand.'

Marc Strong nodded, expression distant. 'In that case, he's all yours.' He clapped Father Luke on the back. 'Just make sure you keep a close eye on him.'

Sid began to edge away from the Range Rover, thinking she might run for the street, but at that moment, Marc Strong said, 'You. Sidney. Go with Father Luke and fetch the boy.'

A scraping sound made them all turn their heads. A light had snapped on showing Gabriel standing in the doorway to the side of the roller door. As they all stared, Gabriel started walking towards them. *Shit,* she thought. He wasn't supposed to do that. He was meant to lure them into the garage.

'No!' Sid gave a shout.

It was as though she hadn't spoken.

Gabriel walked towards Father Luke. He was walking oddly, off-balance, as if he was carrying a great weight. His face was as pale as a moon. He didn't look left or right. He was like an automaton.

'Gabriel!' she shouted.

He didn't look at her.

And then Marc Strong looked at Greg and said, 'Shoot him.'

Greg looked startled, but only for a moment. He reached his hand towards his shoulder holster. At the same time, Sid sprang for him, but Father Luke was faster. He spun on his heel and snapped out an arm, knocking Greg's arm high. Greg brought the gun down hard on Father Luke's head with a sickening crunch. Father Luke fell to his knees. Greg took aim at Gabriel again, but Sid was moving at full force as she barrelled into him. He tried to aim the gun at her. She pushed his arm with her whole body but he was bigger than her and much stronger. He shoved her aside, took aim again.

The shot was small and sharp, like a firework cracker and for a moment Sid didn't think anything had happened, but then Gabriel fell. One second, he'd been upright and walking, the next he was a bundle of limbs on the ground. Sid pelted to his side. Knelt next to him. His face was like chalk, his eyes shut. Frantically she pulled at his puffer jacket, trying to see where the wound was but then his eyes snapped open.

He stared at her, almost in surprise, and then someone yelled, 'POLICE! FREEZE!'

Everything went to hell.

Marc Strong and his henchmen raced for the Range Rover. Sid couldn't see who was driving, but they were too slow. Two men had already dragged the garage gates closed and bolted them. The Range Rover roared straight for the gates, smashing into them with an almighty crash. The gates buckled, but held. The Range Rover reversed, smashed the gates again. This time, one of the bolts popped free. As the car reversed for a third effort, uniformed police flooded the forecourt. Armed officers stood on either side of the gate, weapons raised. The windscreen of the Range Rover was covered in little red dots. Infra-red lasers.

A terrible pause where nobody moved.

Then the Range Rover's engine was switched off.

Slowly, the doors opened and Marc Strong's two security guards stepped outside, hands raised. Even more slowly, Marc Strong joined them.

'GET DOWN! ON THE GROUND! HANDS BEHIND YOUR HEAD!'

All three men dropped onto their fronts. Police kicked their feet apart, handcuffed their hands behind their backs. Two police stood over Father Luke, pointing their guns at him as he knelt on the ground.

Sid didn't watch anymore, she'd turned back to Gabriel, desperately wanting to find his injury.

'Hey, fella.' A man in a black flak jacket, vest and trousers bulging with tasers, handguns and handcuffs, dropped next to Sid. He wore a helmet and balaclava. All she could see were his eyes. Deep brown, as brown as peat, with thick lashes.

Win.

'You okay?' he asked Gabriel.

The boy gave a nod, started to scramble up but stopped when Sid put out a hand.

'Gabriel, where are you hurt?'

He smiled. Pulled open his puffer jacket to reveal a bulletproof vest.

# 58

G abriel sat in the back of Win's tatty old Vauxhall watching the journalists emerge from the garage, cautiously at first, and then they became a flood. Win had only contacted a handful but they'd brought sound and lighting experts, as well as lots of cameras, several of which had been positioned earlier in the day, to cover the garage forecourt. With everyone hidden inside the garage, Gabriel watched events unfold on a screen, heard every word.

Until then, he wasn't sure if he believed Father Luke was responsible for Hannah's death, but now he had no doubts. Which was why he'd walked outside, to face the men who'd killed his sister. Win had told him they'd kill him if they could, but he hadn't really taken it in. Not until one of the men had pointed the gun at him, and pulled the trigger. He could still feel the bullet that hit him, like a fist being punched against his chest.

'Minister!' shouted a man who Gabriel had met earlier, and knew was from the BBC. 'What do you say to the accusations of using bombs to terrify the country into accepting you as a candidate for prime minister!'

'Father Luke!' This from another journalist. 'We heard just now that the bombers were children from the Golden Dawn! What do you say?'

The questions came thick and fast, and Gabriel felt a surge of fierce joy watching Father Luke stare at the ground, unable to meet anyone's eye.

Now, Sid was next to him, looking at him anxiously. 'Are you sure you're okay?'

'Yes,' he said. 'I'm okay.'

They were the first words he'd spoken in days, and they felt as dry and rough as chips of concrete in his mouth. He looked at his feet, feeling as though he'd committed a betrayal. Hannah couldn't speak. She never would.

Sid grabbed his hand, staring at him. 'What did you say?'

She was hurting him, but he didn't pull away. 'I'm okay, Sid. I really am.' He coughed, trying to clear the husk in his throat. 'A bit sore from where the bullet hit me, but it's only a bruise.'

'Jesus, fuck. You can speak!'

When Win hopped into the driver's seat, Sid leaned forward. 'Gabriel can speak!'

Win looked at Gabriel in the rear-view mirror. 'Nice one.'

Gabriel liked Win, and not just because he'd saved him on his motorbike. He didn't talk down to him like some grown-ups. He treated him like an equal.

'Where were you?' Sid demanded of Gabriel. 'When those men took me away at Liz's?'

Gabriel told her the story in fits and starts. He hadn't trusted the man with the beard in the healing centre. He'd made him feel on edge, frightened, and when he'd been woken at Liz's in the middle of the night by voices outside, he'd bolted for the bathroom and the airing cupboard. He'd checked it out earlier – *be prepared* – and had already made a note of the space between the floor and the first shelf, filled with blankets and a spare duvet. He'd simply pulled some blankets free, shoving them on the upper shelves before wriggling behind the duvet until he couldn't be seen. He'd stayed there, as quiet as a mouse.

*Camp Fire Yarn. No. 14*
  *How to Hide Yourself*
  *Remain perfectly still without moving.*

'I heard you change in the bathroom, but I didn't show myself.' He bit his lip. 'It wasn't that I didn't want you to know I was there, but I couldn't be sure one of the men might open the door and see me.'

'You did good,' she told him.

Eventually, he'd had to come out of hiding to pee. Plus, he was hungry. Liz just about had a heart attack when he appeared downstairs and he'd cringed, miming *sorry, sorry* but she'd simply swept him into her arms and hugged him. Which had been nice.

'Liz got your message,' Gabriel told her. 'She found your phone.'

'She called me,' Win said. 'She showed me the text you'd sent her when you'd been in the bathroom. It was enough for us to form a decent plan. When you rang later, we were already pretty much there.'

Sid leaned forward and put a hand on his shoulder. 'Thanks.'

'Thank Gabriel. He was pretty amazing.'

The shine in the boy's eyes made Sid's heart fill.

# 59

As Win drove out of Locksbrook Road, Sid said, 'Where are we going?'

'The police station.'

Sid remained leaning forward. 'Are you a policeman?'

'Sometimes.'

'What does that mean?'

His eyes gleamed like shiny black stones in his rear-view mirror. 'What it sounds like.'

'You're not an accountant?'

'I am, actually. But I'm also a cop.'

'I don't understand.'

'Later,' he said. Weariness tinged his tone and suddenly she saw the bruises beneath his eyes, how tired he was.

'Later,' she agreed. She leaned back, closing her eyes. She felt Gabriel put his hand in hers. She didn't realise she'd dropped into an exhausted doze until Gabriel withdrew his hand and Win said, 'We're here.'

Win smoothed their way through the next few hours. He was at Sid and Gabriel's side when they made their statements, making sure they were looked after, and stayed until every t had been crossed, every i dotted. Gabriel's grandparents had been called but when the time came to take him to their house, he'd looked panicky, and asked to stay with Sid and Win. They looked hurt, but when Sid explained it wasn't personal as much as for his emotional security, they reluctantly agreed.

Gabriel, understandably, had wanted to see his mum, but this was impossible, not just because it was the middle of the night, but the Golden Dawn was now under investigation. Win solemnly promised the boy he'd get someone to check on her as soon as possible.

Now, they were back in Win's humdrum Vauxhall, driving out of Keynsham. 'Where's your Porsche?' she asked.

'At home.'

'How come an undercover cop can afford a Porsche?'

'How come a supernatural scientist owns an original Dali sketch?'

*Touché.*

'Where to now?' Sid asked.

'Somewhere safe.'

Somewhere safe turned out to be Win's place in Oxford. Meadow Barn. The curtains were drawn but she could see lamps burning inside. A security light snapped on as Win approached the front door and then the door was open, and Bert stood there, leaning on a stick.

'You made it,' he said.

Flick arrived, tinkling with bangles. Sid watched, surprised, as she went to Gabriel and gave him a hug. Gabriel hugged her back. 'We've been waiting up for you.'

'You know each other?' Sid stared.

'Gabriel stayed here while we put your plan into action,' Win said. 'We thought it safer.'

They stumbled into the house.

'Bet you're exhausted,' said Bert.

'Just a bit.' Win yawned. It was now 2am.

'Any of you hungry?'

Win shook his head, along with Sid, but Gabriel looked hopeful. 'Beans on toast?' Flick offered.

'Yes, please,' said Gabriel.

Flick's eyes widened. 'You can… well, I hope you don't mind me pointing it out, but you just spoke.'

Gabriel looked away, biting his lip. 'It didn't feel right before. It still doesn't, when…' He took a shuddering breath.

Flick touched his shoulder. 'It's okay.'

He shrugged miserably, and although her soul ached for him, Sid was glad to see he was starting to process his grief.

'I'll let you get on,' said Bert. 'I'll see you in the morning.' He went and kissed Flick on the cheek and with a start, Sid saw their similarities. The same thick hair swept above their ears, the same long noses, same tan colouring of their skin.

'You're all related,' she said, looking between Win, Bert and Flick.

'Of course.' Flick looked surprised. 'This is my grandad, and Win's my stepbrother.'

Sid looked at Bert, skin prickling. 'You're Win's father?'

'For my sins.' His tone was dry but his gaze was affectionate as he glanced at Win.

'You were Marc Strong's tutor?'

He fell still, his eyes growing wary. 'I was. Why?'

'You're one of Marc Strong's most ardent supporters.' Her tone was accusing.

A glimmer of a smile. 'That's what an online search told you, I expect.'

She waited.

'It's all a smokescreen, a ruse to disguise my real intentions. I expect you know all about that in your trade.'

'Real intentions?' Sid repeated.

Bert looked at Win. 'Gathering information.'

Sid lifted her eyebrows at Win, who said wearily, 'Let's not get into that now,' and as Sid opened her mouth to persist, he yawned again, swaying a little. He was, she recognised, just about dead on his feet.

'Let's talk tomorrow,' Bert said briskly. 'You show Sid to her room and I'll see you in the morning.'

Win showed her upstairs to a bedroom with a small coal fireplace. Ancient beams and thick carpets made it snug and cosy. A pair of towels lay on the bed along with a robe. A handful of pictures stood on the chest of drawers. Sid picked up one to see Win in a sharply tailored suit. He had his arm around a striking redhead in an elegant white dress. When Win saw her looking, he came over and put it in the top drawer. 'I'd forgotten that was there.'

'How long were you married?'

'Three years.'

'What went wrong?'

'I got tired of the turbulence.'

Brief silence.

'You?' he asked. 'Have you ever been married?'

She gave a snort.

He raised his eyebrows.

'I was…' She wondered how to put it. 'A bit of a free spirit.'

'And now?'

She considered it. 'Much less so.'

He looked as though he was going to say something, but changed his mind. 'Bathroom's next door,' he told her. 'It's got soap and shampoo and stuff. Flick and I share a bathroom at the other end of the corridor, so this is all yours. Okay?'

'Thank you.'

'See you in the morning.' He gave her a finger salute and padded away.

Sid thought she'd be too tired to do anything but crash on the bed and sleep, but the second she took off her shoes and socks, she felt a fierce urge to wash. She turned the shower as hot as she dared and stood beneath the flow, letting the water play over her, letting the memory of the past few weeks wash through her mind.

It was extraordinary to think this had all started with Detective Kelly showing her her father's postcard, all those weeks ago. His investigating Owen Evans's murder. The four boys grown to men, one missing, one dead, two under arrest. If she hadn't gone looking for her father, who knows how things would have transpired. And after all this, she still hadn't found out what had happened to Dad.

She climbed into bed. With Father Luke and Marc Strong out of the way – at least for the moment – she would return to the Golden Dawn and, police investigation permitting, continue her search. She stared at the ceiling. Closed her eyes. But the questions didn't stop. She was exhausted but couldn't sleep. Her mind went around and around. After what felt like an age, she checked her phone to see it was barely 3am. Finally, she rose, thinking of getting some water, and went to the top of the stairs, peered down. All was still and silent. She was dithering whether to turn on a light or not when Win said softly, 'Sid? Is that you?'

She padded downstairs to find him sitting on the sofa, in the dark. He switched on a side lamp. She saw he had a glass of what might be whisky in his hand. He was still dressed.

Sid folded her arms. 'You followed me on your motorbike.'

He put down the glass. 'Yes.'

'You were behind me when I visited Harriet Evans and the Chalice Well. You were outside the Gloucestershire police station when Detective Kelly drove me to the Golden Dawn. Then you followed me into Bath. I did a U-turn to catch you out.'

'I started keeping an eye on you long before then.'

She blinked.

'The day after we met, to be precise.'

'Why?'

'When you first came to see me, I didn't know whether to trust you or not. You said you were Michael Scott's daughter and were looking for him, but with everything going on, I couldn't be sure if you were genuine. I wanted to see what you were up to.' He swirled his drink, took a sip. 'Later, when I was sure you were who you were, I kept track of you because you were doing such a great job of disturbing things. You were like an eager spaniel rushing around a copse, flushing out pheasants.'

She wasn't sure if she liked the spaniel metaphor but decided to let it ride. 'Why were you at the Golden Dawn?'

Win raised his glass. 'Would you like one? Armagnac. Very smooth.'

'Sure.'

She watched as he rose and fetched a bottle, poured her a glass. She took a sip. He was right, it was smooth, and burned a pleasant trail down her throat. He returned to one end of the sofa. She propped herself on the opposite arm.

'With Dad's approbation, I gained Father Luke's trust as a bit of a financial advisor.' He studied his Armagnac. 'I bugged Father Luke's office.'

Sid felt her eyes widen. 'What kind of police officer are you?'

'The undercover kind.'

Sid digested that. 'The police condoned your listening in to Father Luke?'

'Yes. There were already reports of abuse as well as financial fraud. We were gathering evidence against him.'

Sid leaned forward, cupping her glass in both hands. 'What did you find out about my father?'

He studied his glass some more. 'I wasn't entirely open about things when we first spoke.'

Sid waited.

'As you know, Dad was Marc Strong's tutor. He found Strong alarming. He got several tutors together and they decided to keep an eye on him, along with his cohorts, Luke Goddard and Owen Evans. Dad joined the BLP in Oxford, but the age gap meant he was on the edge of things. So they approached your father with their concerns, who agreed the trio were worrying. He wasn't their friend as such, but he'd been at the same school as them and they trusted him, to a certain degree. Your father became part of their extended circle, and over the years, he heard rumours of a plan they were putting into place. All very hush-hush, but he never found out exactly what it was.'

Sid felt a sharp pinch of dismay. 'You're saying he was a spy.'

'As am I.' His gaze was cool.

She took a breath. 'Did they find out he was spying? Kill him?'

'I don't know.'

'What about your father? Does Bert know what happened to Dad?'

Win shook his head. 'He says not.'

'He's also a spy.'

'I guess you could say that.'

Sid downed the rest of her drink. Thought some more. 'How did you know I was meeting Gabriel in the park?'

'I'd already followed you to SouthGate car park. Saw you swap cars with your landlord.' He gave her an approving look. 'If I'd relied on a tracker, I'd never have known about the swap. Good move.'

She felt ridiculously pleased at his praise.

'From there,' he went on, 'I simply followed you to Europcar, popped a tracker on your hire car, and the rest is history, as they say.'

She put down her glass. Slid down the arm of the sofa, tucked her feet beneath her. 'There was a man watching me in the woods.'

'Yes.' He looked away. 'Sorry about that. He wasn't supposed to be seen.'

A curl of disbelief. 'He was a cop?'

'No.' He gave a rueful chuckle. 'He was a friend doing me a favour. Which is probably why he was so terrible at it. Your farmer friend scared the crap out of him, by the way. As well as your dog.'

'But why put your friend–'

She swallowed her words when Win rose and came to sit next to her. 'Another thing,' he said, voice gentle. 'I didn't say why I continued to follow you.'

'You wanted to catch Father Luke and Marc Strong out. Save Gabriel.'

'It was more than that.' His gaze deepened, making her pulse quiver. 'I followed you to try and keep you safe.'

Long silence while they looked at one another.

'Come here.' He stretched his arm along the top of the sofa. 'I need a hug. And don't worry, I won't jump on you. I'm too knackered.'

Sid wriggled over and lay against him, her head against his chest, broad and warm. His heartbeat was loud and steady in her ear. She felt his arms go around her. She wrapped her hands around him. His skin was like warm stone. He pressed a kiss against her hair. She could smell the sharp acid of man-sweat and something deeper, almost herbal, like rosemary, or thyme. Whatever it was, it was distinctly male, and she felt petals of desire blossom inside her but when she tilted her face to look into his, he was fast asleep.

# 60

Breakfast was noisy and messy, involving Bert's special fry-up with all the trimmings followed by stacks of toast and marmalade for the grown-ups, peanut butter for the kids. Tea, coffee, orange juice, cereals, fresh fruit, yoghurt, butter and cutlery lay scattered across the table. Everyone talked over everyone, passing things, eating voraciously. Sid didn't think she'd ever felt so hungry and from the way everyone else behaved, neither did they.

She'd fallen asleep in Win's arms and had only woken when he went and fetched a duvet, which he wrapped around them. They'd slept as though felled until a pale finger of sun crept across the sofa. Win had swept her up to sit across his thighs. He'd looked at her mouth for a long time before saying hoarsely, 'I don't think I've ever had to exert such self-control in my life before.'

She'd given a little wiggle of her hips and watched his eyes darken.

'You witch,' he gasped.

A laugh escaped her, at which point he picked her up

and carried her across the room for the stairs. She was wondering – hoping? – he was taking her to his bedroom but then a door banged upstairs and he paused. Put her gently down. 'Later,' he whispered against her lips.

'Yes.'

---

Sid didn't watch or listen to the news. It was Win who told her that David Reville was now prime minister, and that Father Luke and Marc Strong had been refused bail.

'They're in jail,' he said with satisfaction. 'Where they will stay until they're sentenced after trial.'

Even behind bars, Father Luke and Marc Strong were pulling every string they could. Their supporters were all over every media outlet, claiming entrapment, that Sid had lost her mind, that she was unreliable, untrustworthy. They even managed to drag out some ex-lovers of hers, making her look slutty and immoral, and when Win mentioned them, she said calmly, 'It was my way of coping with grief. Blocking my emotions.'

He'd reached over and squeezed her hand.

Despite Father Luke and Marc Strong's best efforts, however, the mud Sid had thrown at them began to stick. Her latest video had gone viral, along with her social media posts. She couldn't wait for the cops to find her phone at Golden Dawn, along with evidence of the bombs in the basement. Then she was going to break open the champagne.

Now, Sid was checking her messages. 'Oh my God,' she said.

Immediately, Win was by her side. 'What is it?'

'It's Julia Pemberton. The woman who ran away from

the Golden Dawn. She says she's willing to talk now Father Luke's behind bars. She's left her phone number.'

Sid texted, asking Julia when it would be a good time to call.

Let's FaceTime. Is now okay?

Sid immediately sent a thumbs up.

Julia called seconds later. She was a strong, handsome-looking woman in her late thirties, with threads of grey showing through her wiry brown hair. 'Hello,' she said.

'Hi.'

Behind Julia was a picture window showing a spectacular vista of rolling mountains and pine trees dusted with snow.

'Is that view real?' asked Sid.

Julia glanced over her shoulder. Smiled. 'Yes.'

'Where are you?'

'Er... let's just say I live here because it was as far as I could get from Father Luke.' Her voice turned tight. 'He said no matter where I went, he'd find me and bring me back...'

'But you did it. You got away.'

'Yes.' Her face brightened. 'And now the bastard's locked up I can at last, sleep easy. And talk to you. I couldn't before...' She trailed off, biting her lip.

'You were scared. I understand. Look, when you messaged me before, you told me to talk to someone called Leah about what might have happened to my father.'

'I don't know if she'll know, exactly, but Leah was like my little sister. She'll talk to you if she knows we've spoken. But don't refer to me as Julia because I was rechristened Amelia.'

Sid's fingers spasmed around the phone.

*Owen shouting the names Amelia, Leah and Mike.*

'Leah wanted to run away too but she never made it...' Her voice caught. 'Sorry... but not a day goes past when I don't think of her and little Hannah, Gabriel.'

Sid felt an electric charge form in the air like a storm brewing.

'Leah is Gabriel's mother?'

'Yes.' A sob emerged and she brought up both hands and rubbed her face. 'I'm so sorry about Hannah. All those poor children. But thank the Lord Gabriel is okay.'

Sid gently reminded Julia of her original message where she'd told her about Owen's murder, and that he'd had a postcard from her father hidden in his jeans.

'I want to know what happened to Owen,' Sid said, 'because I'm pretty sure I'll then find out what happened to my father.' She told Julia about his disappearance fourteen years ago. 'Can I show you a photograph of him?'

'Of course.'

Sid fetched it from the sitting room. It was one of the photos the police had used at the time, showing him smiling at the camera, his features clear and his beard neatly trimmed. She was totally unprepared for Julia's response.

'Oh my God, oh my God, oh my God...' The woman clapped her hands to her face, her eyes wide.

'What is it?'

'It's the man from the hospital! It's him!'

'What?'

'I don't know his name. But he was at my hospital. His mother was in my ward. She'd broken her hip. She was sedated but he was there, holding her hand, comforting her...'

'When was this?' Sid asked urgently.

'A long time ago. Years and years. I was...' She

scrunched up her face as she thought. 'Twenty-four. I remember that. Which would make it… 2009.'

Sid felt a surge of elation. 'What date, can you remember?'

Julia thought some more, then shook her head. 'No, sorry. It was November, though.'

'And it was definitely him.'

'Oh, yes. It's him all right, except his hair and beard weren't as tidy. He was altogether rather more shaggy, if you know what I mean.'

'I do.' Her heart squeezed. Dad was always a bit shaggy. It was the perfect description.

'It was your father who rang my mum and dad, told them I was there. They came straight over.'

'Why were you in hospital?'

'Appendicitis. It had burst and I'd nearly died, but I'd had an operation and was on antibiotics, and things were looking up… Brother Isaac usually sat with me, but he'd gone to get a coffee. It wasn't often I was alone, but just this once your father and I got talking. He wanted to know how come my appendix had burst – you can die from a ruptured appendix, you know – and when I told him… well, he went weirdly quiet. At the time, I thought he wasn't interested, but then I realised he was indescribably angry…'

Julia took a breath. Sid was gripping the phone so tightly her hand was beginning to ache.

'You see, I'd told your father that because I'd been caught hoarding eggs – we were always so *hungry* – I was shut in the Shed for a week. No light, no food, just water. My appendix was already hurting pretty badly when Father Luke locked me in but he wouldn't listen. It burst when I was in the Shed. I screamed and screamed, and

Father Luke told me I was a liar and that unless I was quiet he'd extend my punishment.

'It was Leah who let me out later that day. I was in a terrible state, it was obvious I wasn't faking it. Leah got Brother Isaac to take me to hospital. Isaac didn't tell Father Luke. He just did it. If he hadn't, I would have died.'

## 61

Sid returned to the breakfast table. 'I have to see Leah, Gabriel's mum.'

Gabriel's face lit up.

'And he needs to see her too.'

'Yes!' he exclaimed, bouncing up and down. 'Please, please. I want to see Mum.'

'I'm not sure if it's possible,' Win replied carefully. 'I called the police this morning. The Golden Dawn's locked down. They're ripping it apart.'

'Where are all the followers?' Sid asked. 'Aren't they still there?'

'In the dormitories. They're only allowed out for meals.'

'Surely, you can pull some strings, Win. Get us in.'

Win thought it over. 'I'll see what I can do.' He looked at Gabriel. 'What's your mother's name?'

'Lucie,' the boy said. 'But she was reborn as Leah.'

Sid felt the world tilt.

She was having a waking dream with her parents in her bedroom. Her father answering her question:

*What happened to you, Dad?*

*Ask Leah.*

She was sitting with Liz in her maisonette, and Liz was asking, *Who is Lucie? She's really important. Something to do with your father.*

'Lucie is your mother?' Sid's voice was choked.

Gabriel nodded. 'She's been really sick.'

'She's been in the san.' Sid remembered. 'Soul Sickness.' She clicked her eyes onto Win. He knew all about the poisonings to keep the followers compliant to God's, ergo Father Luke's, will. 'I have to see her. *We* have to see her. Julia said Leah would talk to me if she knew she and I had spoken.'

Win caught her urgency and by lunchtime, he'd arranged for them to meet at the Golden Dawn, in a temporary police base which had been set up in the commune's car park.

Bright sunshine greeted them when they arrived. No djellaba-wearing followers stood at the gates to greet – or threaten – them, but two uniformed police officers instead, who checked their IDs carefully before waving them on. The car park was teeming with police and forensic officers, their cars and their kit. Three tents had been erected to one side, from which a variety of people swarmed. There was a police-dog van with its rear door open, two Alsatians sprawled inside their cages, looking bored. The dog handlers were sitting on the tailgate, eating donuts and sipping from steaming Styrofoam cups. They raised their cups, greeting Win as they passed, who gave them a nod in return.

Inside the first tent, labelled TENT ONE, it was hot and stuffy, and seemed chaotic. There were maps and photos on the walls and people were talking, radios and walkie-talkies crackling. Sid's eyes snagged on a man at the far end, talking to a uniformed officer. He was pale and thin and looked exhausted.

She stared.

'What it is?' Win was alert at her side.

'Detective Kelly.'

As she stared, Kelly turned and met her eyes. His expression was haunted.

'Is there a problem?' Win asked.

'The last time I saw him, I hit him.'

Win's eyebrows disappeared into his hairline. 'Did you indeed.'

'He abandoned me.' Fury rose. 'And here he is, acting as though nothing's happened.' She began walking towards Kelly. He met her halfway.

'I told them,' he said.

She lifted her chin. 'What did you tell them?'

'Everything.'

'But only after it all came out. After they'd been arrested.'

He looked away. 'I'll go to jail if that's any help.'

Her gaze intensified. 'Good.'

'I'll testify. I will make sure everything sticks… They've got your phone from that chest of drawers you hid it in. Precursory swabs show bomb residue in the basement. There's even Christmas wrapping paper still there. They may never be released from jail.'

'No thanks to you.'

'No thanks to me,' he agreed. 'But I'll do everything I can.'

Small pause.

'How's your sister?'

'Still not speaking to me. She blames me for–' he waved a hand around the tent, '–all this. But at least she's alive.' His gaze hardened a little. 'I'd do the same again, you know. Father Luke would have poisoned her and kept poisoning her until she died.'

Sid felt a tiny bit of sympathy rise and quashed it. She turned away without another word. Went and rejoined Win and Gabriel, who was anxiously shifting from foot to foot.

Win's phone buzzed. He had a look. 'The lead detective,' he said. 'Leah's in Tent Two.'

'You mean Lucie,' said Sid.

'Tent Two,' Gabriel repeated. Spinning around, he darted through the mêlée as fast as a minnow. Within seconds, he'd vanished.

'Shit,' said Sid. Both she and Win broke into a run for Tent Two.

# 62

Gabriel couldn't stop clinging onto his mother. He'd thought he was grown-up enough not to cry but the instant he saw her, arms outstretched to embrace him, he let go. The dam broke and the monumental torrent of grief that he'd held back, burst through. Great wrenching noises of grief erupted. His mother's arms were around him and she was sobbing with him, holding him tight, rocking him, wailing, tears pouring. They wept for themselves and for Hannah. They wept for all the children who'd died. They wept and wept and when they were finished, his face felt puffy and sore.

They mopped up their tears then cried some more. A woman who called herself a family liaison officer brought them tea and sugar, and biscuits, but Gabriel didn't eat. His mother didn't either, even though she was terribly, horrifyingly thin. She looked like a skeleton and hugging her was like hugging a bunch of twigs except her hug was really strong, and made him feel incredibly safe.

Finally, they wiped their eyes. Fumbled for hankies and blew their noses. When he could talk, Gabriel told his mother what had happened. He wobbled when he came to the bit when Hannah had bolted in the Christmas market, but when he glanced at Sid, sitting quietly to one side with Win, she gave him a small nod, and he found the courage to continue.

'Your sister,' Mum choked. 'She could be impossible.' She gave a watery smile and, reaching up to his face, brushed his hair back from his forehead. 'But we should give thanks because if she hadn't been Hannah and run away, you wouldn't be here.'

Gabriel told her about meeting his grandparents, and that Tinsel the cat was now very old. Mum said that was wonderful, and that she'd be going 'home' to Bath as soon as she could.

'I've tried to escape so often.' Her eyes were sad as she spoke to Sid. 'But after a while, you just give up.'

'I can imagine,' Sid said.

'I didn't know he was poisoning me. He was always–' her gaze grew distant, '–so believable.'

A small silence fell, and then Gabriel remembered. 'I brought your special ring back,' he told her. Reaching into his front jeans pocket, he brought it out. 'I kept it safe.' Carefully, he passed the ring over, watched as his mother raised it to the light and read the tiny words etched on its inside.

'The greatest science in the world,' she murmured, 'in heaven and on earth, is love.'

'What did you say?' Sid had jack-knifed to her feet.

Gabriel's mother looked scared.

'Leah,' Sid said. Gabriel could tell she was trying to contain herself. 'May I see the ring?'

Mum clamped her fingers around the ring.

'Please,' Sid said. 'I won't keep it. I just want to see it.'

His mother's lips tightened into what he knew was a stubborn line. Just like Hannah.

'Go on, Mum,' Gabriel said. 'She'll give it back. I promise.'

Reluctantly, Gabriel's mother gave Sid the ring. As she studied it, Sid turned so pale, so fast, that he thought she might faint. Win did too, because he also sprang up, went to stand next to her.

Sid was staring at the ring.

'This is my father's wedding ring. My mother had it made for him.' Her voice strengthened as she looked at each of them in turn. 'It is my *father's ring*.'

## 63

'How did you get it?' Sid tried not to scare Leah, but the woman was now looking terrified. Sid took a deep breath, let it out. Gentled her voice. 'Leah, Lucie... how did you get my father's ring?'

The woman closed her eyes. She remained silent. Her fists lay clenched on her lap.

Sid brought every ounce of self-control into her being. Steadied her breathing. *Calm, calm, calm.*

'My father has been missing for fourteen years.' Her voice was as gentle as thistledown. 'I want to know what happened to him.'

She pulled out her phone and brought up a picture of her father. 'Leah,' she prompted gently. 'I have a photo of him here. I need you to look at it.'

For a moment, Sid thought the woman would never open her eyes, but then Gabriel said, 'Please, Mum.'

Finally, Leah looked at the photograph. Reached out a finger and touched the screen. 'My Angel,' she whispered.

'That's the man who saved you?' Gabriel looked stunned.

'Tell me,' Sid urged him.

'Mum was in the Shed. She was on her own. No light, no food, just water. She'd stolen an egg, hadn't you, Mum?'

Leah looked up, eyes wet. 'I was seventeen. I was pregnant with Gabriel.'

Sid was appalled but tried not to show it. She didn't want to interrupt.

'After three days, I honestly thought I was going to die. I was petrified Gabriel would be damaged by the experience but then a man came and saved us. He knocked on the Shed door really loudly, banging it, and when I answered, telling him I was being punished for releasing Amelia so she could go to hospital, he broke down the door and let us out.'

'And this is that man, the one in this photograph?'

'Our Angel,' she whispered. 'I pray for him every day.'

'What happened to him?'

'He kicked and kicked at the door. He was shouting. I was terrified but when the wood shattered and he looked inside, he told me not to worry, that Amelia had sent him and I was quite safe, and I could come out now.' Her mouth twisted. 'He looked so very kind. I trusted him.

'Someone had gone and fetched Father Luke. Our Angel...' She gulped. 'I mean, your father went crazy when he arrived. He yelled and shouted at Father Luke. I've never seen anyone so angry. He punched Father Luke, can you imagine? And Father Luke...' Leah paused, her lips trembling. Tears began to rise again. 'I'm so sorry...'

Sid felt a sense of dread descend.

'Please, I need to know.'

'Father Luke... he hit him back. They fought. Wrestled, really. Brothers Saul and Jeremiah tried to pry them apart...' Her gaze grew distant as she remembered. 'But it was Father Luke that finished it. He ran and fetched a shovel. Saul had your father in a headlock, Jeremiah holding his arms… and your father was fighting like a bull, still yelling, and Father Luke hit him on the side of his head with the shovel…'

Leah began to weep again, softly.

'Father Luke killed my father?'

'I don't think h-he meant to.'

Sid was trembling head to toe. She wanted to scream, she wanted to weep. She felt sick to her core. 'Where is he now, my father?'

Leah looked away.

*I have to know.*

Leah closed her eyes. 'We put him in the slurry pit.'

# 64

Leah confirmed it was her who'd let Amelia, real name Julia Pemberton, out of the Shed.

'I couldn't bear it. I got Brother Isaac to take Amelia to hospital. When Father Luke found out what I'd done, he locked *me* in the Shed...' Leah looked at Gabriel. 'I lied to protect you. I hadn't stolen an egg, that was Amelia. But I'd done something even worse. I'd gone against Father Luke's command.'

She took a long breath. 'When your father heard Amelia's story, he stormed out of the hospital and came here...'

'To confront Father Luke.'

'Yes.'

'Who killed him.'

'Yes.'

When Sid spoke, it was as though she was talking from the bottom of the ocean. 'How many people know about this?'

'We all know.'

Collective consciousness, but a court wouldn't see it

371

that way. They'd be accused of collusion by default. Accused of lying to the police.

Leah twisted the ring around and around between her fingers. 'I used to wear it all the time. I hung it around my neck on a little string. It became part of me. But now I think it might be cursed.'

'Why is that?' Sid asked quietly.

'Because two men have died.' Her voice was a whisper.

'You're talking about my father, and...' Trembling a little, Sid found a photograph of Owen Evans and showed it to Leah.

Leah looked at the photograph for a long time. 'That's him. He came to us to be exorcised. I managed to get myself tasked to take him to the church – anyone from Outside was a potential source of escape – but before we headed there, he spotted your father's ring. He wanted to look at it, so I showed him.'

'He saw the initials etched inside?'

She nodded. 'I wouldn't let him take it. I let him have the postcard instead.'

'Postcard?'

'It was really pretty. A view of Switzerland's mountains in the snow.' Her eyes widened as she stared at Sid. 'It was addressed to you. Sidney Scott.'

'Yes.'

Long silence.

'Did you tell Owen what happened to my father?'

She nodded. 'I told him everything. I wanted him to rescue me and my children.'

'What did he do then?'

'He said he was going straight to the police.'

Sid felt as though the oxygen had been sucked out of her lungs.

'Who else knew he was doing this?'

'Father Luke.' Another whisper. 'He saw us talking and when Owen left in a hurry, Father Luke came to me, demanding to know what we'd been talking about. When I didn't answer straight away, he told me that God wouldn't just give me Soul Sickness, but Hannah and Gabriel too. He terrified me into telling him what I'd told Owen. He chased after him…'

*Oh God.* Sid's ears were ringing, her pulse pounding. Her mind became a maelstrom.

'How many people know about this?'

'Just me. When Father Luke came back, he brought me some special holy water. I thought I'd been forgiven but then I fell ill with Soul Sickness. He told me it was God's retribution because I'd betrayed him.'

Sid couldn't bear to remain in the tent any longer. She desperately needed air. She stalked outside, her legs feeling as though they were disconnected from her body. She pictured her father, his broad frame, the freckles on the backs of his hands.

*You're dead,* she said.

*Yes. I'm sorry.* His face was long and sad.

*If you hadn't gone to the hospital… If you hadn't talked to Amelia… Why do you always fucking* talk to strangers?!

He closed his eyes. *My darling daughter. I happen to like people. I can't change the way I am.*

*I wish you were alive.* It was a sob.

*I do too.*

# 65

S id had already testified, and now she was watching Illa being gently questioned on the stand. Illa had, she told the court, tried the bottles of mineral water that had been supplied to Sidney Scott, to reassure her they were safe to drink, but ended up becoming horribly ill herself.

'You were also poisoned?' the barrister asked.

'I believe so.' It was a whisper but the shocked ripple around the court showed everyone had heard her answer.

Sid hadn't missed a day of Father Luke's trial. She'd watched Julia-Amelia give her testimony, along with Lucie-Leah, Detective Kelly and Liz. The rosy-cheeked woman who looked after the pigs at the Golden Dawn, and who Sid had chased the day she'd been drugged and incarcerated, also testified. She had, she said, been ordered to help the Brothers dispose of Michael Scott's body in the slurry pit. No wonder she'd turned bone-white and fled when Sid had shown her Dad's picture. The same woman directed the police to Michael Scott's car, which had been hidden at the back of a Dutch barn and buried beneath stacks of straw.

Rebekah, the elderly woman who worked in the commune's kitchen, testified that when asked to make tea with Father Luke's special Earl Grey, she knew to slip a tranquilliser in the pot.

'How many times have you done this, when asked to?'

Rebekah twisted her arthritic fingers together. 'I can't say.'

'Less than five?'

'No.'

'More than ten?'

'Yes.'

'More than twenty? Fifty?'

Rebekah couldn't remember as it was a regular occurrence. Father Luke would drug the more difficult young girls who would wake up in his rooms the next morning with no memory of what had happened to them.

Brothers Jeremiah, Isaac and Saul also testified against their leader. Nobody defended him. They were like termites leaving a burning mound. But the most devastating was Gabriel's story. As the survivor of the bombings, his image was plastered across the front of every newspaper, at the top of every TikTok and YouTube search. The video of him chasing after Hannah was the most-watched clip in the world.

With Win's support, Sid had decided not to hide Gabriel or herself away, but meet every interview head-on. She wanted the world to know how easy it was for a nation to be manipulated and, without their realising, how easy it could be for a dictator to slip into power.

Interestingly, Marc Strong's *Little Blue Book* had sold out virtually overnight. Needless to say, not everybody was pleased with how things turned out. Like Greg, Marc Strong's minder, who was filmed as he was being arrested, saying, 'It's a f***ing–' the swear word was bleeped out, '–

catastrophe that we've lost the greatest prime minister we'll ever see. How can you not realise he's been set up by the libs, the left? They hate him because he's everything they're not.'

Audrey, Marc Strong's wife, had fallen completely silent. Word was she'd swept her and the kids to hide out on a remote Scottish island until his trial was over. She wasn't standing by her man. No way, no how. She wanted nothing to do with him. She'd made a statement when he'd been arrested, however, declaring she'd known nothing about his plans, and how devastated she'd been when she'd found out what kind of man she'd married.

'They say you can't know the person you married fully.' She stood outside the gates of their country house, shoulders back, erect in Barbour and wellies and looking every inch the country lady with two black Labradors at her side. 'I now know this to be true. I wish I'd discovered a decent man but instead I discovered a self-centred, deceitful and narcissistic creature who I want nothing more to do with.'

*No coming back from that one,* Sid thought.

Marc Strong's trial was the following month, and with the Brothers' desertion, making plea-bargaining deals left, right and centre, it was generally considered he would, like Father Luke, be jailed for life. And that was even before the court took into account the videos and testimonies from the journalists and police who witnessed the scene in the garage, culminating in Gabriel being shot.

Sid still lived in her cottage with Tank, but was now spending more and more of her time at Meadow Barn. Tank came too, of course, which he loved since Flick doted on him.

'He's getting fat,' Toby told her the last time she'd dropped by.

'But he's happy.'

'Like you.' He smiled.

'Like me,' she agreed.

Toby and Harriet had been inundated with journalists initially, wanting to know details of how Sid lived, how much they'd known about her whistleblowing, and they'd been staunch, selling their story to one media outlet, to keep the others off their backs. The police had investigated AgriCredit Corp, the finance company who'd threatened to foreclose on their loan, but hadn't managed to find any evidence of misconduct. They surmised the call had come from the company but been made by a person who'd used a bogus name.

Gabriel was living with his grandparents, but came to stay when he could. Flick and Gabriel had become firm friends, and were already planning their first backpacking foray around South America.

'Dear God,' Sid said to Win that evening. 'They're not even fifteen!'

'It's good to have something to look forward to.'

'Well, yes, but–'

'Take me, for example,' Win interrupted. 'I've been looking forward to travelling across the solar system again.' He trailed a finger down her spine, making her shiver. 'I think there's a constellation I haven't yet explored...'

In one sweep his arms were around her, pulling her to him. His mouth was cool, his lips unbelievably soft. 'How is it,' he breathed, 'I can never seem to get enough of you?'

A long time later, when they were curled together on the sofa in front of the log fire, he continued his gentle exploration. 'This bit,' he murmured as he kissed the skin below her left shoulder blade, 'is the Eagle Nebula. And this bit–' another kiss, '–is the Andromeda Galaxy.'

She'd already explained her tattoo to him, taken from real science and new-age art, where multicoloured universes mingled with healing angels and nature – an homage to her parents – but he still loved tracing the stories and meanings over her skin.

She twisted to look into his eyes. 'If you got a tattoo, what would you have?'

'A socking great anchor with I LUV SID on it.'

She couldn't help but laugh.

When she awoke the next morning in his bed, rain dashing against the window, their limbs entwined, her head nestled on his chest, the warmth of him enveloping her, she didn't think she'd felt so safe or content in years.

'You awake?' he murmured.

'Just.'

'Oh, good.' His hands began to drift over her body. 'Because I wanted to talk about Christmas.'

'What about it?' Instantly, the old her began to bristle.

'I thought it would be nice to have everyone here. Gabriel and his grandparents, Bert, you and me, Flick and Tank. Oh, and Flick's grandmother from the other side of the tracks.' He peered down at her. 'Could you cope with that?'

'I love hearing her Spitfire stories.'

'Liar.'

'I do! I think she's an amazing woman.'

'Amazingly un-PC, you mean.'

'Sometimes,' Sid admitted. 'But since it's only for a couple of days…'

He rolled her onto her back, looked down at her, eyes alight. 'Is that a yes? Oh, do say, *Yes, please, Win. I'd love to spend Christmas with you…*'

'Yes, please, Win,' she said solemnly, 'I would love to spend Christmas with you.'

His smile was like a star exploding against the night sky.

———

Christmas Day and Sid had just opened her present from Flick – a large, personalised dog bowl with TANK on the side – when her parents appeared. They stood to the side of the sparkling Christmas tree and smiled at her.

*Happy Christmas*, said her father.

*And happy New Year*, added her mother.

*But I'm not asleep*, said Sid in her mind, bewildered. *Or drug-addled. What's going on?*

Her mother laughed while her father shook his head. *Don't let your head rule your heart so much.*

Nobody noticed they were there, but then Tank rose and walked over, hackles up, tail stiff. He sniffed the air before her parents and gave a growl. Immediately, they vanished.

She didn't expect to see them again, but they popped by occasionally, to say hello. It was weird, and she could never be sure if she was hallucinating or whether she really was communicating with the dead. Perhaps there was a time-slip somewhere? A wormhole of some sort? She had no idea.

It wasn't until she was walking Tank one day in a rain-soaked field, the sun flashing between deep black clouds, thunder echoing in the distance, when she saw the solution quite clearly.

There were just some things that couldn't be explained.

## THE END

# AUTHOR'S NOTE

One of the themes in this book came from when I visited Berlin on a research trip for a previous novel. I'd been deeply shocked at how fast Hitler had come into power – just three weeks – turning liberal Germany into a dictatorship almost overnight. Liberal, open-thinking Germans thought this would be impossible, so how did it happen?

This turned me to study one of the largest dictatorships today, the CCP, Chinese Communist Party. For my novel, I cribbed China's very real social credit system, where you are given and deducted government credits according to your behaviour. You can gain credits for giving to charity, for example, or be blacklisted from getting a mortgage for not paying your electricity bill on time.

In the UK recently, a poll of 8,000 adults by JL Partners for the think tank UK Onward showed 46% of the public would prefer some form of dictatorship. Within that, the 18-34 year-olds endorsed such a proposition by 61%. Crikey, I thought, what about our free press? Freedom of expression? Because no matter how much we may abhor our messy democratic system – which certainly isn't perfect by any stretch of the imagination – at least we have the means to change things and remove those in power to bring in a new administration.

And so, this novel was born, giving me the opportunity to explore dictatorship versus democracy, and how we risk losing our freedom at our peril.

# ALSO BY CJ CARVER

PUBLISHED BY BLOODHOUND BOOKS:

*Over Your Shoulder*

*Scare Me to Death*

## THE HARRY HOPE THRILLERS

*Cold Echo*

*Deep Black Lies*

---

## THE DAN FORRESTER THRILLERS

*Spare Me The Truth*

*Tell Me A Lie*

*Know Me Now*

## THE JAY MCCAULAY THRILLERS

*Gone Without Trace*

*Back With Vengeance*

*The Honest Assassin*

## THE INDIA KANE THRILLERS

*Blood Junction*

*Black Tide*

## OTHER THRILLERS

*Dead Heat*

*Beneath The Snow*

*The Snow Thief*

# ACKNOWLEDGEMENTS

I would like to thank Dr Janet Seed, for giving me the inside gen on CERN, and even though her scientific take on wormholes and parallel worlds didn't make the pages of this book, it was great fun considering them.

Special thanks to Charlotte Ayres for bringing together such a terrific blurb, and for sharing her insights on digital marketing as well as her timely advice on how to look after bees.

Thanks to Ali and Martin for allowing me to use their cottage as the blueprint for Sid's home.

Thanks to Susan Opie for putting her finger on how to fix the first draft to make the story even better.

To Bazzer and Gill Dix, Karen and Mike Brzezicki, and Serena Gambarini, for chats, laughs, drinks, and loads of moral support.

As always, beyond words, thanks to my husband Steve Ayres.

# A NOTE FROM THE PUBLISHER

**Thank you for reading this book**. If you enjoyed it please do consider leaving a review on Amazon to help others find it too.

**We hate typos.** All of our books have been rigorously edited and proofread, but sometimes mistakes do slip through. If you have spotted a typo, please do let us know and we can get it amended within hours.

**info@bloodhoundbooks.com**